KT-501-389

# A Wartime Promise

C334257461

Ruby Reynolds is a pseudonym for Fiona Ford, author of *The Spark Girl*. Fiona was born in Cornwall and grew up in Bath. As well as having a thirst for books, Fiona had a huge interest in history and adored listening to her grandfather talk about his time in the navy during World War Two. Together they spent many a happy afternoon poring over the large collection of photos he had taken travelling the globe, somehow managing to perfectly capture life during wartime. Although Fiona went on to develop a successful career as a journalist, she never forgot her passion for the past. Now, Fiona has combined her love of writing with her love of days gone by in *A Wartime Promise*.

Find out more about Fiona by following her on twitter @fionajourno, or visiting her website www.fionaford.co.uk.

# A Wartime Promise

## RUBY REYNOLDS

ORION

First published in Great Britain in 2018 by Orion Books,
an imprint of The Orion Publishing Group Ltd
Carmelite House, 50 Victoria Embankment,
London EC4Y 0DZ

An Hachette UK company

1 3 5 7 9 10 8 6 4 2

Copyright © Fiona Ford 2018

The moral right of Fiona Ford to be identified as
the author of this work has been asserted in accordance with
the Copyright, Designs and Patents Act of 1988.

All rights reserved. No part of this publication may be
reproduced, stored in a retrieval system, or transmitted
in any form or by any means, electronic, mechanical,
photocopying, recording, or otherwise, without the
prior permission of both the copyright owner and the
above publisher of this book.

All the characters in this book are fictitious, and any resemblance to
actual persons, living or dead, is purely coincidental.

A CIP catalogue record for this book is
available from the British Library.

ISBN 978 1 4091 7015 0

Typeset by Input Data Services Ltd, Somerset

Printed in Great Britain by Clays Ltd, Elcograf S.p.A.

MIX
Paper from
responsible sources
FSC® C104740

www.orionbooks.co.uk

# Acknowledgements

This book wouldn't be complete without paying tribute to all the wonderful women of the ATS who worked tirelessly for their country during World War Two. Whilst researching this book I was lucky enough to encounter several brave, valiant women who worked as drivers, Ack Ack Girls and sergeants through the Women's Royal Army Corps. I am incredibly grateful to you all for your candour and for helping me see what life really was like as a spark girl.

For me, part of the joy of writing about this period is the research and so I would like to express deep thanks to the staff at the Imperial War Museum and the National Archives for their patience with all my particularly stupid questions. I would also like to thank the lovely people at the Law Society and of course all the wonderful souls in Swansea and Bristol who told me many stories about life during wartime.

A large thank you must also go to my lovely parents, Barry and Maureen who although born shortly after the war have been a mine of information for me, not to mention support. Their sheer belief that I could write these stories, along with their many plot suggestions has been nothing short of wonderful. However, Dad, I'm sorry to break it to you, but I just don't think it would be appropriate for James Bond to turn up in a saga! Whilst I'm listing family members I must also pay special thanks to my great aunt, Brenda Williams who lived through the war as a young woman and gave me a great insight into what life was like during that time.

I would like to say a very big thank you to Kate Burke and Diane Banks at Diane Banks Associates for their belief in me as a writer and of course to my wonderful editor at Orion, Laura Gerrard. Laura's passion for the books and the valuable suggestions she has made, have only helped make this book extra special and I feel very lucky to have her support.

Lastly, and most importantly, thank you very much dear reader for taking the time to pick up this book and read it. There are many wonderful wartime sagas out there and I am so grateful you decided to spend some time with Peggy Collins – thank you!

# Prologue

The early afternoon sunshine flooded through the sash windows, giving the sparkling white hospital ward a warm glow. Outside, the sounds of excited children playing with their friends on the street, together with the gentle swishing of trees in the breeze, told the woman it was a perfect summer's day. But not for her, for her it was all too much; the echo of laughter and joy slicing into her body as painfully as if she were being cut with a knife.

Turning her body away from the sunshine, the woman screwed her eyes up tight and shut out the promise of happiness the beams of light offered. Her mind hurt just from the very fact she was alive and she burrowed her face under the pillow, hoping to find solace in the cool darkness of the cotton sheet beneath.

For the past few weeks she had truly believed there was hope, that she would find happiness. But not now, it was her and her newborn baby against the world.

As if on cue, the sound of an ear-piercing, demanding wail shrilled through the room, causing the woman to jump in shock. Wearily she pulled her head from beneath the pillow and sat upright to look at the cause of all the noise. Peering through tired eyes, the woman saw a baby girl, red-faced and angry, her hands balled into determined little fists as she noisily insisted upon attention.

The baby's cries grew louder and louder and the woman glanced anxiously across the ward to see if she had upset any of the other mothers who were enjoying the luxury of an afternoon's rest. Yet unlike her and her daughter, everyone else was sleeping peacefully. Gingerly, she placed her hand on the baby girl's chest, the warmth of the tiny body stirring feelings of love and longing she thought she had buried forever.

'Hush now, sweetheart,' she whispered, bending her face down close towards the baby. 'I'm right here.'

Gently, the woman leaned over the cot and rocked her from side to side, humming 'Hush Little Baby' to try and soothe her daughter's cries. At first the baby refused to be silenced. Then looking her mother squarely in the eye, she opened her mouth wide, beat her tiny fists against the blankets and let out one final sob before closing her eyes and falling straight to sleep.

Watching her baby slumbering contentedly, the woman smiled and tucked the blankets tightly around her before bending down to plant a tender kiss on her forehead. Standing back, the woman wondered how something so wonderful could come from so much heartache. She was perfect in every way, with ten tiny fingers, ten tiny toes, eyes that were the spitting image of her father's and a character filled with determination.

Suddenly the echo of heavy footsteps trailing down the corridor towards the ward made her heart pound. It was him, she knew it. She would recognise the sound of that heavy tread anywhere. A thrill shot through her as the feelings of hope she had long since abandoned, resurfaced. Finally, he was here. How foolish she was to think he would let her down when she needed him most.

'You came,' she whispered, as he walked through the door.

Looking at him standing in the doorway, staring at her, a mixture of surprise and concern written across his face, she felt a pang of longing. It was all she could do not to run towards him. She thought back to the last time she had seen him several months ago. He had been boarding a train, on his way to God knows where. The platform had been so crowded, he hadn't seen her, but she had seen him, and she had waved and waved, blowing him kisses with tears streaming down her face as the

2

train slunk majestically out of Bristol Temple Meads station and taken him far away. Now he was back, standing before her, and she ached to wrap her arms around him and hold him close.

'You've obviously got a way with him,' he said gruffly, still not moving from the door.

'Her,' the woman corrected. 'She's a girl.'

The man nodded as if it was something he had known all along.

'She's a credit to you,' he replied evenly.

Her heart leapt at the compliment. Even though she was sure he could barely see the baby from where he was standing, the fact he had praised her must surely mean he was pleased to see them both.

'Would you like to hold her?' she said eagerly, bending down to reach for the child.

A flicker of shock passed across his face before his eyes lit up. 'Yes.' He beamed. 'Yes, I would.'

Gently the woman reached into the cot and placed the bundle of warmth into his waiting arms. 'This is your daddy, sweetheart.'

The man took the bundle and she could see his eyes shine with tears as he drank her in. 'She's perfect,' he cried. 'Simply perfect.'

The woman felt tears of joy pool in her eyes. He wanted her, he already loved her, she could see for herself.

'We made her, she's ours,' the woman whispered.

Gently the man nodded and giving her a gentle kiss on her cheek handed his daughter back to her mother.

'I just wanted to see her; I hope that's all right.'

'Of course it is,' the woman replied warmly. 'I'm glad you did.'

The man smiled shyly. 'Well, I'd better go.'

'You don't have to,' she said, a hint of desperation creeping into her voice.

She looked him up and down; even though it had been at least six months since, she was grateful to see his time away in the Army hadn't jaded his good looks. He was still as handsome as he had always been and she found herself smoothing her long hair down, wishing she looked more presentable.

Watching him shuffle uncomfortably from foot to foot in the doorway, she became aware of some of the mothers in the ward starting to stir. The last thing she wanted was to be the source of gossip, yet there was something she had to know.

'We could all be so happy together if you would just give us a chance. We could be a family,' she begged.

The man shook his head. 'It's not that I don't want to, you know how I feel about you, about our child.'

His eyes gazed down at the baby before he looked back at the woman. 'It's just not possible. Not now, not after everything.'

'But why?' she begged.

The man shook his head in sadness. 'You know why. I know you don't believe me but you'll be better off without me. Your husband will take care of you, you will both be happy, I assure you.'

'But I don't want him, I want you,' she told him, her voice trembling.

'I'm sorry, I can't.' His voice contained a note of finality and he turned on his heel and strode along the corridor without turning back.

As she watched him leave, her whole body shook violently as the reality of her new life hit her like a ton of bricks. She realised now she really had lost everything. Her hopes and dreams of a life filled with love for her and her baby had gone up in smoke. She walked across the room and back to the crib where she gazed down at her daughter, who was still slumbering peacefully without a care in the world.

Bending down, the woman stroked her baby's cheek with her forefinger, and then reached into the bedside table for her notepaper and a pen. Deftly, she began to write.

*My darling girl,*

*If you're reading this then you will know that I feel the time has come for you to know the truth about just who you are. Before you start to wonder, or panic, please know, my precious child, that you mean the world to me. You are, without doubt, the very best thing in my life.*

Pausing for a moment, the woman put the pen down, glanced at her daughter and broke into a broad smile; this little girl was her everything. All she wanted was for her to find a life filled with happiness. But as a mother, it was up to her to protect this angel, give her the world and most importantly of all, tell her the truth. That was a promise she was determined to keep.

# Chapter One

## January 1941

The high-pitched whine overhead was unmistakable and it filled Peggy Collins with hate and dread in equal measure. Surging forwards along the pavement, the terrifying sound of the Luftwaffe became louder with every step she took and her skin prickled with fear.

For weeks now the Germans had been targeting her beloved hometown of Bristol and tonight it looked as though the Jerries were going to give it to them with both barrels. Anxiously Peggy looked at the sky and saw it had turned an eerie shade of silver. They were only three days into the New Year and the day had been freezing, with temperatures plummeting to below zero. Peggy had hoped the evening would be full of thick fog, making them safe from attack. Yet, gazing upwards at the full moonlight, she realised with a sickening sense of fear that her city was primed for a raid.

Shoving her hands deep into her pockets to try to keep out the icy chill, Peggy quickened her step towards the house she and her mother Edie shared. Out of the corner of her eye, she saw what looked like sparkling fairy lights dance through the sky, hissing and singing as they fell to the ground. She shuddered and broke into a sprint, carefully dodging the sheets of ice that lined the pavement.

Just as the air-raid siren began its familiar mournful wail, Peggy looked around and saw she wasn't the only one in a hurry. In fact, she was surrounded by passers-by, all running like hell, clearly preferring to take their chances on the ice rather than lie in wait for Hitler to drop his barrel-load of hate.

Remembering the khaki Army uniform she wore with pride, Peggy took care to make sure nobody needed any help before turning the corner into Priestley Avenue. As the corner shop she had grown up in came into view she slowed her pace until she reached the back door. Fishing for her keys in her bag, Peggy noticed the sky was now a fiery shade of orange, and her heart went out to those poor souls dealing with the first few bombs tearing through their homes causing death and devastation in equal measure.

Fingers trembling, she unlocked the heavy wooden door that led to the little shop and looked for Edie.

Mother, where you to?' she called, frantically.

'I'm in here, Peggy love,' a muffled voice called from the cupboard under the stairs, towards the rear of the store.

Relief flooded through Peggy as she saw Edie perched on the makeshift bench they had fashioned from vegetable crates when war broke out.

'There you are! I was worried you'd still be serving, or up in the flat,' Peggy exclaimed, slamming the door shut and sitting down next to her mother.

'No chance. I saw the flares over Clifton, closed the shop and sought refuge in our very own little shelter,' Edie replied. 'Course, Esme Hotchkiss wouldn't leave till I promised to serve her first with her rations when we reopened after the raid, but then she's always been a daft old bag!'

'You'd think she'd be more concerned with getting up home to safety,' Peggy replied.

'There's nought so queer as folk, or Esme Hotchkiss anyway,' Edie muttered darkly. 'Cheeky mare was in here shouting the odds as usual. I've half a mind to tell her where to stick her custom but as her ration book is registered with our shop, I don't s'pose that would be a very Christian thing to do.'

Peggy stifled a smile; there had never been any love lost between her mother and Esme Hotchkiss. One of Peggy's earliest memories was of her mother and Mrs Hotchkiss warring over the till and not a lot had changed since.

'What was the problem this week?' Peggy asked.

Edie shrugged in the candlelight. 'She had the cheek to suggest I wasn't giving her full rations. Accused me of keeping a bit back for myself, said I'd always been selfish!'

Peggy gasped. 'That's awful. What did you say? Were there other customers around?'

'No, it was just me and her. I'm used to the old bag, Peg, and told her where to go if she didn't like it, and then of course the air-raid siren sounded so she had to go. Though if truth be told, I reckon she'd have preferred to have hung about the shop for a row, and I wouldn't have minded putting her straight on a few things, I can tell you. Anyway, where've you been? I was expecting you a while back.'

Peggy didn't miss the rebuke in her mother's tone. 'I just went up Broadmead for a look around the shops, but it's so different now. I didn't know how badly bombed out everywhere was.'

Naturally Peggy had known Bristol had suffered during the raids, but to see so much devastation and wreckage in the city she loved had been heartbreaking. Park Street, where Peggy and her mother had enjoyed many a happy hour ambling up the hill, lay in ruins. As for the old furniture store on College Green, the place had been devastated. It had been awful to witness, and a small part of Peggy had to admit she would be glad when her seventy-two-hours leave was up and she could return to her post at Swansea's ATS barracks.

Despite her time in the Army, Peggy had yet to face a raid, and sitting in the cramped shelter, she did her best to recall her training as the sound of the city's heavy artillery went into action. She knew the most important thing was to remain calm, but with the relentless gunfire filling the air, staying calm felt like the most difficult thing in the world. Instead Peggy tried to distract herself with thoughts of happier times. She remembered how the last time she had spent any real time in this cupboard was when she was a little girl, and she and her dad used to play hide-and-seek when he came back from his job down at the docks. Peggy would spend what felt like hours in the dark waiting for her father to find her, which of course he always did, then he would reward her with a cuddle.

Back then, the cupboard felt like a happy, safe place to be, and she realised that it was still keeping her and Edie safe years later.

'How long d'you think it'll last?' Peggy asked quietly.

Edie shrugged in the darkness. 'How long's a piece of string? Last time they reckoned it'd be over quick as a flash but I was stuck in here hours. That's why I brought us some essentials.'

'How d'you mean?' Peggy shouted over a particularly loud round of shelling.

'I mean I always keep a jug of water on the shelf, a tin of biscuits up the top next to it, but today I made us each a cuppa and brought us some leftover Christmas cake,' Edie explained, pressing a large slab into her daughter's hands.

Peggy giggled and shook her head. Her mother really did think of everything, but then she always had. She had run the corner store in Knowle on the outskirts of the city since she was born. It had been in Edie's family for years and the place had been a lifeline to the pair of them when Peggy's father, William, had been killed five years earlier picking up an extra day's work at the docks. It had been terrible for the pair of them, but the shop had given them a focus, and Peggy had channelled her grief into helping her mother clean and wipe the shelves and fill them with stock.

Edie had always been proud of her beloved store, working tirelessly to provide for Peggy. As a result she was well respected and well known in the community, famous for her hard-working nature and no-nonsense attitude; two things she had passed on to Peggy.

Peggy took a huge bite of the slab of fruit cake, savouring the flavour of the rich sponge and boozy fruit dancing on her tongue. She knew her mother would have used her rations carefully to make it, and yet it tasted delicious.

'I don't know how you do it,' Peggy said, her mouth full.

'Don't know how I do what? Oh, and don't speak with your mouth full, we might be trapped in a shop cupboard but manners cost nothing,' Edie scolded.

Swallowing the cake, Peggy opened her mouth to speak once more. 'I mean I don't know how everything you do turns out so perfectly.'

'Rubbish!' Edie snorted.

'It's true,' Peggy said in protest. 'You run a shop, take care of me, run a home, cook like Marguerite Patten and all on a shoestring with a war raging. I'm just saying you're a marvel.'

But Edie was having none of it. 'Don't talk daft, Peggy Collins. If your father could hear you now, he'd die laughing if he wasn't already six feet under! You do what you have to, girl, like you in the ATS.'

'I s'pose so,' Peggy said nodding. 'But I've still a long way to go.'

It was certainly true that since she had been posted to Swansea last month, her confidence had soared. When Peggy had joined-up just under a year earlier, she hadn't the first idea of the level of responsibility she was taking on. Edie had always tried to protect her from as much of the world as possible. When other kids were out playing hopscotch on the street, Peggy had to remain indoors or in the shop. As a result, the children at school generally regarded Peggy as a bit odd. The only real friend she had ever made was Bess who she had met at Sunday school where she had gone on to be a teacher.

Peggy didn't mind. Edie was her world, and despite her brusque exterior, Peggy knew how much her mother adored her. When William had died, Peggy had seen how devastated her mother had been. It was then, at sixteen years of age, she had made a promise to herself that she would live with her mother and they would run the shop together. She would make her mother her life. Peggy knew Edie would never remarry; although they rarely talked about her father, the pain on Edie's face every time Peggy tried to broach the subject was obvious and so she kept quiet, even though she longed to discuss the happy times they'd all shared as a family.

As neither of her parents had siblings and with both her grandparents long dead, Peggy had nobody she could talk to about her father. So instead she relived her memories of him alone. The opposite of her mother, William was full of love and fun. Where Edie was cold, William was warm. It was him that always read her bedtime stories and helped her grasp her times tables, whereas Edie always said she never had time, citing the shop that wouldn't run itself. There were occasions where Peggy briefly found herself wondering how on earth her parents had wed, they were so different.

Yet, the one thing they had in common was they both wanted the best for Peggy. When her best friend from Sunday school, Bess, suggested they join the ATS Peggy remembered how her father used to tell her wistfully about his own time in the Army during the last war. He had made it sound as though it was one of the happiest times of his life, packed with fun and adventure. Consequently, she found herself at the recruitment office in the city centre the very next day with Bess at her side. Although Peggy had never intended on leaving her mother alone, this was different; she would be leaving to help win the war.

'What's on your mind?' Edie said quietly, interrupting Peggy's train of thought.

'Oh, nothing. Just thinking about when I joined-up,' Peggy admitted, brushing the crumbs of fruit cake from her lap.

There was a brief pause before Edie spoke. 'Remember it well. One of the worst days of my life.'

Peggy's eyes widened in shock. 'You never said.'

'Didn't think I needed to.' Edie sniffed.

Thinking back to that fateful day when she had received her call-up papers and decided to come clean to her mother, Peggy remembered how she had dreaded breaking the news. Instead of saying the words aloud, Peggy had chosen to show her the papers. Edie had read them through carefully, her greying red locks falling into her face as she fiddled with the wedding ring she always wore on a chain around her neck. Reaching the end, the shopkeeper had said nothing, but for the first time in her life had pulled Peggy into her arms, and held her tight. It had never happened before or since, but Peggy had never forgotten that rare display of emotion, and it was something she had treasured during her first few lonely nights in the Army.

'I never meant to upset you, Mother,' Peggy admitted.

'I know that,' Edie said, thin-lipped. 'But your place is here with me, not hanging about the Army with all sorts.'

'Everyone's very nice,' Peggy protested.

'It's dangerous too,' Edie continued as if Peggy hadn't spoken. 'Every night you're away I lie awake wondering if you're still alive.'

Peggy said nothing. She had heard this same speech from her mother since she joined-up, and knew it by heart. Instead she listened to the sound of rapid gunfire, the only thing punctuating the silence.

'I know why you wanted to join the ATS,' Edie said eventually, her voice steady and even. 'You was doing what was right, fighting for your country. But there are dangers out there you know nothing about, people that want to do nothing but hurt you. I only wanted to protect you from all that, like I have all my life.'

Peggy nodded. Her mother's protectiveness had been something she had treasured until she had arrived at Leicester for basic training. There, she grew up quickly, surprised to discover she was the only one of the recruits who had never been to a dance, tried an alcoholic drink, or even been allowed on a day trip alone. As for courting, Edie had drummed it into her that men would only ever bring her heartache and she was better off on her own. Peggy assumed her mother felt that way because her father had died so suddenly and she was left broken-hearted. Not that it made any difference to Peggy; she would always do right by her mother and would never leave her to fend for herself.

'You're not like me, Peg,' Edie continued. 'You're not strong. That's why I've worked so hard to look after you, so you can lead a happy life and not have to worry about the things I've had to worry about.'

In the darkness Peggy rolled her eyes. Even though she had been away from home almost a year, Edie still saw her daughter as a scared little girl rather than the woman she had become.

'So what is it you've had to worry about all these years, Mother?' Peggy asked drily. 'You never have said.'

There was a silence and Peggy wished with all her heart she could take the words back. She had never dared cheek her mother like that before.

'You little madam,' Edie growled. 'It's none of your business. You wanna respect your elders, you hear me.'

'Yes, Mother, sorry,' Peggy said.

'I've never heard the like,' Edie continued furiously. 'If that's what they're learning you in the Army I shall write to your commanding officer and have you withdrawn.'

A sudden fear pulsed through Peggy as she wondered if it was possible for her mother to do that. Although it had taken a while, she had learned to love her new life and wasn't prepared to give it up, especially while there was still a war on. Hitler needed defeating, and she wouldn't rest until Britain had won.

'Sorry again, Mother,' Peggy said, her tone contrite. 'I don't know what came over me.'

Edie sniffed and said nothing, leaving Peggy lost with her thoughts. She could kick herself for being rude to her mother. They had enjoyed such a perfect couple of days, trust her to ruin it all now.

She opened her mouth to speak, when something outside startled her. 'D'you hear that?'

'The guns have stopped firing,' Edie replied matter-of-factly.

In the darkness, Peggy realised you could hear a pin drop it was so quiet outside. Did that mean the raid was over? But listening again, she heard the familiar whistle and hiss, and realised bombs were still falling in the distance.

'Why aren't our guns answering those bombs?' Peggy cried. 'I don't understand.'

Closing her eyes and taking a deep breath, Peggy leaned in towards her mother, rested her head on her shoulder and was immediately transported back to the love and security of her childhood. Too practical to wear perfume, Edie relied on Life-buoy soap and Peggy breathed in that familiar scent now, partly wishing she was still a child again when her biggest worry was whether she would choose a chocolate éclair or caramel from the Saturday Assortment tin.

'See, we've got each other now, Peg. We don't need nobody else,' Edie said quietly. 'You and me, we rely on each other, Peg, don't we? That's why I didn't want you going off playing at war games. There's all sorts of trouble out there.'

'No worse than in here, though,' Peggy replied gently.

'Maybe not but there's all sorts of people out there what'll want to get you in trouble,' Edie pressed.

Peggy groaned inwardly. Her mother was about to start her usual lecture on why all men were bad news. She had heard it a million times before and no doubt would hear it a million times again.

'I mean they have all sorts posted everywhere now, don't they?' Edie continued, warming to her theme. 'I see these fellas in their uniform all about the town. And I know they only want to bring heartache to women everywhere. You remember, Peggy, your place is with me, not going off with some fancy man. You hear me?'

'Yes, Mother,' Peggy said quietly.

She had no intention of courting a man, she simply wasn't interested. But no matter how many times she told her mother that, Edie still felt the need to push the point home.

There was no let-up from the bombs and as they sat in the cupboard, the all too familiar roar of the Luftwaffe in the distance, Peggy found herself drifting in and out of the land of nod.

It was a long night, and by the time the siren blared across the city, finally signalling the all-clear, Peggy was exhausted. Her neck was stiff, her arms and legs cold to the bone and she felt sick from lack of sleep. Checking the small gold wristwatch her father had given her not long before he died, she saw it was just after six in the morning, meaning they had been forced to stay under the stairs for twelve hours. Blearily she looked at her mother, and saw Edie was already on her feet and clearing away the remnants of their picnic.

Stretching her arms out overhead, Peggy stood up and pulled open the cupboard door. Her legs felt as unsteady as a newborn lamb after spending the night cooped up in such a tiny space, and gingerly she walked across the hallway and into the parlour. Opening the blackout curtains, the flash of torchlights from teams of volunteers filtered into the room.

Tentatively she peered out of the window and let out a gasp of horror. The street was all but destroyed. Several of the houses opposite were in ruins with their roofs torn off and windows blown out. Fires blazed through the remains and although the street was teeming with firemen, who were attempting to put out the fires with a network of hoses and stirrup pumps, their job was made even more difficult thanks to the icicles that had formed on their equipment. Peggy's eyes swept over the scene as she tried to take it all in. Spotting what looked like a small stream of red trickling down the street, tears brimmed as she realised what that meant.

Reluctantly, her eyes strayed to a corner at the top of the road where volunteers had started to stack corpses ready to be buried. As a pair of volunteers added the body of a young woman to the mound, Peggy stifled a scream. She had always known the aftermath of a raid would be horrific but to see her friends and neighbours suffering this way was devastating. Much as Peggy wanted to tear her eyes away she couldn't stop staring. It could so easily have been her and Edie amongst the death toll. For some reason, they had survived, and a sudden chill ran through Peggy's bones as she realised how close they had come to having their lives snuffed out as if they were no more than a gaslight.

'Come on then, girl,' Edie said determinedly from behind her. 'We've no time for tears, not when there are folk out there what need our help.'

Peggy whirled around and saw her mother already had her coat on and an arm outstretched with Peggy's greatcoat. Wordlessly Peggy took the garment and together the two women walked out into the arctic temperatures to help in any way they could.

For hours they worked tirelessly, bringing cup after cup of tea to those that needed it, not to mention every blanket and sheet they owned to help keep those that were now homeless safe, warm and dry. Elsewhere, more volunteers had arrived, armed with hot food and more supplies of tea.

Once all the lifeless souls had been stacked into a corner, Peggy joined in with those sweeping the streets free of the wreckage. As she put her back into brushing the streets with the stiff wooden brush, she dwelled on the tragedies of those who had suffered in neighbouring streets. Tales of those who had lost everything in one single night were all too common, but it was the sound of a young boy sobbing as he was led away from the bodies of his parents that caused her to feel a flash of anger.

How dare Hitler try to wipe out the community she had grown up in and loved. Watching the boy cry into his handkerchief, her heart ached for him and his future. Anxiously, she reached for her mother, who was working alongside her.

'You all right, Peg?' Edie asked in surprise.

Peggy nodded. 'Fine,' she replied, understanding that her mother wouldn't appreciate a public display of emotion. 'Just been a long day and night.'

'I make you right there,' Edie said. 'Reckon we could all use a cuppa before you go.'

'You've never gotta go back now, Peggy? Not looking like that,' one of her elderly neighbours gasped in horror. 'The Army'll go spare, surely?'

Peggy smiled as she looked down at her filthy uniform, covered in dust and soot. 'More than likely. But I've a clean one back at Mother's so I'll be shipshape and Bristol fashion for the train later.'

'You'll have a job. Trains haven't been running right since Temple Meads was raided in November,' said the old woman authoritatively.

'It was fine on the way down,' Peggy replied doubtfully.

'Course it was.' Edie sniffed, patting her daughter's arm. 'Give over, Doris; we've enough drama here for one night without you stirring the pot as usual. Don't worry, love, I'll give you a lift over to the station in the Tilly and make sure you're in plenty of time.'

'Thanks, Mother,' Peggy replied gratefully.

Glancing down at her watch she saw it was almost three in the afternoon. She needed to be back at her billet by seven or the Army police – or red caps as they were better known – would hang, draw and quarter her.

'Can we leave soon?' Peggy asked in a panic.

Edie nodded and together the women returned to Priestley Avenue and stood amongst the chaos. It wasn't lost on either of them that they were incredibly lucky to find both their shop and flat above still standing.

'Time for a quick cuppa then?' Edie asked as she opened the front door and walked up the stairs to the flat above the shop.

'Please,' Peggy replied, following her mother straight into the kitchen.

It wasn't much, Peggy thought as she pulled out one of the two hard-backed chairs that sat underneath the tiny wooden table, but it was home. Above the table, a row of cream-painted shelves held near-empty canisters of tea, sugar and flour, while the butler sink stood opposite. While Edie filled the kettle and placed it on the range to boil, Peggy pulled two cups down from the shelf above and looked hopefully in the bread bin. Hearing her stomach rumble, she realised she hadn't eaten since last night. What she wouldn't give for a slice of bread and butter.

'There's nothing in there, but I made you these yesterday for the journey if you want them now?' Edie said, gesturing towards a waxy brown-paper package on the shelf near the larder.

Peggy reached forward and tore at the wrapper. 'What would I do without you?'

Edie raised an eyebrow as she watched her daughter hastily devour a tongue sandwich. 'I dread to think. Now, take your tea upstairs and get yourself ready. We can leave soon as you like.'

Grabbing the cup, Peggy raced up the second flight of stairs and into her childhood bedroom. It was only a small box room overlooking the back of the shop, but Peggy loved it. Running her fingers along the veneer dresser, she smiled as her fingers caught the chip on the side. She had slipped and fallen headfirst into it after daring to try on Edie's good navy dress and shoes when she was eight years old.

Peggy couldn't remember how it had happened, only that one minute she had been admiring her appearance in the little mirror above the dresser and the next she was flat on her face, crying her eyes out, blood trickling down her forehead.

Edie had of course raced up the stairs to see what was wrong, and spotting Peggy's blood dripping all over the most expensive thing she owned had shouted the place down. She had towered over her and threatened to box her ears until William had returned home from work demanding to know what was going on.

William had shaken his head at Edie and ordered her downstairs. Then he had mopped Peggy up, dressed the wound and dried her tears. Edie had said nothing to her daughter until bedtime, when she had strangely offered to read her a bedtime story. As her mother tucked her in, she had read her a passage from the Bible then explained that it was wrong to take others' things without asking, and vanity was akin to one of the seven deadly sins.

Something Peggy was reminded of now as she slipped on her clean uniform and examined her appearance anxiously. She had lost a few pounds since joining the ATS last summer and the jacket that had once hugged her plump curves now fitted flatteringly around her smaller frame.

If only the same could be said of the enormous box-pleat skirt that fell past her knees, she thought, groaning inwardly. It had always been on the large side, but now it practically buried her. Still, she thought, turning her head this way and that in the mirror, at least the cap suited her, especially now her fiery red hair had been recently trimmed.

'Not bad at all,' she said to herself quietly, picking a tiny piece of lint from her sleeve. 'You're as ready as you'll ever be.'

Whirling around to pick up her kitbag from the tiny iron bed that took up most of the room, she jumped as she came face to face with a stern-looking woman.

'Today's peacock is tomorrow's feather duster,' Edie shrilled.

'Mother! You startled me,' Peggy gasped.

'Just as well, preening like that. This morning should've taught you there's more to life than what you look like,' Edie cautioned.

Peggy gave her mother the slightest nod of her head in apology. 'I know that, Mother, I just wanna make sure I look me best for me new job.'

'The job you can't tell me nothing about,' Edie bristled.

Peggy's cheeks flushed with guilt. She knew how much her mother hated not knowing where she was and how she spent her days. But the war meant everyone in the services had been sworn to secrecy. Since becoming a driver, or spark girl as they were better known, for the Army, the phrase 'Careless talk costs lives' had been drilled into her repeatedly. It was something she had tried to explain to Edie, but to no avail, as she frequently tried to convince Peggy that those rules didn't apply to her.

'Anyway, I'll not be so far away from home this time.' Peggy smiled, trying to appease her mother.

Edie's stare was unrelenting. 'Something else you can't tell me about.'

'You know I can't, Mother. I would if I could.'

'Hmmm,' Edie replied, seemingly unconvinced, her eyes taking in every inch of Peggy's uniform.

Peggy shifted uncomfortably from foot to foot under her mother's watchful eye.

'Will I do?' she said anxiously, desperate to avoid any more of Edie's criticism.

'You'll do,' Edie replied, turning on her heel and walking back down the stairs.

Following close behind, Peggy felt a surge of pride. This time she wasn't returning to the pool of ATS drivers. Instead, she had been specially selected as sole driver to Lieutenant Colonel Carmichael and she couldn't be more excited.

'You ready?' Edie asked as Peggy reached the bottom of the stairs. 'I won't have the Army saying my daughter's tardy.'

'They say many things, but tardy's not something I've been accused of yet,' Peggy said as she walked back out into the freezing temperatures, shivering despite her greatcoat.

Pulling open the door of the Tilly truck, she threw her bag into the footwell and clambered inside as her mother started the engine.

The familiar sound made Peggy smile. 'I never understood

why you liked driving this old thing, but I reckon I do now.'

'Oh yes?' Edie's pale blue eyes twinkled as the old truck jumped into life.

'It feels like you've got your freedom. You could go any-where, do anything,' Peggy explained as she watched her mother handle the gear stick as easily as if it were an extension of herself.

Edie paused and glanced quickly at her daughter before turning right. It was just starting to rain, and with the afternoon light already low she was struggling to see the road ahead. 'I can't imagine the Army would take too kindly to you seeing their cars as a chance at freedom.'

'No, but I s'pose it's about possibilities, isn't it? You know, you could go anywhere, if you wanted,' Peggy reasoned as she looked out of the window at the children playing knock down ginger along the streets she knew so well. She shook her head in amazement; there were bombs, rubble and fires still ravaging the city, yet children were out on the streets playing. Life carried on, she thought wistfully.

'Well, I should get notions like that straight out of your head, Peggy Collins,' Edie said firmly as she indicated left. 'Like it or lump it, there's a war on and there's duty to be done. And for you that duty's driving whoever wherever whenever they wanna go. Rules exist for a reason, and you're best off follow-ing them.'

Peggy chuckled as her mother turned into the narrow lane and drove the truck up the slight hill that led to the station. You always knew where you were with Edie Collins, she thought as the truck came to an abrupt halt. But what about her father? What would her dad have made of her joining up and becom-ing a driver? Would he have been proud? Delighted to see his darling girl doing her bit for king and country? Or would he have been like her old ATS pal Mary's father and tried to stop her from doing the job she loved?

Before she could stop herself, Peggy asked, 'What would

Father have thought of me being in the Army?'

Edie visibly jumped at the question and said nothing, her mouth set in a determined line as she gazed through the wind-screen, the rain gathering pace against the glass. Peggy felt the tension between them grow until Edie eventually turned away and smiled as she leaned across her daughter and opened the passenger door.

'You take care of yourself, you hear me,' Edie said evenly as if Peggy hadn't spoken. 'And I'll be expecting you to write me a letter come Sunday as normal or there'll be hell to pay, my girl.'

Nodding, Peggy got out of the truck quietly and slammed the door shut, knowing the subject was closed. Stepping back on to the rain-soaked pavement to wave at her mother, she saw Edie had already put the little truck into gear and driven away, all without saying goodbye.

# Chapter Two

Just over four hours later and Peggy was safely back in Swansea. The journey had been long and difficult, and the train had been continually shunted into sidings to allow others to pass, so she had been extremely grateful for the sandwich and extra chocolate bar Edie had tucked into her kitbag.

Stepping on to the platform, Peggy found luck was on her side, as she recognised another spark girl from her barracks and managed to catch a lift back to the hotel she was billeted in.

Although it was now evening and pitch-black outside, Peggy could make out some of the landmarks of the town she now called home. With the heady sea air, majestic castle and fancy Ben Evans department store on a par with Harrods, Peggy felt a million miles away from Bristol. Yet strangely, she had immediately felt comfortable in Swansea, taking delight in walking through the huge covered market on a rare afternoon off, strolling along the River Tawe or enjoying an afternoon in the Castle cinema.

For now, though, Peggy thought grimly, there was war work to be done. And walking up the steps of the small hotel in the town centre where she had been billeted, she couldn't wait to get started.

When Peggy had discovered she would be stationed in a hotel rather than the barracks, she had been worried. Having gone straight from her mother's house to the Army, Peggy wasn't sure she would be capable of taking care of herself, but thankfully the older couple who ran the hotel, Harry and Ida, had been nothing but welcoming, looking out for her and the two other ATS girls, Annie and Judith, Peggy shared a room with.

Like Peggy, Annie and Judith were also spark girls and co-incidentally sisters. Despite the fact that at twenty-three Judith was four years older than Annie, the sisters could easily have passed for twins; they looked so alike with their manes of jet black hair, emerald eyes and thick Midlands accents. Yet even though the girls were thick as thieves, they took care to include Peggy in everything they did, and in the month they had all been stationed together in the Welsh town, the trio had become firm friends.

Pushing open the heavy white door to the large room at the top of the building that overlooked the sea, Peggy smiled as she saw the sisters sitting on their beds, polishing the buttons of their jackets with their button sticks.

'Peg, you're back, love!' Judith exclaimed, getting off the bed to greet Peggy and help her with her luggage. 'How was your trip?'

'It was all right, ta, Jude,' Peggy replied gratefully. 'Trouble at Temple Meads meant it took ages and of course there weren't a seat.'

'That's no good,' Annie sympathised, rubbing her hands together to warm them through. 'Come on, Jude, let's stick that electric fire on now Peg's here; Ida will never know.'

Judith wrapped her scarf tightly around her neck and sighed, her warm breath clearly visible in the chilly room. 'You know as well as I do, Ida'll break our necks if she sees us turn that fire on again. She nearly crowned us last time, said we'd have the whole place up in smoke.'

'Don't be like that, Jude,' Annie said pleadingly. 'I'm that cold, I can barely move me fingers to clean me buttons.'

Peggy chuckled as she sat on her bed still huddled in her greatcoat, the icicles on the sash windows putting her off removing any of her clothes. 'To be fair, Ann, you don't need an excuse to get out of polishing your buttons, but Jude's right, Ida did her pieces last time so I think we should leave it off.'

'You two are being very unfair,' Annie grumbled, standing up and marching on the spot to try and get some warmth into her body. 'It only started smoking 'cos you two were drying your passion-killers on it.'

Judith bristled with outrage. 'They were your passion-killers, Annie! Peg and I told yer to take them off. It's a blinking wonder yer didn't kill us all.'

Annie opened her mouth to protest and Peggy got to her feet and held her hands out as if to silence the sisters. She had lived with them long enough now to know that although they worshipped one another, one of their rows could last hours, something Peggy could do without after the day and night she had just gone through.

Glancing down at her fingers, she saw they were chapped, dirty and almost blue from the cold. 'How about we go up the teahouse and get warm in there instead?'

'Good idea, Peg,' Judith said.

'I dunno,' Annie said, pouting. 'I've got no money till pay parade.'

'Oh for heavens' sakes,' Judith grumbled. 'I'll stand yer a cuppa, how does that sound?'

'Ta, Jude,' Annie chuckled, brightening immediately and reaching for her coat. 'Come on then, what are you two waiting for?'

Exchanging glances of amusement, Peggy and Judith followed Annie out into the hallway and down the stairs to the foyer. The hotel was small with ten bedrooms, each with a sea or garden view and beautifully decorated with embossed, creamy wallpaper, heavy floral curtains and thick squishy rugs. Yet even though the hotel had been requisitioned by the War Office for use by the ATS, Ida and Harry ran the place with so much care and love, Peggy had felt as if she were staying with family. The couple did of course have strict rules. Breakfast was at seven sharp, supper no later than six and woe betide if you weren't on time. Peggy shuddered at the memory of one new recruit who had arrived ten minutes late for breakfast and faced Ida's wrath head on. It was enough to say the girl had never made the same mistake again. But despite Ida's gruff exterior, she was soft as snow underneath. During Peggy's first week, Ida discovered she had never been to Wales, much less seen the coastline. One Saturday afternoon, when Peggy had been granted a rare few hours off, she had insisted on taking Peggy aboard the little Mumbles train that ran along the beautiful Gower coastline so she could see the glorious scenery that surrounded her.

Although it had been a bitingly cold December day, it had been sunny, crisp and bright; Peggy had never enjoyed herself so much. The Gower had been breathtaking and Ida wonderful company as she told Peggy all about the hometown she was so proud of. Tall, with her black hair greying at the temples and eyes as black as coal, Ida Jones was well known across the valleys. The hotel she ran with Harry, The Empire, had been in his family for generations, with tourists flocking to their establishment. Then war broke out, and life changed for good, as it did for the rest of the country.

Seeing Ida now at the foot of the stairs, her tall, slender frame bent over one of the dining tables as she cleared away the last of the supper things, Peggy shot her a warm smile. 'Evening, Ida.'

'Hello, Peg.' Ida beamed at her, her hands full of leftover bread and dripping. 'You have a good time with your mother?'

Peggy nodded. 'Lovely, ta, Ida. Mother says to pass on her thanks to you for looking after me so well.'

Ida's cheeks flushed at the praise. 'Get away with you. I'm only doing what any mother would do. And besides, with my two boys away in the Army, I like to think someone else would treat my children as if they were their own.'

Annie's eyes widened. 'In that case, Ida, is there any chance of a slice of that leftover bread and dripping seeing as we missed supper?'

Ida snorted with outrage. 'You know the rules, missy. Six and no later. Besides, it was only you that missed out, your sister here managed to get herself down to the table in time.'

Annie rolled her eyes at Judith. 'Oh come on, you're only going to chuck that food out.'

'I am not,' Ida protested. 'Lenny'll be tucking into it shortly, and no doubt he'll be very appreciative.'

'You're giving leftovers to a dog?' Annie gasped. 'Lenny's not serving his country like I am.'

Ida's eyes narrowed with fury. 'Maybe not, but he's never late and a more faithful companion than you, Annie Shawcross. P'raps think about that next time you're at the cinema day-dreaming over Cary Grant, is it? As I hardly think that's serving your country either.'

Annie opened her mouth to speak, only for Judith to lay a hand warningly on her sister's arm. 'That's enough now, Annie. We're just popping over the teahouse, so we'll see yer later, Ida.'

'Yes, see you later, loves.' The landlady smiled as the girls walked outside into the bitterly cold night.

Hurrying towards the teahouse on the corner, the girls quickly found a table by the steaming windows and ordered tea and crumpets. Peggy peeled off her coat, finally feeling warm enough to shed a layer of clothing. The place was a hive of activity; all around her servicemen and -women swapped stories, ate and drank as nippies bustled in between tables, cleaning and jotting down orders on the little pads they tucked into their aprons. Peggy smiled at the scene, it reminded her of basic training in Leicester when she and her friends, Kitty, Mary and Di, had put the world to rights in a teahouse just like this one. They had been happy days, Peggy thought wistfully, as they had got to know one another and learned new skills along the way.

It all seemed like a million years ago now and yet it had been less than a year since she had joined-up, but so much had happened. She had been stationed in Northampton, Exeter and Camberley since leaving Leicester, while the others had been scattered across the country and beyond, from what Peggy could gather. The last she heard, Mary was in France, Di had been moved to Yorkshire and Kitty was in Oxfordshire. At the thought of her old friends, Peggy felt an unexpected pang of longing. She missed them all dreadfully.

When Peggy had joined-up she'd realised how much of a sheltered life she had led under her mother's care. But thankfully her friends had helped her learn fast, and Peggy had been delighted to find her feet and discover she was something of a natural behind the wheel. Lost in thought, it took her a few seconds before she suddenly became aware of someone calling her name. Turning her head back towards the table now full of tea and crumpets, she smiled questioningly at the sisters.

'Sorry, girls, I was miles away. Were you saying something?'

Judith smiled fondly at Peggy. 'We were just asking you about your leave, Peg. Did yer manage to do much, like?'

'Not really,' Peggy admitted, as she reached gratefully for the cup of tea Annie had poured for her. 'I did the flowers for the church with Mother, but last night we were raided so I spent most of today helping people what had lost their homes. It was a tragedy; I've never seen anything like it, but I s'pose it's something folks across the country cope with day after day, though that don't make it any easier.'

Judith grimaced as she smeared a small scraping of butter across her crumpet. 'I heard Bristol's been bombed quite badly, like. I didn't know you'd had another attack so soon into the New Year.'

Peggy nodded mournfully. 'Yes. The city looks so different now, buildings blown to smithereens, chaos everywhere . . .'

Her voice trailed off as she remembered how wretched it had been to see her hometown all but destroyed and her street in ruins. Not for the first time that day she thanked God she and Edie had lived to tell the tale, unlike so many others who had lost not just their homes, but their mementoes, tokens of lives lived and memories made. She shuddered as she remembered the wedding photo she had seen that morning lying in the street. The glass and frame smashed and the picture itself scratched and torn jutting out of the rubble. There was so much devastation and so much loss. Would she ever get used to this war?

Turning her gaze back towards Annie and Judith, she saw a mixture of curiosity and worry in their eyes and felt a flash of guilt. She knew they too had lost their older brother, George, at Dunkirk last year, and since then had joined-up themselves, determined to do more to end the war that had killed their brother. If they could stand it, so could she. An image of Edie flashed into her mind, and she could picture her mother scrubbing the shop floor until it sparkled, telling her that she had made her bed, it was time to lie in it.

'Still,' Peggy said, with forced cheer in her voice, 'at least we weren't hit as bad as some of those poor souls in London.'

'They really did have it bad,' Annie agreed, her top lip covered in strawberry jam. 'I wouldn't have wanted to have been down there when Jerry had his way.'

'No, we've been pretty lucky up home with the raids,' Judith pointed out. 'Apart from Coventry and Birmingham, the Midlands hasn't suffered too much.'

Peggy winced. The raid last November on the Warwickshire city had been horrific, and worse still, her friend Kitty had been caught up in it. Thankfully she had survived, but it could have been so much worse. If anything, the war was teaching her to be thankful for every new day she survived, but there were times, Peggy thought, when it was incredibly hard to feel thankful.

'So, much happened while I've been away?' Peggy asked, changing the subject.

'Not a lot,' Annie admitted, looking at Judith for confirmation who gave a sharp nod of her head. 'New Year was quiet as we were driving a convoy up to Fishguard. We didn't get back till the small hours, 'cos Pat Grimes's truck broke down.'

'She didn't give it a maintenance check before she left,' Judith added in hushed tones.

'Yes! Because she was too busy the night before getting up to no good with that soldier she's been messing about with,' Annie hissed.

'Annie! Don't say things like that,' Judith whispered in alarm, looking around her to see if anyone had heard her sister's outburst.

'Why?' Annie shrugged. 'It's true. Everyone knows she's been up to all sorts, and it's down to her we weren't back at the mess for the music night they'd organised.'

'Is that what you told her?' Peggy raised an eyebrow.

Annie lifted her chin and met her friend's gaze. 'Might have mentioned it. Daft so-and-so should have been more careful.'

'Yer want to be more careful around Pat,' Judith cautioned. 'Yer know she's a nasty piece of work.'

Annie rolled her eyes. 'I can see off the likes of Pat Grimes and her rotten mate May Horobin. Don't you worry about me.'

'Even so,' Judith scolded. 'Don't make trouble where yer don't need to, it's never worth it.'

Annie shook her head and ignored her older sister's warning as she turned to Peggy. 'Anyway, apart from that it's just been work, work, work.'

'Well, there is a war on,' Peggy chuckled.

'Yes, Annie,' Judith pointed out. 'I think it's supposed to be work, work, work.'

'Not all the time!' Annie exploded, banging her hand down on the table to further emphasise her point.

Peggy blanched at Annie's outburst. Wasn't committing to a life in the Army and serving your country enough? There was a time for everything, Peggy concluded as she sipped her tea. And now was not the time for enjoyment; it was a time for fighting back.

'So,' she said brightly, turning to Judith. 'What about the rest of the spark girls? Any news?'

Judith shook her head. 'No, everything's been fairly quiet, Peg. We've had plenty of visitors to drive to and from the station, and of course we've got another convoy delivery to organise up to Manchester next week.'

'Goods for the NAAFI,' Annie added, leaning closer to the girls. 'I don't think Pat will be joining us this time, she's on a CB notice.

'Annie!' Judith hissed, widening her large emerald eyes in annoyance. 'Will you behave and stop gossiping.'

'It's not gossip if it's the truth,' Annie pointed out.

'Is it true?' Peggy asked, curiosity getting the better of her. A confined-to-barracks notice was a serious punishment. Too many of those and you could face court martial or worse.

Judith paused for a moment, before turning her head right and left to check who was listening. 'It is true. The red caps caught her out after curfew one night last week when she was supposed to be on guard duty. That and the truck breaking down was the last straw, I think. So yer see where living a little gets you, Annie.'

'Exactly,' Peggy agreed. 'As my mother says, rules are there to follow not break and if Pat had done the same she wouldn't be in this mess.'

Leaning back in her chair, Annie shook her head so violently a lock of hair escaped from her victory roll. 'If it were down to you two we'd no doubt stay in every night, knitting and listening to *It's That Man Again* on the wireless,' she groaned.

'Sounds like a good night to me,' Judith chuckled.

'And me.' Peggy smiled, as she stifled a yawn.

'Long night?' Judith asked sympathetically.

Peggy nodded. The events of the last twenty-four hours were catching up with her. 'So much for being fresh for my new job tomorrow.'

'Oh yes.' Annie grinned. 'You're personal driver to the lieu-tenant colonel now, aren't you?'

'Certainly am.' She gave the girls her best salute. 'I report for duty at eight in the morning sharp.'

'Do you know anything about him?' Judith quizzed.

'Nothing,' Peggy replied. 'I'm a bit nervous if I'm honest, girls. I can't believe they've asked me to drive one of the bigwigs about.'

'Rubbish,' admonished Annie. 'You're as good as, if not better than any of them. Lieutenant Colonel Carmichael prob-ably hand-picked you himself.'

'She's right,' Judith agreed loyally. 'You're a born driver, Peg, and your mechanical skills are excellent. It's no wonder they chose you.'

Peggy squirmed uncomfortably in the hard-backed chair. 'I just wonder what I'll do if he wants to talk to me. I mean, I don't know much about much, if I'm honest. What do I say?'

Annie sputtered with laughter as the nippy put the bill beside her. 'Give over, Peg, he's hardly likely to start discussing military strategy with yer, is he? If in doubt, get him talking about Lord Haw-Haw; everyone's got an opinion on him!'

'You're right, I'm being daft.' Peggy sighed.

'Not daft,' Judith said comfortingly. 'It's natural to worry about starting summat new.'

Peggy smiled, grateful for the reassurance and turned to Annie. 'How much is the bill, babber?'

Picking up the note, Annie held it at arm's length as she tried to make it out. 'I can't quite read it, the writing's that bad. That nippy wants to go back to school.'

Judith laughed as she snatched the chit from her sister's hand. 'Give us it here.'

Scanning the paper she reached for some coins in her purse and left them on the table. 'My treat.'

Peggy raised her eyes in surprise and gratitude at her friend's generosity. 'You sure?'

'Course,' Judith replied, getting to her feet and shrugging on her coat. 'Call it a good luck present for tomorrow.'

'Thanks,' replied Peggy, genuinely touched as she got up and walked through the crowded tearoom towards the door.

'You'll need more than luck,' Annie said, chuckling as they walked back out into the cold night air. 'Lieutenant Colonel Carmichael's supposed to be a right pain in the backside.'

Before Peggy had time to say a word, Judith whirled around and gripped Annie by the arm, leaving Peggy wide-eyed with surprise. Judith rarely lost her patience with Annie so suddenly.

'How many times have I told yer to stop gossiping, eh?' Judith scolded

'I wasn't, Jude, I swear,' she said, her voice trembling. 'It's true, I heard it off one of the girls up the garage the other day, like.'

'True or not, Annie, there are some things people don't need to hear,' Judith said, loosening her grip. 'The last thing Peggy needs before she starts a new job is your chi-iking.'

As the sisters walked on ahead, Peggy suddenly felt very tired. Usually she tried to help the girls resolve their differences, but tonight she was too exhausted. She had been through far too much for one day and all she wanted was to climb into bed, pull the sheets over her head and sleep. Quickening her step along the now icy pavement, she hurried towards the hotel, hoping against hope her friend was wrong about her new boss.

# Chapter Three

Throwing her sponge into the bucket of murky water, Peggy wiped her hands on the front of her khaki overalls and smiled at a job well done. The Humber she had spent the past two hours cleaning inside and out shone like a new penny and she felt a burst of pride that her car was without doubt the cleanest in the barracks.

Standing back to admire the gleaming bonnet, Peggy rubbed her hands together and pressed them to her lips to try and get the blood flowing again. Despite her long day yesterday, she had got up at four in the morning, unable to sleep. She wanted to get off to the best possible start with Lieutenant Colonel Carmichael and so before reporting to his office, she had wanted to make sure the car she had been assigned was in perfect condition.

Although she had given it a thorough going-over before she went home on leave, Peggy was a firm believer in double-checking, which was why she had not only missed Ida's promise of bacon and eggs for breakfast but had spent two hours in the freezing cold getting the Humber ready.

Now, as dawn began to break and the rest of the spark girls filed into the garage ready to start work, Peggy noticed her hands were red raw and chapped. Shoving her fists into the pocket of her khaki overalls she resolved to get a well-deserved cuppa from the mess just as soon as she had given the car a final once-over. She walked around the vehicle slowly, frowning as she saw a speck of dirt on the windscreen. Leaning over the bonnet to wipe the smear away with her sleeve, she gasped in shock as she felt a rush of icy cold water splash against her face and trickle down her neck.

'What was that for? You've soaked me good and proper,' she blasted.

Yet, whirling around to face the culprit, she was shocked to come face to face with ATS veteran and superior officer, Sub-Leader Sal Perkins. 'Sorry, Sal, didn't realise it was you.'

'No, pet, it's me that should be sorry. Let me get a cloth,' Sal replied apologetically.

Sal handed her a clean rag from her toolbox and Peggy blotted away most of the liquid.

'Sorry again,' Peggy said, handing the cloth back to Sal. 'I don't know what's got into me this morning, I didn't mean to be rude.'

Sal raised her eyebrows, her expression full of mock surprise. 'Nothin' to do with startin' a new job for one of the most important men in Wales, by any chance?'

Peggy looked at the concrete floor before gazing up at Sal and smiling awkwardly. 'Is it that obvious?'

'Not at all, flower,' Sal said in her clear Geordie accent. 'I'd be just the same as you if it were me tasked with drivin' his lordship here, there and everywhere.'

'I was so excited when I was asked to do it, but now I'm just nervous,' Peggy admitted, leaning back against the bonnet of the Humber. 'What if I forget how to drive or say something really stupid?'

'I think we both know that's not very likely, pet.' Sal smiled, her crinkled eyes full of kindness. Leaning next to Peggy, she reached into her pocket and produced a bar of Cadbury's chocolate. 'Here, this'll settle your nerves, no doubt you've got yourself that worked up you've not had any breakfast yet either.'

Peggy gasped in surprise at the unexpected kindness. 'I can't take that.'

But Sal had already unwrapped the bar and pressed it into her hands. 'Course you can, and no doubt you'll feel right as rain when you've finished it.'

Gazing at the bar with longing, Peggy's stomach suddenly let out a loud rumble. She was hungrier than she thought. Smiling shyly, she accepted the bar and took a hungry bite. As the sweet chocolate slid down her throat, Peggy realised with satisfaction how right Sal had been – suddenly her new job didn't seem quite so terrifying.

'So, what's got your knickers in a twist?' Sal asked, as Peggy finished the chocolate.

Scrunching the wrapper up into a tiny ball, Peg shoved it into her overall pocket and eyed Sal with caution. As sub-leader, Sal was responsible for dishing out petrol, driving supplies and keeping the girls on a tight leash when they were out on the roads. It was also her job to ensure every spark girl kept an accurate record of their mileage and their vehicles in good working order.

Sal was in her forties, and with her red hair and matching lips, she made a point of not mincing her words. As a result, Peggy had a lot of time and respect for the matriarch. Sal was widowed with a grown-up son in the Army. When he was called up, Sal felt there was no point staying at home, so decided to do her own bit for the war effort and joined the Army herself. She had an air of trustworthiness about her, Peggy thought, and she could really use a friend. Not that Annie and Judith didn't count, of course, Peg told herself hurriedly. It was simply a case that getting involved in the two sisters' rows took up much of their time together, something Peg found herself confessing to Sal, along with Annie's latest revelations about her new boss.

'Oh, you don't want to take any notice of Annie Shawcross, Peggy,' Sal said in a soothing tone. 'What she doesn't know, she makes up. She's only a kid, Peggy, likes a bit of drama.'

'But Annie seemed to know something I didn't,' Peggy said sadly, the emotion of the situation tumbling out of her like water through floodgates now she had finally opened up. 'What if she's right? I'm not sure I could cope with a bully.'

'I've never heard anythin' like that about Lieutenant Colonel Carmichael,' Sal insisted. 'I'm sure Annie's just made it up for a bit of fuss.'

Peggy hoped Sal was right, she had seen first-hand how badly her friend Kitty had been bullied by a superior officer and knew she wasn't strong enough to cope. Opening her mouth to say as much, they were interrupted by a group of spark girls who had just barged their way past the two women demanding motor fuel and requisition forms from Sal.

'No rest for the wicked.' Sal smiled as she got up from the car to calm the throng. 'Now go and get some real breakfast, there's no sense startin' somethin' new on an empty stomach.'

With a grin, Peggy realised Sal was right. Giving the woman a cheery wave of thanks, she picked up her eating irons and made her way towards the mess. Inside she was delighted to find that it was not only quiet, but that Cook herself was serving eggs and bacon.

Just over an hour later and with a tummy full of food, she marched her way across the quad towards the office of the lieutenant colonel. Nervously she knocked on the heavy wooden door and waited for a response. Just getting near the great man himself had been a challenge. Not only had she had to announce herself three times to various secretaries and guards, but she had been up and down so many wood-panelled corridors that she felt as if she had walked the length and breadth of Wales.

As she waited, Peggy allowed her mind to wander. Although she hadn't known Annie long, there had been several times when the younger girl had got hold of the wrong end of the stick. She had never forgotten the time when Annie was supposed to have been navigating her to Aberystwyth for a pick-up but had got the directions completely wrong, ending up with some very cross words between them.

Chances were she was completely wrong about this as well, Peggy thought as she lifted her hand about to knock again, when the sound of a deep, booming voice shouted, 'Enter.'

Pushing open the door, Peggy walked boldly through and tried not to gasp in amazement. The tall-ceilinged, wood-panelled office, decorated with a range of oil and watercolour paintings, was like nothing she had ever seen before. Noticing that her feet felt unusually comfortable, she looked down and saw her Oxford brogues were pressing into plush red carpet. She felt as if she had died and gone to heaven as she marvelled at the luxury, a fact that wasn't lost on the lieutenant colonel.

'Cat got your tongue, volunteer?' he bellowed, standing up from behind his desk.

Suitably rebuked, Peggy brought her head up sharply and looked at her superior officer with a start. As she had expected, he was a lot older than her, with a head full of grey hair and a determined set to his jaw. Tall, with a portly frame, Peggy saw there was a hint of amusement in his grey eyes and as she walked across the room to greet him, her fears melted away.

'Volunteer Collins, sir,' she said, standing before his desk and saluting him as she had been trained.

Peggy stood there wordlessly, her hand clamped to her forehead as the lieutenant colonel walked out from behind his desk and stood in front of her, hand outstretched for her to shake.

'Pleasure to meet you, Volunteer Collins,' he smiled. 'Lieutenant Colonel Ian Carmichael.'

Gesturing for Peggy to take a seat, the lieutenant colonel walked over to the window and looked out across the barracks. Following his gaze, Peggy tried to see what her commanding officer saw and realised that it wasn't much of a view for a man in his position. The quad was cold and grey, and with the bare trees and even greyer sky overhead it made for a dismal sight.

'Been driving in the Army long, Collins?' he asked, his back still facing her.

'Just under a year or so, sir,' Peggy replied.

'Is that all?' The lieutenant colonel's voice rose in surprise.

'Yes, sir.' Peggy gulped nervously, wondering if he was going to sack her before she had even started.

'Well, you must be jolly good then.' He smiled, turning to face her and walking back towards his desk. 'Either that or the Army's trying to see me off by pairing me with someone inexperienced.'

Peggy coloured at his teasing. 'I hope it's not that, sir.'

'One never knows,' he said, eyes crinkling in merriment as he shuffled some papers across his desk. 'Well look, we've a nice easy day today. Trip over Bridgend way to the air base. I've a meeting with one of the officers over there. Shouldn't take too long, and hopefully we'll be back in time for tea and crumpets. That all right with you, Collins?'

'Yes, sir, of course, sir,' Peggy said meekly as she got up to salute her officer.

'Excellent, Collins. I'll see you in the car in ten minutes. Bring it around to the front for me,' Carmichael ordered before dismissing her.

Wordlessly Peggy left the lieutenant colonel's office and raced down the corridor and out into the quad. She would have her work cut out getting all the way across to the motor garage to pick up the Humber and bring it back in under ten minutes. Still, she was determined not to let her new boss down, and with just seconds to spare, she had the car out the front, just as Carmichael walked down the stairs.

Still panting from her efforts, Peggy got out of the car and walked around to the back to open the door and he smiled at her as he sat in the car.

'Hope I haven't got you out of breath, Collins?' he chuckled.

Peggy's cheeks coloured with embarrassment as she slid the

car out of the gates and turned right into the narrow road. 'Not at all, sir. Fit as a fiddle.'

'Glad someone is, because I'm certainly not.' He laughed.

Glancing into her rear-view mirror, Peggy saw her boss lean back against the back seat and peer out of the window at the bright but cold wintry morning. With ice on the roads, Peggy knew she would have to be careful and she kept her eyes firmly on the road ahead.

'So, what made you join-up, Collins?' Carmichael called, interrupting Peggy's concentration.

'My father was in the Army,' she explained. 'When war broke out, I wanted to do more and the Army seemed a natural choice.'

Indicating left, Peggy turned into the narrow country lane, and hoped the lieutenant colonel couldn't see the awkwardness she was sure was written across her face. She had thought it best to leave out the part where her best mate had encouraged her to join-up for adventure, sensing somehow that her boss was a man of honour and wouldn't appreciate the whole truth.

'Seems to suit you, Collins,' Carmichael called from the back. 'You're certainly a natural driver.'

Peggy flushed at the unexpected praise. 'Thank you, sir, I do my best.'

'You're certainly better than I am, that's for sure. I have always been an absolute duffer behind the wheel. Just couldn't get to grips with it. So it's as well I spend most of my days behind a desk with the pleasure of a bright volunteer to take me wherever I need to go.'

Peggy said nothing as Carmichael continued, 'Of course, I do miss the cut and thrust of being out in the field with my chums. The endless marching in all weathers, the training, but mostly I miss the camaraderie. It's not the same when you're in charge, Collins.'

'I understand, sir,' replied Peggy, slowing down to allow a tractor to pass her in the narrow country lane. Pausing to look again into the rear-view mirror she saw a flicker of wistfulness pass across his lined features. She had a feeling Carmichael was a soldier first and officer second. Just where had Annie got the idea he was a pain?

'Yes, I bet you do, some of my best friendships were forged in the Army, and I imagine you've made a fair few good chums yourself,' Carmichael said, interrupting her reverie.

Images of Kitty, Di and Mary flashed into her mind, and Peggy smiled at the thought of the three girls she had come to adore as if they were sisters. Kitty particularly had become a good friend to Peggy. An orphan herself, Kitty had known just how to comfort Peggy on her first night away from home.

It was thanks to Kitty that Peggy had survived the Army at all, and had gone on to do so well. If Peggy had been left to her own devices she would have been begging her superiors to let her leave after just a couple of days she was sure.

'One or two, sir.' She grinned.

'Yes, it's one of the best things about Army life: the friendships you make,' the lieutenant colonel continued, warming to his theme. 'Your old friends, the people you grew up with or worked with before you joined-up, don't usually understand things the way Army muckers do. Incidentally, where is it you're from, Collins?'

'Bristol, sir,' she replied, 'born and bred.'

He smiled and nodded his head in approval. 'Thought I detected a bit of an accent, Collins. It's a fine city, if I do say so myself.'

'That it is, sir,' Peggy agreed enthusiastically.

'You know, an old pal of mine was from Bristol,' Carmichael mused as he rubbed his chin thoughtfully. 'In fact, he was called Collins too – thick as thieves we were for a time, but of course we lost touch when he was posted abroad, must be twenty years ago now. Don't suppose he's any relation?'

Peggy shook her head. 'I don't think so, sir. My dad never

mentioned you, and I couldn't ask him as he passed over five years ago now.'

The lieutenant colonel flinched. 'I'm sorry, Collins.'

Peggy lifted her hand from the steering wheel and batted her superior officer's concerns away.

'Don't worry, sir, you weren't to know.'

Just then the picturesque rural landscape disappeared and a huge, grey, formidable-looking aerodrome came into view. As they approached the wrought-iron gates, Peggy slowed and wound down the window to announce their arrival to the guard on duty.

Once they were waved through, Peggy parked as instructed in front of a large Nissen hut and opened the door for Lieutenant Colonel Carmichael. The wind was so strong on the airbase it took all the strength she possessed to hold it open, a fact that wasn't lost on her superior officer.

'Get yourself a cup of tea in the mess, Collins,' he shouted above the roar of the gale. 'I'll find you in there. It's far too cold and miserable to sit in the car.'

'Very good, sir,' she said, shutting the door firmly behind him and saluting his retreating back.

Once Carmichael was safely inside, Peggy followed his instructions and walked towards the mess. Hearing a sudden roar overhead, she glanced up at the sky and felt a sudden thrill as she saw a Spitfire coming into land. Unable to tear her eyes from the scene above, she watched in awe as the pilot skilfully tilted the plane to the right before lowering the small wheels that would deliver it safely to the ground.

Watching planes take off and land was a sight Peggy wasn't sure she would ever get used to. Being in the services she had seen several aircraft but the thought of flying still seemed so exciting. She knew the mechanics of it all and understood the science behind the metal silver birds and how they remained in the sky, but it still felt like a little miracle every time she saw a pilot launch one.

Huddling into her greatcoat to keep out the chill of the wind, Peggy saw two airmen rush forward to help the pilot clamber out of the aircraft. As he appeared, she saw the airmen slap him heartily on the back, and despite the roar of the wind, the pilot's voice was so loud, she could hear his plummy tones as clear as a bell, making Peggy wince.

'Jolly good show, sir,' one of the gunners called.

'Thanks, Simmons,' the pilot shouted. 'Gave the Hun a jolly good thrashing, just as Blighty ordered.' The airmen laughed and patted him on the back once more.

'Looked rough out there today though, sir. Did you find the wind tricky?' one of the younger men asked.

The pilot chuckled as if the very idea was something he couldn't fathom. 'Absolutely not. First-rate flying conditions for getting rid of Jerry! Gave him six of the best and a few more from matron besides.'

As the braying laughter continued, Peggy turned away in disgust. She hadn't met many pilots, but those she had come into contact with she had found to be conceited and arrogant. They generally had little time, respect or care for anyone else, and listening to the pilot gloat about how he had swooped in low during a training exercise, getting so close the Hun had been forced to run for their lives, wasn't doing anything to change her mind.

Pursing her lips as she looked at him she shook her head in disgust. He was everything she loathed: tall with blond hair, blue eyes and an easy smile. Privilege oozed out of him and it was clear he had never faced a day's hardship in his life.

Unable to listen to the raucous noise of the pilot and his airmen any longer, she turned her back and walked inside. Feeling the warmth seep into her bones, the anxiety she had been harbouring all morning began to melt away. Her shoulders loosened, the tension in her neck eased and after helping herself to a teacake and strong, warm cuppa, she took a seat by the fire and relaxed. Unwinding the scarf from around her neck, she looked around and saw with surprise the place was practically deserted. More often than not, she ended up talking shop with anyone who was in the mess, but today it looked like she had the place to herself.

Peggy smiled at the unexpected pleasure. If there was one thing she wasn't in the mood for it was making polite chit-chat with pilots. Instead, she took a grateful sip of tea and let the warmth of the liquid thaw out her insides. Instantly feeling better she reached into her pocket for the paperback she had started on the train yesterday and sank back into the battered leather easy chair.

When she had started driving she had always thought it seemed a bit of a cheek to grab a cup of tea and a rest on the job. Thanks to a strong work ethic instilled by the formidable Edie, Peggy had at first taken time to wash the car, or check the mechanics while she waited for whoever she was driving to finish their business, much to the amusement of more seasoned drivers. Now, she not only saw these breaks as a happy perk, but something of a necessity. Long days and sometimes nights as a spark girl could often mean driving for hours without a break and so it was vital, Peggy had realised, to take the opportunity for a rest when you could.

Besides, she thought, taking another sip of tea, her commanding officer had issued her with a direct order and she wasn't going to disobey him on her first day. Peggy began to read, losing herself so heavily in the romance novel of a pair of tortured sweethearts that almost three hours passed in the blink of an eye.

'Hope I'm not disturbing you, Collins,' a loud voice boomed in her ear.

With a start, Peggy jumped to her feet and saw her superior officer standing over her, hands clasped behind his back. Shoving the book she had by now almost finished hastily into her pocket, she saluted him.

'Sir,' she said in what she hoped was a respectful and professional tone.

'At ease, Collins,' the lieutenant colonel barked.

'Would you like to go now, sir?' Peggy asked.

'Yes, better had, dastardly long meeting. Only good thing about it was the toad-in-the-hole Cook provided at half-time,' Carmichael said conspiratorially as he glanced down at his watch. 'Heavens above, Collins, it's past lunchtime. Have you eaten?'

Nodding, Peggy thought back to the teacake she had devoured earlier and thanked her lucky stars she had seen the good sense to eat as well as drink. Something else she had learned early on, she thought with a wry smile as she reached for her scarf and wound it around her neck.

Following Carmichael across the room towards the exit, Peggy noticed the mess was now full of pilots and airmen, chattering and laughing loudly as they tucked into lunch.

At the sound of another jarring laugh, Peggy shuddered and hastened her step, pushing past a group of gunners in her hurry to leave.

Outside, the roar of the wind had become deafening and it had by now gathered so much speed it was all she could do to stay upright as she and Carmichael hurried to the car.

'Don't worry about opening the door for me, Collins,' Carmichael bellowed, as they reached the Humber, which Peggy was alarmed to see was juddering violently. 'It's every man for himself in this weather.'

'Very good, sir,' she said, flinging the driver's door open and hurling herself into the seat.

With the doors safely shut, Peggy was struck by how quiet the car was and took a deep breath before she started the car.

'Are you all right in the back, sir?' Peggy asked as she turned on the starter motor, knowing that checking on the welfare of a passenger was just as important as ensuring they got to their destination safely.

'Splendid, Collins,' the lieutenant colonel replied. 'The bigger question is, are you all right? This wind isn't a problem, is it? I'm quite happy to wait if you would prefer to hang about for more clement weather.'

But Peggy shook her head. She had driven in worse conditions than this and peering at the dark grey sky, which was getting blacker the longer she looked at it, she had a feeling the weather would get worse before it got better. At least there was still technically an hour or so of daylight left, which ought to be more than enough time to get back to Swansea.

'I reckon the best ideal is to proceed with caution, sir, if that's all right with you?' Peggy said in what she hoped was an authoritative tone.

Carmichael nodded his head in reply. 'You're the expert, Collins. I'll leave it in your more than capable hands.'

As Peggy slid the car into gear, she clung to the wheel for dear life as the vehicle rumbled along the tarmac and back out on to the road. Once they were away from the expanse of the aerodrome, the wind wasn't quite so bad thanks to the shelter of the hedgerows on either side of the narrow country lane so she relaxed and loosened her grip on the wheel, confident she had the car under control.

'Bit hairy out there, wasn't it?' Carmichael exclaimed.

Peggy's eyes met his as she glanced at him in the rear-view mirror. 'Let's just say I'm glad we're off the airbase, sir.'

'Yes, me too,' Carmichael agreed. 'If only to get away from those arrogant airmen. Honestly, Collins, of all of His Majesty's services, it's the RAF that are the most stuck-up.'

Peggy raised her eyebrows in surprise and stifled a giggle. She had never heard a commanding officer speak so freely before. Was this what Annie meant? she wondered. Well, if it was she had no problem being her superior's sounding board. But wisdom told her it was best to say nothing in reply, no matter what she heard. One wrong word from her lips could cost her a CB notice, a court martial or even her job, Peggy thought sagely.

Instead, she kept her gaze firmly on the road, marvelling at the beauty of the Welsh countryside. Even on a day like today, she thought, where everywhere looked grey, dirty and miserable, there was something glorious about the way the rolling hills morphed into lush green fields that stretched on forever. Wales was like nowhere she had ever seen before, and, she thought with a smile, she could understand why the country was famous for its choirs: there was after all, so much to sing about.

Slowing the car down as she approached a junction, Peggy indicated left and turned neatly into a narrow lane she knew was popular with farmers. As the mist descended over the hills, she was careful to keep an eye out for farm traffic and even the odd cow or stray goat. In an ideal world, she would put on her lights to see better, but thanks to blackout restrictions cars were only allowed a pinprick of light from their headlamps when it was pitch black, which was usually no good to man nor beast.

'Sorry for the delay, sir,' she called, aware that her superior officer had important work to be getting on with back at the barracks.

'Not at all, Collins,' he replied. 'Better to arrive late and in one piece than not arrive at all.'

Peggy smiled, that was just the sort of thing her mum would come out with, and she felt a sudden rush of longing for home and all the comforts it contained. It was getting darker by the minute and Peggy had never carried such precious cargo. As the rain began to fall, a knot of fear grew in her stomach. She hunched over the steering wheel to get a better view of the road ahead, so much so she didn't even see the car behind her, much less hear it until the sound of a loud *beep, beep* screeching at her like a banshee behind caught her attention. With a start, Peggy peered into her rear-view mirror and saw what looked suspiciously like a sports car.

Squinting, she saw to her surprise it was an Aston Martin

Ulster, a notoriously expensive and rarely seen car since the onset of war. Peggy was no car buff, but everyone knew of the Ulster; it was such a glorious vehicle, she thought, admiring its beauty. Looking into her mirror once more, she frowned at whoever was behind the wheel. He or she was clearly a maniac, judging by the speed and general lack of care towards other motorists.

As the car neared and beeped again, Peggy felt her hackles rise. Not only was this road narrow, but with such poor visibility the driver was just asking for an accident driving like that. Another glance in the mirror told her that the car was now perilously close, and obviously wanted her to pull over so they could overtake, but one look at the road ahead, along with the perilous driving conditions, ought to have told the driver they would have to wait.

'Who is that road hog?' Carmichael demanded, peering out of the back window.

'No ideal, sir,' Peggy replied, her hands gripping the steering wheel as she looked for a safe place to pull over and let the idiot go.

'Well, he's a damn nuisance on the road, Collins, that's who he is,' Carmichael roared.

Peggy couldn't disagree, and rounding the corner, she hoped and prayed that there would be a place she could stop. Yet as she indicated left, the driver behind obviously thought she was pulling in and moved his car violently forward to overtake. As the car neared the Humber with just inches between them, Peggy was forced to pull the steering wheel down hard on the left, causing the car to veer violently off the road. She gasped in horror as they skidded into a ditch then crashed into a tree while the Ulster roared off into the distance.

'Are you all right, sir?' Peggy asked as the car came to a stop.

'I'm fine,' Carmichael roared, his eyes narrowed with anger. 'No thanks to that bloody menace though.'

Before she could say another word, the lieutenant colonel had opened the rear passenger door and clambered out of the car in the pouring rain to inspect the damage. Heart heavy, Peggy climbed out herself, legs shaking. As she joined him, she could scarcely believe her eyes. Despite the gloom, she could see that the front of the car was smashed to pieces, with the bonnet all but destroyed and bent into an upside down V-shape. Aghast, Peggy looked at the damage, feeling sick. She was such a careful driver and had never been in any kind of accident before, and now this on the first day of her new job. As the engine hissed and wheezed like a wounded animal in pain, Peggy felt terrible. The car was clearly a write-off. What would her commanding officer say? How would they even get back?

Tears pricked her eyelids. 'I'm ever so sorry, sir.'

But Carmichael batted her apologies away. 'Now that's quite enough of that, Collins. This was far from your fault. If anything, I should be thanking you from the bottom of my heart for ensuring we both survived. No, if anyone's to blame it's that devil in the Ulster. I tell you, Collins, if I ever get my hands on him he'll regret it, make no mistake.'

As the lieutenant colonel tailed off, Peggy suddenly heard the sound of a car coming towards them. The gentle whoosh of the tyres squelching against the wet ground became louder and as Peggy peered through the darkness she saw the definite shape of a car approaching. Jumping up and down, waving her hands in the air to alert the driver to their plight, she was overjoyed when the car stopped a little way ahead. Screwing up her eyes for a better view, she rushed towards the vehicle. Only her joy quickly turned to anger as she realised it was no ordinary car. It was an Aston Martin Ulster.

Shocked, she watched the driver's door open and a pair of feet step on to the ground. As the rest of the body emerged, Peggy felt anger course through her veins. Of course, it all made sense now. The idiot driver who had run her off the road was none other than the braying pilot she had seen land the Spitfire earlier.

# Chapter Four

Rooted to the spot, Peggy could barely keep her disgust to herself as the pilot's long legs strode easily along the path, clearly illuminated by the Ulster's headlamps, which he had left switched on. Even his walk looked arrogant, Peggy thought as she watched him tilt his head forward to avoid the rain and shove his hands into the pockets of his leather flight jacket.

Turning to the lieutenant colonel, she caught sight of the naked anger in his eyes. Good. She wasn't the only one who was furious.

'You ran us off the road, you young buck,' he roared, the warmth of his breath sending clouds of mist into the cold, dark air.

The pilot lifted his head, and Peggy saw the tight set of his jaw. 'I truly am sorry for what's happened here,' he said in a quiet, well-spoken voice. 'But I think you'll find if you had been driving properly in the first place this would never have happened.'

Peggy gasped in shock. She had been right all along. The pilot was an arrogant pillock. How dare he try and make out it was her fault when he was in the wrong? Anger pulsed through her veins and more than anything Peggy wanted to tear strips off him. However, with her commanding officer standing next to her, she wasn't entirely sure it was appropriate and did her best to remain calm.

Thankfully, Carmichael had no such qualms and took a menacing step towards the man. 'You cheeky upstart. I ought to horsewhip you for your insolence.'

The pilot stared mutinously at them as Carmichael continued with his onslaught. 'This was very clearly your fault. You were driving like a road hog for miles, I saw you with my own eyes. Have you not seen the weather, man? Are you unsure of how to drive along a country lane? Hell, do you even know there's a war on and speed restrictions are in place? You were roaring through the countryside with no thought for anyone else. I'll make damned sure your superior officer knows about this and your insubordination, just look at what you've done.'

Carmichael gestured towards the car and Peggy and the pilot followed his gaze and saw the sorry state of the Humber. Although the steam was no longer hissing into the air, the bonnet and grille were completely smashed and both wheel arches had buckled.

Peggy hung her head in sorrow. The new car she had been assigned as part of her new job had been destroyed. She lifted her head and gazed at the pilot with hatred in her eyes.

'And not only that,' Carmichael continued, bringing his gaze back to the other man, 'but you've given my driver here the fright of her life. What have you got to say for yourself?'

The pilot raised an eyebrow at Peggy, giving nothing away.

'I can see you're upset, but I'm not taking responsibility here. Anyone knows that if you see someone wanting to overtake, you get out of the way, you don't hold your position,' the pilot replied in a bored tone. 'Now if you need a tow or something, I'll be happy to try and organise something for you but that's as far as my part in this goes.'

Carmichael shook his head. 'You're wholly responsible and I'm sure your commanding officer will agree. Now, you can forget a tow, you brainless imbecile, I'm commandeering your car for myself and Collins.'

The pilot jerked his head up. 'You will do no such thing.'

'I will do every such thing,' Carmichael thundered, before addressing Peggy. 'Collins, seize the vehicle.'

The pilot took a step towards him. 'Don't you dare. It's an Aston Martin Ulster, I only collected it yesterday – you won't have a clue how to drive it.'

Carmichael turned to Peggy. 'Collins, I am giving you a direct order, get into that Aston now. As for you, pilot . . . pilot . . . what is your name?'

'Hudson, Pilot Officer James Hudson,' he sneered, drawing himself up to his full height.

'Well, Pilot Officer James Hudson, be under no illusion, this isn't a request, it's a direct order. Collins here is a first-rate driver, and I can assure you she'll make a finer job of it than you will. Now you can either join us or stay on the roadside. Your choice and I don't care which it is.'

Peggy wasn't sure who was more shocked, her or Pilot Officer Hudson who stood speechless, staring open-mouthed from her to Carmichael. Her commanding officer had given her a direct order that she had every intention of fulfilling, but could she really drive a car worth so much money? With a jolt she remembered how she had told Edie how much she loved driving, the freedom behind the wheel. Looking across at the Ulster, she realised that this was her chance to experience a freedom like no other.

Cautiously she looked up at Carmichael again. She still wasn't sure, but her superior officer was clearly in no mood to mollycoddle her.

'Collins! What did I just say?' he roared. 'Get into that car now.'

Trembling, Peggy didn't wait to be told twice. Running down the road, far away from the pompous pilot and her commanding officer, she neared the car, feeling like a child at Christmas. Up close, the car was a beauty, she had never seen anything like it in her life.

Running her hand over the bonnet, she marvelled at its shape.

Despite the gloom, the glossy black paintwork shone, and the twin red leather seats shaped like armchairs looked beyond inviting. Eagerly, Peggy held the door open for Carmichael who had now caught up with her.

'Watch the paintwork,' Hudson snapped, as he clambered in ahead of the lieutenant colonel.

Peggy said nothing. Instead she walked around to the driver's side and got in. Oh, it felt like heaven, so squishy and comfortable, it was as though she was sitting on a hundred feather pillows. But glancing at the walnut dashboard, that familiar lack of confidence began to grow. There were so many complicated-looking instruments and dials she had never seen before and she didn't have a clue what they all were. Earnestly, she tried to make them all out, but they were so difficult she was none the wiser.

'Come along, Collins, stop dilly-dallying,' Carmichael ordered.

'Yes, sir,' Peggy replied, correctly guessing she needed to flick a switch to activate the ignition, magneto and fuel pump before pressing the starter button.

Immediately the car burst into life, and Peggy slid the Ulster into gear, hands gripping the giant wheel as she drove nervously along the road, aware that Pilot Officer Hudson was so close to her she could feel his leg pressed against hers.

His body oozed a warmth that made her uncomfortable, but Peggy refused to let the pilot's presence put her off. Incredibly, within minutes she forgot all about Hudson, the Humber and even Edie. Instead, she lost herself in the car. Although the Ulster was heavier than the Humber, there was no denying it had a certain grace. It gripped the road like no other car she had driven, cornering each turn precisely. Best of all, the comfort meant she barely felt any of the lumps and bumps in the road. It was a driving experience she would probably never have again, Peggy thought, smiling as she drove through the country lanes in silence, imagining what it would be like to drive this car every day.

By the time they reached the aerodrome, Peggy was well and truly in fantasy land. Pulling into a space, she was as shocked as she was sorry when she brought the car to a halt.

Stepping out on to the tarmac, she held the door open for Carmichael and felt a pang of sadness as she watched Hudson step out behind him. The car really was a beauty, it was a shame it belonged to such a prat. He would no doubt run it into the ground rather than treat it with the respect it deserved.

Carmichael tapped her lightly on the shoulder. 'First-rate driving there, Collins, absolutely first-rate. Now, why don't you go back into the mess, get yourself a cup of something hot.'

'Very good, sir,' Peggy replied, saluting her superior officer as he turned his gaze to Hudson.

'And as for you, you can come with me now and explain just how you ran my driver off the road and destroyed my car.'

Peggy looked at the pilot out of the corner of her eye, expecting him to deliver another tongue-lashing. But instead all the fight, arrogance and bravado seemed to have left him as he silently saluted and followed the lieutenant colonel across the quad to the wing commander's office.

Turning up her collar to keep out the wind, Peggy watched the pilot's retreating back and shuddered. Not for all the tea in China would she want to trade places with Hudson right now – even if he did own an Aston Martin Ulster.

Back in the mess, Peggy helped herself to yet another cup of tea and saw her place by the fire was still vacant. She quickly settled in the chair, and pulled out her paperback. She had no idea how long Carmichael would want to tear strips off Hudson, or how long it would take for them to drive back to Swansea, so she decided to make the most of her unexpected break.

But despite her best intentions, she could barely concentrate on her book, so wrapped up was she in the events of the day.

After reading the same paragraph three times, she stuffed the novel back into her pocket and sank back into her chair, allowing the warmth of the fire to thaw her freezing arms and legs.

It had been quite the first day, she thought, remembering with horror the state of her precious car. She had so wanted everything to go well and had fretted over every detail, from how she would cope if Carmichael turned out to be the bully Annie suspected, to how she would manage a difficult driving route. What she hadn't expected was what she would do if she encountered a rude ratbag who drove her off the road, caused her to write off her new car, and refused to take all responsibility. Just the thought of the pilot made her blood boil.

'Penny for them?' A loud voice boomed in her ear.

Turning around, Peggy saw it was the pilot responsible for her misfortune standing beside her chair grinning.

'Even though you've got a fancy car, I doubt you could afford my thoughts,' she said bitterly.

Hudson grimaced and raked his fingers through his hair as he sat in the chair opposite. 'That bad, eh?'

Peggy shrugged and turned her gaze back towards the fire. She avoided confrontation of any kind, but today had taken its toll and she suddenly felt very tired.

'What d'you want?' she said, gruffly.

'I just wanted to apologise,' he said solemnly. 'I was unforgivably rude to you and I'm sorry.'

Peggy raised an eyebrow and turned back to look at the flames dancing merrily in the grate. She knew she ought to be gracious and accept his apology, but the truth was it felt a little too late. No doubt his superiors had blasted him from here to kingdom come and he had been ordered to apologise. Peggy shook her head, she was in no mood for it.

The pilot, sensing her displeasure, leaned forward in his chair. 'Look, I really am sorry. It was my fault not yours. I don't know why I didn't say that at the time, I knew I was in the wrong.'

'So why lie?' Peggy barely even bothered to glance up at him, but something in his tone made her curious.

Hudson sighed and ran a hand through his hair. 'I don't know. Because I'm an idiot, and because I'd had rather a tough day. It was foolish of me and it was foolish of me to run you off the road like that. I certainly never meant to cause you to crash.'

'So why did you?' Peggy blurted.

The pilot's eyes shot up in surprise at Peggy's forthright tone. 'Well, as I say,' he mumbled, 'it was an accident.'

Peggy couldn't help herself, and burst out laughing. She didn't think the day could get any stranger, and if truth be told she really didn't want to listen to a host of excuses from a pilot who was clearly well-practised at getting his own way.

'What's so funny?' Hudson demanded, his brow furrowed in confusion.

'Nothing.' Peggy smiled, remembering that the pilot was not only a good ten years older than her, but also a far higher rank and as such she should treat him with respect, even if he was a berk. 'Nothing at all, sir.'

Hudson sank back into his chair and looked at Peggy questioningly. 'You don't believe me, do you?'

'I'm sorry, sir?'

'You think I couldn't give a damn about the crash,' Hudson said evenly.

Peggy blushed at being caught out and shuffled uncomfortably in her chair. 'It's not really my place.'

'Of course it's your place. I behaved like a prize fool. My commanding officer has just torn several strips off me. I'm to pay for the damage out of my own pocket, and worst of all I'm on jankers until further notice.'

Peggy blanched at the harshness of the punishment. She had been around pilots long enough to know jankers was their slang for a confined-to-barracks notice, which Peggy lived in mortal fear of. As a driver she couldn't bear the idea of losing her freedom, and realised that for a pilot it must be even worse as they spent much of their lives in the skies. As for the cost of repairing the car, Peggy felt a flash of horror at the expense of it all, knowing it would easily cost her ten years' wages to afford to replace an entire a car, let alone a Humber.

'Will you manage?' she asked gently.

Hudson's expression softened. 'I'll be fine. It's no more than I deserve, as your lieutenant colonel was quick to point out, along with how he hoped I didn't pilot planes in the same way I drove motor cars.'

Peggy stifled a smile. She had known her commanding officer for less than twenty-four hours but already she could tell he was as loyal as the day was long.

'So why were you driving like that?' she asked curiously.

Hudson said nothing, instead he raked his hands through his blond hair and sighed. 'It's a long story, but let's just say I had some bad news and was letting off a bit of steam.'

'You looked happy enough to me when you landed that plane earlier,' Peggy pointed out. 'All your mates clapping you on the back, as you told them all about how you gave the Hun a thrashing.'

'You saw that?' Hudson said in surprise.

Peggy nodded. 'It was hard to miss, to be honest with you.'

Hudson roared with laughter. 'Well, you're quite right, Collins. We pilots do show off a bit, not cricket at all. I suppose it's because there's always the worry you might not return from a mission and so we celebrate whenever we come back, more often than not with a drink and a pretty girl, like you.'

A dark crimson blush crept up Peggy's neck and she hated herself for allowing her heart to be sweet-talked so easily. The trouble was she hadn't received many compliments from the opposite sex and had no idea what to do when they came her way. As the cacophony of chatter in the mess grew louder, Peggy searched desperately for something to say, only to be rescued by the pilot.

'I've embarrassed you,' he said quietly. 'I'm sorry, I didn't mean to do that, especially after everything else I've done today.'

Shaking her head, Peggy smiled. 'You didn't.'

Hudson held her gaze and returned her grin. 'I really would like to make it up to you, Collins.'

Peggy felt a knot of fear in her stomach. 'That's not necessary, sir, honestly. You're doing more than enough as it is, paying for all that damage yourself.'

'I'm making amends to the Army, Collins. By the way, what is your first name? Feels a bit odd calling a girl by her last name.'

'Peggy, sir,' she replied nervously.

'A lovely name. Peggy, it seems only right to me that I make amends to you as well. Your superior officer was right, I behaved appallingly. So, what's it to be? Dinner? Dance? Pictures, or perhaps all three if you'll let me?'

Lost for words, Peggy was saved from a response at the sight of Carmichael making his way across the mess.

'Hello, sir.' Peggy quickly got to her feet and saluted him as he approached.

'Hello, Collins.' He spotted the pilot officer and a flash of anger crossed his features. 'What are you doing here?'

'Just apologising to your driver, sir,' Hudson replied contritely, after saluting the officer.

Carmichael pursed his lips and said nothing, before turning to Peggy. 'And I should jolly well think so. Come along, Collins, the wing commander has organised a driver to take us back to the barracks.'

'Very good, sir,' Peggy replied, gathering her coat.

'Bye, Peggy,' Hudson said softly, as she turned to leave. 'I'll be in touch about that dance.'

*

The sun had long since dipped by the time Peggy returned to the hotel. Walking into the foyer, she looked so exhausted that

Ida took pity on her and made her a cheese sandwich, even though supper had finished an hour earlier.

'You look done in, my lovely, if you don't mind me saying,' the kindly landlady said, placing the plate of sandwiches in front of her. 'Just don't tell anyone I gave you food after hours. Folk'll think I'm running an hotel!'

Peggy chuckled as Ida laughed at her own joke. Taking a grateful bite of the sandwich, she sighed with pleasure. She hadn't realised quite how hungry she was. But then, as she had barely eaten all day it was no surprise. By the time she and Carmichael had returned to the Swansea barracks, Peggy had gone straight to the motor centre where she had needed to explain to an irate Sal exactly what had happened to the Humber she had been entrusted with that morning.

Sal had been very understanding, all things considered, but Peggy had still hated letting her down like that. To make amends, she had washed and polished the two new Vauxhalls a couple of the spark girls had driven down from Liverpool. Afterwards, she had been summoned to the lieutenant colonel's office, and given her instructions for the following morning. He ordered Peggy to be at his office for six in the morning sharp for a drive across to Bicester. Peggy had nodded politely and with a heavy heart returned to Sal to beg for another car. Thankfully, Sal had told her she could take one of the new Vauxhalls.

Now, the cheese sandwich Ida had lovingly prepared tasted like heaven and Peggy wolfed it down as though she hadn't eaten for days.

'You looked like you needed that,' Ida observed, taking the empty plate and rinsing it in the sink.

'I've had a right day of it, I don't mind telling you, Ida,' Peggy admitted with a sigh.

'A problem shared is a problem halved, love.' Ida pulled out a chair with one hand and set down a plate of garibaldi biscuits with the other.

Peggy smiled. She was like a mother hen, she thought, as she took a biscuit and bit into it, savouring the satisfying crunch. Ida watched her quizzically, and Peggy found herself telling her everything from her first meeting with Carmichael to her offer of a night out with Hudson.

When she'd finished, Ida had worked her way through most of the garibaldis and was brushing the crumbs from her lap. 'Well, Peg love, you weren't joking when you said you'd had a bad day, were you?'

'No,' Peggy chuckled. 'I don't s'pose I was.'

'Look at it this way, you've made your mark,' Ida said kindly.

Peggy raised an eyebrow. 'But I didn't want to make a mark, Ida, I just wanted to prove myself as a reliable driver. Instead, I've made myself look flighty.'

Now it was Ida's turn to look surprised. 'How d'you work that one out, then?'

'Because Lieutenant Colonel Carmichael was bound to have heard Hudson ask me to a dance. Not only will he doubt my driving skills, he'll think I'm a girl with loose morals as well.'

Ida snorted with laughter. 'Don't be daft. He'll no more think that than he'll think you're a poor driver. Look, you've just had a bit of bad luck is all, and it sounds as though this Hudson was a rude little so-and-so but at least he apologised and took responsibility for what he did.'

'I don't reckon he had much choice,' Peggy replied with derision.

'Maybe so. But that doesn't mean he had to offer to take you out by way of apology. He could have just sucked up to his superiors and then washed his hands of you, but he didn't,' Ida pointed out.

Peggy thought about what Ida had said. Her landlady was right; Hudson could have grunted a sorry at her when he saw her in the mess, but he hadn't.

'So are you going to go?' Ida prodded gently.

'Go where?' Peggy asked absent-mindedly.

'Out. With this pilot fella,' Ida replied impatiently.

'I am not!' Peggy gasped indignantly. 'I shouldn't trust him if my life depended on it. I'm going nowhere with him, especially when there's war work to be done.'

'No, but life's short, Peg love. You should live a little while you can.' Ida stood up to clear the plates.

'I'm not sure going to a dance with a pilot what ran me off the road is living, Ida,' she grumbled. 'To be fair, I think too much time in his company might see me six feet under.'

'See how you feel in the morning, precious. Might do you good to do something different, is it,' Ida said knowingly.

Nodding, Peggy smiled at her landlady and wished her good-night. As she climbed the stairs to bed, she wondered when everyone would realise that as far as Peggy was concerned being an ATS driver was doing something different.

# Chapter Five

Peggy woke to find her bedroom filled with sunshine rather than the gloomy darkness the blackout curtains always provided. Alarmed, she scrambled out of bed and looked at her wristwatch. A feeling of relief moved through her as she remembered that today was Saturday and she had a day off – for once she could sleep all day if she wanted to.

Sinking back on to her pillow she noticed Annie and Judith's beds were empty and freshly made and the curtains pulled back to expose the late January sunshine. Enjoying the warmth of the sun on her face, Peggy snuggled under the covers and luxuriated in the idea of an entire day to herself. It had been three weeks since she had become the lieutenant colonel's driver and Peggy had spent hours behind the wheel. She had driven him to and from meetings across the country and various other barracks to deliver lectures on everything from operations to morale.

Peggy had come to discover that Lieutenant Colonel Carmichael was a well-liked and respected officer. He was talkative, interested in everything Peggy had to say and always had time for everyone he met. In short, Peggy realised, he was an utter joy to work for, frequently worrying about her safety and ensuring they either didn't get back too late or she had a billet for the night.

He really was turning out to be a wonderful boss, Peggy thought with a smile as she reluctantly swung her legs out of bed and got to her feet. Stretching her arms overhead, she thought again about why Annie had said he was a pain, when in fact she had found Carmichael to be nothing short of charming.

Looking out of the window, she grinned as she saw her two roommates walking across the road towards the hotel and waved excitedly down at them.

'All right, girls?' she called, through the open window.

'Not as all right as you,' Judith replied, her tone light. 'We're not still in our pyjamas.'

Peggy chuckled and smoothed her hair down.

'Hurry up and get dressed,' Annie called. 'We're off for the rest of the day and are going up the market. Come with us.'

'Good idea!' Peggy shouted. 'Give me two minutes.'

Quickly Peggy ran some water over her face and pulled on her uniform. Even though it was a day off, being in the Army meant she wasn't allowed to wear mufti even off-duty.

As promised, she was ready in minutes and after saying a quick hello to Ida on her way down the stairs, Peggy ran outside and met the sisters by the hotel front door.

Together the three girls walked through the town and soon found themselves strolling along Oxford Street just yards from the grand, red-bricked market.

'I reckon this has gotta be the poshest market I've ever seen,' Peggy said admiringly. 'I'll never get tired of coming in here.'

'Nor me,' Judith admitted. 'Though I've no coupons left to buy anything.'

'I'll treat yer to a bit of soap, if you like, Jude,' Annie said generously. 'I need some Yardley's.'

'That's kind of yer, love, but spend it on yourself.' Judith smiled, before turning to Peggy. 'So, did yer enjoy your lie-in this morning?'

'Yer looked like you'd died!' Annie added good-naturedly. 'I was going to hold a mirror under your nose to check yer were still breathing, but Judith said to leave yer be.'

'And I'm blinking glad she did, Ann! Honestly, girls, I don't feel like I've seen my bed in weeks.' Peggy laughed.

'You've had a lot of late nights, like, we've barely seen yer,' Judith agreed, as they turned into the turreted market entrance.

Gazing at the fleet of colourful stalls up ahead, Peggy grinned with excitement. 'I always knew driving was hard work, Jude, but the lieutenant colonel's had me all over the shop.'

'Well, I just hope he's been nice to yer,' Annie muttered darkly.

'He's been smashing, Annie. Where d'you hear he was mean, though?' Peggy asked her tone sharp.

'Just around,' she said sulkily, walking away from them towards the stalls at the back of the market.

'Ignore her,' Judith said, raising her eyes heavenwards. 'She's been in a strop all week.'

'How come?' Peggy asked, looking longingly at a sweet stall.

'Oh, she had to drive a lorry down the coast as part of a convoy,' Judith explained, gently guiding Peggy away from the temptation of the stall. 'Sal told her to make sure she got her vehicle signed for by the shipping office and she didn't so Sal gave her what for and she's had her knickers in a knot about it ever since.'

'But why didn't she just do as Sal said?' Peggy asked. 'All she had to do was join the other girls in the office and get her form filled out.'

Judith shrugged her shoulders. 'I've no idea, Peg. Annie might be my sister, but half the time I dunno what's going on in her head.'

Peggy chuckled. Judith was such easy company, she loved being around her.

'You heard off your Al lately?' Peggy changed the subject.

Judith's face broke into a delighted beam at the mention of her fiancé. 'I had a letter this morning, like. Sounds like he's doing ever so well in the RAF.'

'Isn't he a gunner?' Peggy asked, trying to remember everything Judith had told her about her intended.

'Just finished his training, now he'll be posted somewhere

dangerous, I suppose,' Judith replied, her face falling.

Peggy smiled at her encouragingly. 'Come on, it won't be that bad. You can keep in touch and you know what he's doing is ever so important.'

Judith nodded. 'I know, Peg. Ignore me, I'm not normally such a soft so-and-so, I just really miss him. We talked about our wedding in our last lot of letters.'

'What have you decided?'

'Well, I think we'll have a small do at the church up home. And Mother's offered to make us a cake and have a little party at my aunt and uncle's up Alsager.' Judith grinned delightedly. 'We're going to do it soon as the war's finished.'

'Don't you mind waiting all that time?' Peggy gasped. 'We've no ideal when this is all going to be over.'

Judith shook her head as they walked past the fish stall. 'No. I just want everything to be perfect. And when I see my Al up at the front of that church waiting for me, well, it will be. We can start our new lives together in peacetime.'

Peggy nodded admiringly. Judith had clearly got it all sorted. It must be wonderful to have all your life mapped out, she thought.

'Have you ever had a sweetheart, Peg?' Judith asked gently.

Peggy shook her head.

'Well, I'm sure you'll meet someone someday, pretty girl like you, you'll have 'em eating out of the palm of your hand.' Judith smiled.

'That's just it, Jude,' she said, stopping in the market gangway, eager shoppers all around them. 'I'm not interested. I don't want a sweetheart, all I want is to fight this war, do my bit for the country and get home to Mother.'

'But surely you must want to meet someone eventually?' Judith asked incredulously.

Peggy shook her head. 'No. I don't, Judith. It's always been just me and Mother, and that's what I want it to go back to when we've seen Hitler off good and proper.'

'You can't mean that, Peg,' Judith said, raising an eyebrow. 'I mean your mother must want yer to have a life of your own. There's a whole world out there.'

'I know that, Jude, but my world begins and ends in Bristol with Mother. That's the way it's meant to be, and that's the way I want it,' Peggy said fiercely. 'Since Dad died she's been all alone apart from me. I won't let her grow old on her own.'

Judith looked at her, her eyes brimming with concern. 'But what about when your mother passes, Peg? If you've got no family, it'll just be you.'

'It don't matter, Jude. Mother's what matters. I have to look after her. Dad made me promise to always take care of her and I won't go back on it,' Peggy insisted.

As they walked past a flower stall, the smell of fresh blooms hit Peggy sharply, rendering her barely able to breathe. Lost in a daze she cast her eyes along the buckets of flowers, until she saw what she was looking for – the blood-red crimson of chrysanthemums. Before she could stop herself, she leaned right over the bucket, plucked one and closed her eyes. Instantly she was transported back to her thirteenth birthday when her father had come to collect her from school, armed with a beaming smile and a bunch of chrysanthemums.

'For the birthday girl,' he had said, wrapping her in his arms and handing her the blooms.

Peggy had buried her head in the petals and sniffed. 'Nobody's ever given me flowers before.'

William had laughed so hard his brown eyes had crinkled with delight and his whole face lit up as he took her hand. 'I should hope not. You're a young girl, but now you're getting older, I thought you might like them. I loves chrysanths meself. My favourites.'

Peggy had looked down at the bunch of flowers and happily hugged them to herself. If they were her dad's favourite flowers, they were hers now too.

She had held on to them tightly as they boarded the tram

that took them all the way to Clifton Down. But despite the happy chatter between them about her birthday, she could tell there was something on his mind. As they got off the tram, Peggy had noticed William seemed distracted and it wasn't lost on her that she had woken up to her mum and dad arguing that morning. They had tried to pretend that was the last thing they had been doing when she got up, but she knew they had, just like she knew now.

'You all right, Dad?' she had asked.

William had arched an eyebrow. 'I'm fine. Why?'

'You just don't seem yourself. You're doing that thing where you furrow your brow and go all squinty-eyed when you're thinking.'

'Is that right?' William had roared with laughter. 'Well, you don't want me to tell you what you look like when you're thinking, do you? You're concentrating so hard I can see the cogs turning.'

At that, he had grabbed her as they reached the top of the Downs and tickled her until she begged for mercy. Breathless with laughter they had sat on the lush grass together gazing out at the Avon Gorge and beyond.

'There is something, Peg. It's your mum,' William had said quietly.

'Oh,' Peggy replied, deftly pulling grass from the ground.

'I know she's not the easiest mum in the world, but she does love you. She just shows it in a different way to me, that's all. She's not very good at jokes and games, but she'd lay down her life for you, bab.'

Peggy nodded. 'I know that. I've always known that. Mother's way is just not like other people's. Least that's what I tell the girls at Sunday school when they ask me why she's always telling me off.'

'She just wants the best for you, Peg love,' William explained earnestly. 'She frets about all the dangers in the world, and being hard on you, well, it's just her way.'

Peggy said nothing. She had sensed there was more her father wanted to tell her and so she had kept her gaze fixed on the blades of grass, deftly yanking at each one.

'That's why there's something I want you to do for me when I'm not here,' William had continued, his tone serious. 'I need you to promise me that you will always look after your mother.'

Peggy had looked up at him in surprise. 'Where you going?'

'Nowhere. Not for a long time,' he had smiled. 'I just need you to make sure your mum's all right if anything happens to me. She's not as strong as she makes out to be; she'll need help.'

'All right, Dad,' she had said, nodding.

'Good girl.' He beamed at her. 'Now, promise me?'

'I promise,' Peggy had said, not really understanding what her father was asking her to do.

When her father had died suddenly three years later, Peggy had remembered that conversation as if it had been yesterday. Watching her mother become even harder and more brusque to the outside world, she suddenly understood what her father meant. For Edie this was all a front; inside she was breaking, and Peggy was determined not to let either of her parents down. As she'd said goodbye to her precious father at his graveside, she had dropped a single red chrysanthemum on to his grave.

'I promise, Dad,' she had whispered before turning back to be with her mother.

Now, whenever she smelled chrysanthemums on a flower stall, she remembered the promise she'd made. Inhaling deeply, she allowed the heady scent to fill her nostrils, and was so lost in the moment she barely noticed Judith shaking her arm.

'Peg, love,' Judith shouted, bringing Peggy back to the here and now.

'What?' she gasped, staring first at Judith and then down at the flower in her hand.

Judith smiled gently. 'I think the nice florist would like her flower back.'

Peggy let Judith take the flower and hand it back to the

florist. She smiled apologetically and gazed around; the market was teeming with people. There was one woman admiring fabric at one stall and another man counting out his change to the ironmonger.

Judith said nothing. Instead she squeezed Peggy's hand in understanding and started walking back through the market, glancing furtively to her left and right.

'Don't suppose you've seen our Annie, have you?' she asked.

Peggy looked around her but couldn't see the younger girl anywhere. 'She said she needed soap, didn't she? Maybe she's at that beauty stall she always goes to.'

Just then, the sound of shouting rang across the market. Instantly, Peggy and Judith turned around to see Annie jabbing and pointing her finger at a stallholder up ahead.

'What's she done now?' Judith groaned as she hurried across the concourse, Peggy close behind. Nearing Annie, they soon found the younger girl at a sweet stall shouting so furiously she was puce with rage.

'Annie, what's the matter, love?' Peggy asked, reaching the girl first.

'This woman,' Annie blustered, her eyes never leaving the market trader, 'won't serve me.'

'Why?' Judith asked indignantly.

'It's perfectly obvious,' the stallholder replied looking bored. 'I won't serve her, and I won't serve you girls either.'

'Why?' Judith asked again, rounding on the woman, who by now had gathered quite an audience. 'Our money's as good as anyone else's.'

'I'm sure it is, love, but I don't serve nobody in uniform, see. It's the war, it's evil and I don't agree with it. Churchill's nothing but a warmonger and you lot in your uniforms are no better.'

'We're serving our country,' Judith protested fiercely, her cheeks pinkening with indignation. 'We're protecting yer, making sure yer can keep hold of everything yer hold dear.'

'You're killing innocent folk. And this one' – the stallholder jerked her head at Annie – 'is full of cheek.'

Peggy looked at the woman and felt an instant hatred. It took a lot for her to dislike someone, but this stallholder with her gaily coloured floral turban and cocky smile had no idea what life was like for the brave boys on the front line, never mind the girls in the services; all so she could enjoy her freedom. What on earth did she want them to do? Give Hitler a free ride? Over Peggy's dead body.

'So how was my friend meant to know you wouldn't serve her? You could have been polite about it, or even made something up,' Peggy said quietly.

The stallholder looked exasperated as she pointed to a sign above her head. Peggy followed her finger and shuddered in disgust at the large but badly painted banner, 'Uniforms Not Welcome'. If she hadn't been so busy looking at Annie, she was sure she would have seen the sign from miles away, but why hadn't Annie spotted it? Peggy turned to Annie in surprise. Had she genuinely not seen the sign or had she just been looking for a bit of drama like usual?

'Surely you saw the banner, love? Why not just go somewhere else?' Peggy asked.

Annie said nothing, instead she just stared angrily at the woman.

'Did you hear me?' Peggy tried again. 'Let's go somewhere else.'

'I'm going nowhere and I didn't see the sign,' Annie replied, her eyes never leaving the market trader's.

'But it's massive,' Peggy said incredulously. 'You couldn't miss it.'

'You did!' Annie retorted.

'I was looking at you, not the stall,' Peggy replied angrily.

The stallholder chuckled. 'Well, your friend's clearly blind as well as stupid. Still, it comes as no surprise. You lot in the Army are all brawn and no brains.'

There was a deadly silence as Peggy looked first at Annie and then at Judith. The sisters stared at the woman with their jaws clenched and eyes narrowed. Peggy could tell they meant business and there was no telling how this might end. She was as furious with this woman as the girls, but knew no good would come from a fight in the market. Thankfully, people with views like this were rare, but Peggy knew the market trader would never change her mind, and a scrap over a stall certainly wouldn't further their cause. Desperately she tried to think of a way to defuse the situation, when suddenly she heard a deep gravelly voice, shout her name.

'Collins! Hello.'

Peggy whipped around and saw Pilot Officer James Hudson standing just a few inches away. Her heart sank. His brand of rude behaviour was something she could well do without just now.

'Sir,' she said, remembering her manners and saluting the officer.

'Oh please, don't bother with all that nonsense,' he said, glancing across at Peggy and the angry faces of her friends and the stallholder. 'What's going on here?'

Peggy shrugged. 'Something and nothing.'

'It flaming well isn't something and nothing,' Annie roared. 'This mardy-arsed mare thinks I'm no better than a murderer.'

The pilot's eyes popped out on stalks as he looked from Annie to Peggy and then at the stallholder.

'Is this true?' he asked, looking at Annie.

Opening her mouth to reply, Annie was cut off by the stallholder.

'If the cap fits,' she said pointedly.

By now quite a crowd had gathered to witness the show and Peggy felt deeply uncomfortable as she watched people point and stare at the sign overhead. Turning to look at Pilot Officer Hudson, she saw he had now spotted the sign too and his face had flushed red with anger.

'Is this a joke?' he asked, his tone suddenly as hard as steel.

The woman shook her head defiantly. 'It's no joke. It's my stall and I'll serve who I like.'

Hudson said nothing for a moment, instead he looked at the rows of glass jars lined up behind the woman. Each jar was neatly displayed with an array of pink, yellow and green sweets on show.

'Been selling chocolate long?' he asked casually, running his eyes across the display as if he was looking for something.

'All my life,' the woman said proudly. 'This was my mum and dad's stall before mine. It's a family business, see.'

The pilot nodded. 'Must be nice to have had something handed down to you like that.'

'I make you right,' the woman agreed. 'I'm very proud.'

'Perhaps you don't realise, but if Jerry gets his way, chances are you won't be able to sell the sweets you like,' Hudson began, his voice taking on a dangerous lilt. 'You won't be able to decide who works with you on this stall, and I very much doubt you'll be able to pass this stall on to your children and grandchildren.'

The woman blanched and put her hands on her hips ready to argue, but he'd only just begun.

'Because what you perhaps don't realise is that the brave men and women all wearing those uniforms you object to so much are out there putting their own lives on the line day after day, so you can continue to live the life you want and to run your business how you want. And yet you have the nerve to refuse service to these brave men and women fighting for your freedom. Then to add insult to injury, you have concocted this nasty little sign, which frankly, in my opinion, merely serves to highlight your bigotry, selfishness and stupidity.'

As he finished his speech, he stood back with his hands clasped behind his back and his jaw set, glaring at the woman. Despite her stubborn nature, Hudson was clearly not going to give way and Peggy felt a flash of respect for him for standing his ground so eloquently. Peggy glanced across at the stallholder and saw a flash of anger in her eyes, as she leaned forward ready to attack. Peggy shuddered, wondering how she could break up the argument, when suddenly there was a shout from the crowd.

'About time someone put you in your place, you should be ashamed of yourself, Eileen Jones,' a man jeered.

'She's always been a disgrace,' a woman's voice chimed. 'I'm amazed nobody's said nothing about that sign before, is it. It's disgusting it is.'

Peggy turned around and saw the crowd had swollen and was now easily six-deep. Watching almost all of the men and women who had gathered nod approvingly at Hudson, she felt a warm glow inside. She looked at her friends and smiled, their efforts clearly weren't in vain.

'Who is this fella, Peg?' Jude hissed.

'It's that pilot what ran me off the road,' she whispered, her eyes never leaving the crowd.

'Never in this world!' Annie replied in astonishment. 'I thought yer said he was a right berk.'

'I thought he was,' Peg said in hushed tones, as the support from the crowd grow.

'Well, Mrs Jones, it seems the public has spoken, and so have I,' Hudson said calmly. 'Now this sign had better not be here when I come back next week, or I'll take it down myself.'

With that he turned his back on an open-mouthed Mrs Jones and smiled at the ATS girls who stood behind him. 'I don't know about you but I'm gasping for a cup of tea, shall we?'

Pushing his way through the crowd, the girls followed and together they made their way to the market entrance. Peering through the doorway, Peggy was disappointed to see the sunshine from earlier had been replaced with thick, dark clouds.

'That was all rather exciting, wasn't it?' Hudson smiled as

they stood in the doorway. 'I'm James Hudson, by the way, but please call me Jim.'

Judith smiled. 'This is my sister Annie' – she gestured to the younger girl – 'and I'm Judith.'

Jim grinned at them all before pumping each of their hands furiously. 'Delighted to meet you all, but rather a shame it was in such dire circumstances.'

'Yer can say that again,' Judith said drily. 'I'm not entirely sure it's an experience I'd want repeating. Still, it was very good of yer to stand up for our Annie like that.'

Annie nodded admiringly. 'Yer really gave her what for, thank you.'

Hudson held his hands up and shrugged. 'Honestly, ladies, any friend of Collins here is a friend of mine. That woman wanted a dressing-down for that ridiculous sign, not to mention the way she treated you.'

As the rain began to fall and they walked through the town the group fell silent as they each reflected on what had just happened.

'You forget not everyone feels the same pride we do about our uniforms,' Peggy said eventually. 'Mine's a badge of honour and I couldn't be prouder of it.'

'Me 'n'all, Peg,' Judith agreed. 'Still, as our mother says, yer can't please all of the people all of the time. Silly old bat'd be sorry if Hitler won this blinking war though.'

'Now, now, that's enough of all that,' Hudson said frowning. 'That sort of defeatist talk isn't helpful. But you're right, she was an old bat, and I suggest we celebrate our victory with a visit to the teahouse.'

'Good idea.' Judith smiled. 'Let me treat you as a thank you for helping us out and that.'

'Well I'm definitely coming with you, in that case.' Annie grinned. 'Throw in a crumpet and I'm sure me war wounds from this morning will be recovered in a flash.'

'Give over, Annie,' Judith chuckled as she linked arms with

her sister. 'Yer gave as good as yer got, and plenty more besides. I think if anyone ought to be buying anyone anything, it's you. You're coming, aren't you, Peg?'

Peggy stood on the pavement, the rain lashing at her heels. She wasn't sure she wanted to spend any more time with the pilot. She was grateful to him for helping them out like that. But the man spelled danger, of that she was certain.

'I reckon I might just go back,' she mumbled. 'I need to sort out me uniform for Monday.'

With a firm shake of the head, Annie grabbed Peggy by the arm. 'Never in this world. Didn't you hear Jude's buying? I'm not taking no for an answer.'

'No, Collins, neither am I,' Hudson added with a small smile. 'And I can assure you I shan't damage anything this time.'

Peggy smiled. Perhaps she was being daft, and they should celebrate what had just happened.

'All right then,' she agreed, following them to the teahouse.

Inside, the foursome sat down and ordered pots of tea and teacakes. Soon, the conversation turned naturally to the war effort, and Annie and Judith were full of questions.

'Did you always want to be a pilot?' Judith quizzed Hudson.

He nodded. 'Ever since I was a little boy. I wrote to the Air Ministry when I was just sixteen. I was leaving school in two years and hoped they would take me but they told me to write back nearer the time. I wasn't put off, wrote again, and had my selection interview with the RAF for a pilot. They liked the cut of my jib, so to speak, and signed me up on the spot. There was a condition though, my parents insisted I went to Cambridge as planned and if I still wanted to be a pilot I could do so after my graduation.'

'Yer went to university?' Annie whistled in awe. 'I've never met anyone that's been to university.'

'Neither have I,' Peggy breathed, feeling the chasm open wider between them.

'So yer must be really brainy and that,' Judith put in quickly, sensing the discomfort. 'What did your family want you to do?'

'Follow Father into the family firm. He's a solicitor, but my heart was never in it and so I began my RAF training a week after leaving university.'

'Yer make it sound so easy,' Annie sighed. 'The WRENS and the Land Army turned me and Jude down before we were accepted in the ATS.'

Peggy clanked her cup down noisily against her saucer and stared at Annie in surprise. 'Is that true? I thought you and Jude joined the Army because you wanted to be Ack-Ack girls.'

Judith shook her head. 'No, we loved the glamour of the WRENS uniform, but they had too many that had joined-up so then the next recruitment office along the road was the Land Army and they said they wouldn't necessarily keep us together. The ATS was our next stop and they said yes we could stay together and yes we could join-up.'

'So the ATS was obviously a calling then.' Hudson laughed as he topped up the girls' tea before pouring more for himself.

'We just wanted to do what we could to help beat the Jerries,' Judith explained, nodding her thanks to Hudson. 'And we knew we wanted to stay together, and the ATS let us do that, so it all worked out.'

'Never expected driving to be on the cards though, did we, Jude?' Annie giggled. 'Not exactly natural navigators.'

Judith squeezed her sister's arm supportively. 'You've come on leaps and bounds with your map reading.'

Annie grimaced. 'I'm better behind the wheel, though not sure Sal would agree after I rear-ended that Humber the other day.'

'That was an accident, Sal will get over it,' Judith insisted, turning to Jim with mischief in her eyes. 'What about you, Pilot Officer Hudson, any mishaps in your plane, or do you just have trouble with cars?'

'Jim, please, and yes, I suppose we all had hair-raising moments in our Tiger Moths practising our bumps and circuits, but thankfully nothing as serious as the damage I inflicted on poor Collins recently.' He pulled a face.

'Well, the car's been written off now.' Peggy shrugged. 'And you're apparently buying us a new one.'

'That's true.' Hudson nodded. 'And please, let me say again how sorry I am for the other week. I do feel absolutely dreadful about it.'

Seeing the genuine look of sorrow in Hudson's eyes Peggy offered him a small smile. Before today, she could never have imagined forgiving him for ruining her car on her first day, but he had not only gone out of his way to replace the vehicle immediately, but he had leapt to her friend's defence without question.

'So where are yer from then?' Annie asked, changing the subject.

Tearing his gaze from Peggy, Hudson turned to the sisters. 'Clifton in Bristol. Do you know it?'

'No, but I bet Peg does. That's your neck of the woods, isn't it?' Judith offered.

Peggy nodded. 'Not quite Clifton, Jude, but I'm a Bristol girl, yes.'

Hudson's eyes lit up at the discovery. 'Ah, I thought I detected an accent, Collins. Wasn't sure if you were from Devon.'

Shaking her head in mock disgust, Peggy wagged her finger at the pilot. 'And you call yourself a Bristolian. My accent's pure Knowle through and through.'

'Sorry, you're right, Collins, I confess,' Hudson chuckled. 'In my defence, I was sent to boarding school in Taunton from the age of five, so many West Country accents do have a tendency to blur into one.'

'Cor, boarding school, university and enough money to buy a new car outright. You're fancy, aren't yer?' Annie marvelled, as she sipped the last of her tea.

Hudson looked embarrassed, his floppy fringe falling into his eyes. 'It sounds fancier than it was, I'm sure, and, well, the money's there for emergencies, and this was that. If it helps, as a family we're always freezing in winter, sweltering in the summer and my brother and I never have enough to eat.'

'Sounds like us and our family up Stoke, Jude,' Annie cackled.

'What's your brother do?' Peggy asked, ignoring Annie's giggling. 'Is he in Bristol or is he in the RAF like you?'

'No, he works abroad,' Hudson said quickly.

'Now that does sound fancy,' Peggy marvelled. 'Can you tell us any more or is it hush-hush?'

Hudson lifted his cup and drained the rest of his tea, his expression darkening. Setting the cup back down he checked his leather wristwatch, turned to the girls and smiled. 'I really must be going. It's been such a pleasure meeting you all.'

'And you,' the girls replied.

As he stood to leave, he reached into his pocket, pulled out a fistful of change and set it down on the table.

'And I absolutely insist the tea and cakes are on me.' He smiled. 'In fact, treat yourselves to another cup, it really is the least I can do.'

Gazing at him in surprise at his generosity, Peggy got to her feet to thank him properly. 'That's very kind, thank you, Pilot Officer Hudson.'

'As I said before, please, call me Jim, and it's my pleasure.' He beamed, shrugging on his coat. 'And may I call you Peggy?'

A flush of colour crept up Peggy's neck and into her cheeks as she glanced everywhere but at him. 'All right.'

'Good.' Hudson smiled. 'And have you thought any more about letting me take you out properly to say sorry for my outrageous behaviour?'

Peggy's heart banged loudly in her chest. It was so noisy and so fast, she was sure everyone else in the teahouse could hear it. 'I, er, well, er . . .' she stammered as Hudson held up his hands.

'I promise I don't bite, and I'll leave the Aston behind! Come on, let me take you to the pictures when you're next off. What do you say?'

As she looked shyly up at him, Peggy saw his eyes were alive with kindness and his smile radiated warmth.

'All right,' she said in a small voice. 'I'd like that.'

'Excellent,' Hudson replied. 'Next Saturday suit?'

Peggy nodded. 'I've the evening off, so could meet you at six.'

Placing his cap firmly on top of his long, floppy fringe, Hudson rewarded Peggy with another generous beam. 'Looking forward to it, Peggy.'

He swept out of the teahouse, leaving Peggy aghast and delighted at how she had just agreed to go out with a man for the very first time. She had no idea what had possessed her to say yes, and even less idea what Edie would say.

# Chapter Six

Unsurprisingly, Peggy became a bundle of nerves as her evening out with Jim got closer. She struggled to eat or sleep, and by the time Saturday arrived, felt as though she had been put through an emotional mangle.

Although Lieutenant Colonel Carmichael usually had no need for Peggy at the weekend, there were still plenty of other duties for her besides driving her superior officer. The night before she had been on guard duty, which meant patrolling the grounds of the barracks and checking all was safe until dawn.

It made for a long, cold night, and was something Peggy, along with the rest of the ATS girls, had to do at least once a fortnight. However, Peggy also knew it was a worthwhile and vital task and so she embraced the challenge. Usually she went straight back to her billet after a night shift for a few hours' sleep, but today she had felt too churned up and instead had gone to the motor garage to service the new Humber that Hudson had bought.

But it was clear her mind wasn't on the job, despite the best of intentions. Not only did she keep dropping her spanner, but she banged her head on the bonnet twice. When she accidentally poured water instead of oil into the engine of the Humber she was servicing, Sal stepped in. Gently she steered Peggy to a quiet corner of the garage and sat her down on an upturned crate. Pressing a cup of tea that she had just brewed up in a steel bucket into Peggy's cold hands, she sat beside her.

'What's the matter, Peg?' the older woman asked in a kindly but forthright tone.

Peggy glanced up and smiled. 'That obvious?'

Sal ran a hand through her bright red locks and chuckled, her signature red lipstick creasing at the corners of her mouth. 'Only to an old girl like me, pet. Now, out with it.'

Peggy grimaced. 'It sounds so stupid.'

'No more stupid than half the stuff that comes out of some of these girls' mouths. Just spit it out.'

Peggy looked down at the tin mug of tea Sal had given her and wrapped her fingers tightly around the metal, enjoying the feeling of warmth in her fingers. For once the garage was quiet, with only a handful of spark girls fixing a fleet of Lister trucks that had arrived in convoy the night before. As the cold February rain thudded against the iron roof of the garage, Peggy took a deep breath and looked at Sal.

'A fella's asked me up the pictures tonight and I've gone and said yes,' Peggy said quickly.

Sal's eyes filled with confusion. 'Am I missin' somethin', pet, is that all it is?'

'I've not asked my mother,' Peggy wailed.

'Do you usually ask your mam if you're allowed out?' Sal asked.

Peggy shrugged. 'I've never needed to ask her before. Normally she and I would go everywhere together.'

'What, even if you're courtin' a fella?' Sal gasped.

Giving her friend a gentle nudge in the ribs, Peggy laughed. 'I've never been out with a fella before so I've never had to ask.'

A huge laugh erupted from Sal's mouth and she rocked back and forth on the crate she was sitting on, struggling to catch her breath. 'Oh my word, I thought someone had died from your carry on.'

'I wondered if I was s'posed to have got Mother's permission,' Peggy said, clearly embarrassed.

Sal stopped chuckling, cocked her head to one side and regarded Peggy sympathetically. 'I'm sorry, love, I shouldn't have said that. But your face made me think somethin' really terrible had happened. If I'd known all we were doin' was gossipin' over a bloke, well I'd have changed me face immediately. I'm sorry.'

Peggy smiled warmly at the mechanical matriarch. She knew Sal didn't have a bad bone in her body and hadn't meant to cause any pain. 'No harm done.'

Clasping her calloused hand over Peg's cold one, Sal beamed. 'So, why do you need your mam's permission? You're over twenty-one, aren't you?'

Peggy nodded. 'I just . . . I don't know, I feel like I've done something wrong, I s'pose.'

'Give over!' Sal chuckled. 'Mams don't need to know everything. Trust me, there are several things my son gets up to I'm sure that I don't want to know about. Anyway, this is a good thing. You do at least like the fella, don't you?'

Peg grimaced once more. 'I don't know, Sal. I don't reckon I do. He's the fella what ran me off the road the other week and was also really rude to me. I don't know why I said yes. I was worried he'd keep asking I s'pose.'

'But isn't he also the fella that apologised to you for his behaviour, stepped in when that stallholder was rude to Annie and bought the Army a new Humber to say sorry?' Sal gently pointed out.

Peggy laughed. 'Well, when you put it like that, he don't sound so bad after all!'

'Sometimes it's hard to see the wood for the trees, pet.'

'So you don't think I'm daft for agreeing to see him up the picture house then?' Peggy said, her voice filled with relief.

'Course I don't!' Sal exclaimed. 'It's about time you let your hair down and enjoyed yourself. And to be fair, Peg, it's only the pictures, he's not asked you to marry him. It's normal to go out with a fella once in a while. As long as you keep to the military curfew of 11 p.m. there'll be no problem. Count yourself lucky you've been asked; when you get to my age, fellas don't want to court you, they want you to wash their smalls!'

Peggy chuckled, it was nice to listen to the wisdom of someone older and wiser than herself. Taking a deep breath, she decided to confide in Sal about what was really on her mind.

'The thing is, Sal, well, what d'you do when you court a fella?' Peggy whispered.

'It's very easy, flower, you simply talk to them like you'd talk to me. Just ask them about themselves and they'll be happy as Larry,' Sal said comfortingly.

'Is that it?' Peggy asked in astonishment. 'There must be more to it?'

'Let me give you a bit of motherly advice, seein' as I think you need it.' Sal smiled. 'Fellas are simple creatures, Peg, just act interested in whatever they tell you and they'll be more than happy.'

'All right. Is there anything else I should know?'

Sal leaned forward conspiratorially. 'There's one more thing that's probably the most important.'

'What?' Peg asked, her eyes wide with innocence.

'Keep your hand on your ha'penny, flower, that's the most important bit of advice!'

With that Sal erupted into another bout of laughter, leaving Peggy to shake her head in amusement as the sub-leader walked back across the garage.

*

It wasn't until the Humber shone like a new pin that Peggy felt satisfied. Stretching her arms overhead, she stifled a yawn. She was exhausted after all the work she had done. Checking her watch, she saw it was just after three in the afternoon. If she was quick, she could grab forty winks before meeting Jim.

After waving a quick goodbye to Sal who mouthed 'good luck' as she left, Peggy turned and walked out of the garage and

84

headed for the hotel she called home. By now the February rain had been replaced with a cold, strong wind, and Peggy had to push her whole body into the gust to ensure she didn't topple over. Twenty minutes later, she had collapsed on to her small bed fully clothed and didn't wake until someone shook her.

Startled, she opened her eyes to see Judith perched on the end of her bed, smiling.

'Wake up, love,' she said gently.

'What time is it?' Peggy said, sitting bolt upright.

'Quarter past five,' Judith replied. 'I thought you'd have been up hours ago.'

Peggy sprang to her feet, nearly sending Judith flying.

'I'm going to be late,' she gasped, gazing down at her crumpled uniform. 'I was going to clean and press my things, but I won't have time. Look at the state of me.'

'It's all right.' Judith smiled, getting up from the bed and reaching into the little mahogany wardrobe she and Annie shared. 'We're roughly the same size, why don't yer borrow my spare uniform, I only pressed it yesterday.'

Glancing at Judith, Peggy's eyes were filled with gratitude. 'You sure? I don't want to put you to no trouble.'

'It's no trouble,' Judith assured her. 'Now, wash your face, slip these on and I'll get me make-up out.'

'Make-up,' she hissed, patting her cheeks anxiously. 'D'you reckon I need make-up?'

Judith chuckled at Peggy's shocked expression. 'No, love, I don't, but I do know a bit of powder and lippy can give you a boost if you're feeling nervous.'

As Judith shooed her away to the corner of the room to wash her face in the little pitcher and bowl, Peggy tried to quell the rising panic. She knew she was being silly, that make-up was just another step. But she also knew that this was a step that Edie wouldn't approve of, just as she wouldn't approve of Peggy courting. Despite Sal's motherly advice she couldn't bring herself to admit that actually there was no point asking her mother's permission because Edie wouldn't give it. Throughout her life, Edie had drummed it into her that the only man she would ever need or could rely on was God.

When she was twelve, Peggy had tried to ask her mother how true that was. Given her mother was married to a man that Peggy felt was particularly reliable, she was genuinely curious as to what her mother meant. But the moment the words had formed, Edie had given her daughter such a ferocious stare, Peggy had fled from the shop in tears.

Not long afterwards her father had whisked her up to the Downs and made her promise to look after her mother. With a start she wondered if her father would approve of her courting or if he would see this as not keeping her promise. Anxiously Peggy pushed the unbidden thoughts from her mind and instead smiled at Judith as she put on her uniform and allowed her friend to apply some make-up.

'There.' Judith smiled as she applied a finishing touch of peachy rouge to her friend's cheeks.

Peering in the little vanity mirror that rested on the wall opposite Annie's bed, Peggy barely recognised herself. Although she took a pride in her appearance, she never wore make-up, indeed Edie had practically brought her up believing make-up was a sin. Now, her skin looked dewy, the freckles replaced with a warm, radiant complexion and two subtly blushed cheeks that gave the illusion of high cheekbones. Add to that the beautifully groomed eyebrows and beauty spot Judith had artfully drawn just above her top lip and Peggy looked completely different.

'What do yer think?' Judith asked eagerly.

Peggy opened her mouth and closed it again. The result was so shocking, she couldn't quite tell whether she liked it or not. 'I look like a proper woman,' she said finally.

'You are a proper woman, yer daft ha'porth.' Judith laughed. 'And yer look lovely.'

'You sure I look all right?' Peggy asked, turning to her friend anxiously.

Judith nodded. 'I'm more than sure. Now come on, let's not keep the fella waiting. I've got to go back up the barracks for guard duty tonight, so I'll walk up the town with yer.'

'I'd like that.' Peggy reached for her coat.

Together the girls walked out of the hotel and through the winding streets. Thankfully the wind had died down so the precious victory roll that Peggy had managed to quickly pin in place before she left stayed intact.

As the girls waved goodbye to one another at the top of the High Street, Peggy rounded the corner. Taking a deep breath she marched towards the cinema and saw Jim already waiting for her outside. Leaning against one of the stone pillars, cigarette in one hand, chin pointed up towards the moonlight, he looked so handsome that Peggy's heart skipped a beat.

The strength of feeling surprised and shocked Peggy in equal measure. Part of her felt so afraid she wanted to turn around and run straight back to her billet. But just as she was debating whether or not to flee, Jim caught sight of her, tipped his hat and smiled.

'Peggy!' he said warmly, strolling towards her. 'You look beautiful, I'm so glad you came.'

Lifting her hand to his mouth, he tenderly kissed the back of it, leaving Peggy feeling as if she had been scorched. 'Shall we go inside? I've already bought the tickets.'

'All right,' she said shyly, falling into step with him as they walked into the foyer.

Once inside, Peggy shivered with delight. There was something about the glamour of the cinema she had adored since she was a child, and Swansea's picture house didn't disappoint, with its thick carpet and walls decorated with embossed wallpaper. A chandelier hung from the ceiling and a sweeping staircase led to two individual screens promising a glamorous escape to another world.

As Jim guided them down the gangway towards their seats, Peggy suddenly panicked that they were heading for the back row. She might have led a relatively sheltered life, but she knew only too well what some got up to in the rear of the cinema and she had no intention of doing something she shouldn't. But as Jim continued towards the front and gestured for Peggy to take a seat in the middle of the row, she breathed a sigh of relief; he was going to behave like a gentleman. All she could do was hope it continued throughout the film.

As the opening credits to *Ten Days in Paris* opened, Peggy forgot all about the fact she was being courted by a man for the first time in her life and instead focused on the screen. She always enjoyed watching Rex Harrison, and became so engrossed in the thriller that by the time it was over she was surprised to see Jim beside her.

'Did you enjoy that?' he asked as they walked out of the picture house into the cold night air.

'It was smashing,' she said, smiling shyly at him. 'Just my sort of film.'

Jim raised his eyebrows as he turned to her and looked pleased. 'Really? I was worried you would be disappointed I hadn't picked something romantic.'

Peggy shook her head as they strolled down the street. 'No, I likes a good whodunnit! Me and Mother must have seen *The Thirteenth Guest* a thousand times.'

'My favourite film!' Jim exclaimed. 'I love Ginger Rogers.'

'I know!' Peggy gushed. 'She's so beautiful and perfect, I loves watching her on screen. She gets you every time, don't she?'

Drawing level with the teahouse, Jim suddenly stopped and gestured at the white and gold lettering of the shop front. 'Do you have to get back or can I tempt you to a cup of tea and an Eccles cake?'

Peggy fizzed with excitement. By rights she ought to have been exhausted after just a few short hours of sleep, but the truth was she had never felt more alive and could think of nothing she would like more than to sit in a teahouse with the pilot.

'I'd like that.' She grinned shyly.

Jim held the door open for her and she stepped inside, delighted to see the air was as electric as she felt. As usual, servicemen and women were chatting away over tea and buns, but there were others from the town Peggy noticed, recognising some familiar faces. Glancing around, Peggy did a double take as she realised the stallholder who had refused to serve Annie was sitting at a window table with a man she guessed was her husband.

'What is it?' Jim asked, almost falling over her as she stood rooted to the spot in the centre of the cafe.

'It's her,' Peggy hissed.

Jim followed Peggy's gaze, before he turned back and shrugged. 'The obnoxious woman from the market? What of it?'

'I don't want her to cause a scene,' she said quietly, her cheeks flaming with embarrassment at the thought.

'I think there's more chance of us making a scene standing in the middle of the tearoom,' Jim said gently, as he took Peggy's elbow and led her to a table well away from the stallholder.

Peggy sat meekly and fiddled with her hands in her lap as Jim gave their order to the waitress.

'How come you're so confident all the time?' she asked finally.

'I didn't know I was,' he said, looking surprised.

'You know you are.' Peggy smiled. 'You told that stallholder off without a second thought.'

'She deserved it.' Jim shrugged. 'Sometimes people need to learn of their imperfections.'

Peggy giggled. 'Like I did when you were downright rude after ruining my car?'

'Are you ever going to let me live that down, Peggy?' Jim groaned. 'Honestly, I felt, and still do feel, terrible about it. I could kick myself for my stupidity.'

'Everyone makes mistakes,' Peggy said kindly. 'And you did say you'd been having a bad day.'

Jim's face clouded at the memory. 'Yes, well, that's all in the past now. So tell me, Peggy Collins from Bristol, why are you so unconfident?'

Peggy shifted uncomfortably in her seat. 'I don't know really, just the way I am, I s'pose. Mother always did everything for me, and I never really learned to do anything for myself till I joined the Army. I s'pose I'm still learning.'

'I think you're doing yourself an injustice. You're more confident and capable than you think you are. You tore shreds off me, and rightly so, when I ruined your car. And you were standing up to that stallholder when I arrived. Not only that, but I would have thought joining the ATS itself shows a certain amount of chutzpah. You just need to have more faith in your abilities,' Jim told her earnestly.

Peggy raised her eyebrows. 'How d'you make that one out? You barely know me.'

'True,' Jim said with a nod. 'But I think you're lovely, if you don't mind me saying.'

Peggy's neck flushed crimson as tea and a plate of sixpenny fruit pies were placed on the table between them.

'I don't mind you saying,' she said quietly.

Helping herself to a pie, Peggy realised it was true, she didn't mind Jim complimenting her. She smiled to herself, perhaps she had come a long way from her days in basic training, when she would have rather hidden under a table than sit opposite a man and talk to him.

'What's so funny?' Jim asked, interrupting her train of thought.

'Oh, nothing, just wondering if you'd been posted up here long?' she said, changing the subject.

'A few months,' Jim replied between bites of his fruit pie. 'I must say, I rather like it. Wonderful to be so close to the sea. Though of course you do get that in Bristol.'

Peggy smiled at the mention of her home town. 'I remember the first time my father took me up Weston-Super-Mare for the day. I thought I'd died and gone to heaven. It was so beautiful.'

'Still is.' Jim nodded. 'I have an aunt that lives there, I must confess I probably see her more than anyone else in my family, as she has the most spectacular view of the coast from her dining room.'

Shaking her head, Peggy couldn't help smiling at the pilot. She could never quite tell if he was pulling her leg or being serious. 'So, d'you manage to see your family a lot then?'

'Enough,' Jim said. 'Mother and Father always demand a visit whenever I have leave, which isn't very often but they understand.'

'And your brother?' Peggy pressed gently.

'No,' Jim said matter-of-factly. 'Edward works abroad. I haven't seen him since war broke out.'

Reaching for her cup of tea, Peggy nodded. 'You must miss him then. Are you close?'

'Only in age,' Jim muttered. 'He's a year older than me.'

'I always thought it must be nice to have a brother or sister,' Peggy continued. 'Someone to play with and understand you a bit. Life as an only child can be lonely. I bet it must have been wonderful to have a playmate all the time.'

Peggy watched in surprise as Jim's face clouded over. 'Not really. In fact, I can honestly say that there have been times in my life where I have thought being an only child would be highly preferable.'

Peggy blanched at his reaction. She hadn't meant to pry.

'Any other family?' she asked brightly, moving the conversation on.

Jim shook his head. 'Other than heaps of cousins, aunts and uncles like everyone else.'

'Well, I don't have heaps of cousins, uncles and aunts,' Peggy replied. 'It's just me and Mother.'

'Really?' Jim asked. 'What about your father, grandparents, that sort of thing?'

'Dad passed over five years ago,' Peggy explained. 'He was an only child, as is my mother. Both of their parents died before I was born so it's just me and Mother.'

'I'm sorry,' he said, his tone full of genuine sorrow as he reached across the table to clasp her hand.

At the feel of his skin on hers, Peggy let out a tiny gasp of surprise. It felt so strange to be touched by a man, and surprisingly intimate. Peggy gazed down at his long fingers with their neatly trimmed nails and felt something fizz inside her as she realised that Jim's hand on hers felt absolutely right.

Gazing up at his face, something told her he felt it too. His blue eyes were filled with warmth and longing and Peggy wanted nothing more than to stay in the teahouse and talk to this man for hours. Which was just what they did.

The sounds and smells of the tearoom all but disappeared, as she focused solely on the man in front of her and listened, rapt, to his life story. Over the course of the night she discovered Jim adored his parents but had never adjusted to life at boarding school. In fact, he had cried himself to sleep until he met his best friend, Thomas. Together they got up to all sorts of mischief, even joining the RAF after going to Cambridge together.

'Where is he now?' she asked, full of curiosity.

'He died during a training sortie,' Jim replied evenly. 'He had been a pilot less than a year.'

Peggy's hands flew to her mouth. 'I'm so sorry.'

Jim grimaced and gave a quick nod of his head. 'I went a bit off the rails when I heard. I didn't have a death wish, but it's probably accurate to say I wasn't exactly focused on living. Tom was my rock; we did everything together. Without him I felt rudderless, do you know what I mean?'

'I know exactly what you mean,' she whispered. 'When my father died, I felt just the same. He was my world, the one I always turned to. Without him, I didn't know what to do, life felt so empty. Mother was so strict, I loves her but we're not as close as I would like.'

Silently, Jim squeezed her hand. Peggy said nothing and together the pair remained in comfortable silence, locked in their own private world. Peggy had no idea how long they stayed like that, but as a nippy placed the bill beside them, and politely announced they were closing soon, they reluctantly sprang apart.

'Can I walk you home?' Jim asked, as he helped Peggy on with her coat.

'I'd like that.' Peggy smiled.

Jim paid the bill and they left, strolling along the High Street, the night air now freezing and the wind strong. With the blackout in full swing, it was hard to see, and Peggy clung to Jim for support against the strong sea breeze. With the gale whipping around their ears, it was too noisy for either one to say anything, so they kept their heads down against the wind until they reached Peggy's billet half an hour later.

Sheltering in the doorway of the hotel, Peggy smiled shyly up at Jim. 'Thanks for a lovely evening.'

'The pleasure really was all mine,' Jim said softly, as he took her gloved hand and rubbed his thumb over the back of it.

His touch left her giddy and Peggy desperately didn't want to say goodbye.

'I'd very much like to kiss you, Peggy,' Jim said, his voice smooth and velvety in the dark night.

A heady mix of fear and excitement coursed through her. She could think of nothing she wanted more, but at the same time, that next step, her first ever kiss, was terrifying. Unsure what to say or do, Peggy gazed up at him and found herself lost in those piercing blue eyes once more. They seemed so full of honesty, hope and sincerity that Peggy found her chin tilting upwards of its own accord. Then she closed her eyes and shuddered with delight as she felt his hot breath against her face and his lips gently brush against hers. Peggy had always thought kissing would be horrible, like rubbing a slimy snail or something equally disgusting against your face, but feeling Jim's soft mouth press lightly on to her lips, she realised she couldn't have been more wrong and allowed her heart to guide her to a place that felt like home.

Breaking apart, Peggy's pulse raced and her heart thumped against her chest. Looking up at Jim, he squeezed her hand, and she knew he felt the same.

'Can I see you again?' he murmured.

Peggy nodded. 'I can think of nothing I'd like more.'

'I'll call on you,' he replied, his eyes fixed on hers as he bent down to kiss her cheek.

Peggy smiled and waved as he walked back down the hill and she turned to go into the hotel. Climbing the stairs to her bedroom, she cast her mind back over the night. She had never enjoyed herself so much. Every one of her senses felt alive, and she wanted to bottle and keep the feeling, preserving it forever. Her thoughts turned to Edie and what she would say if she could see her now. Peggy imagined the displeasure that would line her face, and the lecture she would no doubt give her on the unreliability and unsuitability of men. Much to her surprise, she found she didn't care.

# Chapter Seven

It was funny the way Peggy had felt brighter and happier since her kiss with Jim. She had found a lightness in her step, and positively bounced out of bed at the crack of dawn each morning when the alarm woke her for daily square-bashing.

Normally in the morning she moaned and groaned her way around the billet with Annie and Judith, but these days she was always up first and humming the theme from *Music While You Work* as she washed and dressed, much to the amusement of Judith and the annoyance of Annie. In the evenings, if she wasn't at the barracks she was in her billet starching collars, darning socks or writing letters home, all while singing 'They Can't Ration Love', which drove Annie back out to the barracks screaming something about blue murder and left Judith glowing inside.

'Someone's in love,' Judith teased as Peggy polished the buttons of her jacket with her button stick, a huge smile plastered across her face one cold evening.

'I am not!' Peggy protested, before returning to her buttons, grin still intact.

'Yes, yer are,' Annie growled. 'And all this singing's driving me up the wall.'

'Annie!' Judith admonished. 'Yer should be pleased for Peggy.'

'There's nothing to be pleased about!' Peggy protested again, raising her voice over the strong Welsh wind that was whipping around the eaves of the hotel.

'Oh yes?' Judith asked, a knowing smile on her face. 'How many times has a certain pilot called on yer this past fortnight?'

At the mention of Jim directly, Peggy blushed. 'A couple,' she said quietly.

'More like four or five,' Annie muttered darkly, throwing herself back on to her bed, crushing her jacket in the process.

'And what's wrong with that?' Judith fired at her sister.

Annie paused. 'Nothing,' she said eventually. 'Sorry, I've had a bad day.'

'What happened, bab?' Peggy asked, her voice full of concern.

'Just Sal had a go at me for not getting me motor spirit form filled out properly at the requisition place. Said if it happened again, she'd report me to me commanding officer.'

'Oh Annie.' Peggy sighed. 'Why don't you just get forms signed like everyone else? It'd make life so much easier. Not everything has to be a battle, does it, Jude?'

Judith glanced at Peggy before fixing her sister with a sympathetic smile. 'Always been a battler, haven't yer, our Annie. Look, don't worry, I'll have a word with Sal, slip her some of those humbugs Mother gave us at Christmas, see if we can't soften her up.'

Annie smiled gratefully at her sister. 'Would yer? Ta, Judith, you're a treasure.'

Judith shrugged. 'Forget it. Now, if you don't mind I think we were in the middle of finding out what's happening with Peggy and Jim. I take it you're obviously courting like?'

Shaking her head at the girls as she put down her button stick, Peggy didn't know whether to laugh or cry. 'We're not courting!' she protested weakly. 'We've only been up the teahouse a handful of times.'

The sisters said nothing, just exchanged knowing looks. Peggy's face flamed with embarrassment and she returned to polishing her buttons. More than anything she wanted to confide in the girls, but the truth was she didn't know what was happening between her and Jim. There was certainly a spark between them, and Peggy had never enjoyed a visit to the tearoom more than when she was with Jim. Together they would laugh, smile and chat nineteen to the dozen as they swapped stories about their lives. As time wore on, it became increasingly clear to Peggy they came from wildly different backgrounds, but there was a real connection between them, one she could neither reason nor explain.

All she really knew was that every snatched moment with Jim made her feel alive and happy, especially after the previous night's bombings. Just after seven thirty, the Luftwaffe had bombed the north of the town in an attack that had lasted more than three hours. Officials thought the docks had been the intended target, but instead incendiaries fell on Kilvey Hill, a well-known landmark, causing it to light up like a burning red ball of fire, visible for miles. The sight had been terrifying,

Tonight, the town was braced for another attack, and Jim had suggested to Peggy they have a quick drink together before it was time to find safety back at their respective barracks. Even though Peggy didn't care much for alcohol, she had said yes, and although it was nothing more than a chilly Thursday evening, she planned on dolling herself up as if it were a Saturday night. Glancing at her wristwatch she saw she had just under half an hour before Jim called. Jumping to her feet, she reached for the make-up she had bought from Woolworths the day before and faced the vanity mirror above the sink. Anxiously examining her reflection, she self-consciously applied a touch of powder and rouge, grateful neither one of the sisters commented.

'Yer look so pretty,' Judith said softly, once Peggy had finished. 'Jim's a lucky lad.'

Peggy smiled awkwardly, she still couldn't get used to compliments. Edie had always told her they were a waste of time, that a compliment was neither use nor ornament. But despite her mother's criticism, she now found the praise gave her more confidence to take this step with Jim

'Yer really do, Peg,' Annie said, smiling as she handed her a crumpled piece of paper. 'By the way, this came for yer today.'

Peggy took the piece of paper from Annie's outstretched hand and saw it was a letter from her mother. To her surprise, the envelope was ripped apart.

'Why has it been opened?' she demanded.

Annie's tone was apologetic. 'I thought it was for me.'

'But our names don't look nothing like each other's. I don't get why you opened it?' Peggy said, puzzled.

Annie stamped her foot on the wooden floor so loudly she made Peggy and Judith jump. 'I just got confused, all right. Don't go on about it. I said I was sorry!'

Judith sprang to her feet to soothe her sister. 'All right, Annie, there's no need to get so upset. Peggy knows it was an accident, don't yer, Peg?'

Nodding, Peggy looked in astonishment at the girls. 'Yes, course, I was just surprised, that's all.'

Comforted, Annie sat back on her bed and looked awkwardly at her sister who gave her a gentle nudge with her elbow.

'It's all right, Peg, I shouldn't have gone on at yer like that,' Annie said quietly.

Peggy smiled graciously at her. 'Let's forget it. Least I got the letter. If I don't write back to Mother on Sunday she'll have me guts for garters.'

'Speaking of garters, you'd better get a move on.' Judith grinned. 'You don't want to keep your Jim waiting.'

'He's not my Jim,' Peggy protested as she stuffed the letter into the pocket of her khaki jacket and reached for her greatcoat.

'No?' Judith smiled. 'Maybe he should be.'

Rolling her eyes, Peggy rushed out of the door and down the flight of steps towards reception. Reaching the bottom step, her pulse raced as she caught sight of Jim, laughing and joking with Ida.

'Peggy!' The landlady chided as she caught sight of her. 'You and your pilot won't have long tonight, you don't want to keep him waiting.'

Jim beamed warmly at Peggy. 'Ida, Miss Collins here is well worth a few hours', never mind minutes', wait.'

Blushing, Peggy hurried towards him and felt her face flush even redder as he gently kissed her hand.

'Look at the two of you. Takes me back to when me and Harry first started courting. He used to look at me like that, you know, Peg.' Ida chuckled as her husband grunted in the corner, rustling the newspaper. 'You'd never know it now, of course. But that's what happens after almost forty years together. Still, you two young things enjoy yourselves while you can.'

'We intend to.' Jim smiled, offering his arm to Peggy. 'Goodnight, Ida.'

'Night you two,' Ida called as they strode off arm in arm. 'Don't do anything I wouldn't do.'

'Not much chance of that,' Jim hissed loudly, leaving Peggy giggling at his cheek.

Outside in the pitch-black, Peggy saw a thick frost had formed on the town's frozen streets. As they walked down the hill, she linked arms with Jim, and huddled against him to guard against the cold.

'So, where you taking me tonight?' she asked, turning to look up at him, his handsome features illuminated by the yellowy glow of the full moon.

'Just to a little pub on the corner.' He grinned back at her. 'I can't have you walking too far in this cold, can I?'

As the snow fell harder, covering the streets with a light dusting of talcum soft powder, she leaned in closer, relieved Jim wasn't planning on walking miles. Glancing up at the bright, moonlit sky, she shivered, realising the conditions were perfect for a raid.

Peggy didn't need much encouragement to be on full alert. After her experiences at home in the New Year, she felt fully prepared to help those in need. She had been devastated at the damage Hitler had done to her city, and later, when she arrived back at work, fuelled by anger, she couldn't wait to get stuck in any way she could. The threat of attack was always high, but Peggy knew that because the Germans hadn't destroyed the quarry, mill and most importantly the docks, they were more than likely to try again that evening.

She had half-expected to be called into work as a result of the impending attack, but her superiors didn't need her for guard duty and Carmichael had assured her he would be holed up in operations all night and wouldn't need her until the morning. Yet she knew it was vital Jim returned to his barracks that night for whatever it was he had to do. Peggy longed to know more about his work, but knew she couldn't ask. Careless talk costs lives, she thought wryly, thinking of the famous expression her mother had taunted her with back in January.

Turning the corner into Castle Street, a flicker of light caught Peggy's eye and she looked up to see the tell-tale signs of twinkling fairy lights dancing high in the night sky.

'Jim,' she said quietly, pointing upwards.

'Blast,' he fumed, as he followed her gaze. 'They're early. Let's get to safety before the air-raid sirens start. Does Ida have a shelter?'

'She's got a large makeshift one in the basement.' Peggy nodded.

They raced back up the hill towards the hotel, making it through the double doors just as the sirens began to sound with their tell-tale wail.

Inside, Peggy saw Ida running the place like a military operation as she herded friends and neighbours down to her cellar. As each one passed, the landlady gave them a blanket so they would be warm and comfortable for the duration of the raid.

'Ida, what can we do?' Jim asked, rushing straight to the older woman.

'Oh, there you are, loves. I was worried where you'd got to, is it.' Ida's eyes shone with relief at the sight of them.

'Ida, you've gotta get yourself to safety now,' Peggy insisted. 'Where's Harry to?'

'He's already down in the basement, Lenny's with him. The two of them are helping everyone get settled,' she replied.

'Which is where you need to be,' Peggy said forcefully, as the whining sound of the Luftwaffe overheard grew closer.

'She's right,' Jim agreed. 'We'll get everyone else down there, you look after yourself.'

'I'm fine, I'll be there now in a minute,' Ida protested.

'Now,' Peggy and Jim chorused as the air-raid sirens grew increasingly louder.

Muttering something under breath, Ida didn't argue and trooped down the stairs. As Jim ran upstairs to check for anyone that hadn't taken shelter, Peggy gave the ground floor a through sweep. Peeping tentatively through the blackout blind that covered the lounge window, she shuddered at the sight of the night sky becoming increasingly orange as the incendiaries fell. With every hiss and screech, Peggy felt a mix of fear and anger that the Jerries were trying to devastate yet another city she called home.

Suddenly she felt a hand on her shoulder and jumped as she saw Jim standing behind her.

'Don't look out there, Peg,' he said softly. 'Let's get downstairs and make sure everyone's all right.'

'What about your job? You need to get back to your barracks, don't you?' Peggy said in an urgent tone, suddenly remembering Jim wasn't supposed to be in Swansea.

'I'll wait until the all-clear,' he reasoned, the orange flares lighting up his face in the gloom of the blackout. 'There's no sense me getting killed on my way back. My commanding officer has given us all orders to shelter if we're ever caught in a raid like this.'

Relief flooded through Peggy. She hadn't realised just how

worried she was about Jim driving back through the raids. Each grabbing a blanket and food parcel of bread and jam from Ida's thoughtfully made up emergency pile, they ran down the wooden stairs towards the basement.

Peggy had never been in this part of the hotel before and was astounded to see how large it was. Thinking it would be a few upturned crates in a cramped and dingy cellar, she was amazed to see twenty bunk beds lined up in pairs, complete with electric lighting overhead. In the corner, behind the beds, stood a large Formica counter where Ida had provided a wireless and tea urn. The effect was strangely homely, Peggy thought, looking around, spotting several neighbours and guests from the few streets surrounding the hotel enjoying Harry and Ida's hospitality.

Speaking of which, Peggy was relieved to see the hoteliers doling out tea to the masses, and even more relieved to see Annie and Judith helping the older couple out. Sorting out blankets, bread and jam for the children, as well as a hug or kind smile for those that were separated from their parents; the sisters made quite a team. Peggy turned to Jim and suggested they join them.

'What d'you need doing, Ida?' Peggy asked as she watched her landlady dole out cup after cup of tea.

'Oh, there's good of you.' She smiled, turning briefly towards the pair of them, while she made another round of tea. 'Could one of you hand pillows out to everyone, Harry will show you where, and the other give a sweet to the children. There are some boiled sweets under the counter.'

'Will do,' Jim replied, walking immediately up to Harry and asking for the pillows.

Handing round the tin of sweets, Peggy glanced across at Jim and felt a sudden thrill rush through her as she watched him share a smile and a joke with everyone he spoke to; he even made a fuss of Lenny, ruffling his ears and encouraging the children to pat and stroke him too.

'He's a dish, isn't he?' Ida whispered, her black eyes dancing with delight

'Ida!' Peggy protested good-naturedly as she watched him shake old Mr Peters' hand before giving him a pillow. His wife had died in the last raid and Peggy intended to offer some words of comfort herself.

'I'm only saying,' Ida chuckled, as she refilled the urn, ready for more thirsty mouths. 'You could do worse.'

Peggy said nothing. Instead she took the cup of tea Ida handed to her and leant against the counter, feeling a flush of pleasure. She knew her landlady was right; Jim was turning out to be a real treasure. Kind, considerate, good with children, she thought as she watched him produce a halfpenny from behind a child's ear. But despite this, Peggy realised with slight frustration, she was conflicted. She was surprised at how much she liked being with Jim. It felt natural, almost as though they were made for each other. But then there was her mother. Edie had made it clear she didn't think Peggy courting a man was appropriate and Peggy had never disobeyed Edie in her life.

With a start, she remembered the letter Annie had given her before she left. Reaching into her pocket, she pulled the note out and began to read.

*13th February 1941*

*Hello there Peggy,*

*How are you? Life's much the same here. The shop's been busy, even after so many of our neighbours were bombed out of their homes. Seems people still want their rations, no matter the fact they've no kitchen to make a round of toast in.*

*I tell you, Peggy, it's heartbreaking seeing some of the people we've known for years homeless and bereft. I've let out your room to the Michaels family after they were bombed out last month. Poor things were sleeping on the street, and that's not right with two kiddies under eight.*

*I said to them it's not exactly comfortable, but it's about making do at times like this and bless Mrs Michaels, she's been a godsend, Peg, cleaning, washing and cooking while I'm in the shop all day on my own.*

*It's been nice to have a bit of company after being alone for so long now, what with you being off playing war. We've got into the habit of playing cards most evenings after listening to the news and* It's That Man Again *on the wireless. Almost makes me feel like part of a family. Course, it doesn't make up for you not being here, but I know we'll be together soon, Peg, once this blasted war is over. You and me, safe and together, running the shop, just as it should be.*

*Love Mother*

Peggy read the note three times over before she stuffed it into her pocket and wiped the tears from her eyes with the pads of her fingers. She felt a stab of guilt as she remembered the promise she had made her father. Her mother was all alone, and she wasn't taking care of Edie now her father couldn't. What had she been thinking, stepping out with a man when her mother was widowed and working tirelessly in their family shop? With a sigh, she cast her eyes back towards Jim. Watching him press a harmonica to his lips, she arched her eyebrows in surprise and couldn't resist joining the back of the little group that had gathered around him.

'What shall we sing, then?' Jim shouted, his face becoming more animated as the suggestions came thick and fast.

Suddenly Peggy couldn't help herself. '"Pack Up Your Troubles",' she blurted, as a sea of delighted faces turned to look at her.

Jim's face broke into a smile at the unexpected outburst. 'The winner is the prettiest girl in the room.'

As he blew gently across the instrument, the cheerful opening notes filled the room and everyone broke into song. Judith walked towards Peggy and stood next to her at the counter. Together the pair watched spellbound.

'He's full of hidden talent, isn't he?' she beamed at Peggy.

Peggy nodded. 'I had no ideal.'

'He reminds me of my Al,' Judith said loudly over the music.

'Really? How come?' Peggy asked, curious.

'He's got that way about him, like the Pied Piper,' Judith explained. 'People just love him; your Jim's the same, I'd say. Look at how good he was with those children, and Mr Peters. Knows just what to say and when, it's a rare skill that.'

'He's the same wherever we go. Could charm the birds out the trees,' Peggy said, a fond smile playing across her lips.

'But has he charmed you, Peggy?' Judith said, her tone becoming serious.

Peggy paused. She didn't want to let her mother down, but thanks to the war she was beginning to see things in a different way and she realised happiness was fleeting. In all her wildest dreams, she had never expected, never wanted, to find someone. And yet she had literally crashed into him, and in turn he had spun her world upside down.

Looking at her friend's beaming face, Peggy realised she needed someone she could talk to, and with a deep breath decided to be honest.

'I reckon he has, Jude,' she confessed. 'I reckon I'm smitten.'

'About time!' Judith exclaimed, wrapping her arm around Peggy's shoulders and squeezing her affectionately. 'And I'd say the feeling's mutual.'

'D'you reckon?' Peggy asked anxiously, afraid that now she had admitted her feelings for Jim, they were one-sided.

'I know,' Judith replied knowledgeably. 'Look at him, his eyes haven't left yer all night. He's barely looking at the people he's singing to, instead he keeps glancing at you.'

Peggy looked across at Jim and saw her friend was right. Her eyes met his and he smiled so warmly, her pulse raced as she lost herself in the look of love he was sending her way. Unable to tear her eyes from his, Peggy knew she was completely and utterly lost to Jim Hudson.

'My mother wouldn't approve,' Peggy said quietly.

Judith raised an eyebrow. 'Why not?'

'Never wanted me to court a fella, thought men only brought yer trouble,' Peggy confided.

Judith squeezed Peggy's arm gently. 'My mother was the same.'

'Really?' Peggy exclaimed.

Judith nodded. 'Thought Al was the devil when he came calling for me. She hated all fellas, thought they were the devil's work. My grandfather was a very cruel man. But I was determined. I showed Mother that I still loved her, that I wouldn't leave her behind, but I made it clear that my future lay with Al.'

'What did Al say?' Peggy begged.

'He was wonderful, Peg.' Judith smiled at the memory. 'Brought Mother flowers, fixed her kitchen tap and always took her a stout on a Sunday. She came around in the end when she could see he was a good lad. But the point is, Al wanted to make that effort for me, and your Jim, well, if it's meant to be, you'll face any problems with your mother together.'

Judith trailed off and Peggy turned back to watch Jim. Everything her friend had just said made complete sense and she suddenly felt very grateful she had confided in her. Just then the song finished, Jim gave a polite bow and Peggy saw that he was making a beeline for her.

This time Jim didn't ask permission, he simply bent down, pulled Peggy into his arms and showed her the depth of his longing with a lingering kiss. At the feel of his mouth on hers, Peggy felt fireworks dance in her stomach and explode into her chest. The feelings of passion ignited her very soul, and she knew she could never give Jim up, not even for her mother.

*

As the night wore on, the screech of the bombs hurtling through the skies above ground grew louder with every passing hour. Despite the fact they were in the basement, it sounded so much worse than the raid she had suffered in Bristol with Edie at New Year and Peggy wondered if it would ever stop. With the main lights turned off, Peggy glanced around her in the flickering candlelight and watched the other townsfolk sheltering against the raid. She noticed that the excited chatter and determined sing-songs of earlier had now stopped and instead everyone was frozen with fear. With the bombs now falling relentlessly around them, there appeared to be an unspoken concern that Jerry would never stop waging his own particular brand of hate and they would never find safety again.

Sadly, Peggy watched mothers clutch children tightly to their chests, whispering words of comfort and planting tender kisses on their foreheads as the very foundations of the basement shook with the force of each blast. Resting her head against Ida's makeshift tea stand, Peggy linked her arm through Jim's and squeezed her eyes tightly shut as the screech and whine of incendiaries crashed down around them.

'You all right?' he murmured into her hair.

Peggy lifted her chin and nodded. 'I'm always all right when I'm with you.'

Silently, Jim bent down, closed his eyes and kissed her with an intensity that left Peggy in no doubt he felt the same. The feeling of his lips against hers was sweeter than any sweet Peggy had handed out earlier and gave her such reassurance that by the time they broke apart she felt powerful enough to take on Hitler single-handed.

Gazing into her eyes, Jim pulled Peggy tightly into his arms. He held her with a force so strong that for a moment she felt as though they were the same person, their hearts and souls entwined with love and belonging.

Resting her head against Jim's chest she heard the sound of his heart beating loud and true despite the sound of the bombs and the hated drone of the Luftwaffe roaring directly above the hotel. The noise was pure evil and reminded Peggy she could very well be moments away from death. Shockwaves crashed through her as it dawned on her that her life could be extinguished in an instant, and what did she have to show for it? What had she done in her twenty-one years? She glanced across at Jim. He might have a few years' head start on her, but he had managed to achieve so much more. What with a university education and trips here and abroad to fight the hun. When would she get her chance to show Hitler what she was made of?

Beads of sweat gathered at her brow and a baby wailed loudly in the gloom as if sensing just how close to danger they all were. Just as Peggy felt panic begin to form, Jim pulled her even closer. With that one movement, Peggy's anxiety was replaced with a sudden sense of calm. Just being with Jim, in his arms, was right where she needed to be; it was where she had always needed to be. It was as though the simple act of finding Jim was what her life had been about and she no longer felt afraid of what Hitler and his band of merry men might throw her way. As this realisation washed over her, Peggy felt comforted. She knew that if she was killed in this moment then this truly would be the perfect way to die, with the man she loved beside her, where together they could go from this world to the next. As she turned her face to meet Jim's, she looked into his eyes and saw her own feelings of love reflected back at her. It still shocked Peggy that her feelings for Jim had changed so quickly, but no matter how fast her love had developed, she knew she could no more live without him than she could her job in the ATS fighting for freedom. There was nothing wondrous about wartime, but knowing you could face danger with the love of your life was a powerful weapon, and one she was very happy to have in her arsenal.

*

By the time dawn broke, the all-clear siren still hadn't sounded. Yet with a definite lull in the bombing, many who had sought shelter through the worst of it wanted to go and check their families and loved ones were safe.

The sudden activity around her caused Peggy to stir. She had only just got to sleep around an hour ago, eventually succumbing with her head lolling against Jim's shoulder. But Jim was no longer beside her and Peggy's bones felt cold and her neck ached. Rubbing her hands together to try and get some warmth back into them, she got to her feet, twisted her neck to the right and left to ease the stiffness in her joints and began to help everyone else to their feet.

Glancing across at the other side of the room, she saw Jim, Annie and Judith doing much the same. As for Ida, Peggy noticed she was pressing cups of tea into the hands of those that wanted something hot inside them before going upstairs to deal with whatever almighty mess Hitler had delivered through the night.

It didn't take long for everyone to leave and once the basement was empty, Peggy raced outside to see the damage for herself. With a sinking heart she took in the devastation. In the half-light, the first thing she noticed was that many of the shops opposite the hotel had been flattened. The wine shop, the stationers and even the gentlemen's outfitters, where Jim always liked to look longingly in the window, had gone.

The next thing she noticed was the smell. The stench of burning wood and dust billowing through the air filled her nose and lungs, while the crackle of flames from the burning buildings up ahead assaulted her ears. Covering her mouth with the sleeve of her uniform, Peggy craned her neck towards the site of a large fire at the top of the street. A team of volunteers from the Home Guard were already at the scene, using stirrup pumps and buckets of water to try and bring the roaring blaze under control. Instinctively, Peggy wanted to help.

Rushing towards the fire she kept her head low to avoid

the flying debris, taking care to tread over the mounds of rubble and glass that littered the street. Reaching the top, her heart was heavy as she realised the inferno was coming from three terraced houses that had been filled with families. Rushing to join Annie and Judith, who were already there, she picked up a bucket and joined them in their bid to do battle with the fire tearing through the street. But with each pail of water she threw, the blaze only seemed to get worse. Turning to the Home Guard, she saw the look of fear and despair on their faces as they realised their efforts appeared to be in vain.

'Where's the fire service?' Peggy begged, picking up another bucket to throw more water on the blaze.

'Too busy across town,' Annie replied grimly. 'Word is Central Hall has been attacked, not to mention Teilo Crescent. Families have been wiped out.'

'That's terrible,' Peggy said aghast.

Teilo Crescent was near the docks, so it appeared the Jerries had missed their target once again.

'What about here? Do we know if everyone's got out safely?' she asked, looking at the fierce blaze.

'We're not sure,' Judith shouted over the roar of the flames. 'But, Peg, there's summat you should know. Jim's inside. He's gone to check if anyone's trapped in there.'

Peggy's eyes opened in horror as she looked aghast at the burning houses. The fire was ferocious, ripping through the old houses as if they were made from nothing more than card. If anyone was in there now, they would surely die from smoke inhalation alone.

'It's not true, Jude, say there's been a mistake, you've got the wrong bloke. It can't be Jim,' Peggy said, her voice trembling.

Judith shook her head in despair. 'I'm sorry.'

Peggy felt the life force drain from her as fear and terror pulsed through every vein in her body. Letting out an anguished wail, she threw her bucket to the floor and raced towards the building, only to be restrained by Annie and Judith.

'Don't be daft,' Annie called, her voice firm as she pulled Peggy away from the blaze. 'There's no point you risking life and limb 'n'all.'

'Annie's right,' Judith shouted, clutching Peggy's right arm tightly to her. 'Jim's a strong and sensible lad, he'll not do anything daft.'

'I've gotta help him,' Peggy screamed, as she tried to free herself from the sisters' grip. 'Look at it.'

Together, the three girls took in the sight of the burning buildings, hearts in mouths as they watched the orange flames destroy what were once homes filled with laughter, love and hope for the future. Peggy wasn't sure she could stand it. All those innocent lives destroyed, and for what? She felt a hatred burn white hot, for what the Jerries were doing to the country she adored. Suddenly Peggy couldn't hold back any more, and tears ran down her soot-streaked face as she sank to the floor and wept for the boy who was by now surely dead.

Suddenly she became aware of someone shaking her by the shoulders. Opening her eyes she saw it was Annie.

'Look,' she hissed.

Turning to where her friend was pointing, Peggy let out a gasp of relief. There, walking through the flames, was her pilot, carrying a small child in his arms. His clothes were burnt and torn, his hair black with soot and he appeared to be missing a shoe, but Peggy couldn't help herself as she ran towards him screaming his name.

'You're safe,' she gasped, trying to fling her arms around him.

'Whoa, steady on, old girl,' Jim rasped, the smoke clearly having affected his voice. 'Let's just get this one out of harm's way.'

Happily, Peggy walked beside him and watched as he delivered the little boy, who was no more than about five, into the arms of the Red Cross who had now arrived along with the fire service.

'He's got a pulse,' Jim told one of the officers who took the child from his arms and immediately set about giving him mouth to mouth.

'What about you?' Peggy asked urgently. 'You've gotta get looked at. You can hardly talk.'

Jim waved her concerns away. Gratefully he accepted a cup of tea handed to him by a WRVS volunteer and slumped on to a nearby bench.

'I'm fine,' he said. 'Just need to catch my breath.'

Peggy looked at him in concern. 'You don't look fine. You look like you need a doctor. What made you go in like that?'

Resting his cup of tea on the ground, Jim turned to Peggy and shot her a small smile. 'It was the right thing to do, Peggy,' he said evenly. 'When I reached the blaze to help, one of the volunteers told me a family hadn't made it to the public shelter. I did what anyone would do and went to save who I could. Just a shame I couldn't find anyone else apart from that little boy. I should have done more.'

Jim picked up his tea and gripped it, gazing sadly at the floor. Peggy's heart went out to him. What else could he possibly have done? It was a miracle he was still alive, never mind the little boy he discovered. If Jim had been inside just a minute more, Peggy was sure he would have been another casualty of war. Resting her head against his shoulder, she felt the scratchy material of his jacket against her chin, filled with the scent of smoke, and let a fresh round of tears fall.

'You're a hero,' she said. 'In my eyes anyway, Jim Hudson, and don't you forget it.'

'I don't know about that, Peggy,' he croaked. 'I was terrified in there, all those flames getting hotter and hotter, licking my flesh; the smoke getting into my eyes and hair. I could scarcely breathe, but do you know what gave me strength?'

Shaking her head, Peggy looked into Jim's blue eyes, and

saw the fire blazing in his pupils. The sight of it chilled her to the core as she took his hand, and ran her fingers across his blackened palm.

'It was you, Peggy. The thought of you gave me the courage not to give up. I think . . .' He paused for a moment then fixed his gaze on the ATS girl. 'No, I know I love you, I would do anything to make you happy.'

Jim took her hand in his, and Peggy marvelled at the sight of her flesh wrapped in another's. She had never once thought she would meet someone and fall in love, yet here she was. She knew she had made a promise to her father, and it was a promise she intended to keep. But maybe Judith was right. Maybe she and Jim could find a way to be together and win Edie round. If so, it was time to make a promise to herself and create her own happy ending. Wordlessly, she leaned towards Jim and kissed him with all the love and passion her heart contained, leaving Jim in no doubt his feelings were not one-sided.

# Chapter Eight

Over the course of the day, Peggy was overwhelmed with happiness, but with so much suffering in the town, she sensitively tried to conceal her joy. Lieutenant Colonel Carmichael kept her more than busy with several meetings to attend following the raids over two consecutive nights and Peggy threw herself into war work.

Reports had already surfaced that the Luftwaffe had dropped six bombs on Teilo Crescent, killing forty-six people and injuring a further forty-four. It was devastating; Peggy had seen the looks of fear and despair on the faces of people all day as they wondered if there would be another raid on Swansea once darkness fell.

Sitting in the car as the sky turned an inky black, Peggy drummed her fingers against the steering wheel as she waited for Carmichael. This was the last meeting of a very long day with the brigadier at his home on the outskirts of the town, and Peggy couldn't wait to get back to the barracks. Truth be told, she was shattered and more than anything wanted a quiet night in stitching and mending with Annie and Judith. Yet peering up at the sky she couldn't fail to notice the full moon glowing overhead and felt a stab of dread at the thought of the Jerries trying their luck on the Welsh town for the third night in a row.

Watching the lieutenant colonel emerge from the brigadier's

house, she got out of the driver's seat, held open the rear door and saluted him as he got inside.

'Where to now, sir?' she asked, catching the weary look in her boss's eyes.

'Back to barracks, please, Collins,' Carmichael sighed.

'Course, sir,' she replied, pressing her foot on the accelerator. 'You might as well know, Collins, we're expecting another attack on the docks. The barrage balloons are protecting the area, naturally, but that's unlikely to be enough and I need you to be my Girl Friday.'

Peggy gave a sharp nod of her head as Carmichael pinched his nose and breathed deeply. He looked as though he had the weight of the world on his shoulders and Peggy knew she would have her work cut out trying to ease some of that burden.

The drive across town was long, with devastation and chaos at every corner. Buildings continued to smoke from the night before and fires burned brightly, as though inviting Jerry across the water. As for the mess and wreckage, it seemed to grow faster than the Home Guard could clear it. Fire patrol wardens paced the streets, checking for infernos, while those who had lost their homes continued to scrabble about in the darkness, searching for mementoes of their lives before the horror of war began. But the one thing Peggy couldn't fail to notice was the look of steely determination on everyone's faces.

Despite the tragedy and heartbreak confronted by so many, there was a single-mindedness in people's eyes that Jerry would not defeat them. It was a look Peggy had seen before, the day she had left her hometown of Bristol following the raids. She too wanted nothing more than to show the Jerries what she was made of, and prove they would never win. So much so that by the time they reached the barracks just over an hour later, Peggy had fired herself up to serve Carmichael in any way he saw fit.

'I'm going to need you manning the phones tonight, Collins,'

Carmichael told her as she opened the rear door for him. 'It's all hands to the pumps.'

'Very good, sir,' Peggy nodded as she saluted him.

The thought of helping her superior officer directly gave Peggy a sudden thrill at the faith he had placed in her. Driving the car into the garage, she nodded a quick hello to Sal then opened the bonnet and performed her usual nightly duty of draining the radiator so it wouldn't freeze.

It was often a fiddly task, but tonight Peggy was relieved to discover someone was smiling down at her, as she finished in minutes. Returning to the operations room to help Carmichael, Peggy gazed around her in awe.

The underground room, built a bit like Ida's shelter, Peggy noticed, was already a hive of activity with several makeshift desks lined up in pairs. Each desk was filled with ATS girls taking calls, making notes and talking to officers. Despite the cold, the dazzling electric strip-lighting gave off a certain warmth, not to mention harsh glare. The air was charged, with everyone prepared for another raid, and wanting to do all they could to stop it.

Spotting an empty desk beside Annie, Peggy sat down next to her.

'Long day?' Annie quizzed.

'You could say that,' Peggy sighed. 'Where've you been?'

'Running deliveries all day,' Annie replied. 'I'm only just back from Wrexham.'

Peggy raised her eyebrows. 'Blimey, that's a drive.'

'You're telling me,' Annie chuckled. 'Still, could be worse, I could've been like poor old Judith. She's out on the ambulances tonight.'

'Is she? Why?' Peggy asked in surprise. Ambulances were usually run by the FANY. Although all ATS girls were trained to drive an ambulance, they rarely needed to except in extreme emergencies.

'She used to help out up the Red Cross in Stoke, so she's

got a bit of nursing experience,' Annie explained. 'Jude's been roped in for a bit of extra support.'

'Bless her cottons.' Peggy smiled as she caught sight of Sal striding towards the desk next to hers.

'You two are a sight for sore eyes,' Sal exclaimed as she sat noisily into the chair.

'What are yer doing here?' Annie asked. 'I've never seen yer out the garage.'

Sal smiled knowingly as she fished in her bag for her trademark red lipstick. Even though make-up was banned at work, Sal paid no heed and her superior officers had never said a word to her about toning it down. Sal Perkins was a law unto herself, and Peggy suspected that was just the way she liked it.

'We're all gettin' stuck in tonight. I've sent out our last vehicle so there's nothin' for me to do apart from make myself useful here.'

'Have you ever been in an office before?' Peg asked in astonishment as Annie's telephone rang.

'Once or twice, pet,' Sal chuckled. 'I used to work in the mail room years ago, before they had the sense to put me in with the hacky mechanics. It suited me and everyone else a lot better.'

Peggy smiled wryly. 'Was it you what sent Judith out in an ambulance? Annie was just saying she's been called out.'

Sal nodded. 'She's got a lovely way about her when it comes to nursin', a real natural. That and the fact she's an excellent driver, she'll be a safe pair of hands for whatever Hitler brings tonight.'

'Who's a safe pair of hands?' Annie asked as she put the phone down.

'Your Judith,' Sal replied, as she arched an eyebrow in Annie's direction. 'Aren't you goin' to write that message down, flower?'

Annie waved Sal's concerns away as she leaned back in the hard, wooden chair. 'It was only someone wanting to check how many girls we had here tonight. Nothing important.'

'Are you sure, Annie?' Peggy asked anxiously.

'More than sure, Peg. You worry too much.' Annie smiled and got to her feet. 'Who's for a cuppa? I'm due a break now, so I'll see if I can't smuggle us a round of brews in, keep us going tonight.'

Not waiting for an answer, Annie left her desk and hurried out of the room, leaving Sal and Peggy to man their own ringing phones as well as Annie's.

The girls had only been at work for an hour when news emerged just after seven thirty that Swansea's worst fears had been realised and the Germans had struck the town for the third night running. Although the girls were underground, Peggy could hear the low whine of the Luftwaffe overhead, swiftly followed by the vibration of incendiaries as they hit the ground. Usually she would have felt terrified, but tonight Peggy felt fired up with injustice at what the Jerries were up to. She put her heart and soul into her work, taking so many messages that her hand ached from scribbling each note so furiously.

It didn't help that every time the phone rang, reports came in thick and fast that the Germans' mission to destroy Swansea was succeeding. So far, bombs had hit the docks and the town centre, with both Ben Evans and Peggy's beloved covered market destroyed.

It was terrifying and heartbreaking in equal measure, but there wasn't the time to dwell on what had happened. Sneaking a glance at Carmichael as she handed her latest message to a passing sergeant, Peggy saw his face was pinched with worry and fear moved through her body. If even her superior officer was anxious, then what did that say about the severity of the situation?

She caught sight of the clock that hung above the door and realised it was almost five in the morning, no wonder she was exhausted. Peggy stretched her arms overhead and tried to ease the tension in her back and shoulders that only came from sitting hunched over a desk all night. She had been at work in the operations room for almost eleven hours, and there seemed to be no sign of the Germans slowing down. Rubbing her eyes, she caught sight of Annie, who appeared to have fallen asleep at her desk. Chuckling, she leaned over and gave her friend a gentle prod in the ribs, waking her just in time to answer yet another call.

Only Sal appeared to be firing on all cylinders, Peggy thought, watching her write down yet another message, her tone clipped and manner efficient. Spotting the mound of teacups pushed to the corner of Sal's desk, Peggy smiled as she realised just why Sal was still on high alert. She had once confided that she did her best thinking with a brew in one hand and cigarette in the other. Although she saw no sign of the Player's that usually resided in the older woman's pocket, it was clear she was turning to her other vice. Thinking yet another cup of tea would do them all good, she stood up to make one when a terrific clatter made her jump.

Alarmed, Peggy saw the noise had come from Annie who had dropped the phone receiver to the floor and turned a ghostly white. Doing her best to stay calm, Peggy picked up the receiver, replaced it on the telephone then wrapped an arm around her friend. She could feel Annie shaking violently and tried to steady her enough so she could explain what had happened.

'Annie, love, what is it?'

But Annie appeared not to have heard Peggy speak as she gazed at the floor, her teeth chattering.

'Did you hear me, babber?' Peggy asked again, her voice firmer now. 'What's happened?'

As though seeing Peggy for the first time, Annie lifted her chin to meet her gaze. At the sight of the younger girl's eyes, Peggy's blood ran cold. They were lifeless and filled with pain so raw it hurt her just to look at them.

'It . . . it . . . it's Judith,' Annie stuttered.

'What about her?' asked Sal, who by now had got up from her desk to join the girls.

'She . . . she's dead,' Annie said shakily.

The large lump forming in Peggy's throat made it impossible to speak for a moment. Surely there was a mistake, Annie must have got hold of the wrong end of the stick; Judith couldn't be dead.

'Sweetheart, are you sure you heard right?' Sal asked matter-of-factly, taking the words right out of Peggy's mouth. 'There's a lot goin' on in here tonight, and mistakes can easily be made.'

'There's no mistake,' Annie breathed. 'I heard it as clear as day. Our Judith's dead.'

'But how?' Peggy croaked.

Annie's face clouded over as she looked despairingly at Sal and Peggy.

'She was driving an ambulance through the town centre,' she began haltingly. 'They'd been called out to deal with some of the fellas who'd been injured dealing with some of the unexploded bombs . . .'

'Go on, pet,' Sal encouraged, her hand now clasping Annie's for comfort.

'One went off,' Annie said in a tortured wail. 'A bomb went off unexpectedly, like, just as the ambulance drove past. They don't know any more than that, but our Judith's dead, me sister's gone.'

Peggy's mind went into overdrive. Nothing Annie had said so far meant Judith had definitely been killed. It could have been anyone driving the ambulance, there would surely have been several out on the streets tonight.

'It was a woman driving the ambulance,' Annie sobbed as if she was reading Peggy's mind. 'I picked up the phone just by chance, Home Guard were the first there and wanted to alert us here as it was an ATS ambulance.'

Peggy squeezed Annie's hand, and turned to Sal who looked

stricken. 'Did anyone else drive an ambulance tonight? Could it be anyone else apart from Jude?' she begged, her voice low.

Sal breathed heavily, as she crouched on her haunches, her face grave as she shook her head. 'I'm sorry, girls, Judith was the only ATS girl out on the ambulances tonight.'

Annie threw herself on the floor, keening like a wounded animal. Despite the continued drone of the Luftwaffe overhead, the room fell so silent you could hear a pin drop, as the reality that one of their own had been killed sunk in. Even the phones stopped ringing, as if somehow everyone knew something dreadful had happened.

Peggy pressed her knuckles to her mouth to stop herself from weeping and instead focused on helping her friend whose high-pitched cries weren't getting any quieter.

'My sister, my sister,' Annie sobbed. 'I need her, where is she?'

'I know, lover, I know,' Peggy soothed, pushing the hair out of her friend's eyes as she exchanged anxious glances with Sal.

Out of the corner of her eye, Peggy saw Lieutenant Colonel Carmichael walking towards them, and sprang to her feet.

'I've just heard,' he said, his face grave. 'What dreadful news. Judith was a good sort, we shall miss her dreadfully, I'm extremely sorry, Shawcross.'

Peggy nodded as the lieutenant colonel glanced around the room, as if assessing the situation.

'Can you and Sub-Leader Perkins take Annie to the mess for a cup of tea,' Carmichael asked gently. 'She shouldn't be expected to cope with all this now.'

'Can you spare all three of us, sir?' Peggy asked in surprise.

'The girl has just lost her sister,' Carmichael replied softly, his eyes filled with kindness and sorrow. 'I think it's the very least I can do while I confirm exactly what has happened.'

He bent down to offer his condolences, and Annie stopped crying as Carmichael patted her shoulder. Like a small child, she allowed herself to be guided out of the operations room by

Peggy and Sal. Together the three of them walked towards the mess, just a few feet away. Emerging into the outside world, Peggy tried to contain her shock at the sight of the sky, which was such a vibrant shade of orange it was as though the whole town had been lit up by Guy Fawkes himself. As they walked across the path, Peggy couldn't fail to notice the overpowering stench of smoke from the buildings burning miles across town. Walking inside, Peggy took one last look behind her with the sinking feeling that tonight, the Jerries may well have bombed the life out of Swansea for good.

*

Peggy had no idea how long she and Sal sat in the mess with Annie, their arms never straying far from the girl as they each tried to find some crumb of comfort to offer. Sal, usually so full of good, practical advice, was for once lost for words, and Peggy felt ashamed to say she had nothing to add, other than more condolences, which she knew were worthless. Not for the first time, she wondered what her own mother would say and realised Edie would probably have been wildly practical, insisting on getting on with whatever needed doing. She smiled at the thought; sometimes her mother's stiffness was difficult to deal with, but there were times when she realised how useful it would be to turn off your emotions.

Word of the tragedy quickly spread, and Peggy was humbled at the way everyone in the barracks banded together to help Annie in any way they could. Nobody passed without bringing a cup of tea, Eccles cake or garibaldi biscuit, which Peggy knew they would never eat or drink, but she was touched all the same at the kindness.

At some point, Peggy became aware that Lieutenant Colonel Carmichael himself entered the mess and confirmed their worst fears; Judith had died. He also revealed that a further three ATS girls had lost their lives during the raid, and that the entire death toll so far over the course of the three nights stood at two hundred, with the figure continuing to rise.

Peggy wanted to howl at the thought of such senseless death and destruction. The Germans were trying to destroy their way of life, but she would never let that happen, she thought fiercely, not after the death of her dear friend. She was consumed with rage, wanting nothing more than to shout and scream. Yet Peggy also knew that her place for now was by Annie's side. Her friend needed her to be strong and so she comforted her until dawn broke and the sound of birdsong rang out, a precursor to the welcome blast of the all-clear siren. By now, Peggy was exhausted. A quick glance over Annie's head at Sal, whose face was grey and ashen despite the red lipstick, told her she wasn't the only one.

Cold and stiff, Peggy turned to look out of the window at the scene before them. She had no idea how bad the devastation across the town was, but the view before her told her Swansea could very well have been obliterated.

Wearily, she watched the recruits file in for breakfast, their faces downcast and awash with grief. Images of Judith filled her mind, and Peggy stifled a sob as she remembered the last time she had seen her friend, how full of wisdom she had been, and how happy she was at the thought of her marriage to Al.

Judith had brimmed with kindness and love, it was a shocking waste she had been taken so soon. She was just twenty-three years old, with a lot of living left to do, Peggy thought. The world would surely be worse off without her friend in it.

'Tea, love?' Sal asked quietly, interrupting Peggy's train of thought.

Peggy nodded. 'Ta, bab. And then p'raps we'd better get Annie to bed.'

Annie shook her head sadly. 'I can't sleep. I can't go back to our billet, Peg. I don't want to see all of Jude's things.'

With that Annie erupted into a fresh round of sobs, and Peggy clung to her, lost for words.

'Maybe we can find you a bed here at the barracks,' she suggested eventually. 'I'm sure Carmichael will want to help, but you need to sleep. Perhaps we can get you a draught from the doctor.'

Annie lifted her head and turned to Peggy, her eyes glassy. 'Don't leave me as well, I don't want to be on me own.'

'Sal's here,' Peggy said gently, glancing across the top of Annie's head at Sal, who nodded. 'I'll only be a minute, promise, and we can get you sorted.'

Reluctantly Annie let go of Peggy's arm, allowing her to get to her feet and walk back to the operations room where she hoped she would still be able to find Carmichael. She had scarcely got one foot out of the door, before she heard the sound of footsteps bounding towards her across the gravelled path.

'Peggy!'

With a start, Peggy saw Jim running in her direction, his face flooded with relief. At the sight of him, her heart leapt and she raced towards him, arms outstretched.

'You're alive.' He beamed, pulling Peggy into his arms. 'I was dreadfully worried you had been caught in the raid.'

Peggy unravelled her arms from his neck, took a step back, tears pooling in her eyes. 'I wasn't, but Judith was. She's been killed, Jim.'

Jim's face filled with horror, but the look in his eyes was steely and resolute as he took a deep breath and clasped Peggy's hand.

'I'm so sorry,' he said, his voice grave. 'That's terrible, I wish there was something I could say that would bring her back.'

Peggy nodded, the comforting feel of Jim's cool fingers against her own warm skin helping calm her down.

'All we can do is keep fighting, Peggy. Keep fighting Hitler and never let him win,' Jim went on earnestly. 'That way we will stop him destroying anything and everything we hold dear and Judith's death will not be in vain.'

'I know,' Peggy whispered, the tears she had kept at bay all night now rolling down her cheeks like rivers. 'I've thought of nothing else all night.'

Wiping her eyes with her free hand, Peggy suddenly became aware of Jim's grip becoming tighter.

'What is it?' she asked, a note of caution creeping into her voice.

'I came as soon as I heard. Peggy, my love, I've just heard that I'm being posted elsewhere,' Jim said quietly. 'These latest attacks mean we have to fight fire with fire. I'm being sent elsewhere.'

'Where?' Peggy begged. 'How long for?'

Jim shook his head sadly. 'You know I can't tell you any more than I have already. But I will write, I can assure you of that, Peggy. You will hear from me far too frequently. In fact, you will be so bored of my letters you will rue the day I ever ran you off the road.'

Chuckling through her tears, Peggy shook her head sadly. 'I'll never be sorry about what happened that day.'

Leaning forward to plant a tender kiss on her forehead, Jim gathered her into his arms and held her.

'Neither will I,' he whispered. 'You are and always will be the very best thing that has ever happened to me, Peggy Collins. Stay safe until I return, promise me?'

With her head burrowed against his chest, Peggy nodded.

'I promise,' she said, her voice muffled but strong.

As her voice trailed off, she allowed herself to soak up the scent of the man she knew she loved while she could and thought of her beloved friend Judith. Despite her best intentions, Peggy knew that remaining safe was one promise she may not be able to keep.

# Chapter Nine

The people of Swansea were understandably shell-shocked after such devastation. In the aftermath, they struggled to come to terms with the loss they had endured. There was no denying that the Welsh town had paid a heavy price in the game of war, with Castle Street and the High Street decimated. Not only had most of the shops that made up the cornerstone of the town been destroyed, but those that had worked in them had lost their jobs. As for the beautiful covered market, which Peggy had adored, it had been reduced to nothing more than a mound of rubble and glass, with the coveted Ben Evans store suffering the same fate.

The town was grief-stricken for days, yet people soon rolled up their sleeves and mucked in together. Temporary shops were set up so shopkeepers could stay in business, and stallholders who had made their living from the market remained afloat thanks to a makeshift bazaar in the old bus station. This ingenious display of enterprise meant staff and employers could carry on regardless and shoppers were keen to show their support.

In short, Swansea was a phoenix rising from the ashes, Peggy thought as she smoothed her khaki skirt and checked her reflection in the tiny mirror that hung in her billeted bedroom. There was no getting away from the fact she looked tired. Straightening her tie, Peggy knew that the events of today were unlikely to do much for her spirit either. Her gaze fell on the empty bed once occupied by Judith. A lump formed in her throat at the thought of her friend. It had been just over a week since the three days of raids and she could still scarcely believe Judith was gone. As Annie burst through the door, Peggy pinched her cheeks to stem the ever-flowing tears that threatened to run down her cheeks.

'Hello, love,' Peggy said in as bright a tone as she could manage. 'How was your walk?'

Annie shrugged as she flopped face down on to her bed. 'Fine.'

'D'you want me to do anything before it's time to go up the church? Meet your parents or something?'

'They're already here,' Annie said, her voice strained. 'I'll see you up there. Mam and Dad want us all to go up together.'

'All right,' Peggy agreed, checking her watch and seeing there was just an hour to go until Judith's funeral. 'Have you eaten anything? I'm sure Ida won't mind making you a butty.'

'I'm not hungry,' Annie replied.

Peggy perched awkwardly on the edge of Annie's bed. 'You should try and eat something, bab. You've gotta keep your strength up.'

'I said I'm not hungry,' Annie snapped, her eyes flashing with anger. 'I know yer mean well, Peggy, but I just want to be left alone. You're as bad as me parents.'

'All right, all right.' Peggy held up her hands and got to her feet. 'I'll see you up the church then.'

As Peggy walked out of the room, she glanced back at Annie and saw the girl was staring vacantly out of the window. More than anything Peggy wanted to comfort her, but knew that was the last thing Annie wanted. Everyone who had known Judith was struggling to come to terms with the loss of the young woman who had been full of hope and joy, but Annie in particular had taken it very badly.

In the immediate aftermath of Judith's death, Annie barely uttered a word. After sobbing her heart out on the final night of the raid, she retreated into herself and only spoke when she had to. Peggy, Sal and Ida were all desperately worried about her, particularly when she refused Lieutenant Colonel Carmichael's offer of a seventy-two-hour pass to spend time with her parents. Like Annie, they were devastated at the death of their daughter but Annie nobly insisted on working, throwing herself into every driving opportunity and working from dawn until dusk, never pausing for breath or complaint.

Peggy kept a close eye on her, particularly as Judith's funeral approached. She couldn't help notice Annie's upset had turned to anger and she lashed out at anyone and everyone over the slightest detail. Walking down the stairs to meet Ida and Harry in the foyer, Peggy hoped that his dreadful day would at least give Annie as well as everyone else the chance to say goodbye.

'You look nice today.' Ida smiled as Peggy joined them. 'Very dignified.'

Peggy smiled at her landlady's kindness. 'I look the same as I do every day, Ida. Khaki uniforms have a way of blending us all together.'

'Nonsense,' Ida scolded. 'You look lovely, doesn't she, Harry?'

'Tidy,' he agreed solemnly, as he extended his arm for Ida to hold on to. 'Come on, it's going to take a while to get up the church, with all the road signs and what have you.'

Harry was right. Since the raid, fears of unexploded bombs lying amongst the wreckage meant warning signs littered the roads, advising people to tread with caution.

Following the older couple as they left the hotel, Peggy shuddered as she walked down the steps and out into the cool air. She knew she ought to be used to the sight of the bombed-out shops and homes by now, but the truth was Peggy found the sight of so much torment increasingly hard to bear.

A strong February wind sent the dust from the rubble soaring into the air, causing Peggy to bend her head low as she walked behind Ida and Harry. Not only did the destruction remind her of the loss of her friend, but it brought home to her the true cost of war. It seemed every day was filled with some fresh new round of terror, and the little Bakelite wireless she and Annie used to listen to the news in their bedroom did nothing to ease her worry about her loved ones.

If it wasn't for her job in the ATS then Peggy wasn't sure what she would have done with herself, particularly after Judith passed away. Like Annie she had found comfort in work, but unlike Annie she wasn't suffering violent mood swings; instead she just felt sad and in a strange way guilty that she had survived and Judith hadn't.

'There but for the grace of God,' Ida consoled when Peggy had confessed her feelings one night.

But making her way into the church to say her final farewell to her friend, Peggy wondered if all it really boiled down to was a case of wrong place, wrong time. Her mother was all alone in Bristol, despite her repeated assurances that the family that had moved in with her were a treasure. And as for Jim, well Jim would be heaven knows where after today. He would be leaving straight after the funeral for his posting and Peggy was dreading a life without him. From nowhere, an image of his handsome face flooded into her mind's eye and she smiled at the thought of his floppy fringe.

News of Jim's posting had hit Peggy much harder than she had anticipated. She hadn't expected to become so attached to him so quickly and whenever she pictured a day without him, she felt a growing sense of despair rise within her. She could kick herself for the way she felt. She knew there were much more important things to worry about, particularly during this dangerous time, but the truth was, just the thought of only hearing from Jim by letter made her physically ache in a way she never had before. Trudging up the hill behind Ida and Harry, Peggy thought back to her conversation with Sal, where she wondered how to talk to a man. She smiled at the memory; talking to Jim now was as natural as the sun rising each morning. As for the love she felt for the pilot, that felt as easy as slipping on her khaki jacket each morning and tying up the laces of her heavy Oxford brogues. Jim had slipped so seamlessly into her life, the profound, unexplainable connection they shared as deep-rooted and strong as a thousand-year-old oak tree. Peggy was dreading the moment she had to say goodbye to him, but was thankful for the note she had received from her old friend Kitty just that morning, offering, as usual, the perfect mix of support and advice.

Reaching the church and realising that she had a few moments before she took her seat, Peggy pulled Kitty's letter from her jacket pocket.

*22 February 1941*

*Dearest Peg,*

*What a treat to receive your last letter. I thought I'd take a minute to reply when I've a rare night in starching my collars, but of course I'd far rather talk to you.*

*I'm sorry to hear what happened to your pal Judith, love. What a terrible thing, and sadly, as we both know, it's not a rarity either, is it? You must be heartbroken, Peg, but I know first-hand how war work will comfort you in your hour of need. More than ever you need to throw yourself into it all. Trust me, when all else fails, your job will get you through. When Joe died it was the only thing in the world that made me want to get out of bed in the morning; that and a few pals, of course. Sounds like you've got a few around you that you can rely on too, they'll help you more than you realise and I'm only ever a letter away.*

*You'll need your pals too when your sweetheart leaves. Try not to worry, Peg love. Easier said than done, I know that. There isn't a day that passes where I don't miss my Arthur, but I'm so proud of him for doing his bit, fighting for our country and that's how you should feel about Jim. Not only that, love, but look how far you've come since*

*we first met at basic training all that time ago. You said
then you'd never look at a fella, now look at you, courting
and fallen in love as well! Be proud of yourself, Peg, you've
grown ever such a lot since you've been in the ATS. I don't
want to speak out of turn but you're so much stronger than
your mother ever gave you credit for, have a bit of faith in
yourself, promise me. You and Jim might only have been
together a couple of months, love, but when you know
something's right in your heart, time's not important. All
that matters are your feelings, and you and Jim have found
a natural bond neither one of you could deny. I know it'll
be hard without him, but this war is so much bigger than
us, one day when this is all over and we're living the life
of Riley with our husbands and our babies, we will have
forgotten all this suffering.*

*Now, I've gone on for long enough so I'll sign off.
Besides, if I don't starch me collars no doubt I'll be for it.
Take care of yourself, love.*

*Your friend forever,*

*Kitty*

As Peggy finished the letter, she found herself smiling at Kitty's advice. Her friend always knew the right thing to say, and no doubt knew that a letter was just what she needed. Clutching it to her chest, she felt Kitty's warmth and affection flood through her, almost as if she were right beside her. Kitty was right, of course, she and Jim may only have been together for a short period, but already Peggy knew that no distance would keep them apart. They were meant to be together, connected with a love so strong only the two of them could understand. It would be tough to say goodbye to him after the funeral but Peggy was proud of her sweetheart for doing even more in this fight against Hitler, and she only wished she too could take to the skies and gun down all of the enemy. If nothing else, she wanted to make them pay for what they had done to Judith. But Peggy knew her place was here in Swansea, fighting the good fight in her own way, and if truth be told there was nowhere she would rather be.

As the clouds darkened, threatening rain, Peggy turned to go inside when she caught sight of Jim walking up the hill towards her. Despite the sadness of the occasion, her heart leapt as she watched his familiar long stride lope towards her, and she revelled in the grin that lit up his entire face when he caught sight of her standing in the doorway. Reaching her side, she allowed herself to be pulled into his arms.

'How are you bearing up?' Jim asked, his voice muffled as he buried his head in her hair.

'Fine,' she replied in a small voice. 'I'll be glad when the service is over.'

'Me too.' Jim nodded. 'It's such a shocking waste.'

Peggy pulled away and looked him up and down. 'And what about you? Ready?'

Jim smiled sadly. 'As ready as I'll ever be.'

'And you're leaving straight after the service?' Peggy asked, squeezing his arm for confirmation.

Jim nodded. 'Yes, all my kit's bundled in the Aston,' he said, jerking his head towards the car that was his pride and joy.

Peggy glanced across at the vehicle and felt a sudden thrill at the sight of it. It was that car that had brought them together, though, naturally, she hadn't known it at the time. She wasn't sure if she would ever see such a beautiful car again, but if she did, she knew this particular make and model would always have a very special place in her heart.

Glancing at her watch, she saw it was time to go in and pay their last respects. Linking her arm through Jim's, they made their way into the chapel and prepared to say goodbye to Judith.

Although the vicar who performed the service hadn't known Judith for very long, he had no trouble talking about the work she did in the community. Not only did she make time to visit the sick and injured at the hospital, something Peggy had no idea about, but she had also helped out with the church, regularly taking part in fundraising activities and visiting the local orphanage to read stories to the children. Then of course there was her role in the ATS, which was the light of her life. The vicar talked fondly about how Judith had proudly given her all to the Army, and the friends she had made, who she considered family.

At that, Peggy, who was grateful to have found a space next to Annie, squeezed the younger girl's hand. Despite her best efforts, Annie was clearly finding the service hard, and Peggy wanted to offer her as much support and comfort as she could.

As Peggy listened to the vicar's sermon, she glanced around and saw the church was standing room only with Army recruits and officers, townspeople as well as friends and family from Stoke, crammed into the tiny room. She realised with a heavy heart how Judith had truly thrown herself into life, making an impact on everyone she met.

Although Al was unable to attend the ceremony as he was serving with the RAF and unable to obtain official leave, he had written to Judith's parents, requesting that Judith's favourite hymn, 'Abide With Me', was sung during the service. As the opening notes rang through the church, the congregation got to their feet clutching their hymn books, ready to sing their hearts out in honour of the young woman who had left a gaping hole in their lives.

The only one who was silent was Annie, Peggy noticed. Up until now Annie had done a good job of remaining stoic, though there had been many times Peggy herself had shed a tear. Yet as the singing got under way, Peggy saw that Annie barely glanced at the book in her hand, instead she seemed to be entirely elsewhere as she mumbled her way through the chorus.

Sympathy flooded through her, and she squeezed Annie's hand once more, resolving to try and get her to open up once the ceremony was over and share her pain. What was it Kitty had always said, Peggy thought, a problem shared was a problem halved? And while Peggy knew there was nothing she could say or do to bring Annie's sister back, she could at least offer her a shoulder to cry on when she needed.

After the hymns, David, Judith and Annie's father, walked towards the altar to deliver his eulogy. Reaching his daughter's coffin, he dropped a single rose on to the top, and let his fingers linger there, as though wanting to hang on to his oldest girl forever.

Peggy felt his pain as keenly as if it were her own, particularly as he told the congregation of the love that would always bind him to his daughter. Thoughts of her own father's funeral flickered through her mind, and she remembered how she had lingered by the graveside, unable to say a final goodbye to the dad she had adored.

Outside in the graveyard, the committal of Judith's body to the ground was mercifully short, but Peggy was highly tuned to Jim's presence beside her and the salvation it offered. Yet even Jim couldn't stop the cruel truth dawning on her that she would never see Judith's sweet face again. Waves of despair coursed through her body and as she wondered just how many more lives had to be lost in order for this war to be over, she felt Jim reaching for her hand, stroking her palm gently with his thumb. Peggy felt calmer immediately and ached with love for him. In that moment, she realised Jim had mastered the art of letting her know he was there whenever she needed him without her ever needing to ask.

Once the final clump of sod had been thrown on top of the coffin, Peggy whispered one last tearful goodbye before turning away to follow the rest of the mourners through the cemetery gates. Whispering polite thank yous and making promises to talk properly to people at Judith's wake, Peggy felt herself slip further into a whirl of grief. The time for the second goodbye of the day was getting closer, and once she and Jim were the last ones standing outside of the church, she knew there was no putting off the inevitable any longer.

The rain that had been threatening all morning began to fall, and Peggy threw herself into Jim's outstretched arms. She said nothing as she buried her head into his chest and inhaled his familiar musky scent, committing it to memory, to store up and remember whenever she needed to feel he was close.

'I wish you weren't going,' she said, her voice trembling. 'I hate myself for saying it, even thinking it, Jim, but I wish you were staying here in Swansea with me. It feels like I've only just found you, I can't bear to let you go.'

Jim pulled Peggy even closer and held her so tightly she could hardly breathe. 'I feel the same. You're my world, Peggy Collins, you're the first person I think of when I wake up and my last thought as I go to sleep. I never thought I would be so lucky as to find love with the girl of my dreams, but I found you, Peggy, and I never want to let you go.'

She nodded, her head against his chest, as Jim continued. 'But you know I have to go,' he said with a tremble to his voice. 'You know I have to see Jerry off once and for all so you and I can have a life together without the threat of war hanging over our heads.'

'I know,' she whispered, pulling away and looking into his eyes, the rain hitting the back of her neck, soaking her collar. 'And that's why I love you, Jim Hudson, because you know right from wrong, because you're as loyal as the day is long, and because you aren't afraid to risk your life for your country. I want you to know I have never been prouder of anyone. You're looking danger head-on for the sake of your country, and to me that's incredible. It was me that got lucky the day I met you. Before you, I didn't know what happiness was, you've shown me what's possible. It's as though I've been asleep all my life and you've woken me up.'

'Like *Sleeping Beauty*,' Jim smiled, pushing a lock of stray hair behind Peggy's ear and gazing into her eyes, his own filled with nothing but love. 'Except this isn't a fairy tale. But, Peggy, I can promise you I want nothing more than to treat you like a princess.'

'You're my very own Prince Charming.' Peggy smiled forlornly. 'I never expected to find you, and now I have I can't stand the thought of losing you. Look after yourself, promise me. No heroics!'

Jim lifted her chin with his finger and returned her grin. 'I will, but, Peggy my love, if it's not too much of an imposition, I would rather like to have an incentive to keep my promise to you.'

'How d'you mean?' Peggy asked warily

As Jim swept his gaze over her face, Peggy felt her heart pound as he began to speak.

'So if I said I wanted you to become my wife once this awful war is over, could I reasonably expect you to make me the happiest man on earth and say yes?' he choked.

Shocked, Peggy's hands flew to her mouth. 'Are you asking me to marry you?' she gasped.

Looking at her adoringly, Jim nodded. 'If you'll have me. I know we have only been together a few weeks, Peggy, but, my love, I can't tell you how right this feels. It's as if when I saw you I knew that you were the one for me. Being with you is as easy as slotting the last piece of a jigsaw into place. We're meant to be together.'

'We are,' Peggy cried, the tears she had managed to keep at bay now running down her cheeks like a waterfall. 'It sounds silly, but it's as though you're the padlock and I'm the key; we just fit.'

'So is that a yes?' Jim asked, smiling, his eyes filled with love, as he wiped the tears from Peggy's cheeks with the pad of his thumb.

'It's a yes,' Peggy babbled. 'Jim, I want nothing more than to be your wife and to cherish you with all my heart.'

'And I you, Peggy,' he said gently. 'Nothing would make me

prouder than becoming your husband. I'll give you the world, I promise, if you'll only let me.'

'I'll let you,' she whispered. 'But, Jim, let's not say this is goodbye, let's say this is until next time. I don't reckon I can stand to say another goodbye today.'

Jim seized Peggy's hands and kissed each one of them, before fixing his gaze on her. 'All right,' he said softly. 'In that case, until next time, Peggy Collins.'

The moment for Jim to leave was almost upon them, but before they parted, Peggy gazed up at him, determined to commit every feature to memory. His startlingly blue eyes, the slope of his nose, the floppiness of his fringe and his strong, tapered fingers that she knew as well as she knew her own. This man was her past, her present and her future. As she looked deep into his eyes, she was sure she could see the very essence of his soul. She realised there were so many things she wanted to tell him, before they said their final goodbyes, but there simply wasn't the time. Instead, Peggy tilted her chin upwards and pressed her lips against Jim's and the unexpected jolt of electricity that surged between them both shocked and delighted her. Feelings of love swept through her body as wildly as stormy seas crashing against a rocky shoreline and she revelled in every perfect second of their last kiss. Lost in a world where it was just the two of them, Peggy savoured the feel of Jim's eyelashes fluttering on her cheek, his stubble against her chin and the softness of his lips that told her with certainty, in a way words never could, that he loved her and this would never be, goodbye.

*

As Jim roared off down the lane in his Aston, Peggy walked back across town towards the hotel where Ida and Harry were hosting a wake in honour of Judith. With every step, she felt like she was soaring high above the skies, floating on the clouds. Was it really possible that she, Peggy Collins, was getting married? Yet with a sudden start she realised the feeling was bittersweet. Not only did she have no idea when or even if she would see the love of her life again, it would be impossible to share her good news with anyone for quite some time, out of respect for Judith. Then there was the fact Peggy knew she had to tell Edie, something that would be difficult as her mother had no idea she was courting. With a frown, Peggy wondered what Jim would say if she told him about her mother's views on men. So far she had only mentioned briefly that her mother was protective of her and of course Jim had promised to win Edie around. She could only hope that he would show as much patience as Judith's Al had, as Peggy had a feeling it would be no easy task.

With a heavy heart, she pushed open the hotel door and walked into the dining room. Once inside, Peggy felt a surge of love for her landlady and the trouble she had gone to. All the tables, lined with Ida's best white table linen, had been pushed together to make one long surface, while on the top it looked as though the couple had used their rations for a month to lay on a huge feast. Cucumber, tomato and even an occasional egg sandwich stood on large plates, while sausage rolls, watercress salad, fairy cakes and almond biscuits were spread amongst an urn of tea and bottles of stout, showed no expense had been spared.

Elsewhere, vases of nasturtiums stood in the windows, and the sweet perfume filled the room, offering a sense of hope, Peggy thought as she sniffed the air appreciatively. Watching Ida stride into the room with another tray of sandwiches, Peggy walked towards her.

'How d'you get all this?' she asked in amazement.

'We managed to use quite a bit from our rations and friends and neighbours donated what they could,' Ida explained, as she placed the tray on the already overcrowded table. 'People have all been so kind.'

Peggy nodded. 'Judith was well-loved.'

'She'll be missed.' Ida sniffed, reaching into the sleeve of her tea dress for a hankie. 'She was one of life's good 'uns.'

'If anyone knows that, it's Annie,' Peggy said sombrely, looking across at the younger girl standing in the corner of the room alone. 'I don't know how she's going to get through this, Ida, she's hardly said a word and when she does she just bites your head clean off.'

Ida smiled comfortingly. 'It's early days yet, Peg. She and Judith were closer than most sisters and shared everything, her dad told me. It's going to be very hard for her, Peggy, we've got to be patient.'

'I just wish there was something I could do,' Peggy sighed. 'I can't stand seeing her so unhappy and I feel I owe it to Judith to look out for her.'

'You're one of life's good 'uns as well, precious,' Ida soothed. 'Just keep doing what you're doing, Annie'll talk to you when she's ready, I'm sure.'

As Ida walked back into the kitchen, Peggy turned back to survey the room. It was filled with girls from the ATS who wanted to pay their last respects to one of their own. Turning her gaze back towards Annie, Peggy noticed she was still standing by the window, looking forlornly out into the garden. Somehow she had managed to make her uniform look smarter than usual with her buttons and shoes gleaming and hat perched squarely on her head. But her red eyes and tear-stained cheeks ruined the effect, and it was all Peggy could do not to rush over and comfort her. As it was, she noticed, her mum and dad were doing a good job of that, standing on either side of Annie trying to get her to rally.

Peggy felt for the girl, she looked as though she was barely listening to her parents' well-meaning words, and she crept closer, determined to try to save her if she could. But nearing the family she realised Annie's parents weren't trying to comfort her, instead it sounded very much as though they were encouraging her to leave the Army.

'Yer know yer can't stay here now, Annie, you'll have to accept that,' Annie's dad insisted. 'We'll let the Army know, of course, but yer see it's impossible now, don't yer? I'll let your bosses know, they'll understand.'

'Course they will, Annie love,' her mother, Mavis, coaxed. 'Your place is back home with us now. Yer can join the WRVS if yer like, do your bit for the war effort up home. But after losing George, now Judith, we can't lose another child to this war, duck.'

Annie turned away from the window to face her parents. 'I want to stay here, I belong here, I'm doing a good job, I like the Army.'

Mavis sighed and exchanged frustrated glances with her husband. 'Forgetting how we feel for a moment, duck, that might well be true, but now our Judith's gone, how do yer propose to manage without her?'

Hovering at the edge of the table, not quite close enough to join in the conversation, Peggy heard Annie draw breath. 'I just will. The Army's important to me, I'm not going anywhere.'

'But, Annie, yer must see it's not practical, like,' David insisted. 'Now, enough of this nonsense, you'll come back with us—'

'I won't,' Annie roared, interrupting her father and pushing past him through the throng of mourners and out into the street.

Peggy turned, about to go after her, when she suddenly felt a hand on her shoulder, gently pulling her back.

'Let her go, Collins,' Carmichael said gently. 'She needs time to think.'

'Yes, sir,' she said reluctantly.

'I took the liberty of procuring a port and lemon for you, Collins,' he said, pressing the drink into her hand. 'You rather look as if you need it, and we have yet to toast young Judith.'

'Thank you, sir.' Peggy smiled, clinking her glass against Carmichael's. 'To Judith.'

'Judith,' he echoed, taking a large slug of stout. 'And how

are you faring with all of this, Collins? I know you and Judith were close.'

'We were, sir. If I'm honest it still hasn't really sunk in she's gone. She had her whole life ahead of her. Well, it all just seems so cruel.'

'War is cruel,' Carmichael said quietly, 'which is why you have to make the most of life while you can.'

Peggy grinned to herself, she had been thinking just the same thing herself of late.

'Something amusing you, Collins?' Carmichael asked, noticing the small smile on her lips.

'No, sir,' she replied. 'It's just, well, I've wondered if I've been making the most of my life up until now.'

'I see.' He paused. 'Well, from the gossip I hear amongst the volunteers, you're courting Pilot Officer James Hudson. That rather sounds as though you are making the most of things.'

At the mention of her relationship with Jim, Peggy blushed crimson and took another sip of her drink, fighting the urge to reveal just how serious their relationship had recently become. 'It's early days yet, sir.'

Carmichael let out a loud chuckle. 'I hear the two of you are inseparable, or were before he was posted abroad. That doesn't sound like early days to me.'

'Well, yes, sir,' Peggy replied earnestly. 'But war work's more important than me and Jim courting, we both think so.'

'Glad to hear it, Collins,' Carmichael said. 'We need all hands on deck, and you are a very good set of hands.'

'Thank you, sir.'

'I've come to be very fond of you, Collins, so I do hope you won't mind me saying this.'

Peggy braced herself for whatever her superior officer had to say.

'Collins, are you quite sure this pilot is good enough for you? Have you forgotten how he almost ran us off the road?' Carmichael continued.

'I haven't forgotten,' Peggy replied, somewhat stung by her commanding officer's bluntness. 'I just learned to forgive him, you know, like it says in the Bible.'

'Yes, I forgot you were a Sunday school teacher,' Carmichael remarked. 'So you've turned the other cheek, so to speak.'

'Something like that, sir, yes. Jim's sorry for what happened and he's proved hisself to be a loyal, faithful and respectable young man that loves his country,' Peggy said in a forthright tone.

Lieutenant Colonel Carmichael said nothing. Instead he took another large gulp of stout, before turning to Peggy. 'Are you quite sure?'

'Yes, sir, he's a good man,' Peggy insisted. 'Honestly, he's not a wrong 'un, he's shown me that. I'd trust him with my life.'

Carmichael's expression softened. 'Very well then, Collins, perhaps I've got it wrong, it just strikes me that a decent man would never have behaved as he did on the road that day, regardless of the circumstances, and if I'm honest I think you deserve better. Be careful, that's all I'm suggesting.'

Visibly shocked, Peggy took a deep breath before she spoke. 'I hope you won't think I'm speaking out of turn if I say I think you have got it wrong, sir. Now, if you'll excuse me, I reckon I'd better see how Annie's getting on.'

Not bothering to wait for a reply, Peggy put her drink down on the table beside her and stalked through the crowds and out of the hotel looking for Annie. She knew Carmichael meant well but his words had stung. Jim had made a mistake and he had done all he could to put it right, that ought to be the end of it. If he hadn't, well then, she would never have fallen in love with him and she certainly never would have agreed to his proposal.

It didn't take long to find Annie, sitting at the bottom of the steps, head in her hands and cap to the right of her on the cold concrete. Glancing up at the sky above, Peggy saw the rain had stopped but the large grey clouds loomed large above her. There was every chance a storm could be on its way. Turning up the collar of her khaki jacket to guard against the chill, Peggy sat beside her friend.

'You all right?' she asked gently.

'Why does everyone keep asking me that?' Annie replied wearily, still staring at the floor. 'I'm fine, or as fine as anyone would be who's lost their sister, like.'

'I'm sorry, Annie, I feel like I keep putting my foot in it with you, I'm only trying to help.'

Annie sighed. 'I know yer are, Peg, and it's me that should be sorry for snapping at yer.'

'I reckon I'd probably snap at everyone as well if it was me what had lost my sister,' Peggy replied, her hand never leaving Annie's.

'I just miss her so much, Peggy.' Annie's body convulsed with sobs. 'I don't know how I'll carry on here without her.'

'But you want to though, don't you?' Peggy asked anxiously. 'It's just I overheard your parents trying to get you to go home. You're not going, are you?'

Annie shook her head, her body still shaking with grief. 'They mean well. I don't think they realise that once you've signed up you can't get out. I'm not sure Judith would have mentioned that bit when she told them we'd joined-up, like.'

'Well, that's good.' Peggy smiled. 'I'd really miss you if you left.'

Annie gave Peggy a watery smile. 'You're a good friend, Peggy. Our Judith was ever so fond of yer.'

'I'm fond of both of you,' Peggy said, clasping Annie's had firmly. 'If you need anything at all you've only gotta ask, I'll help any way I can.'

'I know you will, but it was Judith that always helped me, and without her, I'm not sure I know what to do, I don't think I can cope . . .' Annie's face crumpled.

Peggy let go of her hand and instead wrapped her arms tightly around the girl, holding her as if she were as fragile as a newborn baby. Finally, when Annie had managed to get her tears under control, she looked Peggy in the eye.

'There's a reason why my parents want me back home, Peg.'

'Well, I s'pect it's 'cos they miss you, and probably after everything what's happened with Judith, they're worried about losing you too,' Peggy pointed out, not unreasonably.

Annie shook her head. 'That's not it. The thing is, Peg, I've never been able to get through life without Judith, I've never had to. She's always done everything for me, my big sister.'

'I s'pect that was nice.' Peggy smiled sympathetically, as she let go of Annie. 'I always wanted a big sister, and if I could have had one I'd have loved her to have been like Jude.'

'She was the best sister anyone could hope for.' Annie's eyes lit up at the thought of happier times. 'She stuck up for me at school when I got bullied, taught me how to plait my hair and when I was old enough, apply make-up to my face.'

'You were lucky to have had her, I was always in awe of how close the two of you were.'

'We were.' Annie sniffed, her gaze fixed firmly on the floor. 'But now she's gone.'

Peggy could only imagine how bereft Annie must be feeling, and knew no words could bring her the comfort she craved. Now Judith's life had been celebrated amongst family and friends, it was time for them all to face the bitter truth, accept Judith had gone and move forward with their lives. It would be hard for all of them, but for Annie who, despite her gruff exterior, had a soft centre, it would be an almost impossible task.

Although Annie was famous for her bluster, Peggy had seen how the younger girl had routinely called upon her sister to help her out of any kind of trouble. Without Judith, Annie was going to have her work cut out standing on her own two feet and Peggy's heart went out to her. She too had been in Annie's shoes not so long ago when she joined-up, but had been fortunate enough to have the support of some wonderful friends who had encouraged her to grab life with both hands and make her own decisions. Thanks to them, Peggy had done an awful lot of growing up, and if she could help Annie do the same, then she would gladly step into the hole Judith's sudden death had left.

'Look, babber,' Peggy said gently in her West Country burr, 'I know how tough things are for you, but it seems to me that the best way you can honour Judith's memory now is to rise up and be strong for her sake.'

Annie said nothing, and continued to stare at the ground, tears dripping down her nose. Peggy continued. 'Look at all she did for the church, for the community and for the Army. Hard work is what'll get you through this, I knows it's the last thing you feel like, but it's the best medicine, and I promise I'll be there for you every step of the way.'

Wondering if she had gone too far with her advice, Peggy gazed anxiously at her friend, wishing, not for the first time, that she had something better to offer in her hour of need than words.

Slowly Annie lifted her head and turned to face Peggy, the cool breeze gathering pace and blowing her hair away from her face.

'Thing is, Peg, I know you mean every word, like, you're a nice person, but being there for me is a bit harder than you might think.'

'What d'you mean?' Peggy frowned in confusion.

Annie laughed mawkishly. 'I mean that there was a reason me and Jude were so close and it wasn't just because she was my sister. She helped me out more than yer know, Peggy. She was there for me all the time.'

'I know.' Peggy tried again. 'I saw. I can do that for you, Ann. Just let me help.'

'Yer still don't get it, do yer?' Annie said bitterly. 'Judith was there for me because she had to be.'

Peggy shook her head. 'No, Ann, she was there cos she loved you, not 'cos she had to be.'

'Listen to me, Peggy, I'm not sure I'll have the courage to say this again,' Annie said firmly. 'Jude was definitely there for me because I needed her. I can't read, Peggy.'

# Chapter Ten

Ever since Judith's funeral, Peggy had been unable to stop thinking about her friend's revelation. She kept going over the fact Annie couldn't read, and began to see recent events in a new light. Missing paperwork, the row with the stallholder in the market, the unread bills in teahouses, even the way Annie had barely glanced at the hymn book during Judith's funeral. These things were all because Annie couldn't read, not because she was slapdash or simply uncaring. With a jolt, Peggy realised that not only was Annie bereft at losing her sister, but that she had a very real fear that she wouldn't cope without the woman that had helped her live her life.

All Peggy wanted to do was be the shoulder to cry on she knew Judith would want her sister to have, but since the funeral Peggy had barely seen Annie. As February turned into March and winter slowly turned into spring, bringing with it the warmth of some early sunshine, Peggy found she was busier than ever.

Following the three-night raid, Carmichael had been tasked with meetings in London. Consequently, Peggy was regularly driving for hours at a time and frequently billeted in lodgings as the distances were so great. She had never seen so much of the country and had never been to the capital before her commanding officer ordered her to drive him there. She had, of course, heard on the wireless how bad the bombings had been in London, but even so, when she got there, she was astounded at just how much the city had suffered.

One Thursday morning, she found herself in the heart of the West End after delivering Carmichael to a meeting near Whitehall. The unexpected warmth of the early spring sunshine had encouraged Peggy to leave the car and walk through the city.

Wandering through St James's Park, enjoying the sight of the greenery and the lake, it was almost possible to believe that there was no war and she was just enjoying a day trip in London.

Thrusting her hands in her pockets, she turned her face towards the sun that was peeping through the clouds and exited on to Piccadilly, excited to see the famous London architecture she had heard so much about. Yet the sight before her left her stricken and she shivered at the sudden change. She thought she had grown accustomed to chaos after being caught up in the raids of Swansea and Bristol, but London was on a different scale. The streets appeared grey, soot-ridden and broken. There were no green fields to gaze at to break up the horror, or shimmering blue sea to prove there was life before and after war. In fact, the famous architecture was hidden under shells of buildings, mounds of rubble and the near constant smell of burning. Walking past the infamous Café de Paris, Peggy thought her heart would break at the sight. The nightspot had supposedly been one of the safest places in London because it was deep underground. Yet the bombs that had fallen a week earlier on Coventry Street and beyond proved nowhere was safe from the Luftwaffe, with incendiaries killing thirty-four and injuring around a hundred.

Looking up at the brilliant blue sky above her, Peggy tried not to think about the poor souls that had lost their lives, and instead turned her thoughts to Jim. She had received a letter from him yesterday and although she had read it over and over, she couldn't resist bringing it with her to savour during a quiet moment. Sitting on a nearby bench, Peggy reached for the envelope and began to read.

3 March 1941

*My darling Peggy,*

*Well, here I am, and so far things aren't half bad. I awoke at four this morning for an exercise on a De Haviland with my navigator, Wilf, and what a glorious sight we had. Flying high in the sky just as dawn broke was a truly wonderful experience. I don't think you can say you have lived until you have seen that first mist soar above the clouds, before it's broken by the hot and fiery sunshine signalling the start of a new day. It really was quite beautiful, and to be perfectly honest, Peggy, it was you I ached to share it rather than Wilf.*

*I have been thinking of you an awful lot, my darling, and long to see you. It's picturing your face just before I go to sleep that has become the favourite part of my day, when I know my thoughts of you will remain uninterrupted and we can be together.*

*Wilf is married with four children at home in Bermondsey, and misses them all dreadfully. He says the children were supposed to have been evacuated to the country but that his wife, Mary, couldn't bear to part with them and refused to send them, saying one absent from her table was enough. I'm not sure whether Mary's actions are courageous or downright foolish but I do know she must feel consumed with love to have done such a thing, and that's how I feel about you, Peggy. I feel dreadful I left you so soon after Judith was killed. I wanted to be with you and comfort you during such a horrendous time but I know, Peggy, just how strong you are. You are one of the most courageous women I know, and I rather think that sometimes it's me that relies on your hand to hold rather than the other way around. I can't wait for us to be married, my love, for us to spend the rest of our lives together as husband and wife. Since you did me the very great honour of agreeing to become my wife I have thought of nothing but our future. Everything suddenly feels ever so much brighter and being apart is easier to cope with knowing that you are mine.*

*Well, I fear that it is time for me to sign off, more circuits and bumps practice to attend to. Write to me soon, Peggy, I cannot wait to hear all your news.*

*Your own devoted fiancé,*

*Jim*

Peggy clutched the paper to her chest, the very act of doing so bringing her sweetheart closer to her. Holding the letter to her nose, she hoped to find a trace of Jim's familiar clean and musky scent, but any trace of him had been washed away as the note was carried however many miles overseas towards her.

Yet in a way it didn't matter. Jim and all her memories of their time together were safely stored in her heart, along with the fierce and intense love she felt for him. It seemed funny to her now, looking back on their first outing to the cinema together, how nervous she had been. Very quickly, Peggy had found loving Jim felt as natural and beautiful as a caterpillar turning into a butterfly. Although they had only been together for two months, it seemed impossible to remember a time when Jim wasn't in her life.

She stuffed the envelope back in her pocket. It was almost lunchtime and she had a feeling the lieutenant colonel would be more than ready to leave his meeting. Walking back towards the car through St James's Park, her thoughts turned to Annie. With a jolt of surprise, she realised her friend wouldn't be able to enjoy the simple act of reading a letter from a loved one. The thought of her friend missing out on such a basic, yet vital pleasure tugged at her heart, and she vowed to help Annie the first chance she could.

Since Annie had told her that she couldn't read or write, Peggy had tried to find a moment to get the girl to open up and tell her more, yet the chance constantly evaded her. Annie had been given a thirty-six-hour pass following Judith's funeral, and when she returned, had been made a staff driver like Peggy, responsible for driving Captain Davis. Carmichael had confided in Peggy that he felt Annie needed a challenge to throw herself into and being a personal driver to a senior officer would do her the world of good.

Privately, Peggy thought it was a terrible idea. She worried that the added pressure of such a serious job when she was already carrying such a huge burden could have devastating consequences for her friend. However, she had kept her thoughts to herself. Annie had managed to keep her illiteracy a secret this long, it wasn't down to Peggy to tell all and sundry. But she'd made a promise to herself to help Judith's little sister and she sincerely believed she could. As a Sunday school teacher, Peggy had occasionally come across children and teenagers who couldn't read or write and she had been proud to help get them started on their reading journey.

For the life of her Peggy couldn't understand how Annie, a girl of almost twenty, had managed to get away without reading or writing for so long, let alone how she had joined-up and learned to be a spark girl. Then there was the fact that Annie seemed to come from a loving, supportive home. How had her parents allowed their daughter not to read or write all this time?

It beggared belief, Peggy thought as she neared the car, and saw Lieutenant Colonel Carmichael walking down the steps of the government building. Hurrying to the Humber, Peggy opened the back door and saluted him as he approached.

'Collins! You're a sight for sore eyes, I can tell you.' Carmichael sighed as he got into the back of the car. 'Take me to my club for lunch, would you? After such a dull meeting with an incredible bunch of half-wits I could do with a Scotch.'

Catching sight of Carmichael's furrowed brow, Peggy smiled. She had never met an officer so forthright before and had to admit it was a refreshing change. Naturally she was more than aware of the importance of discretion during wartime, and always ensured nothing she heard Carmichael say ever left the car.

'We'll be there in no time,' she promised, firing the starter engine.

'Good,' he replied, brightening considerably. 'What did you do while I was stuck inside? Take in the capital as I suggested?'

Peggy nodded as she explained where she had been, and the devastation she'd witnessed.

'Terrible shame about the Café de Paris. In my younger days, I used to spend many a Saturday night there. In fact, it's where I met my wife.'

'Really, sir?' Peggy quizzed, unused to hearing Carmichael talk about his personal life.

'Yes, love at first sight.' He smiled. 'Best day of my life meeting Belinda.'

Looking at her boss in the rear-view mirror she caught a flicker of wistfulness pass across his features. 'Of course, it was all such a long time ago now, and the world has changed so much.'

Peggy said nothing, and left him to his trip down Memory Lane. If she was honest she was enjoying the few moments of silence to get her bearings around the large city. Although she had taken care to check the map thoroughly before she left Swansea that morning, there was still so much to remember and think about in London.

The rain had begun to fall softly on to the windscreen. Turning on her wipers so she could see better, Carmichael's voice suddenly boomed from the back seat, wrenching Peggy from her train of thought.

'I've had an idea, Collins.'

'Sir?' Peggy said, her voice containing a note of worry.

'I think we should put on a company variety show at the barracks. Boost morale. It's been such a dreadful time for everyone following the raid on the town and of course Judith's death. It's hit the troops hard, what do you think, Collins?'

'A variety show?' Peggy murmured.

'Yes, you know the sort of thing: songs, dances, sketches, jokes,' Carmichael went on, warming to his theme. 'We haven't had anything at the squadron like that in months, we didn't even have a pantomime at Christmas as we were all so busy. A terrific shame.'

'Yes, sir,' Peggy agreed, although secretly she had been glad the squadron's infamous panto had been cancelled as she had been dreading the prospect of being forced on stage.

'Excellent, Collins,' Carmichael replied, brightening immediately. 'So you'll be able to get it organised, say in three weeks?'

Peggy's eyes shot up in alarm. 'Three weeks? You want me to organise a show in three weeks?'

'I have every confidence in you.' Carmichael grinned, as Peggy pulled up outside a grey, unassuming building in the heart of London, which she knew to be his club. 'It doesn't have to be a huge great thing, just a few songs and jokes, you know. You can put it on in the mess. I've cleared it with the powers that be.'

'Right, sir,' Peggy said, paling at the thought of so much work.

Stepping out of the car to open the door for Carmichael, he caught the look of despair on Peggy's face.

'No need to look so worried,' he told her with a low chuckle. 'I've asked Davis to get Annie to assist you. Like you, she could do with the extra work to throw herself into and I'm sure between the two of you, it will be marvellous. Oh, speak of the devil, here she is now.'

Mind reeling, Peggy followed Carmichael's gaze and saw

Annie's Humber had turned into the road with Captain Davis in the back.

'There's a Lyons Corner House up ahead,' Carmichael suggested to Peggy after greeting Captain Davis. 'Why don't the two of you get started on some variety plans now, and we'll see you back here at two p.m. sharp.'

'Yes, sir.' Peggy nodded miserably.

The two men walked up the stairs and into the stone building, and Peggy turned to Annie and flashed her a bright smile. 'I take it you heard the good news then?'

'The show, yer mean?' Annie said morosely. 'Captain Davis just told me. I tried to get out of it, but the more I insisted, the more he said it would do me good. Said Lieutenant Colonel Carmichael had asked for me especially like.'

Peggy nodded. 'Yes, he did. Thinks it'll help you get over Judith.'

'This is why I can't stay in the Army, Peg. My parents were right; I'm no good here without Judith. I'm going to be found out, and the Army'll have me thrown out on me ear for lying,' Annie said sadly.

'Don't say that, Annie,' Peg soothed. 'I know I don't know an awful lot about what you've gone through, but I do know that to have got away with keeping it a secret for this long, you've gotta have something about you, bab, it can't all have been down to Judith.'

'D'you think so?'

'I'm sure of it, lover.' Peggy took a step towards Annie. 'And you know I'll help you, any way I can.'

Annie suddenly reached out and clasped Peggy's hands firmly. There was no mistaking the gratitude in her eyes.

'I didn't know if yer were serious,' Annie said quietly. 'I thought yer were making it up.'

'Why would I do that?' Peggy asked bemused. 'I meant it. I often helped the children at Sunday school with their reading, I can teach you too.'

Annie gave her a flinty stare. 'I thought you said yer were going to help me like Judith did.'

'I will help, I'll teach you to read,' Peggy replied earnestly.

Annie snatched her hands away so quickly she nearly fell straight into a passer-by. Peggy couldn't miss the look of fear in her friend's eyes.

'It's no good, Peg,' Annie blurted, 'I've tried in the past and couldn't do it. Please, I just need yer to cover for me like Judith used to.'

Glancing up at the sky, Peggy saw the clouds had knitted together to form a thick dark blanket. Realising her collar was now soaking wet with rain, she slipped her arm through Annie's and whisked her in the direction of the Corner House just as a clap of thunder echoed above them.

Ten minutes later both girls were safely settled in a cafe, a pot of tea and plate of almond biscuits between them. Grateful for the warmth, Peggy dabbed at the sodden collar of her khaki uniform with a napkin and turned her attention to her friend.

'So, just what was it Jude did for you?' Peggy asked quietly.

Annie said nothing as she poured them each a cup of tea but then began, 'She filled out forms for me, read signs, posters and notes, wrote letters and even took any tests I had to sit for me.'

Peggy's eyes widened in astonishment. 'But, how? What . . .?'

Her voice trailed off, and Peggy realised there were so many questions, she didn't even know where to start.

'At school, the teachers said I was stupid,' Annie began. 'Said I was too thick to learn, like, so they never bothered with me. Course Mam and Dad tried to teach me letters and the alphabet, but it wouldn't stick and I used to get ever so angry with 'em for trying that they ended up agreeing with the teachers. Everyone told me that some people weren't meant to be clever with books and that, I just went along with it.'

'And Judith?' Peggy prompted gently.

At the mention of her sister's name, Annie's eyes brimmed with tears. 'Judith was a godsend. I used to get bullied at school because I couldn't read or write and Judith would take them all on, until I learned to stand up for meself, of course.'

Peggy nodded, suddenly aware just where Annie's bravado stemmed from. She had a feeling that Annie was about as tough as a Walnut Whip, hard on the outside, but soft as snow in the middle.

'I left school as soon as I could,' Annie continued. 'Got a job as a seamstress in one of the factories in town, but when war broke out, me and Jude both wanted to join-up, it was all we talked about.'

'So how did you and Jude get round it?' Peggy asked, already guessing the answer.

'We knew the Army had a rule that sisters were kept together, like,' Annie explained. 'When we went to our local recruitment office, Judith filled out all the paperwork for me, and when we were sent to our postings for training, she did the same. We always found reasons to drive together so she could help me, and when it came to tests, she wrote the answers on her piece of paper and mine.'

'What about map-reading or if you had to sign something in front of someone?' Peggy asked.

'I've got a good memory. I learned the shapes of place names, and if I had to sign summat, I usually did a squiggle, but only if I had to,' Annie admitted. 'I always worried that if someone pressed a pen in my hands they'd want me to write proper, like.'

'You've not half been lucky to have got away with all that.' Peggy whistled as she helped herself to a biscuit. 'What would you have done if you were caught?'

Annie shrugged. 'I dunno, we'd have come up with summat, Judith was always very good at thinking on her feet.'

Peggy shook her head, lost for words. The whole tale was such a sad one, she didn't know what to say. Turning her head she scanned the room. Despite the fact the Corner House oc-cupied a very glamorous building in the West End spanning five floors, once you were inside, it felt very much like any other. Misted windows and the scent of freshly baked cakes filled the air, while nippies of all shapes and sizes weaved their way across the crowded floor, deftly writing orders in their little notebooks. There were old friends gossiping, servicemen and women taking a well-earned rest, and even a couple of sweethearts, Peggy noticed, feeling a tugging at her heart at the sight of them. No matter what problems you were facing or even war you were fighting, life carried on.

'Is that why you thought Carmichael was horrible?' Peggy asked suddenly. 'Does he know you can't read?'

Annie shook her head. 'No, it's like I said, you're the only one that knows, like. Carmichael gave me a roasting one day 'cos I never filled a form in proper. Tore strips off me he did for laziness.'

Peggy looked at the younger girl quizzically. 'Doesn't sound like him?'

'No, I suppose it wasn't his fault. Sal'd told me off three times in a row for the same thing. I expect she got that fed up she told him about it. I shouldn't have said that to yer when yer were just starting with him, like, it wasn't fair.'

Pursing her lips, Peggy said nothing. What a dreadful mess it all was.

'I'm sorry, Annie, but I can't lie for you like what Judith did,' she said eventually, her tone sombre. 'When I said I'll help you, I meant I'd teach you to read, not cover up your lies.'

'It won't work, Peg,' Annie replied, a note of bitterness creeping into her voice. 'Mam and Dad tried and Judith, they all tried to get me to read and they couldn't. Sometimes people can't do things, and for me, reading's one of 'em.'

Peggy looked at her pleadingly. 'Annie, from what I can tell, love, you haven't got a lot of choice. I'm offering to give you a chance but if you won't take it then it strikes me your parents might be right and you might have to go home. What have you got to lose?'

Peggy leaned back in her seat and watched Annie's face

flicker first with anger and then acceptance. As a nippy slid the bill down on the table, Annie's eyes met Peggy's.

'All right, I'll make a deal with yer,' she said confidently. 'We'll try it your way, but if it doesn't work, then yer have to help me out like Judith did.'

Peggy couldn't help herself and smiled at Annie. How anyone could ever accuse her of being thick when she could haggle like that was beyond her.

She chuckled, holding out her hand for Annie to shake. 'Deal. But I want you to do your best. No messing me about so you win, otherwise I won't help you at all.'

'All right,' Annie agreed, shaking Peggy's hand. 'But one more thing, promise me yer won't breathe a word.'

'What d'you take me for, Annie?' Peggy rolled her eyes. 'Nobody but me will know, but we start lessons straight away.'

Annie nodded once more and Peggy twisted in her seat to reach for the little canvas bag she always carried with her. Pulling out a notepad and pen, Peggy turned to a fresh page, licked the nib of her fountain pen and started to write.

'Surely you didn't mean we were going to start right now?' Annie gasped in horror.

Roaring with laughter, Peggy put down her pen. 'No, bab, not right this second. But we have got to think about this show. I thought we could make a few notes and we'll start your lessons back in Swansea.'

Relief flooded Annie's face. 'Thank heavens for that. I know I said we'd do it your way, but there are limits.'

'You're not kidding.' Peggy laughed. 'Now to business, how on earth are we going to put on a show in three weeks?'

Annie shook her head. 'Three weeks brings us to the weekend just before Easter. Should we make it a festive show, do you think?'

Peggy raised an eyebrow. 'I reckon that's making it even more complicated. Come on let's have a proper think.'

As the rain continued to pour down outside, the girls

remained holed up in the Corner House, ordering more drinks and planning the show. They decided that Peggy would make a poster and put it up in the mess later that night, inviting people to audition in a week's time. That way, they reasoned, they would have almost a fortnight to rehearse.

Annie said that one of the kitchen girls had a beautiful singing voice, while another of the spark girls she had trained with was an excellent mimic and could even take off Lord Haw-Haw. With the ATS choir to give the show a lift, Peggy was sure that between them they could put on something halfway decent. There was just the question of what they could do for a finale.

'What about something in honour of Jude?' Annie blurted. 'Or do you think that's not right?'

'I reckon that's a brilliant ideal,' Peggy gasped. 'What about a song? Your Jude adored a good old sing-song during our Tuesday night stitch-in.'

Annie nodded, smiling wistfully at the memory. 'She'd love that we could get everyone up on their feet.'

'Perfect.' Peggy grinned, catching sight of the clock on the wall. 'Annie, love, it's ten past, we've got five minutes to get back.'

Hurrying to their feet, the girls paid, then rushed out of the teahouse and down the street towards their cars. Thankfully the rain had given way to sunshine, and as the beams of light peeped through the clouds, Peggy felt as if the world was spurring her on. Yes, it was horrific that Judith had died, and she knew it would take a long time for them all, Annie especially, to come to terms with it. But crossing the road, Annie's arm linked through hers, Peggy felt pleased with the progress they had made that afternoon. Not only had they sorted out a show, but they had also come up with a plan to sort out Annie's reading. Looking up, she smiled in delight at the clear blue sky, wondering if the sunshine was Judith peering down, cheering Peggy and her sister on to victory.

*

When Peggy returned from London, she was full of enthusiasm, vowing to do all she could to help her friend. Fresh pens, pencils, exercise books and notepaper were organised into a neat pile for Annie to get started. Now, as they sat in their billet the following morning, after a breakfast of porridge and several cups of tea, Peggy was keen to make a start.

'Are you ready?' Peggy asked, shoving a clean exercise book Annie's way.

Annie eyed the plain white notepaper with mistrust. 'I'm still not sure about this, Peg. I know what I'm like, and I really don't think I can do this.'

Peggy shook her head. 'Yes, you can, Annie. We talked about this last night, and over breakfast. You're more than capable and you know it. Why don't you use some of that energy you're using to get out of learning to read and spend it on doing what you're told?'

'Yes, boss,' Annie said mutinously.

Peggy ignored the barb, and instead carried on writing the letters of the alphabet out in long hand. 'Right then, I'm sorry in advance if this seems a bit basic, but I reckon we should start at the very beginning and then we'll both have a better idea about what you know and what you don't.'

'I've told yer, I know nought!' Annie said, rolling her eyes.

'Then there's no harm starting at the beginning,' Peggy said firmly. 'Now d'you know what these are?'

'I'm not thick, Peg,' Annie sighed. 'I know that's the alphabet.'

'Good, but how many of these letters can you read?' she asked gesturing at the page.

Turning her gaze from Peggy, Annie looked pointedly at the floor.

'None,' she admitted in a small voice.

'Then let's change that right now,' Peggy coaxed.

Together, the girls went through the sound and shape of each letter. Peggy could see instantly why nobody had enjoyed much success getting Annie to read or write before, as the girl became frustrated and difficult when she struggled to get something right first time. But life as a Sunday school teacher had given Peggy the gift of patience, as well as a thick skin, and she refused to give up.

'Come on, bab, you nearly had that one then,' Peggy encouraged, pointing at the large letter e she had drawn in her pad. 'Have another go.'

'I don't want another go,' Annie spat, snatching the pad from Peggy's hands and throwing it to the floor. 'I told yer I couldn't do it, this is useless.'

Wordlessly, Peggy picked it up. Glancing at Annie she saw her face was red with rage and frustration. Not for the first time, Peggy wondered what she could say to the girl when she so obviously didn't want her assistance.

'I don't even know why you're helping me like this,' Annie snarled.

Peggy shrugged. 'I'm not sure I know myself at this particular moment. But what I do know is I'm not giving up on you, Ann, and you shouldn't be giving up on yourself neither. So things have got a bit difficult? So what? That's life, get used to it.'

As Peggy finished her speech, Annie stared at her in shock. 'You've never spoken to me like that before.'

'No,' Peggy replied, her voice shaking. 'I don't think I've ever spoken to anyone like that before in my life. I'm sorry.'

Annie shook her head firmly. 'No, you were right. You've nought to apologise for, Peg, you've done nothing but try to help me and I'm sat here throwing it in your face. It's me that should be sorry.'

'Then let's both forget it and move on,' Peggy said gently.

Opening the book and turning to the last page, Peggy tried again. 'So, where were we?'

By mid-morning, Peggy was delighted with the progress they had made. Annie had mastered much of the alphabet and could easily identify a lot of the sounds of each letter without any prompting. Peggy knew they had a lot of work to do, but seeing just how far Annie had come in one morning, she felt proud of all they had achieved.

Reaching the barracks for their afternoon shift, it was clear to Peggy that Annie was pleased with her progress too. Her mood was lighter, and she seemed almost excited to be going to work.

'Fancy a cuppa?' she asked as they neared the NAAFI van. 'I'll even throw in a bar of chocolate as a thank you.'

Peggy smiled at the unexpected gesture. 'You feeling all right?'

'I'm feeling fine,' Annie grumbled. 'I just want to say ta for all your help this morning, that's all. But if yer don't want a bit of chocolate when I'm buying then I won't force yer.'

'Now, now, don't be hasty,' Peggy chuckled. 'I never said that. It's just not like you to put your hand in your pocket, that's all.'

'Any more of that sort of talk and I'll throw the chocolate bar at yer!' Annie teased.

As the girls doubled over with laughter, Peggy suddenly heard the sound of footsteps behind her.

'Collins,' a voice roared.

Spinning on her heel, Peggy came face to face with Volunteer Pat Grimes. She sighed. Pat was a stocky, thick-set girl and fellow Bristolian who had never forgiven her for beating her to the job of Lieutenant Colonel Carmichael's driver. What could she want with her now?

'Lieutenant Colonel Carmichael wants to see you in his office immediately.'

'Now?' Peggy whined.

'No, next week!' Pat jeered. 'What part of immediately didn't you understand?'

Annie burst out laughing. 'No, next week,' she mimicked in a thick Bristol accent.

Peggy sighed as she saw Pat's eyes narrow with rage. There had never been any love lost between the two girls, and it looked like trouble was brewing.

'And who the hell d'you think you're talking to, Annie Shawcross?' Pat growled. 'You wanna watch your manners.'

'Or what?' Annie jeered.

Pat looked menacing as she took a step towards her. 'Or I'll knock your block off. You and your sister always thought you was better than the rest of us. Well now your big sister's not here to step in for you every time you get in a bit of trouble, I'll be waiting.'

Peggy glanced nervously at Annie and saw a flash of anger in her eyes. Inwardly she groaned, Pat was a known troublemaker and no doubt knew just which of Annie's buttons to press for a reaction. As if on cue, Annie flew at Pat and grabbed a handful of her long brown hair.

'Don't you ever talk about my sister like that, you hear. You've no business even mentioning her name,' Annie screamed as she pulled Pat to the ground.

In a flash, the two volunteers were rolling around in the mud, a tangle of arms and legs as they tugged, slapped and pulled at each other's clothes. Soon a small crowd had gathered but rather than do anything to break up the fight, they watched agog, keen to make the most of this unexpected burst of entertainment.

Peggy shook her head in fury. If any of their superiors caught the girls fighting they would be put on a CB notice if not more.

'That's enough,' she shouted, getting between the warring women and pulling them apart. 'You'll both be for the high jump if there's any more of this carry-on.'

Breathless and red in the face, Pat and Annie stood on either side of Peggy, looking for all the world like a pair of boxers in the ring fighting out a grudge match.

'Look at the state of the pair of you,' Peggy hissed, turning to each of them. 'Pat, you said Carmichael wanted me, well I suggest we get going. And Annie, go and clean yourself up.'

Reluctantly, the girls got to their feet and Peggy let go of each of them, but Pat couldn't resist one last jibe. 'Like I said, Shawcross, your sister's not here now, I'll be waiting.'

Turning to Annie, Peggy watched aghast as the younger girl went to fly at Pat once more. Just in time, she managed to grab hold of Annie and restrain her.

'That's enough, Ann. Don't let Pat get to you, can't you see that's what she wants?'

The girls turned to look at the volunteer and the smug expression on Pat's face was unmistakable.

'All right, Peg, you win,' Annie hissed. 'But if she ever says anything about our Judith again . . .'

Peggy nodded soothingly. 'I know, lover. Now go, don't give her the satisfaction.'

Wordlessly, Annie turned away and walked back down the hill. Once Peggy was sure her friend wasn't coming back to give Pat another slap, she turned to the volunteer.

'Ready?'

Pat nodded and she brushed mud from her jacket. 'I would just like to say though, Peggy, it was good of you to stop Annie going for me like that. I thought she was going to kill me. Thank you.'

Peggy levelled her gaze. 'Don't be under any illusion, Pat. I didn't stop Annie having another go at you for your benefit, I did it for Annie's. If it was down to me I'd have let Ann rip your hair out – it's what you deserve for that remark about Judith.'

Angrily, Peggy turned on her heel and stalked past Pat up the hill towards headquarters, muttering under her breath. By the time Peggy reached Carmichael's office she had calmed down. Straightening her tie, she tapped lightly on the door.

'Come in,' his voice boomed.

Pushing open the door, Peggy walked towards his desk and saluted.

'You wanted to see me, sir.'

'Indeed, Collins.' Carmichael sighed. 'Take a seat, would you?'

Obediently, Peggy sat down opposite him, noting his weary features. He looked as if he had aged overnight and Peggy felt a flash of sympathy for the man and all he had to endure.

'Now, Collins,' Carmichael began, his face grave. 'I've asked you here because I have some rather difficult information to impart.'

Peggy furrowed her brow. 'Is this about the show, sir, because I can assure you Annie and I have some very good ideas.

Carmichael raised his hands to silence her. 'No, Collins, it's not about the show. There's something else.'

Looking at her commanding officer, his face grey and rich with concern, Peggy felt chilled to the bone. Whatever was the matter? Was something wrong with her mother? She steeled herself for the worst. As he opened his mouth to speak, the door opened and his assistant Jenkins appeared with two large brandies.

'Just set them down on the side, there's a good chap,' Carmichael instructed, gesturing towards the small table that rested beside him and Peggy.

'Now, Collins,' Carmichael began as Jenkins silently retreated and shut the door. 'There is no easy way for me to say this, and by rights, there is no reason you ought to know this as you and Pilot Officer Hudson are not related, but I have some news I feel you ought to hear.'

Leaning forwards on her chair, Peggy felt almost sick with the dread that unfurled in her heart. 'What is it?'

Carmichael cleared his throat. 'As you know, Collins, Hudson was posted elsewhere, the details of which I cannot go into.'

Peggy nodded, doing her best not to scream at her boss to get to the point. 'Yes, of course, sir.'

'As part of his work at his new posting, he was required to take part in what's known as a sweep and escort exercise.'

Trembling with fear, she scanned Carmichael's face for clues as to what he was about to say. Whatever he had to tell her about Jim wasn't going to be good news and she needed to feel in control.

'Go on,' she begged.

'There is no easy way to say this, Collins, but it's believed that two days ago, whilst carrying out this exercise, his plane was shot down by the Hun over the Channel,' Carmichael continued. 'I'm very sorry, but Pilot Officer Hudson is missing, presumed dead.'

Peggy felt her world shift on its axis. The loving, happy future she thought she had found, snuffed out as quickly as she had discovered it.

# Chapter Eleven

Peggy had no memory of what happened after Carmichael broke the news. She vaguely recalled him taking her elbow and steering her outside, but she had been completely unaware of anything going on around her.

Now she saw she was in her bedroom, the sunshine streaming through the windows. With a start, she checked her watch and saw it was just after eight in the morning. The events of yesterday flooded through her and Peggy felt a sharp pain tear through her insides, as surely as if a surgeon was slicing her in two with his scalpel. Jim was missing. Jim was thought to be dead. She would never see him again. She wanted to howl with the agony of it all. And yet a part of her didn't believe it could be true. After all, she had only just received a letter from him, how could he suddenly have gone like that? At the thought of something terrible happening to the love of her life, panic enveloped her and she gripped the bed frame for support. Was he hurt? Was he in pain? Had he been captured by the Germans and interred in some dreadful prisoner-of-war camp? Or was he just as Carmichael said, dead, never to be seen or heard from again.

An image of Jim lying bloody and hurt amongst the wreckage of his plane came unbidden into her mind, and Peggy stifled a scream. Her poor, precious love: hurt and suffering and all alone. The thought of it sent a fresh pain soaring through her body, as real as if she had been injured herself. She couldn't stand the thought of him dying out there not knowing how much he was cherished. Although Peggy knew it would have half killed her to see Jim take his last breath, she wished she could have been there for him, to have held his hand, kissed his beautiful face one last time, tell him that he was loved and always would be.

Despite the tears, Peggy knew there was no time for idling in bed. Reluctantly she roused herself from her blankets but felt overcome with tiredness, her legs as wobbly as a newborn lamb's as she tried to stand. Steadying herself, she saw the door suddenly swing open, with Ida bearing a cup of tea.

'Come on now, precious, sit down, I've brought you something wet and warm, is it.' Ida smiled, bustling her way towards Peggy and helping her to sit back on the bed.

'But I've got to get up for work, I'm late as it is,' Peggy protested weakly.

'Don't be silly,' Ida said gently. 'Your boss, Lieutenant Colonel Carmichael is it, had a word with me yesterday after he drove you back here.'

'Carmichael drove me here?' Peggy gasped.

'Yes, but he told me to tell you not to worry, and to take the day off today if you felt like it. He's no need to be driven anywhere at all,' Ida assured her.

As the landlady perched beside her on the bed, Peggy felt her resolve leave and she gave in to wracking great sobs. Ida wrapped an arm around her, and pulled her close.

'I'm so sorry, love, your Lieutenant Carmichael told me what had happened after I helped you up the stairs to bed. I can't believe it; Jim was such a lovely fella.'

'He was, he is, I don't know what to think. Missing presumed dead. Though I don't reckon there's any surviving that,' Peggy said, her voice wild with grief.

'There's terrible,' Ida agreed. 'But that's why we have to keep fighting, Peggy love, for the likes of Jim and Judith, all taken from us far too soon.'

'It's not fair, Ida.' Peggy sniffed. 'We just found each other, we were going to have a life together, it's not fair. Those bleedin' Jerries – how much more destruction have they got in 'em?'

Ida patted her shoulder, as if she were no more than a baby, and rocked her gently from side to side. 'I know, precious, I know. Nothing about this war is fair.'

Peggy nodded, her head bent low. 'I don't know what I'm s'posed to say, Ida. We were gonna get married.'

Ida pulled away, clearly dumbstruck, 'Oh, I had no idea.'

Peggy shook her head bitterly. 'He only asked me as he left. We just knew we wanted to be together forever. It felt so natural when we were with each other. Jim said he wanted me to give him a reason to come back.'

Remembering how happy they had been the last time they saw one another caused Peggy to break off into a fresh round of tears. Feeling helpless, Ida gently rubbed Peggy's back and tried to soothe her tears.

'You made a lovely couple,' Ida told her. 'You really did – everyone said it. The love between the two of you, well, it was as obvious as the nose on your face.'

Peggy smiled in between the sobs and wiped her face with the back of her hand. 'D'you reckon so?'

Ida nodded. 'I know so. You and Jim, well even Harry said you two were the real thing. A love like that, it's hard to find, sweetheart, but you did find it. Take comfort in that where you can.'

'I'm never going to see him again, am I, Ida?' Peggy whispered.

'I don't think so, love,' Ida replied quietly. 'But those memories you have of your time together, nobody can ever take those from you, love, not even Hitler.'

Peggy nodded allowing the truth of Ida's condolences to sink in. She was right, of course, those memories she and Jim had made would now be stored away in her heart, as precious to her as the crown jewels surely were to the king himself.

'Will there be a funeral, do you know, or will there be more of a wait for confirmation?' Ida asked.

Peggy shrugged. 'I've not got a clue. Carmichael never said.'

'His poor mother.' Ida shook her head in despair. 'She'll never get over something like this. She'll be under the doctor, mark my words. It's every mother's worst nightmare, to outlive their child.'

'I wonder if I should write, offer my condolences or something? I know Jim said he mentioned me to her,' Peggy murmured.

'I think that would be a very nice idea, sweetheart,' Ida said softly. 'She may not have met you, but she'll appreciate the sentiment, is it.'

'I'll do it now,' she said, getting to her feet and fumbling in her bedside locker for her writing pad.

Pulling it out, she saw the beginnings of a letter to Jim she had started only yesterday. Catching sight of the words she had so hopefully scribbled on the page, a scream caught in her throat. Was life always this hard?

Glancing at the sheet of paper resting in Peggy's lap, Ida gently pulled the pad away and laid it to one side. Then she pressed the cup of tea into Peggy's hands, and stroked the hair away from her face.

'Drink up and we'll start to make sense of all this.'

'I don't reckon I ever will,' Peggy said, her voice shaky, and her eyes red-rimmed and raw from so much sobbing.

Ida paused, before getting to her feet. 'I know it doesn't feel like that now, but I promise you'll find a way to live with this. Everyone does.'

With that Ida closed the door behind her leaving Peggy alone with her thoughts. She sank back on to her bed, her mind a whirl of emotion. From nowhere, she heard Edie's voice, telling her that this was the sort of thing that happened when you looked to find happiness with a man. She felt a wave of panic wash over her as she wondered if Jim had woken on the day he died knowing it was his last. She had often wondered the same thing after her father had passed away. Had he known it was his last day on earth? Had either one of the men she adored spent their last days carefree and happy until it was time to meet their maker? Or had they felt petrified for whatever lay ahead?

Sitting upright, Peggy reached for her pad once more and tried to write. But suddenly she felt tired and very confused. No matter how hard she tried, the words wouldn't come. After screwing up the notepaper, Peggy realised it was pointless to even try to scribble something to Jim's family at this time, perhaps it was better to wait until later when they knew more. Wearily she got to her feet; she had to get out of this room and do something, but what? Casting her eyes to the floor she saw her khaki overalls had fallen from the chair and knew the only comfort she would find today would be in work. Lieutenant Colonel Carmichael might not have any need for her, but she was sure Sal could make use of her in the garage. There were always cars to repair and trucks to tinker with. At this very moment, Peggy could think of nothing she would like more. Something told her that when she reached the garage she would be able to think straight. Stepping into her overalls she splashed cold water on her face, reached for her jacket and fled down the stairs towards salvation as quickly as she could.

The irony of the cloudless azure blue sky and bright sunshine as she walked briskly through the town wasn't lost on her. Today of all days Peggy wouldn't have objected to the sight of thick black clouds and pouring rain to match her mood, but like so many things in life, as she was beginning to realise, it wasn't to be.

Minutes later she arrived at the barracks and as she half-walked, half-ran towards the mechanic centre, she was grateful to see Sal standing at the doorway. Catching sight of

Peg, Sal immediately held her arms out for the younger girl and offered a much-needed hug.

'Word's spread, pet, I'm ever so sorry, you must be beside yourself,' Sal said, squeezing Peggy so tightly she could hardly breathe.

'I don't know what I'm s'posed to say or think, Sal,' Peggy mumbled into her friend's shoulder.

Sal smiled. 'You don't have to think, do or say anythin', pet. You do what's right for you, all right?'

Pulling back from Sal's embrace, Peggy fixed her friend with a stoic smile. 'That's why I'm here, Sal. I wanted to work to take my mind off things. I feel like I'm in such a dither, this place seemed like the best solution.'

Sal let out an affectionate laugh as she gestured towards the fleet of muddy Lister trucks that were lined up outside the garage. 'Hard work's the best medicine for a broken heart, flower, I can swear to that. Why don't you get started servicin' this lot and I'll make you a cuppa.'

Smiling gratefully at Sal, Peggy took the spanner from her outstretched hand. 'Sounds like the only good ideal I've heard all day.'

The day flew by for Peggy as she threw herself into her work, repairing trucks, servicing cars and even cleaning out the inside of a couple of Bugs. By the time darkness fell, Peggy was exhausted but in no mood to go home, despite Sal's insistence that it was time for her to get some rest. The truth was, Peggy didn't want to be alone with just her thoughts for company. Even though every bone in her body ached, she would clean a whole fleet of Lister trucks if it meant she didn't have to think about what had happened to poor Jim.

Sinking on to the floor, as she rubbed her aching back she suddenly became aware of a car approaching the garage. Shielding her eyes from the pinprick of light the car's beams gave off, she saw it was Annie in her Humber.

'You're late,' Peggy piped up, as Annie clambered out of the car.

'Davis had a late meeting over Cardiff way,' she explained, sauntering towards the garage. 'Anyway, I could say the same. Yer sure yer should be working after everything that happened yesterday?'

Peggy said nothing as Sal appeared in the doorway, her greatcoat slung over one arm.

'You're wastin' your breath, flower,' she said pointedly. 'I've been tryin' to persuade the bairn to go home for the past two hours, but she won't be told.'

'Yer really should listen to Sal, Peg,' Annie said, walking towards her friend and crouching down before her. 'Yer need your rest, you've had ever such a shock.'

'I need to work,' Peggy replied miserably. 'If I stop, my mind, well it goes places it oughtn't to go.'

'I know, Peggy, but you'll make yourself ill. If anyone should know, it's me,' Annie said, her face filled with worry.

Sal nodded. 'It's not often I say this, Peg, but Annie's right. Let her take you home, you'll sleep like a baby tonight after all this work today.'

'I can't,' she sighed.

Sal and Annie exchanged concerned looks. Wordlessly, they sat on the cold concrete floor next to Peggy, and arranged themselves in a little circle.

'Well, we can't leave you here,' Sal said gently. 'If you're stayin', pet, then so am I.'

'And me,' Annie nodded.

Lifting her chin, Peggy smiled gratefully at her friends. The last thing she wanted to do was worry them, but she had to admit it felt nice not to be alone.

'Thanks, girls.'

There was a pause before Sal spoke. 'I can't begin to know how you're feelin', pet, but I do know somethin' about grief, and I do know that this will get easier with time.'

'And work.' Annie shuffled closer to Peggy. 'Since Judith passed, work's been the only thing that has kept me going.'

Sal leaned over and clasped Annie's hand. 'Your sister would have been so proud of you, for stayin' put and carryin' on.'

'I don't know about that,' Annie snorted. 'Judith did far more than I ever did. But she was always the same, since we were nippers, always put other people first.'

'You're doing the very same thing now,' Peggy said gently. 'Don't tell me you wouldn't rather go home and get warm instead of sitting here with me.'

Annie raised an eyebrow and said nothing, while Sal wrapped her free arm around Peggy. 'You girls are doin' better than you think. There's not a day that passes where I don't think about Norman, God rest his soul. My world came crashing down around my ears the day I learned he'd been killed in a tram accident. We'd been together twenty years, a lifetime. There were days I didn't think I could carry on, and plenty more where I didn't want to. When Tommy, our only boy, told me he wanted to join-up shortly after his dad passed, I thought my heart would break.'

Pain was etched clearly on the redhead's face as memories of her husband and son flooded her mind. Peggy didn't want to pry, Sal so rarely spoke about anything personal, but she got the feeling it would do her good to open up.

'But you did carry on, Sal, you carried on enough to join the Army yourself,' Peggy told her.

'What else could I do, pet?' she replied, her eyes glistening with tears. 'My grief wasn't goin' to bring Norm back, or put a stop to the war. I channelled my feelings into war work, I carried on, and I realised it was the little things that get you through life.'

'Like what?' Annie demanded. 'Cos I don't think I'll ever get over losing Judith. Every morning I wake up and for a few brief seconds I forget she's gone. Then I roll over and see her empty bed and it hits me all over again. We'll never share a Sunday roast around Mam's table, we'll never cycle through the lanes, we'll never go to the pictures or the teahouse, and worst of all I'll never see her wed her Al. My heart's breaking, she was the kindest, big sister in the world and I just can't see how I'll ever get over losing her, she was my world . . .'

Through the orange glow of the candlelight Sal had lit behind them, Peggy watched Annie inhale deeply as she swallowed back her sobs. Her heart went out to her. What right did she have to grieve like this when Annie had lost a sister, her flesh and blood? Peggy could imagine Edie telling her to pull herself together and was about to say as much to the group, when Sal broke the silence with her gentle northern burr.

'You won't get over losin' her, pet, that's the honest truth of it. But both of you will learn to live with this pain. It doesn't matter whether someone was in your life for five decades or five minutes, love is love and it hurts like hell when it's gone.' Sal's voice was rich with sorrow and wisdom as if she had somehow read Peggy's mind. 'But trust me, there'll come a time when you'll appreciate the sight of the sun shinin' in the mornin' or a smile from a friend. Some days even a hot cuppa when it's brass monkeys outside will see you through a rough day. These small kindnesses show you that life carries on and you can as well, even when you think it's the most difficult thing in the world.'

The three women looked sombrely at one another in the half-light, each hoping to find peace and comfort during their own private hell.

'But it hurts so much,' Peggy said, breaking the silence. 'I didn't know how bad it would feel, but this, this is . . .' Her voice trailed off and Annie gave her an understanding smile.

'None of us ever do, flower,' Sal comforted, her forehead lined with worry. 'But we owe it to the loved ones we've lost to keep fightin', now more than ever before.'

Annie looked impassively towards the blacked-out windows while Peggy nodded and hung her head in deep thought. She knew Sal was right, that she had joined-up to help put an end to this war, and she was more determined than ever to do that now the losses had hit her so close to home.

'How d'you keep 'em alive, like?' Annie blurted suddenly.

Peggy and Sal looked up in surprise.

'How d'you mean pet?' Sal asked.

'I'm scared I'll forget Judith. I'm frightened one day I'll forget what her face looks like, the shape of her nose, her eyes, the way she laughed. How d'you keep your Norman alive?'

Peggy was taken aback at the pleading in Annie's voice. It was loaded with fear and it was all Peggy could do not to sweep the younger girl into her arms and never let go. Instead she looked across at Sal who slowly raised her right hand and placed it on her heart.

'You talk about them, pet,' she said fiercely. 'The love you shared doesn't go anywhere, you share the memories and the good times, and that's what keeps them alive in your heart.'

Feeling the tears well, Peggy got to her feet with a renewed sense of strength. 'All right then.'

'All right what?' Annie quizzed, brow furrowed with concern.

Peggy smiled weakly. 'All right, let's go home and get some rest. Another day dawns tomorrow, let's see what it brings.'

'That's the spirit, girl,' Sal beamed.

'Most sensible thing you've said all day,' Annie added, holding out a hand for Peggy to help her up.

Sal locked the garage behind them and Peggy allowed the older woman to pull her in for a hug.

'You'll get there, sweetheart,' she whispered in Peggy's ear, before releasing her into Annie's care.

Annie took her elbow and gently steered her home. They walked in silence, but Peggy's mind was in overdrive as she dodged mounds of rubble and shelled-out buildings that continued to litter the street.

Reaching the hotel, the girls hurried inside into the warm. It was gone nine now, and Ida would have long since shut the kitchen, not that she was hungry anyway. Just the thought of eating made her feel sick. Unenthusiastically, she followed Annie up the stairs and into their room, which was spick and span, as Ida had obviously given the place a thorough going-over that morning.

Casting her eye over her neatly made bed, Peggy shucked off her clothes and without even bothering to wash her face, climbed into bed. Snuggling under the blankets she closed her eyes and brought Jim's face to mind. As she pictured his floppy blond hair and sparkling blue eyes she smiled; his face was a respite from the nightmare she would surely face tomorrow and beyond.

# Chapter Twelve

True to her word, Peggy spent every waking hour working her fingers to the bone. Whether she was driving Carmichael, helping Sal in the garage, teaching Annie to read or organising auditions for the variety show, she went to bed exhausted, falling asleep as soon as her head hit the pillow.

It was only in her quieter moments, where she was tinkering under the bonnet of a Lister or polishing the Humber in the March chill, that she allowed herself to think about Jim. She had started to wonder if in fact he wasn't dead, and that he was just missing as initial reports had suggested. Every day she hoped there would be fresh news that would confirm he was still alive, but it never came. Peggy wasn't stupid, she knew that as time wore on the chances of finding Jim living and breathing became slimmer.

She did her best to put her grief on hold during the daytime, realising that the more she wondered what had happened to her beloved pilot the more she would torment herself. Instead, Peggy focused on the advice Sal and Ida had given her when they urged her to treasure him always in her heart. Peggy had done just that and she carried her recollections of him like a precious talisman, only to be pulled out when she could really indulge in his memory.

Thoughts of Jim had become her favourite way to fall asleep. Safe in her bed, while the Jerries wreaked havoc on the world,

Peggy would allow herself to give in to the fantasy of a future where she and Jim were married and had a family, never to be apart. This indulgence meant she fell into a deep sleep every night, though she found her pillow was always wet with tears when she woke.

Yet this morning had been the first time since she had learned of Jim's disappearance the week before that Peggy hadn't woken in tears. Feeling brighter than she had for some time, she had seized her good mood, and before breakfast insisted she and Annie go over some of her letters.

'Oh, Peg, come on, I'm tired,' Annie grumbled as Peggy handed her the notepad. 'I was on guard duty till all hours last night.'

'Just a few minutes,' Peggy insisted. 'We didn't have a lesson yesterday 'cos you were too wiped out and we need to be studying together as often as possible, it's the only way you'll learn. Besides, you're doing ever so well. You improve every day.'

'If yer say so,' Annie sighed, sinking on to her bed and opening up her pad. 'What do yer want me to do?'

'I thought you could write down the letters I call out, without looking anything up,' Peggy suggested, ignoring the look of fear on her friend's face. 'I'll be nice, I'll only pick letters from the first half of the alphabet. You'll get this.'

'I'm not sure, Peg,' Annie replied doubtfully. 'I don't think I'm ready.'

'I do,' Peggy said firmly. 'Now come on, we've not much time before work, so the sooner you start writing the sooner we can get going.'

Despite Annie's reservations, Peggy was right and the younger girl did well. Not only did Annie get just two of the letters Peggy called out wrong, but she didn't bat an eyelid when Peggy went back on her word and started calling letters from the second half of the alphabet. By the time the girls reached the barracks and reported for duty, Peggy was feeling happier than she had in days, and knew it was all down to her friend's progress. She had every faith in Annie's abilities and knew she was picking up reading and writing faster than either one of them anticipated. Annie was a clever soul and with the ability to read and write under her belt, there was no telling what she could achieve; the thought made Peggy smile.

Sadly, this unexpected feeling of joy only lasted until she dropped Carmichael off at his first engagement of the day. Sitting in her trusty Humber waiting for her boss to finish his meeting, Peggy was horrified to find she was sobbing into her hanky. She didn't normally cry when there was a chance other people could see her, but for the first time since Jim had gone missing Carmichael had needed to go to the airbase where she had first met the pilot and the outing had all become too much.

She had done a good job of pretending all was well, yet the moment her superior had gone inside, Peggy hadn't been able to stop the tears from falling. Surrounded by memories of Jim, she was aware of his presence everywhere, and her loss felt as raw as it had the day she had learned he was gone. Looking through the rain-spattered windscreen into the grey gloom she could see the runway where he had landed his plane the very first time she had seen him. Remembering how arrogant she had thought he was as he stepped out of the plane, cock-a-hoop at an expert landing, his pals clapping him on the back at a job well done, Peggy's eyes welled with a fresh round of tears. What she wouldn't do to relive that moment right now.

Carmichael had suggested that she use the mess to get a cuppa and something to eat while she waited, but Peggy had refused. She couldn't bear the idea of leaving this car and going out into what had once been Jim's world. To his credit, Carmichael hadn't pressed the issue. Instead he had fixed Peggy with a look of quiet concern as she held the rear door open for him and paused briefly, as if about to say something, before walking towards the office.

Dabbing her eyes with the sodden handkerchief, Peggy hastily shoved it into her pocket. Her fingers grazed the envelopes she had received in the mail that morning. She hadn't had a chance to read them in her haste to get Carmichael to his meeting on time, but now with the hours stretching out before her she wanted to savour each message.

Spotting the lazy scrawl of her best friend Bess, Peggy smiled with genuine delight. She hadn't heard from Bess in weeks. Despite the fact Peggy had sent her numerous letters of late telling her about Jim, she hadn't heard a peep from her friend and could only assume she had been incredibly busy with her own ATS work as an orderly in the stores. In her last letter, she had discussed trying to arrange leave together but Peggy knew such a request was unlikely.

The last she heard, Bess had been stationed up in Blackpool, a million miles away from their West Country roots. What a treat to hear from her now, just when she needed a lift. Tearing open the envelope, Peggy pulled out the note.

*11 March 1941*

*All right Peg,*

*Firstly, I owe you a massive apology, bab, for not writing sooner. I've been so busy and my commanding officer put me on a CB notice last week after I missed my curfew. Wasn't my fault, I got held up in the town, and there were no trams, but you know what the red caps are like, they never believe nothing you tell them and even if they do, they don't let you off! As a result, I've spent the week scrubbing the life out the loos and peeling spuds!*

*Anyway, enough of all that, how are you? I was so sad to hear what had happened to Jim. I wish there was something I could do or say to make you feel better, I know you must feel like you're in hell. I've been praying for you, lover, you don't deserve none of this. I know you always thought you and Edie would grow old together in the shop but if I'm being honest, I always felt you deserved to find your own happiness, Peg. You should find a future for yourself that's yours and not live in the shadow of your mum.*

*Look, I don't want to poke me nose in and with
everything that's happened with Jim, now's not the best
time to be making decisions, to my mind, Peg, but what I
will say is that you seem like you've found your feet with
the Army and I reckon the hard work the Army brings will
do you the power of good. Blimey, if anyone knows that it's
me after the hard work I've clocked up this past week. If
it wasn't tactless I'd suggest that a cure for grief was a CB
notice, but I'd never be that daft, Peg!*

*Just think on, and take each day as it comes. If you've
learned nothing else, you've learned you can love and that's
a powerful thing. Some people never find what you found
with your Jim. Cherish the memories, Peg, they'll be sweeter
over time.*

*With love as always,*

*Bess*

The sight of Bess's handwriting offering her the words of salvation she hadn't known she longed for gave Peggy a surge of hope. Bess was right, Peggy thought gratefully, and she would have known just how much Peggy needed to hear from her.

Looking back out of the window into the mist that framed the Welsh skyline, she found herself thinking back to all the happy times they had shared. Friends since they had met in Sunday school at the tender age of five, Bess had always been the more adventurous one. The daughter of the postmaster and his wife, Bess had been brought up in a similar vein to Peggy: to respect the community. She did, of course, but unlike Peggy, Bess also respected the need for fun. They both became Sunday school teachers, but while Peggy always followed the rules, Bess wasn't afraid to do what she liked. She would think nothing of taking her charges to run around the park on a bright, sunny morning, claiming they were closer to God when they were amongst nature rather than sat in a stuffy church hall.

Then there was the time Bess had diligently drunk a parishioner's homemade pea wine, just to check it for quality purposes. The parishioner had intended to give it to Bess's father as a Christmas present, but Bess had insisted on conducting a taste test, just to ensure it lived up to her father's exacting standards.

Peggy had of course refused to try a drop, but she hadn't batted an eyelid when Bess threw up most of the contents of the wine in the church's font, then sworn afterwards, nothing ventured, nothing gained. She had topped up the bottle with water, knowing her father would never know the difference and she was never caught out – she so rarely was.

For so long Peggy had wanted to be like Bess. She had adored the way she never seemed to plan her life, or care what happened next. Bess lived for the here and now, and growing up beside her, there were times Peggy could see the value in that attitude towards life. When Bess had suggested they join-up, Peggy had for once decided to hell with the consequences. If nothing else she was serving her country and that was always a good thing.

*

The moonlight was shining as brightly as a torch when Peggy finally dropped Carmichael back at the barracks. As she brought the Humber to a graceful standstill inside the motor garage, Peggy rested her head gently against the steering wheel and closed her eyes – she could have sworn she had seen the entirety of Wales in just one day. Enjoying the peace and quiet the darkened garage offered, she found herself drifting off, until a sharp rap on the driver's window brought her abruptly back to the present.

With a start, she turned towards the glass and saw it was Annie, smiling wickedly down at her. Wearily, Peggy wound down the window. 'What d'you want?'

Annie arched an eyebrow. 'Charming! I was only asking if you were ready to go to the mess?'

'Why?' Peggy grumbled.

'Don't tell me you've forgotten!' She gasped in horror. 'It's the auditions tonight, for the variety. I thought Carmichael would have been on at yer all day about it.'

Peggy let out a groan as she sank her head back on to the steering wheel. She had completely forgotten. Reluctantly lifting her head from the wheel, she turned back to Annie.

'Don't s'pose you fancy doing it on your own?'

'Not on your nelly!' Annie cackled, opening the door for Peggy and ushering her out. 'Come on, sooner we get on with it, the sooner it's over. Isn't that what you said to me this morning? Besides, some of them might be quite good.'

'Since when did you become such an optimist?' Peggy chuckled.

'Since when did you become such a pessimist?' Annie quipped.

Together the two girls walked across the quad towards the mess. With the night sky now an inky black and only a handful of stars to show them the way, they walked gingerly up the hill, doing their best to avoid the muddy puddles.

Reaching the red-brick building, Peggy pushed the door open and walked inside. She was pleased to see someone had gone to the trouble of creating a small stage area using a few upturned crates by the noticeboard. The little piano that usually gathered dust in the corner had been wheeled out and cleaned, ready to be played, and a series of chairs had been lined up in rows.

'How many are you expecting?' Annie gasped.

'Possibly hundreds, the girls are that excited,' a voice piped up from behind them.

Swinging round, Peggy's face broke into a delighted smile. 'Sal! What are you doing here?'

'Thought I'd give you a hand, pet, and play the piano for the girls when they audition,' she chirruped. 'Plus, I wouldn't mind castin' me eye over a few of these acts meself.'

'That's very kind of you,' Peggy said, beaming.

'Not really, flower, I haven't had a good laugh in weeks, and it beats a night in stitchin' and mendin' in me billet.' Sal sniffed. 'Now what time are you expectin' the first one?'

Peggy glanced at the clock above the door. 'Any time now, I reckon.'

'Shall I see if anyone's waiting?' Annie asked.

Nodding, Peggy glanced at Sal and gestured for her to take a seat at the piano.

'So, have you got any idea who's auditionin'? Anythin' Carmichael particularly wants to see?' Sal asked, pouring three cups of tea from the urn resting on top of the tiny trestle table.

'Not really,' Peggy replied, gratefully taking the cuppa Sal handed her. 'All he kept saying was he wanted variety. Not all singing, not all music, but some jokes and sketches as well.'

'Christ!' Sal muttered, rolling her eyes heavenwards. 'We'll not move for girls who think they're Mae West.'

Peggy chuckled, as Annie opened the door and showed the first girl to the stage. Taking a seat, on the other side of Peggy, Annie started sniggering. Fixing her friend with a firm glare, Peggy turned to the ATS recruit and smiled welcomingly.

'Hello, lover, what's your name?'

'Volunteer Michaels, but my first name's Helen,' the girl replied confidently.

Licking the tip of her pencil, Peggy wrote the name carefully in her notepad, and took the time to appraise the girl standing before her. Tall with a button nose, brown eyes and long blonde hair, Helen was clearly a beauty. There was something about her that Peggy thought made her look haughty.

Still, she thought, underlining the girl's name, it wasn't fair to judge just yet. And besides, to stand up in front of a group of strangers and belt out a tune or a sketch, you would need to have something about you.

'And what are you doing for us?' Peggy asked pleasantly.

Helen took a step forward and smiled benevolently at the trio sat before her. 'I'm going to be singing "I'll Take Romance".'

'Lovely.' Peggy beamed as she turned to Sal. 'You got the sheet music for that one, bab?'

Sal shook her head. 'I don't need it, flower, it's one of my favourites. Are you ready, Helen?'

The girl nodded and as Sal began to play the opening notes she stepped forward to the edge of the makeshift stage and readied herself to hit the right note.

But the moment the girl began to sing, the pianist's face dropped like a stone.

'Stop,' Sal called, cutting the singer off.

'What's the matter?' Helen asked.

Peggy glanced at Sal and saw she looked mutinous.

'You came in too late. And you were out of tune.'

'I was not!' Helen replied indignantly.

'You flamin' well were, flower,' Sal fired. 'I know better than anyone how it should be sung.'

'So do I,' Helen spat. 'I frequently sing this at home with Father. I think if anyone was out of time it was you.'

Noting Sal's furious expression, Peggy groaned inwardly, covering her face with her hands and sinking lower in her seat.

'Is that right?' Sal fumed, getting to her feet.

Alarm spread through Peggy and she knew she had to take charge of the situation. 'All right, ladies, come on, there's no need for this. Let's just try again.'

There was a pause as Sal narrowed her eyes. 'Fine.'

'Fine,' Helen echoed, walking back to the centre of the stage.

Immediately, Sal struck up the opening chords and Helen walked towards the front of the stage as she sang the opening line once more.

Peggy couldn't help herself and began to wince as the girl tried to hit the right notes. Her tuneless screeching resembled a bag of kittens being strangled, and as Annie nudged her sharply in the ribs, Peggy turned and was horrified to see her friend laughing.

Torn between wanting to tell Annie off for her rudeness and encouraging Helen to get to the end of what was frankly a painful rendition, Peggy did the only thing possible and faced front. However, it was impossible to ignore the look of fury on Sal's face. Every time she sneaked a glance at the ATS veteran, she saw the woman scowl and thump the keys even harder as Helen murdered the tune.

Silently Peggy willed her to say nothing and instead let Helen get to the end, so none of them had to listen to any more of her tuneless wailing. Looking back at Helen to see if she could find anything positive to say about her performance, Peggy was amazed to see the girl had no idea how bad she was. If anything, she was a confident performer, commanding the stage with a self-assurance that saw her walk to and fro and even attempt a dance across the makeshift stage.

As the song came to its conclusion, Peggy watched in surprise as Helen attempted a rather graceless flourish that saw her end with a series of energetic high kicks. Clearly putting her heart and soul into the final moments of her performance, Peggy watched in horror as Helen's last kick saw her teeter at the edge of one of the upturned crates.

Watching the girl try to steady herself, all with a smile on her face, Peggy's hands flew to her mouth as she crashed to the floor, khaki passion-killers on display for all to see. Quickly, all three girls rushed to her aid, only for Helen to wave their concerns away.

'I'm fine.' She smiled, doing her best not to wince as Peggy helped her to her feet. 'So, what did you think? Will you make me the star turn?'

Sal patted the girl's shoulder comfortingly. 'We've got a lot of other girls to see, pet, but we'll definitely let you know.'

Helen's face fell. 'It was the high kicks, wasn't it? I can assure you I won't fall off on the night.'

'I know, bab,' Peggy soothed. 'But it wouldn't be fair if I gave you an answer now without seeing everyone else.'

'All right.' Helen nodded as Annie led her gently by the elbow towards the door. 'But you'll let me know, won't you? I'll get Mother to send my best dress up especially for the occasion.'

Once Helen was safely out of the room, Peggy slumped into the nearest chair and covered her face with her hands. 'Please tell me they're not all going to be that bad.'

Annie chuckled. 'I shouldn't count on it, Peg.'

'Neither would I,' agreed Sal. 'Did you see how high she was gettin' her legs at the end? It was a miracle she didn't break somethin'.'

'She did, her pride,' Peggy quipped, turning to Annie. 'I s'pose you'd better show the next one in, lover.'

'Flamin' Nora, it's going to be a long night,' Sal grumbled as she walked back towards the piano.

\*

Unfortunately for Peggy, Sal turned out to be right. Not only was the night long, but it was arduous too as the girls sat through more tuneless singers, unfunny sketches, jugglers who couldn't juggle and one incredible act featuring an ATS girl and a live budgie. It was mind-boggling, disheartening and in parts disastrous.

As Peggy looked at her watch she saw that it was almost ten, and stretched her hands over her head.

'We done now, Annie?' she said with a yawn.

Annie nodded. 'Carmichael's got a few more he wants us to see tomorrow night.

Peggy's face dropped like a stone. 'You're not serious! We've gotta sit through more of this?'

'Afraid so,' Annie chuckled.

'Well, all I can say is I'll be goin' on the hoy after,' Sal exclaimed.

'I reckon we all will if they're as bad as Helen,' Peggy agreed.

'Speaking of which, shall we pop to the NAAFI? They've not got booze but they should have a nice strong cuppa? I think there's time,' Annie suggested.

'Are you buying?' Peggy asked, astonished.

Annie rolled her eyes. 'No need to make such a big deal out of it.'

'No, but I will mark this date in me diary,' Sal teased, opening her notepad in jest only for a letter with Annie's name to fall to the floor.

'What are you doing with a letter for me?' Annie asked, picking up the envelope.

'I picked it up earlier and meant to give it to you sooner,' she explained. 'Sorry, pet.'

'That's all right.' Annie smiled, stuffing it into her pocket.

'Don't you want to read it now?' Sal asked puzzled.

'No. Right now, all I want is a cuppa.'

As Peggy followed Sal and Annie through the door, she turned a wistful look back at the mess. She knew it was only a little variety show they were putting on for the troops, but she sincerely hoped that tomorrow would be better. Snapping off the lights, she couldn't shake the nagging voice that told her trouble was just around the corner.

## Chapter Thirteen

The following morning, Peggy woke to find Annie was already washed, dressed and sat on her bed, hunched over an exercise book. Blinking the sleep from her eyes, Peggy saw that to her delight Annie appeared to be copying out the letters they had been going over yesterday.

Keen not to disturb her friend's concentration, Peggy gingerly clambered out of bed, and padded across the floor to peer over her shoulder. With surprise, Peggy saw Annie had managed to write her name, all without looking at the book. It wasn't bad. The writing was uneven, but it was neatly spaced and better yet, mostly spelled correctly.

'This is brilliant,' she said encouragingly.

'No, it's not,' Annie groaned, throwing the pad on to the floor in frustration.

Peggy bent down and picked up the battered notebook. Smoothing the creases from the pages, she was about to show it to Annie once more, when something stopped her. The younger girl looked broken, her eyes filled with defeat. Icy fear gripped Peggy's heart as she saw just how frail Annie was.

Putting the pad aside, she wrapped an arm around the younger girl. Instinctively, Annie's shoulders stiffened, before she relaxed them and leaned into Peggy's embrace.

'Our Judith always told me I was capable of more than I

thought.' She laughed bitterly. 'Shame she's not here for me to prove her wrong.'

'You shouldn't be so hard on yourself. I reckon Jude was right; you can do whatever you put your mind to, least you could if you didn't give up at the first hurdle.' Regret coursed through Peggy's body as the words left her lips. 'Sorry, Annie, I shouldn't have said that.'

Annie shrugged. 'Don't worry, Peg, it's the truth. Nice to hear it. Judith was the only one that ever gave it to me straight. Everyone always says I'm too difficult.'

'I wouldn't say difficult, bab.' Peggy shifted uncomfortably on the bed. 'Mind, you do take offence easy. Makes it harder for people to help you, if you keep shutting them out all the time.'

'I know.' Annie sighed and leaned back on the bed, her small frame crushing the notepad Peggy had recently straightened. 'But it's really difficult. I'm me own worst enemy. I think I got so used to people telling me I was stupid at school that I always thought I might as well give up now, before I'm forced to.'

'That's daft,' Peggy insisted. 'You're a bright girl. You were doing ever so well just then.'

'I don't know about that, Peg.' Annie sighed again.

'I do,' Peggy replied determinedly. 'And anyway, what's your alternative? Go home to your mum and dad?'

Sitting bolt upright, Annie looked stricken. 'I can't go back. I want to stay here, carry on Judith's work, win this war for her sake and stop good, decent people like me sister being killed by Hitler. Judith means too much to me to go now.'

'She was a good girl,' Peggy remembered fondly.

'She was more than good, Peg. She was a hero. I only joined-up cos of her. Now I'm here, I'm not going back without a fight.'

Peggy fixed Annie with a determined glance, and handed her the notepad she had sat on. 'Well, then, you know what to do.'

The next couple of hours slipped by like minutes as Peggy

and Annie pored over her notepad. Since her outburst, Annie had returned to her work with a new enthusiasm, and Peggy couldn't have been prouder. She knew just how difficult it must be to learn something many people took for granted, but to do it at a time when she was bereft with grief was something else entirely. Casting a sidelong glance at Annie hunched over her work, painstakingly writing out the word 'cat', Peggy felt a rush of admiration.

'I can't get over how much you've learned so quickly, Annie,' she blurted.

A deep flush coloured Annie's neck as she shied away from Peggy's praise with embarrassment. 'I'm only writing "cat", it's nothing.'

Peggy gave her friend an affectionate nudge in the ribs. 'You're a marvel. Don't sell yourself short, you've done brilliantly.'

'D'you think so?' Annie asked shyly.

'I wouldn't say it if I didn't. Same time tomorrow?' Peggy beamed.

'I'd love to, if that's all right.' Annie smiled. 'But will yer have time, what with having to get the poster done for the variety show?'

Peggy's hands flew to her mouth. 'I'd completely forgotten about that.'

'Don't worry, I'll help,' Annie assured her. 'How about I do the drawings and yer do the words?'

'Would you really?' Peggy breathed gratefully.

'Course, what else are friends for?' Annie grinned.

Returning her pal's smile, Peggy suddenly remembered the letter Sal had pressed into her hands last night.

'D'you want me to read that letter for you?' she asked.

Annie looked at her blankly for a second, before remembering the note she had stuffed into her uniform pocket.

'I'd forgotten all about that. Thanks, Peg, Jude always used to do that for me but now . . .'

Annie's voice trailed off and Peggy took the envelope from her friend's outstretched hand and looked at it. Surprisingly, it only had Annie's first name written on the envelope in thick capitals. It must be from someone local, she thought, tearing it open.

Turning the note over, Peggy saw the letter was only a few lines long, but as she scanned it she felt sick. This was the most disgusting thing she had ever seen.

'What is it?' Annie asked anxiously.

Peggy glanced up from the note, keen to shield her friend. 'Erm, it's nothing.'

'It doesn't look like nought to me, Peggy Collins,' Annie said firmly. 'What's the note say?'

A feeling of dread coursed through Peggy. She didn't want to lie to her friend but she didn't want to cause upset either. She had already endured far more than she should.

'Peggy, I'm serious, tell me what it says,' Annie said, a determined glint in her eye.

'All right.' Peggy sighed. 'Just remember whoever wrote this wants locking up.'

Smoothing out the paper, Peggy read aloud:

*Dear Annie or should I say thick girl what can't read,*
*    Stupid girls like you make me sick! How you reckon you can serve our king when you can't read or write is a joke. You're a disgrace to the ATS! You'd better tell Lieutenant Colonel Carmichael or I will!*

*    A friend*

Hands trembling, Peggy folded the letter back in its envelope and looked at Annie. Her cheeks were flushed with anger and her breathing was shallow. Reaching out to clasp her hand supportively, Annie pushed her away.

'Who'd do this?' she gasped.

Peggy shook her head sadly. 'I dunno, love. Some sick mare, I reckon.'

Annie glanced up, brow furrowed. 'Did yer tell anyone? About me not being able to read, I mean?'

'Course not!' Peggy gasped. 'It's not my secret to share. I can promise you, I've told nobody.'

Annie nodded. 'Then who? You and Judith were the only ones who knew about this, and she's hardly likely to have let it slip.'

Silence fell across the two girls as they turned their thoughts to who could possibly have written such a nasty note. The very idea of someone in the ATS doing something so appalling was unthinkable.

'I have to say I don't know, Ann,' Peggy said finally in a low voice. 'I can't think of anyone we know who would do something so vile.'

Annie turned to face Peggy, her green eyes flashing with anger. 'Neither can I, but I can tell yer this, Peggy, I'm going to find out and when I do they'll pay all right.'

*

The rest of the day passed in a blur as Peggy drove Carmichael around Swansea, her mind full of the poison pen letter Annie had received. Every ATS girl Peggy met or spoke to she wondered if they were the ones who had sent the note and why. Annie was certainly forthright and had a bit of an icy reputation but she never meant anyone any harm, and she certainly didn't deserve to be on the receiving end of such unpleasant abuse.

Just as worrying was the issue that someone other than Peggy knew Annie's secret. For the life of her she couldn't understand how anyone could find out. She knew she hadn't said anything and Annie was hardly likely to have blabbed. Just thinking about it all was exhausting and by the time Peggy clocked off her driving duties and returned to the mess for round two of the auditions she was ready for bed.

Walking inside, she was delighted to see Annie and Sal

already waiting with a handful of ATS girls keen to watch the acts. Just as before, there was a trestle table filled with a tea urn alongside the makeshift stage and it looked very much as though Sal had managed to lay her hands on some almond biscuits to keep their spirits up.

'You two should be made saints.' She beamed at them.

'I'd find a port and lemon more useful tonight, pet,' Sal chuckled.

As the girls burst into laughter, the door opened, and in walked their first act of the night. A company commander who Carmichael had warned Peggy had to be put in the show no matter how terrible, otherwise she would make his life a misery.

'What are you doin' for us?' Sal asked, walking across the stage towards the piano.

'Just an impression,' the woman replied.

'Whenever you're ready,' Peggy called encouragingly.

As she sat back in her chair with Annie beside her, Peggy felt a feeling of dread moved through her body. Talented mimics were hard to find, and this lady, no matter how high her rank, looked as though she took herself far too seriously to be any good. The woman, with her pinched face, raven hair and harsh expression, looked as though she couldn't find an ounce of fun in a music hall. But as Sal started to play the theme from the film *Grand Hotel*, Peggy watched in astonishment as the company commander she knew to be called Gloria transformed herself, with just a look in her eyes, into a very convincing Greta Garbo.

'I want to be alone,' she called, slinking across the stage in a very Garbo-like way.

Peggy and Annie grinned as they broke into a thunderous round of applause. She was actually brilliant! Finally, they had found one decent act to put into the show.

Luckily, the rest of the night passed in much the same vein, and Peggy managed to uncover some wonderful diamonds in the rough including a talented dancing troupe, a trio of sisters who sang in harmony and a fire-eating sergeant from the neighbouring Army base. Peggy wasn't entirely sure if his act was safe or on Carmichael's wavelength but she did think her boss would approve of the violinist who played Beethoven as naturally as if she had composed the pieces herself. And she knew he would also adore the rhythm tap dancer who performed effortlessly despite having only one leg.

'Is that it?' Peggy asked, stifling a yawn,

Annie peered out into the corridor. 'Just one more, by the look of it, but she's not in uniform and gripping her coat to her chest as if it was as precious as a newborn.'

'You sure she's here to perform and isn't waiting for that fire-eating sergeant?' Peggy teased. 'Still, you'd better show her in, Ann love, I was ready for me bed when I got here.'

Quickly, Annie got to her feet and held the door open. Peggy smiled at the woman and gestured for her to stand on the stage. She looked to be a few years older than her, Peggy realised, and smartly dressed in a floral tea dress and violet cardigan. She was holding a red coat bundled against her chest. Her long blonde hair fell in soft waves around her shoulders, but her eyes looked tired, and her jaw was clenched, as if she was somehow expecting someone to run off with the jacket she was holding so tightly.

Looking closer at the woman, Peggy saw, with a start, that the bundle was a baby, and the woman had wrapped her coat around the infant. Feeling a pang of sympathy that she had been made to stand in a draughty corridor for hours, Peggy gestured to the urn Sal had kept filled all night.

'Cuppa, love?' she asked kindly.

The woman shook her head. 'No thank you. I shan't stay long.'

'What's your name?' Peggy called, ready to scribble it down on her pad.

'Hilda,' she replied. 'And this is Iris.'

As Hilda gestured towards the bundle, Sal hurried across the parquet floor.

'What a beautiful bairn,' Sal gushed as she peered over the baby and gently stroked her cheek. 'How old is she?'

'Just eight weeks.' Hilda smiled as she looked down at her child.

'Which ATS company are you in?' Annie suddenly called from across the room.

The woman looked up from her baby, startled. 'Oh, I'm not in the ATS.'

'But you are here to audition for the variety show?' Sal said, breaking her gaze away from the baby and looking in bemusement at the woman.

Hilda shook her head. 'No, I didn't even know that's what this was. I'm looking for a girl named Peggy Collins and was told she'd be here.'

The girls exchanged surprised looks, before Peggy raised her hand.

'I'm Peggy,' she replied cautiously.

Immediately, the strained expression on the woman's face returned.

'Well then, I want a word with you,' she said, her eyes alight with fury.

Peggy looked at the woman in astonishment as she got to her feet. 'How d'you mean?'

'I mean, stay away from my husband,' Hilda hissed as she stepped from the stage and advanced towards her.

There was a collective gasp from the ATS girls who had gathered behind Peggy.

'What?'

'Don't you give me what,' Hilda spat, her voice taking on a dangerous edge as she continued towards Peggy, the baby held steadfast in her arms. 'I know about you Army girls, you're all a bunch of tarts.'

Sensing mutiny, Sal turned quickly to the group of volunteers who were watching, mouths open in amazement

'You lot, out now. And as for you, just hang on a minute,

you've no business comin' in here, makin' your accusations,' Sal snapped, reaching for the woman's arm and pulling her away from Peggy.

With the volunteers begrudgingly leaving the mess, Hilda spun angrily on her heel and came face to face with the northerner.

'I've every right. This woman,' she spat, briefly turning back and jabbing her finger menacingly in the air towards the spark girl, 'has been carrying on with my husband and I won't have it. We've a child, for God's sake, has she no morals?'

Eyes wide and arms held up in defence, Peggy spoke firmly. 'Look, babber, I reckon there's been some sort of mistake. I'm not carrying on with nobody.'

The woman snorted in disgust. 'Course you're not, love, you girls never are. Christ, d'you think I just fell off the turnip truck?'

The shouting clearly woke the baby who began to stir and suddenly the mess was filled with the sound of Iris's cries as she screamed at the top of her lungs.

'Now look what you've gone and done,' Hilda said, as she tried to mollify the baby by letting her suck on her little finger.

As the baby nuzzled contentedly at her mother's flesh, the cries subsided and Annie got to her feet.

'Look, I'm sure there's been some horrible misunderstanding or summat,' she said quietly, her hand resting comfortingly on Peggy's arm. 'Peggy's not the sort to go off with a married bloke.'

Hilda's head snapped up as she looked sharply at Peggy. 'I don't reckon so. I've heard all about you. Bristol girl, aren't you?'

Peggy nodded.

'Me 'n'all, from Redland way. Well, my husband's Jim Hudson. Know him?'

Nausea rose at the mention of her sweetheart's name and she sank unsteadily into the chair behind her.

'Well, me and my Jim met up the Hippodrome one night over ten years ago and we've been together ever since,' Hilda continued, unaware of the effect her words were having on Peggy. 'He's the love of my life, knew it from the moment I met him.'

Sal shot a concerned glance at Peggy who had turned a deathly shade of white.

'Are you sure we're talkin' about the same Jim Hudson, love?' Sal asked quietly. 'Jim's a common enough name. Do you think you've got him muddled up?'

'I reckon I know my own husband!' Hilda laughed scornfully. 'One of the best pilots in the RAF, blond hair, piercing blue eyes and an accent that would cut glass. Sound about right?'

Wordlessly, the girls nodded as Hilda continued her tirade.

'And I reckon I've got the measure of her 'n'all. As for this baby' – she thrust the child under Peggy's nose – 'can't you see the resemblance to Jim Hudson? My husband, father of my child. You want to be ashamed of yourself, you're nothing but a common tart.'

Peggy gasped in shock at the insult as she looked down at the sleeping bundle lying contentedly in Hilda's arms. There was no getting away from it, the baby was the spitting image of Jim, from the gentle slope of her nose to the cleft in her chin. Drinking in the sight of what she knew to be Jim's daughter, Peggy was filled with disgust and loathing. Had Jim really taken her in like that? Had she really allowed herself to be courted by a married man? Just what sort of a person was she? But then what sort of a person was he? They had talked about a future together. He had asked her to marry her! Was he planning on having two wives?

A stifled sob escaped Peggy's lips as she caught sight of a simple gold band on Hilda's wedding ring finger. Was this real?

'I don't understand any of this,' she whispered, thunderstruck.

Hilda stood upright, her shoulders arched, as though braced for attack. 'Lucky for you that I do. You're the talk of the family, and brought shame on us all as well as yourself. Now leave him alone.'

'Well, that won't be difficult,' Annie fired angrily, coming to the defence of her friend, 'seeing as he's gone missing.'

Hilda blanched at the news, before quickly rearranging her features. 'What are you talking about?'

'Jim, your husband, by all accounts. Went missing a couple of weeks ago, but surely you know that?' Annie snarled, laying a protective hand on Peggy's shoulder.

Rooted to the spot, Hilda looked from one woman to the next before she finally spoke.

'Well, of course I know, I've just been to the base, they wanted to talk to me, give me more details, you know, as his next of kin,' she said pointedly, looking straight at Peggy. 'While I was in the area, I thought I'd tell you to get any ideas out of your head about stealing my husband from under my nose when he does return.'

Sal cocked her head to one side and regarded the woman thoughtfully. 'You think he will come back then?'

'Course,' Hilda replied, seemingly recovered from Annie's questioning. 'This isn't the first time Jim's done a disappearing act, he's probably holed up in some French port drinking champagne and befriending some other silly innocent girl.'

Searing agony ripped through Peggy's heart as she realised that she was just as Hilda had described, a silly innocent girl who had fallen for a married man. Peggy may not have had much experience in affairs of the heart but she knew it was a story as old as Father Time himself.

Getting to her feet, she squeezed Annie's hand gratefully and looked Hilda straight in the eye.

'I promise you, I didn't know your husband was married—'

Hilda cut her off with a peal of laughter.

Peggy raised her hand to silence her and continued, her voice containing a dangerously steely edge. 'If I had known he was married I would never have gone near him. My mother raised me to know the difference between right and wrong, and I would never in all my days have gone with a bloke what was someone else's. I appreciate you've come here to warn me off, but I'll tell you this, you don't need to because even if Jim Hudson is alive and well, he's very much dead to me now.'

With that Peggy squared her shoulders, pushed past the women and stalked out into the cold night air. Racing down the hill, away from the mess, she only stopped running when she reached the motor garage. Rounding the corner, away from the main barracks, she sank down on to the cold earth and allowed the tears to fall as she wept her heart out for the future she knew she would never have. She had been a fool, a stupid little girl. Well, never again, Peggy vowed furiously – she had fallen in love once, it was a mistake she would never make again.

# Chapter Fourteen

The moment Hilda dropped her bombshell, the gossip spread through the ranks like wildfire. Immediately, everyone seemed to know all about Peggy's personal life, a fact she found deeply embarrassing.

Whether she was enjoying a cuppa in the NAAFI, square-bashing or simply getting on with her job, Peggy found the stares and whispers hard to bear. It had only been three days since Hilda had paid her a visit but more than once she had fled from the mess, her meal untouched, because she heard the word 'trollop' bandied about.

Naturally, Annie and Sal leapt to her defence. Particularly when a few of the girls from the variety show auditions dropped out, saying they didn't want to work with a tart like Peggy. But the truth was, Peggy didn't blame them and although she appreciated Sal and Annie's efforts to do something she didn't feel capable of doing herself, she wasn't altogether sure she wanted or even deserved defending. The truth of the matter was that she had fallen in love with a married man, a cardinal sin according not just to the teachings of the Church, but her mother as well. The only silver lining in this impenetrably dark cloud was the fact Edie had no idea about Jim. Peggy knew her mother would never forgive her and would insist she had cast a shadow over the family's good name. As for her father, Peggy thought miserably, no doubt he would be turning in his grave if he could see her now.

Since discovering the truth about Jim, Peggy had felt bereft. Her heart was breaking, but she was also furious with herself and with him for leading her such a merry dance. If it hadn't been for work, Peggy was sure she would have gone under and as a result had thrown herself into every driving and vehicle repair task Sal could give her.

That morning, she had received a letter from Edie. Sitting outside the NAAFI van, the sun doing its best to peek through the clouds as she took a break with a cuppa, she glanced at Edie's familiar handwriting and felt a surge of comfort. Just when she needed her most, Edie had written.

*17 March 1941*

*Dearest Peggy,*

*I'm writing this in our front room after a day at the shop and I don't mind telling you I'm exhausted. I'm sure you've heard about Hitler's latest attack last night, the fifth on our beloved city, would you believe. It was horrific and lasted seven terrifying hours.*

*They destroyed St Pauls, Eastville, Redland and had a good go at the docks. You could see the fires for miles around, and the dazzling blue lights of the bombs in all directions. All of us gathered close and wondered if it would ever end.*

*Now, I don't want you to worry, I'm fine. But to be blunt, Peg, the Michaels family were killed in the raids. I can scarcely believe it, even days after the event. They'd gone over to Easton to see Mr Michael's cousin and were killed in the blasts trying to find shelter. Apparently the all-clear sounded too early and they made their way out of the underground shelter only to be wiped out by a screaming bomb less than fifteen minutes later. Mrs Hooper from two doors down was the one what told me. She'd spoken to Robert, their son and sole survivor of the family, and said* they died as soon as they stepped on to the street. It's awful Peg, I don't half miss them. They were a lifeline for me, what with you gone. Not only that but I can't stop thinking of how they suffered. Honestly, I wonder how much more the people of Bristol can take; folk are getting fed up with this bombardment. We feel helpless, Peg, it's time this war was over, and I can't honestly say I blame those that are leaving their homes every night for safety in the country. I know some people say they're the Yellow Convoy but if I didn't have the shop to open up for, I'm not sure I wouldn't do the same thing.

Which leads me on to my next point, Peg. I've been doing some thinking, and I want you home. It's not safe for you in the Army, people are dying left, right and centre. Look what happened to your friend Judith, out driving, trying to help people. And I know things are no better here, but I thought we could perhaps sell the shop, go and open a little store over Clutton way. We would both be safe there, Peggy, and think how lovely it would be to breathe in the fresh air every morning and see the green fields. Course, you might have that where you are, Peggy, but you don't have safety. You might not be on the front line, but you're putting yourself in harm's way every day being in the forces and I can't stand the thought of it.

I understand it might be difficult for you to leave like that so I'm quite happy to write to your boss and tell him I need you here. But you must leave the Army, Peggy, there's no choice. Your place is here with me.

Your loving Mother

Peggy dropped the letter to her lap as if she had been burned. She was shocked Edie could ask her to leave a job she knew Peggy adored. Edie had always been a staunch believer in doing your duty, frequently trotting out the expression, you've made your bed, now lie in it. In horror, Peggy realised that her mother was asking her to give up the one thing that was keeping her afloat at the moment, and the idea was as shocking as discovering her beloved hometown had been raided so many times.

Peggy shook her head bitterly. She just couldn't do it. Even though everyone at the barracks was giving her the cold shoulder, her job as a driver was the only thing keeping her upright. When it was just Peggy, the car and the open road, everything else paled into insignificance. War work made sense to Peggy in a way that her job with her mother or as a Sunday school teacher never had.

Putting the letter back into the envelope, Peggy sighed and pushed a loose strand of hair back under her cap. It was true that war had done funny things to people but it seemed to have hit Edie hard. She had become a changed woman in the eighteen months Britain had been at war. She had gone from a strong woman to a frightened, weak one and Peggy couldn't help feeling worried about her. But still, going home wasn't an option, she thought grimly as she got to her feet and walked back across the quad towards the garage.

Pushing open the door, she was relieved to see the centre was empty. She took off her jacket, put it on the back seat of her trusty Humber, then she wrapped a scarf around her head and picked up a bucket from the stack near Sal's makeshift office. Filling it with soapy water, she started cleaning, keen to make the car as shiny as a new pin for her trip to Cardiff later that day with Carmichael. Slopping lukewarm water over the windscreen, her mind soon began to wander and inevitably all thoughts turned to Jim, just as they always did. Since Hilda had paid her a visit, Peggy had gone over and over the way she had met Jim, trying to find some clue that he was married. Admittedly he hadn't worn a wedding ring, or even mentioned a wife, but shouldn't she have asked?

Tearfully, she dipped her cloth into the bucket and rubbed hard at the mud that still spattered the windows following yesterday's drive through the country lanes. There were days, Peggy thought, where simply getting out of bed and facing the world seemed like the hardest thing to do, never mind throwing herself into war work. Naturally she had tried to put a brave face on things, insisting to everyone that she was fine, but in private, it was a different story. Alone with only her thoughts for company, Peggy felt bereft, unable to believe that the first man she had fallen in love with had broken her heart in such a cruel way. She had thought Jim was many things, but he had never struck her as unkind. And yet the way he had deceived her, manipulated her, encouraged her to love him, as though he truly were a free man, seemed very heartless to Peggy. She had believed the sun rose and set with him each day, and to discover he had deceived her on such a shocking scale was quite simply unfathomable.

She wanted to hate him for what he had done, but the truth, buried deep inside her very core, meant she couldn't. Peggy still loved him, much to her great shame. She ached for him and longed to feel his hand in hers or the weight of his arm wrapped around her shoulder. Despite what had happened, she still fell asleep thinking of him. Her favourite memory was the last time they had seen each other, and the way Jim's face had lit up when she had told him she would marry him. He had looked so happy, so hopeful, the love she clearly felt for him radiated back in his sparkling blue eyes. And yet, the truth was Jim already had a wife, a woman he had pledged to spend his life with before God and witnesses. It was when she felt the sharp pain of reality that she felt blindsided. Peggy knew she really had no business feeling anything for the man who had tricked her into loving him. Worse, he didn't deserve her love or her tears. She had never felt more conflicted or wrong-footed. How badly she had misjudged the man she thought was the love of her life.

Leaning back against the car, she heard the rustle of paper in the pocket of her overalls. In her haste to start work and think about something other than Jim, Peggy had clean forgotten she had shoved her notepad and pen into her pocket, keen to write a letter to her old friend Kitty when she had time. Sinking on to her haunches, she rested the pad on her lap and, in the silent garage, she took five minutes away from her duties and began to write.

20 March 1941

*Dear Kitty,*

*Thought it was my turn to drop you a line and I hope you won't mind but I don't think this note is going to be very cheerful. To be honest, Kit, I've had a bit of a shock – yes, another one, would you believe – since my last letter where I told you Jim was missing presumed dead. What with time being precious and all with a war on, I'll get to the point – it turns out Jim's married.*

*I can picture the look on your face now as you read this, your jaw's dropped with shock and then you're doubting what I'm saying to you because how can such a thing be true? After all, didn't I say Jim was perfect, that he was so perfect he had asked me to marry him? Well, it is true, Kit, and I know it's true because I met his wife, Hilda. She turned up at the barracks here a few nights ago, with their baby daughter, and she was the spit of Jim, Kit.*

*You're the one person I thought might understand this. Not because you know what it's like to court a married man, but because you know what it's like to have your heart shattered and how to live to tell the tale. Oh Kit, I've been such a fool to fall for all of Jim's tricks and his lies. He must have seen me coming a mile away, and had a good laugh at my expense. I wonder if he told all his mates, and they were in on the joke too. Poor defenceless and stupid little girl from Bristol. Yet I fell for him, Kitty. I fell so hard, and I allowed myself to believe that we belonged together, that we had a connection only the two of us could*

*understand. And now look what's happened. What Mother
would say if she only ever knew I dread to think.*

*Thing is, I didn't know what to say when Hilda told me
she was his wife, Kitty, it was a wonder I didn't fall to the
floor in shock. Truth be told, I don't know how I'm upright
now. I'll admit this to you, and only you, mind, but the very
worst part of all of this is that even after everything I've
learned about the man I thought would be my husband, I
still love him! Just what sort of a wicked person am I?*

*I don't know how I'll ever come to terms with this. I've
lost the man I loved with all my heart, the man I thought
was my future. I spent my stitching and mending nights
fantasising about our house in the countryside, wisteria
up the door and our three adorable children (yes three,
two never seemed enough). I allowed myself to picture a
different future to the one I always expected to have with
Mother, and it turns out I was on a fool's errand. None
of this was real, not a single word. Jim just thought I was
some silly girl he could have a laugh with, yet my traitorous
heart's still breaking, Kit, and there isn't a day that passes
where I don't miss him and wish he'd come back to me. I
keep thinking that you can't really miss something that was
never really yours, and Jim was never really mine, was he,
he was someone else's. I should hate him for everything that
he's done, but no matter how hard I try, I just can't.*

*I'm going to sign off now, Kit, this will turn out to be a
very long letter otherwise. I hope you're well and I hope
things aren't as dramatic in your world.*

*With love as always,*

*Your friend, Peg*

Looking back over the letter, she suddenly felt overcome
with exhaustion. Recent events taking such a toll she couldn't
remember the last time she had enjoyed a proper night's sleep.

Closing her eyes for just a moment, Peggy allowed herself to give in to the wretchedness burning inside her until a pair of loud voices entering the garage startled her. Blinking her eyes open, she was about to stand up and say hello, when she heard something that made her stomach lurch.

'What I don't understand is how she could court him all that time and not know he was married,' a spark girl Peggy recognised as May Horobin said.

'You didn't fall for that old flannel, did you? Course she knew,' snorted another woman, who Peggy realised was Pat Grimes.

'No! D'you reckon?'

'I more than reckon, I know,' Pat trilled authoritatively. 'Rumour has it she didn't give a monkey's about his missus or his kiddie. She got what she wanted and that was all what mattered to Peggy Collins.'

'Well I never.' May let out a low whistle. 'If that's what Peggy Collins's really like, it's no wonder girls are dropping out of the show left, right and centre. I mean who'd want to spend time with a common tart like that?'

'Exactly,' Pat agreed. 'I mean, she had a reputation back in Bristol for being a good-time girl so none of this surprises me. All I can say is Carmichael'd better look out. Mark my words, he'll be next on her list.'

Peggy's stomach lurched in horror. Was this what people really thought about her? That not only did she know Jim was married but that she made a habit out of carrying on with men that were wed?

'Give over, Pat,' May chuckled.

'I'm serious,' Pat cried. 'That Peggy Collins is a proper trollop, mind.'

'Well, I s'pose you'd know, wouldn't you—' May began.

'However do you mean?'

'Only that you know her, don't you, that's what I'm saying.'

'Oh right,' Pat replied, mollified. 'Well, I know of her, let's put it that way, May. I mean, my family don't mix with girls like that.'

'Course not,' May agreed.

Fury coursed through Peggy's veins. She and Pat Grimes no more knew each other than either of them knew the pope.

Pat sniffed loudly before she spoke. 'But what I will say is this variety show that Carmichael thinks will entertain the troops will be nothing short of a shambles 'cos of Peggy Collins. She should be ashamed of herself.'

May sighed. 'You're not wrong there, Pat. It's the lieutenant colonel I feel sorry for, after all it was his idea.'

'Well, he's only got hisself to blame. If he will go giving cheap little mares like her ideas above their station, then he's going to get what's due,' Pat said smugly.

'True,' May agreed. 'This would never have happened if he'd given you that driving job.'

'My point exactly. Still, this'll learn him. Now, come on, we'll be getting what's due if we don't get this Lister truck out on the road for delivery.'

Peggy heard the girls open the doors to the truck near the entrance and fire the engine. As they drove away, she stood up, and found her legs were trembling with shock. More than anything she wanted to put those girls straight, but what was the point? She would only be adding further fuel to their gossip. It was best not to give them the satisfaction.

'Are you all right?' sang a voice from the office behind her.

Whirling around, Peggy smiled weakly as she came face to face with Sal, arms folded, concern etched across her face.

'I'm fine. Bit shaken, I s'pose.'

Sal nodded. 'I only caught the tail end of what they were sayin', otherwise I'd have given them what for.'

'Thanks, Sal.' Peggy smiled gratefully. 'But you don't have to keep fighting my battles for me.'

'I know,' Sal replied. 'But those girls have no business talkin' about you like that. Neither Pat Grimes or May Horobin are any better than they should be. Pat's been thievin' out of the NAAFI, which is why she never got the drivin' job, and May's no stranger to courtin' a different fella every week.'

Peggy arched an eyebrow. 'But I don't imagine any of them are married.'

'I wouldn't like to say.' Sal shrugged. 'What I will say is, those girls will soon get bored and move on the moment someone more interestin' comes along to gossip about, nobody cares what they think.'

'But in the meantime, girls are still dropping out of the variety show,' Peggy sighed.

Sal smiled comfortingly. 'They'll get over it, I promise you, pet.'

'And if they don't?'

'Then those girls will be the ones missin' out because there'll be no show!' Sal insisted. Walking towards Peggy, she draped an arm around her shoulders and squeezed her tightly. 'Forget them, and focus on your job. That's what matters now.'

* 

Peggy did her best to follow Sal's advice and spent her days throwing herself into her driving duties, offering to take on other spark girls' jobs when Carmichael didn't need her. In the evenings, Peggy concentrated on Annie's reading and writing lessons, which were fast turning out to be the only highlight of some very trying days. There were still times when Annie became frustrated, but Peggy could see progress, and amazingly so could Annie.

It was only at night, as Peggy lay silently in bed, waiting for sleep to find her, that she allowed herself to think about Jim, and the situation she now found herself in. Despite Sal's words of comfort, the girls of Swansea barracks had proved unforgiving. And as gossip continued to spread and the rumours worsened, Peggy found more and more girls were pulling out of the show.

Tonight, just days after Peggy had overheard Pat and May run her down, she felt filled with despair as she lay in her narrow bed, eyes wide open, staring at the ceiling. Yet another girl had refused to take part that afternoon, and the full horror of a show with only a handful of acts was beginning to sink in.

She knew she ought to apologise or at least somehow atone for the sins she had committed, but the truth was that although Peggy felt guilty about what had happened, she realised no amount of apologising to her fellow volunteers would be enough. They were out for blood; Pat and May had shown her that. But Carmichael deserved better and she would do anything to save the show for him.

Then there was her mother. She still hadn't replied to Edie, unsure what to say that would cause the least amount of trouble. She wasn't going home, that much she knew, but how she could get that point across without a row she wasn't sure.

As she closed her eyes and tried to go to sleep, Jim's face came unbidden into her mind and it was all Peggy could do not to cry out with pain as she remembered the simple joy of just being with him. Eventually, she fell into a fitful sleep, and surprisingly woke a few hours later to find that she felt as bright as the spring sun outside, knowing just how she was going to save the show.

Feeling unburdened, she washed and dressed then hurried through the town towards the barracks, ready to take action before drill practice. Walking along the corridor towards Carmichael's office, she smiled at his secretary who fixed her with nothing but a cold sneer.

Peggy said nothing and simply waited for the secretary to show her into her superior officer's quarters. Despite the fact she had been working for the lieutenant colonel for some time now, she still felt a thrill every time she entered his office. It was so grand and imposing, it made her feel a little overwhelmed, something that was only going to make her next task that more difficult.

'Collins, this is a nice surprise, at ease.' Carmichael beamed as Peggy entered his office and saluted him before his desk.

'Sir,' she replied, lowering her hand and regarding him carefully. 'I'm sorry to arrive unannounced.'

Carmichael waved her concerns away and gestured for her to take a seat in the wooden chair opposite his desk. 'Nonsense. Now what can I do for you?'

Peggy took a deep breath. 'Well, I've been doing some thinking, sir, and I think it's only right I withdraw from organising the variety show.'

'I see,' Carmichael replied, his brow furrowed with concern. 'And may I ask why?'

'It's a few of the girls, sir,' Peggy told him, biting her lip. 'They're not happy working with me and truth be told I can't say I blame them. I reckon it's best for everyone if Sal and Annie take over, they've been doing a smashing job.'

The superior officer regarded Peggy quietly before he spoke. 'I'm sorry, Collins, but the answer's no. I'm afraid I simply won't accept your resignation.'

'But, sir,' Peggy protested, 'there won't be a show at all if more girls drop out. I reckon it's a good ideal.'

'I am aware of that, but I disagree, Collins, and what I say goes.' He got up and walked around to the front of his desk, perching casually opposite Peggy. 'Look, I can't pretend I haven't heard about what happened,' he said, his tone gentle. 'But this will blow over and those girls that say they can't work with you ought to examine their own lives. How many of them can say they aren't guilty of making an honest mistake at some point or another?'

Peggy opened her mouth to argue her point once more, but Carmichael raised his hand to silence her. 'Believe me, Peggy, to give up organising this show would be giving into scurrilous gossip. And if anyone is the victim here, it's you. You weren't to know Hudson was married. If anyone should suffer it's him. Speaking honestly, it's a good job he's missing in action, because given my current disposition towards him I would argue hanging is too good for his crimes.'

Peggy blanched at the severity of her officer's words. 'I feel such a fool. You were right – I should've listened to you. Mother always says I'm too trusting.'

Carmichael smiled and leaned forwards conspiratorially. 'There's absolutely nothing wrong with being too trusting, Peggy, it's a nice quality to have. Just in future learn to spot who's worth trusting and who isn't.'

'You're right, sir, I'll do my best.'

'Good.' Carmichael smiled as he walked back around to his desk. 'Now, I don't want to hear any more nonsense about you leaving the show because of this. If people want to leave, let them, you've suffered enough because of what that cad has done, there's absolutely no need for you to wear a hair shirt over it.'

Peggy nodded, and as Carmichael dismissed her, she walked out of the office, feeling lighter than she had in days. Smiling once more at Carmichael's secretary she was surprised to find the lack of friendliness from the woman hardly bothered her, and she headed out into the spring sunshine.

With the gentle spring breeze whipping through her hair, Peggy breathed the salty sea air deep within her lungs and turned her attentions to the variety show. Time was running out fast and with acts dropping out left, right and centre it was vital they made sure what remained was a success. There were rehearsals to organise, costumes, programmes and posters, not to mention seating. Thankfully, Sal had offered to play the piano for the night and so they would at least have music, and Peggy would see a friendly face on stage.

Although Peggy had had every intention of handing over the reins of the show to someone else, she was secretly pleased Carmichael had turned her resignation down. She had believed in the show, as much as she believed in the Army, and with the truth about Jim now out she was glad of a chance to redeem herself.

Ignoring the pointed stares of some of the recruits, Peggy walked determinedly towards the garage. Carmichael had made her realise she had done nothing wrong, and she would hold her head high.

Catching sight of Sal at the doorway, she waved and smiled at the redhead, who returned her grin.

'Peggy,' Sal called with a wink, 'just the girl. I've got a job wants doin'. Carmichael need you today?'

Peggy shook her head, and allowed herself to be steered towards another volunteer who Peggy knew to be Maggie Archer. Smiling politely, she turned to Sal and waited for her to explain.

'Two girls are off in the sanatorium with a flu bug or somethin'. Maggie here was due to take a delivery up to Wrexham with one of them, do you mind fillin' in?'

'Course not, bab,' Peggy said, returning Sal's smile. 'You ready to go now, Maggie?'

The volunteer, who was not much older than Peggy herself, tugged her khaki cap into place over her thick black hair, and sneered at Peggy before turning to Sal.

'You're all right, Mrs Perkins,' she said coldly. 'I can manage this one on me own.'

Sal drew herself up to her full height. 'It's Sub-Leader Perkins to you, flower, and I've just given you an order to make a delivery with Volunteer Collins, is that understood?'

'I'm not spending the day with this tart,' Maggie hissed angrily. 'My mammy would never forgive me.'

'And I'll never forgive you if you don't.' Sal glowered.

Mouth set in a mutinous grimace, Maggie glared at Peggy before speaking.

'With respect, Sub-Leader Perkins,' she said in her lilting Belfast brogue. 'I'm choosy about the company I keep.'

'Well, you're in luck,' Sal fired back. 'Peggy's usually very choosy about the company she keeps, yet for today she's kindly chosen to overlook the feelin's she normally keeps in reserve for girls like you and help out instead. Isn't it kind of her to think about the fact there's a war on rather than the fact she probably can't stand you?'

Suddenly Peggy felt very tired. She was tired of having to apologise for something that wasn't her fault, tired of people talking about her, and tired of her fellow recruits judging her when there was clearly something far more important happening in the world than her love life.

Glancing at Sal, Peggy felt a surge of affection for the redhead and opened her mouth to speak.

'Sub-Leader Perkins is right,' Peggy said mischievously. 'Being a tart with a heart, I usually prefer the company of married men, but today I'll have to make do with you. Come on, Maggie, sooner we get there, sooner I can start looking for another fella what's taken to get me claws into.'

With that she walked past Sal, who rocked with laughter, and opened the cab door of the Lister truck. Visibly shocked, Maggie clambered in wordlessly beside her. Firing the starter engine, Peggy drove out on to the open road, and glanced at her companion. Maggie's eyes were facing firmly forward. Changing gear, Peggy sighed, it was clearly going to be a long day.

# Chapter Fifteen

Sadly for Peggy, it wasn't just the day with Maggie that was long; it was the rest of the week. Everywhere she went her fellow volunteers gave her the cold shoulder, or gossiped behind her back. By the time the weekend arrived, Peggy was sure she could count on one hand the girls who were still talking to her.

She knew she ought to have been upset, and perhaps a few days ago she might have been. But as far as Peggy was concerned, as long as her boss and friends thought well of her, then there was no reason to feel anything at all. She had a job to do, and nobody was going to prevent her from doing it, least of all a bunch of gossipmongers.

Swinging her legs out of bed, she tiptoed across the room towards the window. Opening the blackout blind, Peggy smiled as she was greeted by a sunny Wednesday morning and peered out across the length of Swansea Bay.

'It's too bright,' came a muffled voice.

Peggy chuckled as she threw back the covers from Annie's bed and on to the floor.

'Oi!' Annie groaned, sitting bolt upright. 'I've got a day off today, I fancy a lie-in.'

'Lie-in? On a day like today?' Peggy smiled, opening the window and breathing in the sea air. 'You want locking up saying things like that. It's beautiful out there.'

Annie threw her a mutinous look and gathered the blankets

back over her. 'Why are yer in such a good mood anyway? You've been in the doldrums for ages now.'

Peggy smiled, filling the little bowl with water from the pitcher and washing her face. 'I can't feel sorry for myself forever. The show's in three days and we've got rehearsals this morning.'

'Well, that'll take all of five minutes, given hardly anybody's in the show any more,' Annie grumbled.

'And we've no chance of pulling off anything decent if that's your attitude,' Peggy argued.

Drying her face, she threw the covers back again. 'Come on, I'm leaving in ten minutes to set up the mess for rehearsal and you're coming with me.'

'I don't feel like it,' Annie replied mutinously, pulling the covers over her head.

Peggy raised an eyebrow. This wasn't like Annie, she had been more than happy to help muck in with the show recently.

'What's the matter?' she tried, perching on the edge of the hard bed. 'You not feeling well?'

'I'm not sick,' came the muffled voice. 'I'm fed up.'

'What with?' Peggy asked.

'Look on my bedside table,' Annie replied sullenly.

Casting her eyes across to the table, she saw immediately why Annie was so upset. Propped up against the little oil lamp was another envelope with Annie's name in thick black letters.

'Read it to me,' Annie said, as she heard Peggy rip the letter open forcefully.

'I doubt it's anything worth reading, bab,' Peggy replied angrily.

'Probably not,' Annie said, 'but I'd like to know what I'm up against.'

With a sigh, Peggy began to read:

*Dear Annie,*
*You still haven't taken my advice, but then I'd expect no*

*less off a thicko. We're watching you, we know you haven't got what it takes. You might want to ask for a transfer to the dud division, where you belong.*

*Your friend*

Once Peggy had finished, she felt a flush of rage. Who was this coward, she thought, shoving the letter back into the envelope, and pulling the covers from Annie's head.

'You all right, bab?' she asked gently.

Annie nodded as she sat upright, though the redness to her cheeks suggested otherwise. 'Fine. Stuff 'em, what do they know?'

'Nothing, lover, but I reckon the time has come to do something. What d'you think about telling Carmichael?' Peggy suggested in a gentle tone.

'No!' Annie blurted. 'I don't want anyone knowing that doesn't have too. We must be able to sort this out ourselves.'

Peggy let out a long sigh as she regarded Annie warily. 'I'm not sure, love. I keep going over and over it, and I've no idea who would do this. I mean there are a few cows dotted about the barracks, but I can't think of anybody that'd do anything as rotten as write a poison pen letter.'

'Me neither,' Annie admitted.

'Who gave the letter to you?' Peggy asked turning the envelope over in her hands looking for clues.

'Sal. She said she picked it up in the mail when she got her things.' Annie sighed.

Silence descended as the same thought flitted through the girls' minds. Sal had given Annie both of the letters so far. Was it possible she was involved in this somehow?

'I don't reckon Sal would know anything about this, bab,' Peggy said, breaking the stillness. 'She's our friend, it's not in her nature. She'd tell you what she thought rather than write something down.'

'D'you think?' Annie asked doubtfully. 'Before Judith died she was always giving me stick about summat.'

Peggy raised an eyebrow. 'Usually because you gave her something to give you stick about. Look it's not Sal, but p'raps we can ask her what she knows. She might have seen someone put the letter in our mailbox or something like that.'

'All right,' Annie agreed, yawning dramatically as she got out of bed. 'Why don't you go on up to work, I'll see you there. I want to finish that writing exercise you gave me last night.'

*

When Peggy arrived at the mess later that morning to stage rehearsals, her positive attitude had disappeared and she had worked herself up into a full state of anxiety. What if nobody turned up at all? What if everyone else had decided they no longer wanted any part of the show? It would be down to Annie, Sal and Peggy to lay on the entertainment and Peggy was sure her tuneless wailings wouldn't go down well.

Thankfully, Sal had already got started. Not only had she arranged the stage again in the corner by the noticeboard, but she'd started to line up a couple of rows of chairs and had even made an urn of tea.

'Blimey, you done this all yourself?' Peggy asked admiringly.

Sal chuckled as she heaved the final chair into place. 'I'll get my just rewards in heaven, don't you worry, pet.'

'What shall I do?' Annie asked, loitering by the door.

'Tune the piano?' Peggy suggested as Sal shook her head.

'Already done. We're ready to go, why don't you two have a cuppa and go through your notes. I want to have a look at the sheet music anyway.'

Peggy nodded and made her way over to the mess itself. Although lunch was a good couple of hours away, the tell-tale scent of Woolton Pie wafted through the room and her stomach rumbled appreciatively.

'Annie, if you've got your writing books with you we can go through what you did this morning.' Peggy pulled out a chair at a table near the window.

Annie looked around the mess cautiously. A handful of recruits were drinking tea, but otherwise they had the place to themselves.

'Come on, nobody's going to see, I promise,' Peggy reassured her.

'All right,' Annie replied reluctantly, reaching into her bag for her book.

'Now, where were we?' Peggy muttered to herself as she flicked through Annie's pad. 'Ah yes, we were going to get you to write some simple three-letter words without any books.'

Annie's eyebrows shot up. 'I don't think I can, Peg.'

Sliding the notepad back across the wooden table to Annie, she noticed a look of fear cross the younger girl's face.

'You won't know until you at least try, babber.' Peggy smiled at her. 'Just do what you can, it don't matter about nothing else.'

Peggy left her to it and walked back to the staging area to get them both a cup of tea. Pouring a fresh cup for Sal, who was looking through the sheets of music, she walked towards her and rested the cup on top of the battered wooden piano.

'You all right?'

At the sound of Peggy's voice, Sal jumped. 'Oh Christ, pet! I didn't see you there, I was away with the fairies.'

'Yes, you looked like you were anywhere but here,' Peggy said kindly.

Sal smiled, and folded her hands into her lap. 'I'm sorry, I didn't sleep too well last night.'

'You were on guard duty, weren't you?' Peggy said, puzzled,

'That's why I didn't sleep well.' Sal yawned as if to demonstrate the point. 'We've more girls out sick in the sanatorium so we were a few down on the rota and even less keeping watch at the gates. Course all of that meant muggins here had to spend three hours patrollin' the barracks on her own instead of two.'

'No wonder you're tired, love,' Peggy replied. 'Walking up and down those cold paths is miserable enough for anyone, never mind when you have to spend an extra hour on your feet.'

'It wasn't too bad,' Sal sighed. 'At least there was plenty of tea in, and there was no raid so we were quiet.'

'Well I hope it's not like that tonight,' Peggy said in alarm. 'It's my turn for guard duty and after these rehearsals are finished I've got to drive over to Cardiff with Carmichael. I'll be knackered if I've got to spend three hours parading up and down.'

Sal laughed. 'You'll be all right, pet. I'm just a tired old woman, that's my trouble.'

'Give over,' Peggy laughed, nudging Sal gently in the ribs. 'You're not old.'

'I'm twice the age of Annie and a few more years on top,' Sal told her, as she gulped her tea down.

Glancing across at the younger girl beavering away at her books, Peggy turned back to Sal. Was it possible she knew anything about the letters?

'Sal,' Peggy asked hesitantly. 'You know you've given Annie a couple of handwritten notes lately, d'you remember where you got them?'

'Notes?' Sal peered at Peggy quizzically.

'Yes, you picked up some of her post last week. D'you recall where you found them?' Peggy said cautiously.

Frowning, Sal thought hard. 'I think I just picked them up with me own, pet?'

'You sure? Nobody gave you anything to give to Annie, did they?'

'What are you on about?' Sal exclaimed, shaking her head in disbelief. 'I've just said I picked them up with me own stuff to give to her, didn't I? Now, look, a couple of our turns have arrived.'

As Sal turned away to welcome the new arrivals, Peggy had a sneaking suspicion something wasn't right.

*

The rest of the day passed with next to no excitement, much to Peggy's relief. The rehearsals were a dream with every act knowing their lines and hitting their mark. As for the drive to Cardiff, the sun continued to shine for the rest of the afternoon, so Peggy enjoyed the warmth of the spring and knitted Edie a new scarf for next winter while Carmichael endured yet another meeting.

By the time she returned to the barracks to start guard duty, Peggy felt refreshed. Knocking on the door to the security room she was delighted to find that her superior officer for the evening was Sergeant Hooper. He was a kindly, older gentleman with greying hair who had seen and done everything in the Army. He always had a twinkle in his sparkling grey eyes and believed kindness was more likely to get the best out of a volunteer than a talking-to. As a result, he was one of the more popular sergeants, and Peggy always looked forward to a more relaxed evening when he was in charge.

'Evening, Collins,' Sergeant Hooper greeted her, smiling warmly. 'We've still got several girls out sick tonight, so you'll be on your own for a bit longer than usual. Still, we're not expecting any trouble, so you should be in for an easy time of it.'

'That's not what Sub-Leader Perkins told me.' Peggy chuckled as she did up the buttons of her great coat.

'Ah well, you know Sal, she tells it how it is.' Sergeant Hooper smiled again. 'Tell you what, you've been hard at it all day, I'll take first shift so you can have some supper and relax, then you can come and relieve me.'

'Thank you, sir,' Peggy said gratefully.

Making her way back to the mess for a tomato sandwich, she ate in silence as her thoughts turned to the poison pen letters. She had been going over and over it all day in her mind, and was still no closer to working out who the culprit could be. There was also something about Sal's response to the notes that troubled her. The older woman hadn't asked why Peggy was interested and had seemed keen to change the subject. Peggy didn't like to think her friend could be involved, but was it possible she knew more than she was letting on?

Peggy took her final mouthful and got up to clear her eating irons. None of this made any sense to her and she was unlikely to solve it tonight. As she walked across the quad, she stopped suddenly, convinced she heard the tell-tale whine of a German plane. Rooted to the spot, she glanced up at the star-filled sky, looking for signs of the Hun. There was nothing. Warily she walked back to the guardroom to give her kit one last check. Although volunteers weren't allowed to carry a weapon, they didn't patrol the area completely unarmed. Instead of a gun, the girls were given a pickaxe handle and a radio transmitter, which they carried in their pockets to exchange messages with their duty officer. These two items were often the volunteers' only defence against the enemy as they patrolled up and down in the dark and Peggy always liked to make sure they were in full working order before she started her shift.

Suddenly the little radio crackled into life. 'Collins, are you receiving me? Over.'

'Loud and clear, sir. Over,' Peggy replied.

'Excellent. All quiet out here but there are reports of fires over to the north of the town. Prepare for possible raid. Over.'

'Understood, sir. Over.'

Peggy clicked the radio off, sank back on to the hard, wooden chair and rubbed her face with her hands. The burst of energy she had enjoyed a short while ago had gone, and now Peggy was exhausted. She hoped the Hun would give her an easy night, especially when they were so short-staffed.

Still, it could have been worse, she thought as she checked her watch and saw it was almost time for Sergeant Hooper to return. She could have had to spend the night working for Sergeant Grayling and he had wasted no time bandying the word tart about where Peggy was concerned, she was not in the mood to deal with that as well as everything else.

Wearily she stuck her hands into her greatcoat and reached for her pickaxe handle just as Sergeant Hooper walked through the door.

'Everything all right here?' he asked.

Peggy nodded. 'Yes, sir. No problems at all.'

'Good,' Hooper replied, removing his coat. 'It looks as though the fires from earlier aren't attracting the Luftwaffe this way so you should be all quiet.'

'Very good, sir.' Peggy saluted him and walked out of the door.

Outside, the scent of smoke invaded Peggy's nostrils. Scanning the horizon, she saw that the flames continued to burn to the north of the city and beyond. She shuddered at the thought of the poor souls suffering once more at the hands of the Jerries.

Peggy's thoughts turned to her mother. She wondered how she was coping without the Michaels. She knew they had been a lifeline to her, and no doubt had they still been living with Edie she wouldn't have insisted Peggy leave the Army. Guilt filled her as she rounded the hill and walked towards the back of the motor garage. She still hadn't written to her mother to ask her to reconsider. A small part of her hoped that if she ignored the problem it would go away.

Sending a flurry of stones flying along the path, Peggy wondered if Edie would have the audacity to write to Lieutenant Colonel Carmichael. Would she demand that he send her home? Could she even do that?

Peggy gulped. She knew her mother would definitely have the nerve to do something like that. For the umpteenth time in her life she wished she had more self-belief. If she was more confident, hadn't led such a sheltered life and had experienced more of the things she knew lots of other spark girls had, then no doubt she would have told Edie she wasn't leaving the Army, she would have noticed Jim was a married man and she would probably have asked Sal outright if she had anything to do with the letters.

As she sent another flurry of stones into the air, a sudden movement in the bushes at the back of the garage caught her eye. Nervously she padded towards the greenery, listening for any more signs of activity. Just a few seconds later she heard the rustling sound again.

'Anyone there?' she called in a voice she hoped sounded braver than she felt.

Silence

'Come on, show yourself,' she called shakily.

But apart from the noise of the wind gathering speed in the trees around her, there wasn't a sound to be heard. After a moment, Peggy chuckled at her stupidity. Of course there was nobody there. This place was like a fortress. Nobody came in or out without the guards at the front knowing about it. Most likely it was probably a rat or a squirrel that caused the movement. She should stop being so paranoid, she thought as she continued her walk down to the garage to check all was as it should be.

Stifling a yawn, she rolled her shoulders backwards and forwards. She was so stiff and tired, it was no wonder she was seeing things that weren't there. What with the show, driving duties and not to mention her heartache and anger over Jim, it was a wonder she was upright, let alone at work. Peggy reached for the khaki torch she always kept in the pocket of her great-coat along with a ball of string she hung on to for emergencies and checked the time with the heavy light. She had been on duty for an hour. In two hours, she would be back in the guards' office with a steaming cup of tea, she thought brightly.

Through the gleaming white torchlight, she suddenly saw the shape of what looked like a foot peeping out from underneath the thick foliage. Peggy craned her neck to get a closer look and saw it was a boot, a man's Army boot, although she didn't recognise it as a British issue one.

Her blood ran cold. Was there an intruder in the grounds? Hands shaking as she tried to get a better look, the torch slipped from her grasp, landing with a thud on the muddy ground.

Plunged into blackness, Peggy heard more rustling coming from the bushes. This time she wasn't taking any chances. Swallowing her fear, she reached in the pocket of her greatcoat for the radio she carried with her and with one eye on the possible intruder she backed quickly away.

'Sergeant Hooper. Can you hear me? Over,' she hissed across the airwaves.

It felt like an eternity before the little transmitter crackled into life. 'Loud and clear, Collins. Go ahead. Over.'

'Request assistance, sir. Possible intruder. Over.'

'Copy,' Hooper replied immediately. 'What's your location?'

As Peggy pressed the button on the side of the radio to reply, a rapid noise from the bushes distracted her. Frozen to the spot, Peggy heard the heavy tread of footsteps hastening towards her. Her heartbeat roared in her ears as she willed her legs to move, to run, to do anything to get away, but she couldn't move. The footsteps stopped just in front of her.

'*Sprichst du Deutsch*?' he asked in a low voice.

A scream caught in Peggy's throat. She was face to face with a German. Although it was too dark to make out his features, she was aware of the monster standing so close to her she could feel the heat of his breath against her cold skin. Opening her mouth to speak, she willed herself to find the words to ask him what he wanted when Sergeant Hooper's voice sputtered over the radio.

'Collins. Where are you Collins? Do you read me? Over.'

Peggy felt menace radiate from the man standing just inches away.

'Turn it off,' he ordered in near perfect English.

Peggy gulped and tried to stay calm. Nobody had told her

what to do if she came face to face with the enemy. She felt a hollow laugh rise within her as she thought back to all the lectures she had received on marching, pay parade and the importance of personal hygiene within the camp. Where was the lecture on how to deal with an enemy soldier?

'Just a minute,' she said, her voice rising an octave.

Reaching into her pocket, she switched off the radio with trembling fingers and stalled for time. Searching her memory for anything that might be useful, Peggy found herself flailing. She thought back to the stallholder in the undercover market who disapproved of anyone in the Army, and how she had been lost for words. How it had been Jim who had come to her rescue. She wanted to cry out in pain at the memory; she was all alone. If Peggy wanted rescuing she was going to have to do it herself.

A debilitating wave of fear crashed over her as she realised she could hear nothing but the sound of the German breathing heavily into the night air. She was frozen to the spot and she knew there was nothing to stop this man overpowering and killing her in a heartbeat if he wanted to. She had read numerous things in the papers about how the Jerries could kill a man with one single movement. Although she couldn't make out his features, she could sense he was a good foot taller than her. It wouldn't take much to see her off, she realised, and she wasn't even sure she would be able to put up much of a fight.

'Give me the radio,' he said, his accented voice calm yet chilling. 'Now!'

'And if I don't?' Peggy replied with a bravery she certainly did not feel.

The German didn't bother to reply, instead he took a step towards her, his heavy tread crunching quickly across the undergrowth. Realising he was on the attack, Peggy felt a cold trickle of terror creep up her spine. This was it, this was her moment to choose whether she lived or died.

Instinctively, Peggy galvanised her body into action. Turning back towards headquarters she sprinted up the bank towards what she hoped was safety, grateful to the PT sessions that had kept her so fit. The German chased after her, his footfall uneven and heavy on the muddy path.

As Peggy continued to pound up the hill, the pickaxe handle that was her only weapon fell to the ground. She could hear the German getting closer all the time. Fear prickled at her scalp and her heart was pounding so quickly she thought it might explode, but she wasn't giving up. Using the adrenaline coursing through her body like a drug, she propelled her body forwards and focused on reaching safety. The German was still just behind her, his breathing as heavy and laboured as her own, when she reached a fork in the path. She could have kicked herself for dropping the pickaxe handle and hoped that the German hadn't picked it up himself. Then it struck her that she had one weapon in her arsenal the German did not. Her regular patrols and marches around these barracks meant she knew every inch of them in daylight as well as darkness. It was time to press home her advantage.

Quickly, she made a sharp right, turning away from the open path and racing through the small woods at the centre of the barracks. Dodging tree stumps and potholes, she ran along the uneven trails. Sanctuary was almost within her grasp and she could no longer hear the sound of the German's breathing. Elation surged through her as she realised she must have outwitted him in the greenery. She carried on, focusing on her own course, every step she took bringing her closer to the outline of her headquarters, now visible thanks to the starlit sky.

The sense of relief at being out of danger almost took Peggy's breath away. And as she neared the edge of the trees, she used the time to slow her pace and catch her breath.

It was the loud thwacking sound that caught her attention first. Then the agony of being hit around the back of the legs moved swiftly through her body. Gasping in pain, Peggy crumpled to the muddy floor, just as she was bathed in light.

Squinting at the sudden brightness, Peggy saw the German had found the torch she had dropped when she first discovered him and had used it to strike her. Now, as the soldier shone it upwards, Peggy shuddered. His face was filled with loathing and contempt and his mouth twisted into a cruel smile. She squealed in horror as she saw her precious pickaxe handle lying at his feet. But there was no time to think about that as the German swiftly reached into his waistband and pulled out a pistol and pointed it at her forehead.

Peggy's blood ran cold.

'What d'you want?' she gasped.

'I want you to stop and talk to me,' he replied, his tone mocking.

Peggy looked at the man properly for the first time in the torchlight. She saw that he was young, probably the same age as her. Tall, blond, with cuts all over his face, he appeared to have some sort of head wound, as blood was trickling down his right cheek. He was dressed in what she recognised as the uniform of the Luftwaffe and she guessed he was a German pilot or gunner forced to bail out of his aircraft.

'Where's your plane?' she asked suddenly.

The German looked wrong-footed at her outburst.

'I am asking the questions, not you,' he snarled, bringing his face towards hers.

Peggy flinched and the airmen laughed bitterly. Despair pulsed through her as the German picked up the pickaxe handle in one hand then hauled her roughly to her feet. Pushing her forwards, she gulped in shock as he wrapped his forearm around her middle while still clutching the handle. Then with his other arm, she felt him press the gun firmly into the small of her back.

'Now, I think we will go back to my hidey-hole and we will wait there while I think about what to do with you.'

Peggy looked down at his calloused hand, and found any trace of fear disappeared to be replaced by a white-hot anger.

All of a sudden, she felt very tired, and not just because it was the middle of the night. Peggy was tired of being pushed around by people who had no respect for her. How dare a married man break her heart. How dare half the girls in these very barracks treat her like something they had trodden in and her own mother demand she leave a job she loved. Now, this rotten Jerry had the cheek to come into her barracks, her home, and treat her like this. She had reached breaking point.

Fuelled by fury, Peggy didn't even think about what happened next. Lifting her right leg behind her, she brought it deftly down towards the German, kicking him in the knee.

He roared with anger and reached down to rub his leg. But Peggy wasn't finished and went to kick his other kneecap. This time, the German was too quick, and despite the pain he was in, he grabbed Peggy with his left arm and held her tight, the pickaxe handle still in his grasp. Quickly Peggy glanced at the gun and saw it was still firmly in his other hand, pointing away from her.

'You think you can get away from me?' he laughed cruelly. 'You are so funny. And yet you English say it is us Germans who have no sense of humour.'

Peggy's heart beat like a drum, but she refused to give up. In that moment she would rather die here in these woods, than be in the enemy's pocket even for five minutes. She looked down at the arm he had wrapped around her waist, and at his gun still pointing towards the trees. Before she could change her mind, she leaned forwards and bit his forearm, causing the soldier to drop the pickaxe, and fire the pistol into the woods.

The sound of gunshots rang through the forest, sounding as loud as if the Luftwaffe themselves were dropping bombs over their heads. Although Peggy had now been in plenty of raids, she had never come face to face with a gun.

'*Flittchen! Genug, du Flittchen*!,' he shrieked, dropping his arm for just long enough to allow Peggy to move.

Fiercely she kicked him again, this time in the shin, and he fell to the floor like a line of dominoes. Peggy wanted to make sure he stayed that way. With a strength she didn't know she possessed she kicked him again and again, each strike harder than the last, leaving him screaming in pain. Once she was sure the German was going nowhere, she calmly reached behind her for the pickaxe handle and torch and laid them at her feet.

'*Aufhören, du Hure*!' he howled, his face pressed into the mud.

But Peggy had no intention of stopping now. Spotting the gun lying next to him on the floor she picked it up then held her finger over the trigger, pointing it just inches away from his face.

The feel of the weapon in her inexperienced hands was overpowering, and Peggy realised she could kill this man in a second. One bullet would be all it took to avenge Judith's death, and even Jim's. To make the Jerries realise the ATS girls weren't taking this war lying down.

She looked down the sightline and saw the back of the man's head, his blond hair slick with blood and sweat. For a split second she pictured herself pulling the trigger. The enemy's brain would be all over the forest and the world a better place with one less Nazi.

'You'll never do it,' the German jeered, his face still pressed into the ground. 'You don't have the guts, or the courage we Germans have, you silly little English girl.'

Peggy said nothing as her index finger hovered over the trigger. She was so consumed with rage that she felt almost drunk on the knowledge that she could end this right here by killing this German. As her finger went to squeeze the trigger, reality hit her like a bucket of cold water; she couldn't kill a man. Not even if he was an enemy soldier. But just because she couldn't kill him didn't mean he was getting away. Holding the gun in one hand she used her other to rifle in her pocket for the ball of string. Giving the man yet another kick to each of his kneecaps she sat on the back of his legs.

'You're right, I can't kill you,' she growled, expertly wrapping the twine tightly around his wrists and ankles so he looked like a contortionist. 'But I can make sure you don't torture any more innocent people. I hope you like prison food.'

Once she was satisfied her prisoner couldn't escape, Peggy reached into her other pocket for the radio and turned it back on.

'Sergeant Hooper, d'you read me? Over,' she said calmly, the gun still pointed at the German's head.

Hooper's voice sounded immediately over the airwaves. 'Collins! We heard gunshots. We're looking for you. Are you all right? Where are you? Over.'

'I'm fine, sir. I'm in the woods by headquarters. I've got a prisoner at gunpoint. Over.'

There was a brief silence before Hooper spoke again. 'Copy that, Collins. Sit tight. Over and out.'

Peggy breathed a ragged sigh of relief. Looking down at the man underneath her, squirming to get away, she yanked hard on the string that bound his hands and legs. Nobody was taking advantage of Peggy Collins again, least of all a Jerry.

# Chapter Sixteen

There was a hero's welcome waiting for Peggy when she arrived at the barracks the following morning. Walking into the mess hall for a well-earned cup of tea after square-bashing, she was astounded to find herself on the receiving end of a standing ovation. The moment she stepped inside, everyone was up on their feet, clapping and banging on the wooden tables, singing a rousing chorus of 'For She's a Jolly Good Fellow'.

Peggy felt her cheeks flame with embarrassment as her fellow volunteers whistled, beamed and applauded. If truth be told, she hadn't expected anyone to know, let alone say anything about what she had done last night. As far as Peggy was concerned she had only done what anyone else would do in the same situation. Taking a seat in the corner opposite Annie, Peggy did her best to appear gracious as colleagues stopped at her table to congratulate her and pat her on the back. The spark girl hated being the centre of attention and it didn't help that she was still exhausted from the previous night's adventures.

Sergeant Hooper and a team of volunteers had found Peggy sat rigidly on the pilot's legs, still holding him at gunpoint. The officer had stared at Peggy incredulously for just a moment, before gingerly taking the pistol from her hands, then rousing everyone into action. Once the relevant authorities had been alerted by Hooper, he was taken away to a prisoner-of war-camp where Peggy hoped he would never see the light of day again.

The German pilot, who Peggy later found out was called Hans Bergenschloss, had indeed bailed out of his plane after launching a bomb on the town. Unfortunately for Hans, while his plane had landed somewhere near the river, he had landed in the ATS barracks, and hoped to make his escape. However, Bergenschloss hadn't expected to meet Peggy, or find himself held at gunpoint with his own weapon.

Afterwards, she had been given a brandy from Sergeant Hooper's hip flask, to help her with the shock. Then she had slept on a camp bed in the guardroom, for what was left of the night.

Waking a few hours later, Peggy was amazed she had given such disregard to her own life. And now, as she nursed a cuppa, all she wanted to do was give in to the exhaustion and shut her eyes. Yet she had promised Annie another writing lesson and despite the constant interruption, Peggy was determined to keep her word.

'Let's have a look at what you've done then?' she said, bleary-eyed.

Anxiously, Annie passed her book over to Peggy. 'I spent all night on it while yer were chasing Germans.'

Peering down to look at Annie's work, Peggy smiled. After everything she had endured, this was just the tonic she needed. Not only had Annie's handwriting improved, but the spelling was completely accurate. She had written out the alphabet and managed to write an entire sentence with the words cat, dog and baby.

'This is brilliant, Ann, just brilliant,' Peggy exclaimed in delight, running her fingers over the words.

Annie raised an eyebrow. 'Give over.'

'I'm serious, you've come on leaps and bounds lately, I can't get over it.' Peggy smiled. 'I knew you could do it, Ann, I really did.'

Just then there was the sound of a girl coughing behind her.

Whirling around she saw Pat Grimes and May Horobin standing either side of Annie. Pat appeared to be leaning over her friend, while May stood with her hands on her hips, her eyes dancing with merriment.

On the surface it looked innocent enough but Peggy knew better.

'Hello, ladies,' she said, a flinty edge to her voice.

'Oh hello, Peggy dear,' May said sweetly. 'We were just admiring Annie's handiwork here.'

'That's right,' Pat added. 'Not often you see a grown woman sitting down practising her letters.'

'And getting it wrong.' May chuckled, nudging Pat in the ribs as she pointed to Annie's notepad.

'Yes, it's almost like this is the first time Annie here has ever written the alphabet,' Pat said snidely.

'Which is impossible, isn't it, Pat?' May added sneeringly. 'Because it'd be impossible to join the women's Army if you couldn't read or write.'

As the women stared at Peggy, she was reminded of a pair of cobras ready to strike. Their lips were pursed and their little tongues were on show, ready to deliver another dollop of deadly poison. Saying nothing, Peggy glanced at her friend and saw Annie was trembling. Her arms hovered around her notepad protectively as she tried to hide the first few letters of the alphabet she had scrawled.

Suddenly, Peggy's blood was boiling. Abusing poor Annie, when all she was trying to do was educate herself was downright disgraceful. Never mind the fact that the only thing Annie should be feeling was a huge surge of pride that she had achieved so much. Peggy knew that if either May or Pat had to face the same hurdles as Annie, they'd founder. In that moment, all Peggy wanted to do was wipe the smile from these poisonous women's faces. Not caring who was listening, she slammed her fist down hard on the table, making them jump.

'If you must know, she's trying out some lettering for our show posters,' Peggy thundered. 'But what the hell it's got to do with you pair, I don't know.'

'Just taking an interest, Peggy.' Pat smiled sweetly. 'Why are you getting so upset? Something to hide?'

'Wouldn't surprise me,' May said in a low voice, her green eyes glinting menacingly. 'I bet she's got a whole cupboard full of secrets.'

'Along with all those married men she's been seeing,' Pat added spitefully.

'What did you just say to me?' Peggy gasped.

'You heard,' May jeered. 'Once a scrubber, always a scrubber.'

'And if anyone should know it's you, you little tart,' Peggy shot back quick as a flash.

Suddenly there was a collective hush in the mess as Peggy felt several pairs of eyes bore holes straight into her flesh. Usually she hated confrontation, but after recent events, she felt a courage she had never felt before sweep through her.

'You two want to be ashamed of yourselves,' Peggy continued, her tone hard and unyielding. 'All you ever do is run your mouths off, doing everybody down instead of concentrating on what you should be doing, which is war work.'

'Well said,' a voice boomed across the floor.

Peggy turned and saw Sal had joined her. 'That's quite enough out of the pair of you.'

'She started it,' Pat said childishly, pointing at Peggy.

'I very much doubt that,' Sal roared. 'I know you of old, Pat Grimes, we served together down in Cornwall, remember? You were a cow then and you're a cow now.'

Red with fury, Pat opened her mouth to protest but Sal raised a hand to silence her. 'I've heard enough out of all of you and if you don't want to be put on a CB notice for the next fortnight I suggest you bugger off! Do I make myself clear?'

'Yes, Sub-Leader Perkins,' the girls mumbled as they shuffled off out of the mess.

Once they were gone, Sal glanced at Peggy and Annie quizzically. 'Anything you two want to tell me?'

They both shook their heads. Sal's expression softened and she turned her gaze back to Peggy.

'Well, you're a dark horse all right, aren't you, pet? Holdin' enemy pilots at gunpoint, shoutin' the odds with a pair of witches. I didn't know you had it in you.'

'Neither did I!' Annie said, eyes wide with amazement.

Peggy chuckled at her friends' shocked faces. 'I didn't myself. I just did what needed doing at the time; I reckon anyone would have done the same.'

'I dunno about that. You know I've already had almost all the girls who dropped out of the show come up to me this mornin' and ask if they can be in it after all,' Sal said, pulling up a chair next to the girls.

Surprise flashed across Peggy's face. 'Really? Why?'

''Cos you're a hero, you daft mare,' Sal exclaimed.

'Still a tart though, aren't I?' Peggy said in a low voice, remembering Pat and May's taunts.

Sal shrugged. 'All of us sat around here know the truth, pet, and we both know you're worth a million of those stupid girls who were silly and daft enough to judge you for what happened.'

Annie nodded in agreement. 'Use them to your advantage, Peg. Put on the show of a lifetime and tell them to get stuffed afterwards.'

Peggy chuckled. Sal and Annie both had a habit of saying just the right thing at just the right moment. Sipping her tea, her eyes strayed to the floor. Spotting a familiar white envelope, she reached down and picked it up. Heart heavy, she turned it over and saw the one thing she didn't want to see – Annie's name written in thick, black capital letters.

'That what I think it is?' Annie asked, her face ashen.

Peggy nodded. 'D'you want me to open it?'

'Where did you find it?' Annie asked, avoiding the question.

'On the floor by your feet,' Peggy replied.

Annie ran her tongue over teeth. 'Coincidence, isn't it?'

'What is?' Peggy looked at her blankly.

'That these letters appear whenever you and Sal are about,' Annie said quietly.

'What are you saying, bab?' Peggy asked in a low voice.

'Yer know fine well what I'm saying,' Annie hissed. 'It's all a bit convenient, don't yer think, that every time the two of yer are together one of these spiteful notes appears. I can't believe I didn't see it before.'

'You can't think that,' Peggy began in protest before Sal cut her off.

'What the flamin' hell are you on about, Annie Shawcross? Have you been breathin' in too much motor spirit? Fumes have addled your brain?'

Annie gathered her notebook and pen together and angrily got to her feet. 'I know I'm right, and the two of yer should be ashamed of yourselves.'

Watching the younger girl storm out of the mess, Peggy groaned and sank her head on to the Formica table. After all they had been through together, how on earth could Annie think she was capable of such a thing? Lifting her head to glance at Sal, the unwelcome thought that the matriarch could be responsible flitted through Peggy's mind again. Although it was something she had considered in the past, Peggy had dismissed it as ridiculous. But was it?

'So are you goin' to tell us what that was all about then, or am I to guess?' Sal asked.

Peggy shrugged. If Sal was responsible she was going to have to tread carefully.

'Annie's been getting some poison pen letters,' she explained. 'Always the same envelope, same handwriting, and so far they've appeared whenever you or I have been around.'

'And you think I'm the one that's doin' it?' Sal remarked, getting straight to the point.

'I didn't say that, bab.' Peggy blushed.

'You didn't have to, flower, it was written all over your face!' Sal snorted.

'Look, I'm sorry, Sal, but now it's out in the open, I'll ask. D'you know anything about it?'

Sal shook her head. 'Do you really think I'd do somethin' like this?'

'No, if I'm honest, I don't.' Peggy sighed. 'But Annie's in bits about it and when I asked you if you knew who had given you the letters you couldn't wait to change the subject. I must admit I did wonder.'

'I didn't want to talk about it because there was nothin' to say and we had a show to organise, pet,' Sal exclaimed. 'Believe me, if there was somethin' I wanted to tell Annie, then I'd say it to her face, I'd not hide behind some anonymous note.'

'I know,' Peggy said. 'I'm sorry, Sal. I had to ask.'

'I understand, flower. But I swear on my Norman's head-stone it's not me,' Sal replied gravely. 'How many notes have there been now?'

'Three,' Peggy said sadly. 'All the same thick, black handwriting.'

Sal nodded. 'And are these notes blackmailin' Annie?'

'No.' Peggy shook her head. 'They're just spiteful, it seems to me. Whoever's doing it just wants to rattle her.'

'And what are the notes about?'

Peggy shuffled awkwardly in her seat. 'I shouldn't really say, Sal. It's not my secret, its Annie's.'

'Fair enough, pet.' Sal smiled. 'I respect you for not gossipin'.'

Peggy said nothing as Sal got to her feet and cleared away her tea things. 'Seems to me then it's a nasty little coward with nothin' better to do. If you want my advice, go over the notes again. Chances are you'll find a clue. Bullies get cocky and slip up in time.'

With that, Sal walked away leaving Peggy feeling wretched. In that moment, she hated herself for thinking badly of the woman who had offered her nothing but kindness. But running her fingers over the sealed envelope, it was possible Sal was right.

*

Sitting in Lieutenant Colonel Carmichael's office, drinking yet another cup of tea, Peggy reflected on the events of the night and morning as she leaned back into the mahogany leather chair. The spring sunshine streamed through the windows and Peggy shut her eyes, allowing herself to relax while Carmichael barked orders into his telephone. The warmth of the sun was working its way through her bones, and finally the chill that had set in last night began to disappear.

'Well then, Collins,' Carmichael said abruptly, causing Peggy's eyes to fly open. 'You've had quite an evening, I hear.'

'Sir,' Peggy said, stifling a yawn.

'How are you feeling?' Carmichael smiled.

Peggy paused for a moment and caught the kindness in her boss's eyes. 'Honestly?'

'Of course.'

'Tired, sir.'

Carmichael threw his head back and roared with laughter. 'That wasn't what I was expecting you to say, but I can quite see how you would feel like that. Jenkins,' he said, turning to the sergeant standing behind the desk. 'Get Collins another cup of tea, would you. And see if you can't find her a biscuit or two to keep her energy up.'

Jenkins swept out of the office and Carmichael turned back to Peggy. 'So now we're alone, how about you and I speak candidly? You must realise what a hero you are after last night?'

'I don't see it that way, sir,' Peggy said evenly.

He shook his head. 'Nevertheless, I want you to know I'm recommending you for a special commendation. Tackling a German soldier single-handedly as a woman and unarmed,

241

was both dangerous and incredibly brave. Between you and me, Collins, there are some men who wouldn't have had the courage to do what you did. It's only right and fair your extraordinary endeavours are recognised.'

Peggy bowed her head and thought for a moment. She was incredibly touched by her commanding officer's suggestion, but how could she tell him it simply wasn't a good idea? Although she was aware that what she had done was out of the ordinary, she knew that if there was any kind of medal for bravery then Edie would explode with fury. Not only would she accuse her daughter of showboating, but Peggy was painfully aware that this would prove her mother's point: that a life in the Army was dangerous. If Edie got wind of what her daughter had done then her Army career would be over in a heartbeat.

'You look hesitant, Collins.' Carmichael leaned forwards over his desk.

'Not hesitant, I'm just not sure I deserve an award, though of course I'm grateful to you for suggesting it.'

Carmichael narrowed his eyes. 'I'm not sure you're telling me the entire truth, Collins.'

'It's my mother, sir,' Peggy admitted. 'She reckons the Army's dangerous and wants me to leave. I'm afraid if she hears about this she'll pull me out.'

'I see,' Carmichael said thoughtfully. 'And is that what you want?'

Peggy's eyebrows shot up in alarm. 'No, sir. I loves my job.'

'Very good, Collins. You're a wonderful volunteer and personally I'm very glad to have you as my driver.'

'Thank you, sir,' Peggy replied meekly.

Carmichael turned away from her and looked out of the window towards the quad. With the sun beating down, it looked like a glistening sapphire jewel, and as Peggy followed his gaze she tried to read his mind. She hoped Carmichael wasn't angry. There was a war to fight, the last thing he needed was to worry about something as silly as this.

'Mothers are wonderful creatures, Collins, and a mother's love is something we should never take for granted,' he said, his gaze still fixed on the window.

'I don't, sir,' Peggy said quickly. 'My mother and I have always been close and I've always appreciated everything she's done for me.'

Carmichael turned his gaze from the bay and looked at her. 'But now it's time to make your own way in the world?'

Peggy smiled. 'Something like that, sir. I knows it's been difficult for Mother since my father died. Until war broke out, I always thought she and I would live and grow old together, run the shop. I never thought about any other kind of life until . . .'

Her voice trailed off and she looked at Carmichael. He was smiling benevolently. 'I do understand, Collins. My two sons and daughter are all serving and I worry about them every day.'

'I didn't know you had children, sir,' Peggy said in surprise.

'Oh yes, I've another life entirely away from the Army,' Carmichael chuckled. 'My wife Belinda has had to put up with a lot from me over the years. Now of course our two sons are in the Navy and my daughter's in the ATS like you.'

'I had no ideal, sir.'

'No reason you should have,' Carmichael replied. 'But I'm telling you this because I want you to know I can see every parent's point of view. When their child enlists, they are giving this country their greatest treasure.'

'What d'you think I should do, sir?' Peggy asked forlornly.

'Nothing, Collins. I'll write to your mother personally,' Carmichael said firmly.

Panic washed over her. Edie disliked outside interference. 'No, sir, I can't ask you to do that.'

'You didn't ask, I volunteered. The two are very different things. Not only that, but as a parent myself I have a feeling I will be able to offer your mother some words of comfort you may not be able to.'

Peggy looked at her officer in surprise. 'If you're sure, sir.'

'It's the least I can do after all you did for your country last night. Allow me to take this burden from your shoulders, Collins. You should concentrate on the show, which I understand is now bursting with acts.' Carmichael's eyes crinkled with merriment.

'You heard about that too then,' Peggy said sheepishly.

'It's the talk of the barracks,' he told her with a broad smile.

Peggy shrugged. 'I'm not sure what to say or even make of it all, sir, if we're still being honest.'

'We are,' Carmichael replied, resting his chin in his hands. 'So allow me to be honest with you. There are plenty of people in this world, never mind the Army, who want to be associated with glory. These people are not your friends, but that's not to say you shouldn't take advantage of their vanity and stupidity. Let them bask in your reflected glory, Collins, and afterwards you can tell them all to go to hell.'

Peggy couldn't help herself and burst out laughing. 'That's just what Annie said.'

'Then Annie Shawcross is a very wise volunteer, Collins,' Carmichael chuckled. 'If there's one thing I hope you'll take away from this, it's that you're far more capable than you think you are.'

'Yes, sir,' she said, standing up as he dismissed her.

'I'll see you at two for my meeting in Cardiff. But until then, Collins, get some sleep,' Carmichael ordered.

Walking across the quad back to the guardroom, Peggy intended to do just that. Sergeant Hooper had already told her that she was more than welcome to use the bed in there any time she liked and she intended to take him up on the offer.

Seeing Annie up ahead, the hem of her jacket crumpled from driving, Peggy called out to her.

'Wait up, I want to talk to you.'

Annie whipped around. 'So you can tell me more lies? Pretend to be me pal when you're secretly trying to do me down.'

Peggy looked at Annie sympathetically. 'D'you honestly think after all we've been through that it's me what's doing this?'

Annie sank on to the damp grass cross-legged and rubbed her eyes. 'I'm sorry, Peg. I know you've done so much to help me, Sal too. I was lashing out. I just don't know what to think any more.'

'Well, lucky for you, I do,' Peggy said gently, joining her on the ground. 'I spoke to Sal after you left and I'm fairly sure it's not her either. You know Sal, love, if she wanted to tell you something she's brassy enough to do it to your face.'

'So who else could it be?' Annie wailed.

Peggy shook her head and reached into her pocket for the letter. 'I don't know, but Sal did say she reckoned the coward would slip up soon enough. Do I have your permission to open this latest one and see if they've made a mistake?'

Wearily, Annie nodded. 'Go on then.'

Ripping the envelope open, Peggy pulled the letter out and began to read:

*Dear Annie,*
    *What's it gonna take for you to get the message, babber? We don't want your kind here. GO HOME before we make you!*

    *A friend*

'Is that it?' Annie asked in disgust. 'We're not going to get a lot from that, are we?'

Peggy smiled. 'Sorry, lover, but that's just where you're wrong. The culprit has just given themselves away entirely.'

'Are you sure?' Annie asked, her face a picture of confusion.

Peggy rested the letter on her lap and fixed her friend with a triumphant grin. 'I'm almost sure. Let's bide our time and have a bit of fun of our own until we can be a hundred per cent certain.'

Despite Peggy's desire to sleep for a week and a day, she knew the chance of any rest would have to wait until much later, as would Annie's letter. Although she was now fairly sure who had written the letters, Peggy didn't want to do anything until she had confirmed her suspicions. After she drove Carmichael back from his meeting in Cardiff, she stopped at the mailbox to check her post. There was just one in a familiar hand, and as she tore the contents open, she smiled with delight.

*28 March 1941*

*Dear Peggy,*

*It was lovely to receive your last letter, and you were right, I was shocked at what you told me. I'm stunned, Peg love. To think someone would behave like that is downright disgusting. You hear all sorts these days, this war seems to bring the worst out in folk, but being married to someone else and then proposing to you and all with a kiddie as well? Peg I truly dunno what to say. But what I will say is that I think you're being too hard on yourself. You fell in love, Peg. You fell in love with the wrong man, but you didn't know he was wrong at the time, you believed him and that's to your credit. Of course you still love him, sweetheart. You thought you were planning a life with this man, you didn't think he was telling you a pack of lies. Your mind might tell you that you should hate him for what he's done, but the heart, well that's a different story, love. You'll get over this, I promise you, but in the meantime don't punish yourself for feeling the way you do. You didn't commit the crime, he did, so don't make yourself pay, do you hear me?*

*Now, have you got any gossip for me? I heard from Di recently, she and my brother (it's still funny for me to write*

*those words, my brother) are still going strong. Mary's met
some fella as well by all accounts, in Ceylon of all places.
Still, she was never going to hang about with the likes of us
for long, was she?*

*As for me, well, I've got a lot to tell you, but I'm not
going to write it down here, Peg. Instead I'm going to save
it up, because, I'm coming to see you! Yes, that's right, I
heard this morning I've been billeted at your lodgings for
two nights on the 3 April and I can't wait to lay eyes on
you.*

*I'm sure you'll be busy, but I hope we can spend a little
bit of time together – it'll be just like old times. In the
meantime, take care of yourself, Peg, and I'll see you very
soon.*

*Yours fondly,*

*Kitty*

Peggy reread the note three times before she put it back in
the envelope and hugged it excitedly to her chest. She could
scarcely believe Kitty was coming to see her! And tomorrow of
all days, the night of the show. Peggy thought back to the last
time she had seen her old friend. It had to have been six months
at least since they had laid eyes on one another when she had
left Northampton for pastures new.

Kitty had given her and Mary a lift to the station to start
their new lives and Peggy remembered how upset she had been
as she had hugged Kitty goodbye.

Now Peggy felt even more motivated to ensure the show was
a success. Pushing the letter into her kitbag she hurried across
the quad towards the mess to get started. With a rehearsal to
organise and so many last-minute changes she would need her
wits about her. Walking inside, she could see she might have
underestimated the problem as a queue of recruits snaked out
of the door, all chattering excitedly to one another.

'What's going on here?' Peggy asked, pushing her way through the throng to reach Sal who was tuning her piano.

Sal looked up at her friend and chuckled. 'It's called hero worship. All those silly mares that said they didn't want anythin' to do with you, flower, have turned up wanting to be in the show.'

'But these are all the girls we cast originally,' Peggy said in astonishment.

'That's the power of being a hero rather than a tart, pet.' Sal grinned. 'Make the most of it.'

'But the show's tomorrow! We've one more dress rehearsal after today and then that's it! We'll never manage,' Peggy cried.

'Course you will. These girls know their routines inside and out, it's not like they've got lines to learn. Just put 'em on the stage and let 'em go.'

Peggy arched an eyebrow as Pat Grimes and May Horobin strode through the crowd and walked right up to her.

'Hello, Peg,' Pat simpered. 'Thought you might like a biscuit. You need to keep your strength up after all your hard work last night.'

Peggy looked in bemusement at the plate of garibaldis Pat was holding out towards her. 'I'm fine thanks, Pat.'

'I'll have it though, if it's going beggin'.' Sal all but snatched the plate from Pat's outstretched hand.

'What can I do for you both?' Peggy asked warily.

'Oh, nothing,' May gushed. 'We just wanted to congratulate you after last night. What a heroine you are.'

'What a heroine,' echoed Pat. 'Taking a German soldier down all by yourself. I don't know if I'd have dared, mind.'

'And holding him at gunpoint!' May breathed. 'I couldn't have done that.'

Pat shook her head knowingly. 'But then you're not the daredevil Peggy is, May.'

Peggy ignored the backhanded compliment and fixed what

she hoped was a cold stare on Pat and May. 'Was there something you wanted, ladies?'

There was a brief pause while the girls exchanged looks, then May piped up. 'Well, we were thinking we could help you out with the show. It's only a day away now and you must be exhausted after your recent antics, shall we say.'

From nowhere Peggy felt laughter rise within her, and more than anything she wanted to tell Pat and May just what she thought of them. Instead, catching Sal's eye, she gave her a wink.

'I'd love you girls to help me out. Anything for the troops.'

'Exactly.' May grinned delightedly. 'We can sing, dance, whatever you want just so long as we put on the best show this barracks has ever seen, that's all that matters.'

Peggy nodded, and pretended to think for a moment. 'I'm so glad you said that, because you see there's a very important role we just haven't found the right girls for yet, have we, Sal?'

'That's right, Peg,' Sal agreed, not having a clue what Peggy was about to say.

'Well, now you have,' Pat purred. 'What can we do?'

Eying the girls carefully, Peggy beamed. 'Well, what we really need is a team to clean and scrub the loos before and after the show, tidy up, sweep and clean the stage. D'you reckon you can manage that?'

'Oh, I'm sure they can manage that,' Sal put in, before they had the chance to protest. 'These two want to help the troops! They just said as much, right, girls? We'll see you at five o'clock sharp tomorrow, flowers. Don't worry, I'll show you exactly what needs doin'.'

'I don't reckon you'll need to do that, Sal,' Peggy smiled, standing up. 'These two are cleaning experts, after all they're not known as a pair of scrubbers around the barracks for no good reason.'

Without bothering to wait for a reply, Peggy swept past a speechless Pat and May and marched out into the corridor, with

Sal closely behind. The moment they were alone, they collapsed to the floor in a fit of giggles.

'The look on their faces. I can't believe you said that,' whooped Sal.

'I can't believe you let me,' Peggy chuckled. 'Still they had it coming.'

'They've had it comin' for a long while,' Sal said in agreement. 'Did you see the looks they got from everyone else? They'll be gettin' the cold shoulder for quite some time, make no mistake.'

'Pair of old cows.' Peggy was still laughing. 'It's no more than they deserve.'

Sal wiped the tears of laughter from her eyes and looked at her friend. 'I dunno what's got into you lately, Peggy Collins, but whatever it is, I have to say I approve.'

# Chapter Seventeen

The Saturday morning of the show, Peggy woke early to find the heavens had opened as she pulled back the blackout blinds. Outside, the sky was a thick blanket of dark grey cloud and the rain was sheeting down like stair rods.

Looking over at Annie's bed, she was surprised to see her friend had already left. Her greatcoat was missing from the small hat stand they kept in the corner, and her bed was already made. Shivering, Peggy washed her hands and face quickly then dressed in her uniform. Although Carmichael didn't need her to drive him anywhere today, she had an awful lot to do in order to get everything ready for the performance that night.

Spotting the other empty bed by the window that had been neatly made up, Peggy smiled with delight at Ida's thoughtfulness. Usually the sight of Judith's bed gave her the shivers, but tonight, knowing her old friend Kitty would be sleeping between the sheets, Peggy felt a sudden surge of joy. Buttoning up her last clean shirt, there was a sharp knock on the door.

'Lovely day for it.' Ida came in, beaming and holding a cup of tea. 'Hope you're taking your galoshes out with you? Still, I'm sure it's lucky somewhere.'

'Not sure about that, but thanks for the tea, Ida! It's almost like breakfast in bed.' Peggy smiled gratefully, taking the tea from her landlady's outstretched hand.

'I wouldn't go that far,' Ida chuckled. 'I just thought

that with the show, you might like a cuppa while you got ready.'

'You were right, thank you. And thank you for making up Kitty's bed too. She'll be ever so pleased she doesn't have to do it herself, mind.'

Ida rubbed her hands together to keep warm. 'It's no trouble. Especially not when you've got me and Harry front row seats to tonight's performance. You have got us tickets, haven't you, Peg love?'

'Of course,' Peggy soothed. 'Don't worry, you'll be next to Lieutenant Colonel Carmichael and his wife, you won't miss a thing.'

'I can't wait,' Ida squealed. 'Harry and I haven't had a night out since the last war ended.'

Peggy stifled a giggle. 'Well, I hope you won't be too disappointed. I'll be honest, Ida, putting it all together's been a bugger's muddle, I don't mind telling you.'

'You'll have done a sterling job, Peg.' Ida sniffed. 'Still, I bet it wasn't easy slotting in all those extra acts like that.'

Perching on the edge of her bed, Peggy cooled her tea by blowing gently across the top of her cup. 'I've done the best I can, that's all I can say.'

Thinking back to last night's dress rehearsal, Peggy knew that wasn't strictly true. The evening had been a complete and utter disaster from start to finish. The juggler repeatedly dropped everything she was juggling, the choir were out of tune, and the fire-eater couldn't light a match. When the talking parrot had flown out of the window, Peggy had decided to call time on the entire thing, assuring everyone that it would be all right on the night.

Now Peggy was pleased the madness would soon be over and she would be able to relax and forget the whole thing.

'I've seen the posters all over the town,' Ida said, interrupting Peggy's train of thought. 'Annie's done a wonderful job.'

'She has.' Peggy beamed. 'Her drawing's terrific.'

'And her writing's come on a treat too since you've been helping her, Peg,' Ida said quietly.

'You know about Annie?' Peggy gasped, regarding her land-lady over the top of her cup.

Ida gave a gentle nod of her head. 'Course I did, love. It was obvious, to me at least. It was why I let a lot of Annie's behaviour go, I knew she was struggling. But the change in her attitude and her reading and writing since you've been giving her lessons is nothing short of incredible. It'll be the making of her.'

'But how did you know?' Peggy asked her tone gentle.

Peggy had the feeling that Ida was holding something back. Although she had no wish to pry, if the older woman wanted to confide in someone, then Peggy could assure her it would go no further.

'Because I used to be like Annie,' Ida said simply. 'Until I met Harry I couldn't even write my own name. My mother and father showed no interest in me. Pair of drunks, they were. I was an inconvenience until I was five and could go to the shops for them on my own for more alcohol. They didn't care about my schooling, and of course as a youngster I was hardly going to make myself go.'

Peggy tried to keep her shock hidden. Ida was such a strong, capable woman, how she had survived such a terrible child-hood, let alone married, had children and run a business, was nothing short of a miracle in Peggy's book.

'Did anyone know?' she asked, trying to keep the pity out of her voice.

Ida snorted with derision. 'Well, my mother and father knew, and my aunts and uncles, but of course they lived up Aber-gavenny, I never saw hide nor hair of them. My grandmother tried to step in, said they ought to raise me right, but my father gave her such a slap, she never dared open her mouth again.'

'What did you do?' Peggy whispered.

'What could I do?' Ida replied matter-of-factly. 'I kept my

head down until I could get a job in a kitchen when I was thirteen. I was lucky. Wife of the chef took pity on me and gave me a roof over my head. That's how I met Harry who was working in the kitchen as a porter at the time.'

'But I thought you said Harry had always worked in this hotel,' Peggy said puzzled.

'He did, love. The job I got in the kitchens was in this very hotel, and the lady who took me in was none other than Harry's mum, God rest her.'

Peggy smiled in delight at the way everything had worked out. Sometimes there was no arguing with fate. 'Then what happened?'

'Then I showed Harry and all his family that although I came from nothing, I wasn't afraid to work hard,' Ida said forcefully. 'Course, all of Swansea knew about my parents, and nobody was sorry, least of all me, when they died a couple of years after I left home.'

'Oh, Ida.' Peggy's eyes flashed with sympathy.

'Oh Ida nothing,' the landlady snapped, her eyes full of fury. 'Best thing I ever did was leave them behind. With Harry's family's help I learned to read, write and make something of myself. I've never forgotten their kindness, and that's why I was touched when I saw what you were doing for Annie.'

'But we did our best to keep our lessons a secret,' Peggy said softly. 'Though someone's found out.'

'How d'you mean?' Ida asked.

Peggy frowned. 'Someone's found out about Annie's illiteracy. They've been sending her poison pen letters!'

'Never in this world!' Ida gasped. 'D'you have any idea who it is?'

Peggy's face broke into a broad smile. 'I got more than an ideal, I'm fairly sure I knows! I've been biding my time waiting for the culprit to slip up.'

'Good on you, love.' Ida nodded approvingly. 'You've got some sort of revenge lined up, is it?'

'Something like that,' Peggy chuckled.

Nodding again, Ida gave Peggy a small smile. 'I'm ever so proud of you, Peg. You really are a marvel, don't let anyone tell you no different, you hear me?'

Head bowed, Peggy could feel the flush of embarrassment creep up her neck. She wasn't used to so many compliments.

'Thanks, Ida,' she said, her voice muffled.

'Don't you start going all shy on me.' Ida chuckled. 'If you can't take praise off me, you'll be in for a high old time by the end of the show tonight.'

Peggy's head snapped up. 'How d'you mean?'

Ida's face fell. 'Oh, love, I'm sorry, I shouldn't have said anything.'

'What oughtn't you have said? Come on, Ida,' Peggy urged.

Ida paused as if trying to decide what to say, and it was all Peggy could do not to drag the information out of her.

'Lieutenant Colonel Carmichael's got a special presentation planned for you afterwards.' Ida sighed. 'It's a thank you for all your hard work organising the show, but mainly it's because he wants all those rotten devils who were so hard on you over that pilot to sit up and praise you for tackling that Jerry all by yourself.'

Sinking her head into her hands in despair, Peggy could scarcely believe what she was hearing. Carmichael knew she didn't like a fuss.

'Are you sure it's tonight?' she said eventually.

Ida gave a firm nod of her head. 'Quite sure. He asked me what I thought and I told him I thought it was a wonderful idea. And it is, love. You've done ever so much and have had a bad time lately. It's nice he wants to reward you like this.'

'But—' Peggy began, only for Ida to cut her off.

'That's enough of your silliness,' she said firmly, reaching across Peggy for the now empty teacup on her bedside table. 'I bet every single one of those girls would give their right arm for an award like the one you're getting tonight. So, even if you're embarrassed, be nice for Lieutenant Colonel Carmichael's sake.'

With that, Ida gave Peggy a warm smile and walked downstairs. Once she was sure her landlady had gone, Peggy sank back on to her bed and wished she could stay there all day.

*

It was the soft-topped Tilly truck appearing over the brow of the hill that caught Peggy's attention. There were no trucks around the barracks at the moment, and just a single one driving towards headquarters was always unusual. Training her eyes on the vehicle, Peggy realised with a start she could just about make out the driver. As the truck swung into the driveway towards the motor garage she dropped her spanner and raced up the hill.

'Kitty, Kitty,' she squealed in excitement.

The truck came to a halt and an attractive woman with twinkling eyes and matching smile all but threw herself out of the driver's door.

'It's so good to see yer,' Kitty cried, wrapping her arms around her old friend.

'And you,' Peggy said, breathing in the familiar scent of her friend before she pulled away. 'Let's have a look at you then.'

Standing back to admire each other, Peggy took in Kitty's appearance. She was delighted to see that apart from a new shade of lipstick, Kitty hadn't changed a bit. Tall, pretty with bobbed brown hair, Kitty was as gorgeous as ever.

'Yer look well, Peg.' Kitty smiled, breaking the silence.

'So d'you,' Peggy beamed. 'I can't believe you're here. It's so nice to see you, but what brings you this way?'

'I've got some papers to deliver and collect for my commanding officer, Major Thomas,' Kitty explained. 'But when they told me where I was being billeted for two nights, I couldn't believe my luck!'

'I couldn't neither.' Peggy linked arms with her friend. 'Cuppa?'

'Is the pope a Catholic?' Kitty chuckled.

The clouds gave way to sunshine as Peggy led Kitty around the corner to the NAAFI van and ordered two teas and an Eccles cake each.

'No expense spared for you, Kit,' she giggled, setting the cups and cakes down with a flourish.

'I wouldn't have expected anything less.' Kitty's eyes danced with merriment. 'So, come on, how are yer?'

Peggy shook her head. 'You first. I've been on tenterhooks since I heard you were coming.'

'All right, all right.' Kitty smiled. 'What do you want to know about? Di and Peter?'

Peggy burst out laughing. 'Fancy you calling Sergeant Hopson 'Peter'. You hated him before you found out you were related. I reckon Sergeant Hopson was the most polite thing you ever called him.'

Kitty arched an eyebrow. 'It was no more than he deserved and he knows it.'

'Still, he's made up for it now?' Peggy looked quizzical.

'He has.' Kitty nodded, taking a sip of tea. 'And he's treating Di like a queen with gifts galore. Ooh, speaking of pressies, I've got summat for yer.'

While Kitty rifled through her bag, Peggy felt a burst of excitement. She so rarely received treats that just the thought of a little something was gift enough. Eventually Kitty pulled out a small wooden box.

'Don't get too excited,' she warned.

'Dates!' Peggy cried in astonishment as she removed the lid. 'Wherever did you get these?'

'Arthur,' Kitty admitted. 'He's in Egypt serving at the moment. He does spoil me.'

Replacing the lid on the box, Peggy fought the urge to devour the entire lot there and then. Instead she looked back at her friend.

'Sounds like it's all going well with you two, then?'

Kitty nodded, as she took a bite of the Eccles cake. 'It's going very well.'

'That it?' Peggy chuckled. 'I've not seen you for six months and that's all I'm getting?'

Setting the plate down, Kitty cleared her throat nervously. 'Well, actually there is summat I need to tell yer.'

'Go on then,' Peggy coaxed.

Kitty took a deep breath. 'Well, there's no good me pussy-footing about. Thing is, me and Arthur, well, we got engaged when he was on leave last month. We're getting wed.'

Peggy didn't think she had ever been so happy for another person in her entire life. She wrapped her arms around Kitty, sending their cups of tea and shared bun flying.

'Oh, Kitty, I can't believe it,' Peggy squealed. 'It's wonderful news.'

'Ta, love,' Kitty said, her face buried in Peggy's shoulder. 'It was a surprise but a very happy one. It just feels right.'

Peggy pulled away from her friend and searched her eyes for any sign of worry. Kitty had joined the ATS after her fiancé, Joe, had been killed in the Navy, wanting to carry on his work, as well as heal her broken heart. She had successfully done both, and found love when she was least expecting it in the form of her best friend Elsie's brother.

However, Peggy knew Kitty had always felt uneasy about finding happiness again, and fretted she was hurting Joe's memory. She and Peggy had exchanged many a letter over the winter months on the very subject and Peggy had always been firm that Joe would want Kitty to find happiness.

Now, Peggy was grateful she could find no trace of un-happiness or worry on her friend's face. This was a time of joy, and she would encourage Kitty to revel in every precious second.

'So tell me everything,' Peggy gushed. 'How did it happen?'

'It was very romantic,' Kitty said, the memory of it all still so recent. 'He took me to the pictures to see *Bringing up Baby*. On the way out, I tripped over and went flying. Arthur caught me in his arms and said it would be his greatest honour and privilege if he could be there to catch all my trips and falls.'

Peggy smiled at the sweet and oh-so-simple romance of it. 'And what did you say?'

'Yes, of course!' Kitty laughed. 'I know a good thing when I see it.'

'So when are you getting married? Where will you live? Where's the ring?' Peggy demanded with excitement.

Kitty raised her hands. 'Slow down, love. We'll get wed after the war. We both want to wait until we're in peacetime and can enjoy ourselves properly without a flaming air raid sounding! We'll probably live with Arthur's mother in Coventry at first, and the ring is right here.'

Loosening the top button of her blouse, Kitty fished out a simple gold chain, with a gold and ruby ring hanging from it.

'It's beautiful,' Peggy gasped.

'Thank you,' Kitty replied softly. 'I know we're not really allowed jewellery but Major Thomas, who I drive for down in Southampton, well he's ever such a softie and said I could wear it around my neck.'

'It suits you,' Peggy whispered, as she watched the ruby glint in the afternoon sunshine.

Kitty delicately replaced the chain and straightened her shirt. 'Now, it's your turn. Come on, love, are yer coping?'

Peggy thought back over everything that had happened since January. Was she coping? Looking at her old friend, sitting before her, eyes shining with happiness, Peggy saw that life could deal you the very worst of hands, then the very best just when you were least expecting. She felt a sudden hope that life was about to get a lot better.

*

With just two hours to go before curtain-up, Peggy was a nervous wreck. She had barely touched the tongue sandwich Ida had prepared for her back at the hotel, and was now pacing up and down the mess room staring blankly at the stage Sal had set up.

In fact, Peggy thought turning around to look at the room properly, Sal appeared to have done everything. The scent of floor polish filled the air, neat rows of chairs stood in front of the stage, heavy blackout material hung from the eaves to form a makeshift theatre curtain, and there was even a little trolley to the left, which Peggy knew would be filled with tea and rock cakes during the interval.

Despite the fact everything had been done to ensure the evening was set for success, Peggy couldn't shake the nervous sense of foreboding that had been following her around all day. Sitting on one of the wooden chairs, she took a deep breath and tried to calm down. She knew she had done everything she could to ensure the evening went well, but juggling so many last-minute acts with so little time could only spell disaster.

Aware that her body was as tightly wound as an overworked clock, Peggy cast her mind back over the past few days. There had been so much disaster she couldn't help wondering if she should have done things differently. Should she have apologised straight away for her relationship with Jim, for example? Was that something that would have made people more forgiving?

Not that she had anything to apologise for, she reminded herself crossly, remembering Kitty's pearls of wisdom. As her friend had pointed out, she had no way of knowing Jim was married. Anxiously she thought back to how Jim had never introduced her to any of his RAF friends, whereas she had been so keen to immerse him into her life. Was that because they were all too busy enjoying a giggle behind her back? After all, Peggy had wasted no time introducing him to Annie, Judith and Sal. And, of course, Ida and Harry had worshipped the ground he walked on after his help in the raids. For the umpteenth time, she wondered just how she could have got it so wrong.

At the sound of a clatter at the door, Peggy's head snapped up as she came face to face with a beaming Kitty.

'Thought I'd look in on yer before the show starts,' she said, looking around the room with interest. 'It looks great, Peggy love. You've done brilliantly.'

Peggy gave a quick shake of her head. 'Not me. Annie and Sal have done all the hard work.'

'You're still doing that then, I see,' Kitty said, her lips pursed.

'How d'you mean?' Peggy asked in surprise.

'Still putting yourself down, not taking credit for the things you ought to be taking credit for.' Kitty frowned. 'You've worked hard here, under tough circumstances as well by the sounds of things, and what do I find? You're still blarting about how you've not done anything. Yer need to stop this, Peg, and let people congratulate you on your achievements.'

'You're talking about this award thing Carmichael wants to present me with, aren't you?' Peggy said softly. The thought of getting up on the stage and accepting it in front of all those people made her feel sick to her stomach. 'I wish you weren't here to see this.'

Kitty folded her arms indignantly. 'I'm flaming glad I am here to see this! You may not be proud of yourself but I am. Imagine what Mary and Di will say when they find out. They'll be chuffed to bits for yer, so stop ruining it for me and enjoy it.'

The vexed look on Kitty's face made Peggy giggle. 'You're too kind for your own good, Kit. What would I do without you?'

'Drive yourself and everyone around yer barmy, I expect.' Kitty sniffed as she checked her watch. 'Looks to me like you've not got long before curtain-up, so I'll take me seat.'

Kitty scraped her chair noisily across the floor until she was settled. 'Get on with it then.' She chuckled good-naturedly. 'This is the highlight of my year so far; I don't want to be disappointed.'

Peggy didn't need her old friend to tell her twice. Giving Kitty's shoulder an affectionate squeeze, she rushed backstage and found Sal and Annie putting the finishing touches to the programmes and costumes. Clearing aside a small area for the acts to come in and get ready, Peggy then started to organise refreshments for the cast and made a mental note to remind Sal to check the piano had been tuned.

As the girls and the acts prepared themselves for the show ahead, Peggy could barely hear herself think. Fretfully, she watched the performers chatter amongst themselves as they painted their faces with stage make-up and dressed in their costumes. Sal was busy helping the choir into their dresses and Annie had turned into a temporary hairdresser, pinning locks into victory rolls at the speed of light. Eager not to just stand and wait for curtain-up, Peggy became a Girl Friday, fetching, carrying and cleaning in order to get everything ready. Just a few minutes before eight o'clock, she was wrung out, and had never been more grateful for the port and lemon someone pressed into her hand.

Taking a large gulp, she felt the liquid trickle down her throat, giving her a much-needed dollop of Dutch courage. Arching her back to stretch out her aching muscles, she stood to the side of the stage and listened to the sound of the audience filing noisily into the mess. Even though she knew she shouldn't, Peggy couldn't resist sneaking a peek from behind the curtain to see who was filling the rows. The view surprised her; there were people arriving from all directions, and it looked as though it was a sell-out. Knowing more than two hundred people would be looking at her later left her feeling both terrified and delighted, and she took another gulp of her drink, allowing the alcohol to soothe her fractured nerves.

Sal sidled up alongside her. 'What do you think?'

'I think I need another port and lemon,' Peggy quipped. 'Seriously, Sal, however did we sell all these tickets?'

'The troops want cheerin' up.' Sal shrugged. 'A night like this has been a long time comin'.'

'Nothing to do with watching me fall flat on my face when it's a disaster, then?' Peggy chuckled.

Sal shook her head. 'No, I think the big draw is the missin' parrot and the fire-eater that can't light a match.'

Rubbing her face with her hands, Peggy groaned. 'I can't wait till this is over.'

'Give over,' Sal said sharply. 'What will be will be, pet. Worryin' won't change anythin'.'

'I know, I know.' Peggy sighed, checking her watch yet again and gesturing for the first act to get themselves ready.

'Now get this down you,' Sal said, handing her a cup of tea. 'And for cryin' out loud, relax.'

But relaxing was easier said than done. Annie pulled the curtain up and the audience let out whoops of delight, but with her heart roaring loudly in her ears, Peggy scarcely heard a thing. As the evening wore on, her heart continued to pound and she struggled to hear whether each act was any good, and had to rely on Sal, Annie and even Kitty, who gave her a large thumbs up from the front row, to tell her if things were going well.

After the interval, Peggy started to unwind. So far all was going to plan; in fact it was going better than she could have dared to hope as even Pat and May had arrived to perform their cleaning duties. Admittedly they hadn't looked pleased when they were sweeping the backstage area, but Peggy was surprised they had turned up at all.

As for the acts themselves, every single one of them had arrived. It was as if all mention of Peggy the tart had been forgotten, and everyone took to the stage with enthusiasm and gusto. The opening mime act had warmed the audience up nicely for the Laurel and Hardy duo, while the ATS cook who had the voice of an angel had all but brought the house down with her aria. Even the fire-eater had successfully managed to not only create fire with a lit match but swallow it whole, prompting gasps of amazement from the audience.

Peggy could scarcely believe that despite all the worry, the evening appeared to be a huge success. From her vantage point at the side of the stage she could see the audience who seemed to be enjoying every moment. Lieutenant Colonel Carmichael and his wife were laughing and smiling just where they should be, as were Ida and Harry who had chuckled heartily at the George Formby impersonator.

The last act of the night saw the entire cast take to the stage and perform 'Over the Rainbow', in honour of Judith and the other ATS girls who were killed during the three-night raid. There wasn't a dry eye in the house as the poignancy of the lyrics took hold of the audience and they thought of those that had lost their lives. Watching from backstage, Peggy fervently hoped that, just as the song said, when all the world is a hopeless jumble, dreams can come true. She looked across the stage at Sal and Annie who were perched on the edge of the wings and saw Annie weeping silently into her handkerchief. Peggy felt a rush of love for her friend. She knew just how much she missed her sister each day, but she had thrown herself into her work, her education and even the show with a kind of bravery Peggy knew she didn't possess herself.

The variety show had seen some terrific acts, but as far as Peggy was concerned the star turns were Sal and Annie. As the song finished, all eyes turned to Peggy and the cast beckoned her on stage to join them for a final bow. Reluctantly, she walked into the limelight and was delighted and horrified in equal measure to find everyone propelling her to the front.

Staring at the audience, Peggy beamed bashfully as they stood up to cheer and whistle with excitement. Never in a million years did she expect the show to be such a hit, but the glory wasn't just hers and the cast's. Turning to Sal and Annie, Peggy beckoned them on stage and the three of them stood together and took a well-earned bow.

As she straightened up, she was astounded to see that Carmichael had jumped out of his seat to thunderous applause and was now on the stage, walking towards her. Grinning at Peggy, he pumped her hand as well as Sal and Annie's before turning back to the audience.

'Thank you, thank you,' he boomed, urging everyone to quieten down. 'I'm not usually one for speeches, so I'll keep this short. But I'm sure you will all agree when I say that everyone involved in this wonderful production has done a simply marvellous job this evening under the stewardship of our very own ATS Volunteer Peggy Collins.'

The audience clapped politely as Carmichael paused for breath. 'As some of you may know, Volunteer Collins is not only an excellent director, but she is also something of a hero in Swansea. Recently, Peggy came face to face with a German pilot who held her at gunpoint while she was performing her usual guard duty.'

There were sharp intakes of breath from the rare few who hadn't heard about what had happened to Peggy. As she felt the stares and whispers of the strangers standing before her, a deep and uncomfortable heat rose within her. She hated everyone staring at her as though she were a museum exhibit, no matter how well-intentioned Carmichael's motives. Smiling across at him, she found herself urging him to hurry up so she could go back to her room and go to bed.

'Now, as you can see, Volunteer Collins not only escaped unharmed and is alive and well here with us today,' Lieutenant Colonel Carmichael shouted above the din. 'But she also captured the pilot, ensuring his detention in a prisoner-of-war camp, all without a weapon of her own, I might add. There is no doubt that she went above and beyond for her country, in the most frightening of circumstances. Our country needs more women like Peggy Collins who are a credit to our Army. It is for this reason that the powers that be followed my recommendation, which is why I have the very great pleasure, on behalf of the ATS, to give Volunteer Collins this commendation for bravery.'

By now everyone was on their feet, applauding and cheering with delight. Peggy remained rooted to the spot, unable to tear her eyes away from the audience. There was Ida, clapping as loudly as she could, her face a picture of pleasure and delight. Next to her stood Harry who had, unusually, even managed to smile for once. On the other side of the row stood Kitty. She was jumping up and down, much to the annoyance of the man standing next to her, but it was clear to Peggy that her old friend didn't care. Tears were streaming down her face as she looked at Peggy, her eyes filled with pride.

Suddenly she heard Sal who was standing behind her whisper, 'Well, go on then. Carmichael's goin' to get fed up if he has to stand there on his own much longer.'

With a jolt, Peggy accepted the certificate and medal Carmichael held out to her. Then he nudged her forwards, muttering the word 'speech' in her ear.

Feeling suddenly wrong-footed, she turned to back to see Sal, Annie and Lieutenant Colonel Carmichael smiling and applauding. Meanwhile the audience were still on their feet, their cheers and claps getting louder by the second.

Clutching the certificate and medal, Peggy looked down for just a minute and felt a stab of pride. Next to the words 'Commendation for Bravery', was her full name, 'Margaret Elizabeth Collins'. She could count on one hand the number of times she had been called Margaret and it seemed funny seeing it written down in an official way like this. If only Bess could see her now, she smiled, running her fingers over the embossed parchment.

Peggy had never won anything in her life, not even a spelling competition at school – something she hadn't told Annie. But this was something else. She looked up and out at the sea of faces, her eyes shining with tears as she listened in delight and surprise to the applause that was all for her.

Nervously, Peggy cleared her throat. 'Thank you, everyone, I won't take up much of your time, but I'll just say a few words. Firstly, I'd like to thank Lieutenant Colonel Carmichael not only for nominating me for this award, but for giving me the courage and confidence every day to be a better volunteer. I'm no different to any of the girls here what serve their king each day. All of us work hard because we love our country and don't want it to change. What happened to me was scary, mind, but what kept me going was knowing that every single ATS girl would do just what I did. I know all of you girls'd put your lives on the line and I know you'll all agree with me when I tell you I'd wrestle that Jerry all over again, blindfold if I had to.'

Pausing for breath the audience whistled and clapped, only stopping when Peggy continued to speak. 'It's an honour to serve with girls as brave and courageous as you here at these barracks. Which is why I want to finish by saying that although I'm extremely happy to be given this commendation, I don't reckon what I did was brave. I was only doing my job, just like what all you girls do every day. So, if I'm being awarded for my bravery, so are you, mind. That's why I'm dedicating this commendation to all of you. Here's to us.'

Bringing her speech to a close, Peggy stood back to observe the audience who were up on their feet once more, shouting and cheering her name. This time tears more than pricked her eyes, they streamed down her cheeks like rivers as she took in the joy on everyone's faces. Casting a glance at Kitty she saw her old friend was crying like a baby. As their eyes met, Kitty raised an imaginary glass to her, toasting her success.

Turning to the performers as well as Annie and Sal who were standing behind her, she saw everyone's eyes were shining with happiness. Facing the audience once more, Peggy thought it was high time to bring the evening to an end. She was shattered, and like everyone else, more than ready for bed. Stepping forward to take one final bow, the sound of a door banging loudly in the wind caught her attention, followed by rapid footsteps racing down the corridor.

Craning her neck over the mass of people, Peggy tried to get a better view, but struggled to see. Her first thought was that it was the German pilot Hans Bergenschloss, back to wreak his revenge on her for having him incarcerated in a POW camp.

But then, as the footsteps ground to a halt, she glanced up and the colour drained from her face as she saw something she had prayed and hoped for, but never expected. Because walking towards her through the throngs of people staring at him as though he was the second coming, was the one person she thought she would never  see again – Pilot Officer James Hudson.

# Chapter Eighteen

It was Sal who galvanised Peggy into action. As the audience stood open-mouthed in shock, Sal led her down the stairs and out towards the makeshift dressing room. Silently, the matriarch sat  Peggy down on an upturned wooden crate. Then she reached into the pocket of her greatcoat for the hip flask filled with brandy she almost always carried and held it out to her.

Peggy needed no encouragement. Taking the flask with trembling hands, she pressed the bottle to her lips and drank it down, hoping the sickly liquor would offer her salvation.

As the brandy trickled down her throat, Peggy tried to make sense of what had just happened. One minute she was on the stage being applauded for her bravery, the next she was mute with shock at the sight of a man risen from the dead.

It was the shape of him she had noticed first. In the half-light of the corridor Peggy hadn't been able to make out the man's face. But his height and build, coupled with the slope of his shoulders and the way he leant against the doorframe, told Peggy it was Jim. His form was as familiar to her as her own, and the moment she had seen him, she had known just who it was.

Watching him slowly walk towards her, pushing his way through the crowds, his face had finally come into view. At the sight of it, Peggy thought she would pass out with shock. The floppy fringe and sparkling blue eyes were two things she thought she would only ever see again in her mind's eye, and yet there they were, just inches away from her. She hadn't had much time to take in his appearance properly, but Peggy remembered his hair was streaked with dirt and his cheek grazed with dry blood. He had fixed his gaze on her then and smiled the lovely smile she once thought was reserved only for her.

Now, with just Sal for company, her body trembled and even her teeth started to shake. Had she imagined the entire thing? Was she simply overwrought?

'It was him, pet.' Sal nodded, as if reading Peggy's mind. 'He's turned up here, bold as brass, all right.'

Peggy had gone white with shock. 'But why?'

Sal shrugged, and took the hip flask from Peggy's grasp. 'I don't know, pet, but I do know that whatever's happened he's got a nerve showin' his face around here again.'

'I don't get why he's turned up out of the blue like this. I know that technically he was missing, but I was so sure he couldn't be alive,' Peggy gasped, sinking her head into her hands.

Sal took a slug of liquor then squeezed her shoulder affectionately. 'I can't believe it meself, flower. When you hear someone's gone missin', especially durin' wartime, well, you think that's it, don't you? You don't expect them to swan back in from the bloody dead!'

'But he has.' Peggy sighed. 'And I've no ideal what to do now.'

'Send the selfish twerp packing,' growled Annie, suddenly appearing from behind the curtain.

In spite of the seriousness of the situation, Peggy found herself chuckling at Annie's outburst. Patting the upturned box next to her, she gestured for her friend to sit down and join her.

'Is all hell breaking loose out there?' she asked as Annie took a seat.

'Yer could say that.' Annie nodded. 'The cast are all getting changed, Harry's taken Ida home and Kitty's trying to get rid of the audience.'

270

'That's kind of her.' Peggy smiled.

'It is,' Annie agreed. 'And hard work 'n'all, given the audience don't want to leave.'

A flash of surprise crossed Peggy's face. 'Why not?'

'Because no doubt they think the best part of the show is yet to come,' snorted Sal. 'Still, I may have only just met your Kitty, but I reckon she'll not stand for any nonsense.'

Peggy chuckled at how right Sal was. 'Where's Carmichael?'

'Talking to Jim,' Annie replied quietly. 'He's taken him back to his office.'

Peggy closed her eyes and pictured the conversation. She was sure no good would come from her superior officer whisking Jim into his quarters. She cast her mind back to Judith's funeral when Carmichael had made his feelings on the pilot perfectly clear.

'I thought being held at gunpoint was the worst thing that could ever happen to me,' Peggy sighed miserably. 'I was wrong. This is. When Jim first went missing all I could think was I would do anything to lay eyes on him again. Now he's turned up and as horrible as it sounds, I wish he hadn't.'

Sal smiled sympathetically as she perched on the end of the box next to Peggy. 'It doesn't sound horrible at all, flower. It sounds perfectly reasonable. You'd just started to come to terms with all that had gone on. You'd begun to move forwards, even with Hilda turning up out of the blue like that.'

'She's right,' Annie put in, leaning over to squeeze Kitty's hand. 'You've been through ever such a lot lately. It's no wonder yer feel the way yer do.'

'If there's anyone that ought to feel bad it's that swine,' Sal muttered. 'He's the one that led you a merry dance.'

'But why has he turned up now?' Peggy let out a tortured wail as she realised she was going round in circles.

Annie yawned as she got to her feet. 'How about we find out in the morning? You're too tired to deal with this now. Let's go back to the hotel and yer can get some sleep.'

At the thought of sinking into her warm bed, relief flooded through Peggy.

'But there's all the clearing up to do,' she protested weakly. 'We can't leave it till morning, Cook'll have a fit.'

Sal pressed a finger to her lips and shushed her. 'Let me worry about that. I've got a Tilly outside, d'you girls want a lift back?'

Wearily, Peggy got to her feet and smiled at all her two friends had done. What she would have done without them she didn't know.

\*

When dawn broke the following morning, Peggy felt drained but grateful for the fact she had such wonderful friends. Despite taking a sleeping draught at Ida's insistence when she got in, Peggy hadn't slept a wink. Instead she had lain awake all night staring up at the ceiling, wondering what on earth she was going to say to Jim when she saw him – because she had no doubt that Jim would insist on talking to her, no matter what Carmichael had said to him the night before. There were a million and one questions rushing through her mind, but without any answers Peggy was at a loss and knew she would have to steel herself before she sent him packing.

She listened to the gentle sounds of Kitty and Annie breathing and smiled with fondness at the thought of her friends. Annie and Sal had been pillars of strength last night, but when Peggy had got home, Kitty had been waiting with a warm embrace, not to mention a cup of hot cocoa.

Once Annie was fast asleep, Kitty had sat on the edge of Peggy's bed and stroked her hair while she'd sobbed her heart out. All the tears she had shed over Jim's disappearance, as well as the ones she had wept over his deception, covered her pillow and Kitty had sat patiently beside her until she was calm.

Silently she offered a prayer of thanks to God for giving her not only the strength to get through this nightmare, but for sending her the very best friend she had in the world as well.

But now it was morning and as Peggy swung her legs out of bed, she yawned and stretched her body into action before walking briskly to the window. Throwing open the curtains, she washed her face at the tiny sink and dressed quickly. Although it was Sunday, they would usually be expected to work. Yet she, Annie and Sal had been given a precious day off after their efforts in putting on the show. Glancing across at Kitty and Annie who were still slumbering gently, she smiled, realising it was just as well.

Making her way downstairs, she caught Ida at the bottom of the stairs, hurrying from the dining room to the breakfast room, her hands full of dirty plates.

'Morning, Peg,' she called cheerfully.

'Morning, Ida. You recovered from last night?'

'I think it's me that ought to be asking you that, love.' Ida beamed, a strand of jet black hair falling loose from the hairnet she had wrapped over her curls. 'How are you feeling?'

'I'm all right.' Peggy smiled weakly.

Ida looked her up and down, her keen eyes scrutinising every inch of Peggy. 'I hate to say it, precious, but I shouldn't like to see you if you weren't all right. You look exhausted.'

'I didn't sleep all that well. I'm just a bit tired,' Peggy admitted.

The landlady pursed her lips together as if considering what to say next. 'I can't say I'm surprised, love. Look, there's a visitor here for you in the dining room. Me and Harry both did our best to get rid of him, but well, he wouldn't leave and started to make ever such a fuss, he did.'

Peggy's smile slipped. 'Is it Jim?'

Ida gave a curt nod of her head. 'I'm only telling you now in case you want to slip out the back way. He's sat down waiting for you but I don't think he'll cause any trouble.'

A deep heat began to rise within Peggy and for a minute she wondered if she might faint. After all this time, she'd heard nothing from him, now it felt like he was hounding her. More than anything she wanted to take Ida up on her offer and run out the back, but knew that she would only be putting off the inevitable. It was far better to face it now than prolong the agony.

'You're all right, Ida. I'll see him.'

As she walked towards the dining room, Peggy was shocked to find her knees were knocking together with every step. She felt as though she were facing the executioner rather than about to sit opposite the man she had thought she was going to marry.

Seeing him sitting by the window, his face turned away from hers as he peered out at the view of the sunshine-filled street, her heart skipped a beat and she cursed herself for it. How she could still have any feelings left for this man after all he had done was a mystery. He was clearly lost in thought and Peggy stood by the table and took in his appearance until he glanced around and saw her. He looked tired, she realised. His once beautiful eyes were dull and grey and his appearance sallow. He looked as though he had lost weight too, she thought, his clean uniform was hanging off him and it was all she could do not to race around the table and wrap him in her arms.

Instead she slid into the seat opposite and folded her hands into her lap. 'You're alive then.'

At the sight of Peggy, Jim's face lit up. 'You came. I was rather afraid you wouldn't.'

'You didn't leave me much choice,' she said, a hint of defiance creeping into her voice. 'Where've you been?'

Jim cleared his throat and gazed at her, his eyes full of longing. 'Well, last night after I'd spent hours with Lieutenant Colonel Carmichael, he was good enough to drop me off at my former RAF base. But I couldn't sleep, Carmichael told me that you had heard some rather unpleasant things about me, but I can explain. I had to see you, Peggy.'

Listening to the lies fall easily from his tongue, Peggy found she could hardly bring herself to look at Jim. Clearly his time away had taught him nothing and he thought he could wheedle his way back into her affections. Peggy seethed, Jim Hudson had another think coming!

Noticing the sudden silence in the room, Peggy looked around and saw that every ATS recruit had stopped eating their tomatoes on toast and were instead gawping at her and Jim. After finding herself the unexpected star turn at last night's variety show, she didn't want to repeat the performance.

'Not here,' she said in a low voice, getting up to leave the table.

Without waiting to see if Jim was following her, she walked across the dining hall, pushed open the heavy doors and walked outside. Despite the fact it was only eight in the morning the sunshine was already incredibly warm. The irony of this sudden burst of heat wasn't lost on Peggy. Whereas passers-by seemed to enjoy this unexpected drop of spring sunshine that softened the edges of the bombed-out buildings, Peggy found herself wishing for grey skies and pouring rain to match her mood.

'Wait for me.' Jim's voice cut through her thoughts as he sidled up alongside her. 'Where do you want to go?'

Peggy said nothing. She looked at the shelled buildings around her, the sight echoing her own sadness, and her eyes alighted on the tearoom at the end of the street. She walked briskly towards it, Jim matching her pace. It wasn't until a wait-ress showed them to a table in the corner and they'd ordered a pot of tea and some scones that Peggy trusted herself to speak.

'I was heartbroken when you were reported missing,' she said, her voice faltering. 'I prayed for your safe return for days, scoured the papers, begged my superiors for information, but nobody could tell me anything; you'd vanished, presumed dead.'

Jim furrowed his brow and looked down at the table in sorrow as Peggy carried on.

'I grieved for you every day. I prayed someone, somewhere was looking out for you and that you'd be happier in heaven.

You were my world, and my world disappeared from underneath me when I learned you'd gone.'

'I'm sorry, my love,' he said, not noticing Peggy flinch at the endearment. 'Do you know anything about my disappearance?'

Peggy shook her head and fixed her gaze on his face as he began to explain.

'I was posted to the South Coast and given a mission to escort our bombers who were planning an attack in Germany. We left our base and all was fine, the sun was shining and we had good visibility. But as we flew over Belgium, the Hun opened fire. One of my men was killed instantly, the bullets piercing his aircraft as easily as if they were slicing through butter. Of course, I had seen the Jerries attack before, but this seemed savage. There were more of them, we were surrounded.'

Jim's voice grew angry at the memory and he took a brief pause before carrying on. 'I turned to look at him, just for a moment, and saw his plane had burst into flames. It was horrific. Westerby was a good man, one of the best, he didn't deserve to die like that. I wanted to help him, hated the fact there was nothing we could do, and it was then the Jerries moved on to me. I saw one of them before they opened fire. His face was contorted with pleasure, it looked as though killing was the thing he lived for. As he began firing, it was written all over his face just how much he wished me the same harm as Westerby.'

'So what happened?' Peggy asked, her tone gentler now.

Jim's face was grave. 'I managed to bail out of my plane in a cornfield. I was bruised and battered, but otherwise unharmed. However, I was also miles from anywhere and I trekked for hours without seeing a soul. I thought the best thing would be to reach the coast. Not having much French money on me, I ended up stowing away on various trains, before reaching Calais. It was there I hoped to get a boat back across the Channel, but of course in the occupied zone that was easier said than done.'

Peggy glanced up from the white tablecloth she had been focused on. 'What did you do?'

Jim closed his eyes as he relived the horror he had endured.

'I hid in the town for a while living off scraps, dodging Germans who I knew would take me as a prisoner of war. Everyone was terrified of the Jerries, but eventually I found a Resistance fighter who took pity on me. They hid me in the bowels of a cafe, and told me they would get help.'

'And did they?' Peggy shivered despite the warmth of the day. Jim's story was haunting her.

'After a few days. But there was no light, and it was horrendously cold, yet they couldn't allow me upstairs in case the Germans found me. After about a week, Helene, one of the Resistance members, had good news. She told me she had found a French fisherman who would take me across the Channel to safety. The crossing was awful and choppy and it was all I could do not to bring up the very little food I had been eating.' Jim paused again, his face lighting up at a memory. 'But it was you, Peggy, the thought of your face that kept me going and, well, here I am. The moment I touched British soil I had to see you.'

'So you haven't reported back to your commanding officer? Do they even know you're here?' Peggy gasped incredulously.

Jim shook his head. 'I hitched a lift back to Swansea. But after my meeting with Lieutenant Colonel Carmichael last night, where he told me what had happened while I had been away, he assured me he would tell them this morning. I only had one condition, that I see you before I returned for duty. No matter what the outcome, I had to talk to you first.'

Her voice rose an octave. 'Not your wife or even your child then? Just me, your tart, you had to see first!'

A flash of hurt and confusion crossed Jim's features. 'Peggy please, I'm sorry, but—'

'But nothing!' she said cutting him off with a hiss. 'You've led me a merry dance, haven't you? And your wife Hilda told me all about it! She even brought your kiddie along. So I'm sure you won't mind my asking why you've not been to see them yet, given they're your family!' Peggy sat back in her chair, arms folded and lips set in a mutinous line.

Jim's face dropped like a stone. 'Please, Peggy, let me tell you the truth,' he begged.

Peggy's body shook with anger, the agony of sitting across the table struggling to control her emotions too hard to control any longer.

'The truth! You'd no more know the truth if you fell over it and it bit you on the backside, Jim Hudson!' she growled, leaning across the table and fixing the pilot with a glare. 'Because I've no ideal how you can explain your wife turning up here with your child. She came here and told me I was nothing more than a cheap tart. Did Carmichael tell you that? Did he tell you your wife told me that I was a woman with loose morals who had no business messing about with her husband, the father of her child? And you know the worst part is, she's right! You've turned me into something I'm not because you lied to me.'

Peggy slammed her fist down on the table so hard the teacups rattled in their saucers, slopping brown murky liquid all over the cloth. Jim said nothing, instead he reached for Peggy's hand, only for her to snatch it away and bury it in her lap.

'I'm sorry,' he said quietly, his gaze never leaving Peggy's. 'But I promise you, there is an explanation. Please give me a chance.'

'What's the point?' Peggy said bitterly. 'How can I believe anything you say now?'

Jim cast his eyes downwards at the rebuke. 'I appreciate how you must feel, Peggy, I should have said something. I wanted to tell you, but I didn't want to spoil what we had. I was terrified you wouldn't understand.'

'How would anyone understand this?' Peggy replied miserably.

Jim's eyes were earnest. 'You're right, but please, hear me out, then I'll leave you alone for good if that's what you want.'

This time Peggy gave a quiet nod of her head. 'It is what I want. I never want to see you again, d'you hear me?'

'I understand, Peggy, but please, just let me explain, then I'll go. I promise.'

'You've got ten minutes,' she sighed.

'Where to start?' He smiled nervously.

'At the beginning, I should think,' Peggy snapped, her patience wearing thin.

'Yes, of course,' he said hurriedly. 'Well, the first thing you should know is that I'm sorry, I'm so, so sorry Hilda came to see you.'

'You're not denying that, then?' Peggy snorted. 'She is your wife.'

Jim nodded. 'I had no idea she knew about you. I never expected her to find you.'

'I can't honestly say it was the best day of my life,' Peggy remarked. 'If I'd known you were married I would never have come near you. You do know that, don't you? I'm not that sort of girl. I thought what we had was special, Jim. You asked me to marry you, for Christ's sake! Then when Hilda turned up here with Iris, well, it goes to show what sort of fool you really took me for.'

'I never thought you were a fool, Peggy,' Jim said quietly. 'I think you are the brightest, kindest, loveliest girl I've ever met.'

'Tell that to Helene as well, did you?' Peggy snorted.

Confusion flickered across Jim's face. 'Helene? What's she got to do with any of this?'

'One of your tarts you've got lined up in every port, I shouldn't wonder. You've no need to lie, Hilda's told me all about it. Tell me, just how many of us are there, Jim?'

For the first time since she had met him, Peggy saw a flash of anger cross his features.

'What else did she tell you?' Jim fired. 'Did she tell you that when we met it was love at first sight? That when we laid eyes on one another at a concert in the Hippodrome we both knew we had found one another's soul mate.'

'She did as it goes, yes,' Peggy said.

Jim leaned his face across the table and spoke quietly. 'And did she also tell you that we're no longer married?'

Peggy snorted with derision. 'Don't give me that load of old bunkum. The very least you can do is be honest with me, you owe me that much at least.'

'I'm not lying,' Jim said bitterly. 'Hilda's the one that's lying. I never so much as glanced in another woman's direction until I met you. It's true Hilda and I were married, but not any longer.'

'How d'you mean?' Peggy asked.

Jim looked over each shoulder to see who was listening before he spoke again, keeping his voice low. 'I mean Hilda and I are divorced.'

Peggy couldn't keep the shock from her face. As a Christian she had been taught marriage was for life, you faced problems together. 'Until death us do part' meant something. How could Jim give up on his wife so easily? Not only that, but what about their child, Iris? What sort of man left their wife to bring up their child alone?

'I don't know what to say,' she said shakily.

'It's true,' Jim said earnestly. 'Hilda and I divorced in January this year. The day I crashed into your car, actually, was the day I received my final papers.'

'Is that why you were driving like a madman?' Peggy whispered.

Jim gave a brief nod of his head. 'Something like that. Even though it was me that divorced her, seeing the papers like that, it was painful to realise Hilda and I had reached the end. We had been married for almost ten years, and when I said "I do" in church before all our family and friends, I meant every word of it.'

Peggy looked across at Jim for a sign he was lying but surprisingly could find none.

'I don't understand how you could let go of your marriage so easily,' she said evenly. 'Especially not when you've got a nipper together. Divorce is just plain wrong, Jim. It goes against the teachings of the Church and God hisself. Surely you can see that.'

Jim's shoulders sank as he ran his hand through his hair. He seemed so pained at having to tell this story, Peggy almost felt sorry for him.

'Of course I can see that,' he snapped. 'I didn't want to divorce Hilda but I had no choice.'

'You're making no sense.' Peggy frowned.

Jim bit his lip. 'My brother Edward and I had always been close. Just a year between us.'

'Yes, you told me,' Peggy put in matter-of-factly. 'But that's about the only thing you ever did tell me about him.'

'There's a reason for that.' Jim grimaced. 'Edward was my best man when Hilda and I married. But then he betrayed me in the worst way possible by having an affair with my wife.'

Peggy stared at him in undisguised shock as Jim continued.

'I found out much later that it started a couple of years after we got married. But when war broke out of course I was away from home a lot more frequently,' Jim said quietly. 'As an engineer, Edward was in a reserved occupation and remained in Bristol. He assured me he would take care of Hilda, ensure that she would want for nothing. Well, he did that all right.'

'How did you find out?' Peggy whispered.

'I caught them.' Jim chuckled at the absurdity of it. 'I returned home from leave a day early and planned to surprise Hilda, take her out for dinner, that sort of thing. Instead I found her and Ed in our bed together.'

The colour drained from Peggy's face, but Jim hadn't finished.

'Of course they were full of apologies, each of them told me it meant nothing, that they were sorry, that they had never done anything like that before. The cheek! I didn't want to hear any of it. I returned to my unit straight away and didn't speak to either of them again, unless it was through a solicitor.'

Tears welled in Peggy's eyes at the sadness of it all. The pain of seeing something like that between the two people you loved most in the world must have been devastating. Before she could think about what she was doing, she reached across the table and took Jim's hand. The feel of his warm flesh sent a wave of longing through her body and she gasped in surprise, snatching her hand quickly away as if she had been burned.

'But what about Iris?' Peggy begged. 'If you couldn't stay for Hilda's sake you should at least have stayed for her. Every child has a right to get to know their father.'

'I couldn't agree with you more,' Jim replied evenly. 'Every child should know their father.'

'So why leave, Jim?' Peggy reasoned.

Jim sighed and ran his free hand through his hair. 'Because I am not Iris's father, Ed is, and he is the one that should be taking care of her, not me.'

Peggy gasped as the pieces of the jigsaw fell into place. When Hilda had shown Peggy her child, the likeness to Jim had been unmistakable. It had been all the proof she had needed to believe that Jim had been unfaithful. Yet, if Iris had actually been fathered by Edward, there was every chance she would have a look of Jim.

She felt a sudden stab of guilt. How quickly Peggy had jumped to conclusions. She should have asked questions, found out more about Hilda. Why had she been so quick to think so badly of him? Because the evidence had seemed unquestionable, Peggy thought to herself. Hilda had seemed every inch the wronged woman, complete with wedding ring and child the spitting image of Jim. Yet there was still something troubling her.

'If all this is true, why is Hilda claiming you're still her husband and why's she insisting you're the father of her child?' Peggy asked, perplexed.

Jim reached for his teacup and took a sip before he continued.

'Hilda never wanted a divorce, but of course when I named Edward on the papers she had no choice. I think she hoped she could cling to a bit of respectability by marrying my brother. But when he discovered she was pregnant with Iris, Ed turned out to be quite the cad. He visited her in hospital, held the child then fled the country. Last I heard he was in New York forging a new life for himself there.'

Peggy shook her head in disbelief. 'That's dreadful. Poor Iris.'

'Yes, poor Iris,' Jim agreed. 'And poor Hilda too, to some extent. Our divorce has caused her a huge amount of shame. Like you, she was a Sunday school teacher in Clevedon, which is where we married. Her family have all but shunned her. I believe she's living in Stokes Croft and trying to start afresh now. Unfortunately, part of that new start is insisting she and I are still married and I am the father of her child, obviously away fighting for our country. It's as though she's rewritten history and truly believes her affair with Ed never happened.'

'What about your parents?' Peggy asked. 'What do they think of all of this?'

Jim raised a smile. 'Incredibly, they have ended up colluding with Hilda and her delusions. Naturally, they were shocked at Ed's behaviour. But reputation is everything to my family and before Iris was born, Mother tried to persuade me to call the divorce off. She suggested I raise Ed's child as my own, but I refused. Hilda had made her bed and she could lie in it as far as I was concerned. I wanted rid of the woman, and as for Ed, well, I never want to see him again.' Jim shook his head in despair. 'But my father is a well-respected lawyer with offices in London and Bristol. He and my mother didn't want to lose standing in the community so they brushed it under the carpet and with Father's help our divorce was processed much quicker. Now, with Ed out of the way, it's easier to pretend to people that Iris is mine, especially with me far from home in the RAF. Finally, the war with Germany has been useful for something as far as my family is concerned.' Jim smiled slightly at the irony of it all.

'But I don't understand how your name weren't splashed across the papers,' Peggy said cautiously. 'When folks get divorced, well, it's everywhere.'

'That's the beauty of having a lawyer as a father. He was rather persuasive with newspaper editors, and ensured my name was kept out of the press,' Jim explained. 'It was in his interests as well, of course. Ensured he and my mother could keep their good name intact and avoid a scandal.'

'Did anyone know the truth?' Peggy asked.

'My commanding officer knew, but I only told him after I had run you off the road. He wanted to know why on earth I had behaved so stupidly so I told him everything. That morning I had received the final paperwork nullifying our marriage. That was why I drove so badly and that was why I was allowed to get away with buying you a car and no further punishment.'

'So what was the big plan then? Was Hilda going to pretend forever you and she were still married and Iris was your child?' she asked.

'I don't know,' Jim sighed. 'I hoped everyone would come around eventually. I certainly wanted no part of it. When our divorce papers were finalised I hoped she would give up the pretence. That's why I wrote to Mother and told her all about you. I wanted her to know the truth was going to come out eventually now I had finally met the love of my life.'

'The love of your life?' she echoed in disbelief.

Jim held Peggy's gaze, a look of pure adoration flowing from his eyes. 'I told Mother I had never loved Hilda the way I loved you. I told her I had known from the moment I saw you in the road, your pretty little face so cross with me for ruining your precious car, that you were my future and I wasn't going to let my duplicitous ex-wife keep me from true happiness.'

'Oh, Jim,' Peggy said, her voice faltering. 'Why didn't you tell me all this straight away? Things could have been so different.' Jim was silent, so Peggy carried on, 'Is that how Hilda found out about me then? Through your mother?'

He nodded. 'I think so, yes. I didn't think she would tell Hilda though. I thought I would turn up, find you at the barracks and you would be delighted to see me. I spent the entire boat crossing picturing our reunion. Then when I arrived and saw you on stage and heard how you had bravely evaded capture by a Jerry only to turn the tables and capture him yourself, I knew I had to make you mine. I wanted to suggest that we married immediately, to forget waiting until this war is over, but then . . .'

He broke off and Peggy was shocked to see he was struggling not to cry.

'But then you saw me and I have never seen anyone look so angry and I didn't understand why. I thought you would be shocked to see me, certainly, but that you would be overjoyed. I couldn't understsand it, I was terrified you had met someone else. Then when Carmichael told me why you were so unhappy about my reappearance, I hated myself. I hated the fact that it was me that made you feel that way.'

Peggy looked at him with compassion. 'I'm sorry.'

'Don't be,' he said softly. 'This is my fault and I'm furious. Furious with Hilda, my parents, but most of all myself. I should have told you the truth, I do know that now, but, Peggy, you must understand that after so much heartache I didn't want to risk losing you before our relationship had even had a chance to begin. Divorce, well, it's a terrible stigma, I didn't think you would be able to see past that. Please tell me you understand?'

'I do.' She smiled, resting her soft palm on top of his rough hand. 'And I do see how hard this must have all been for you. Discovering your wife had an affair with your brother, knowing she gave birth to his child. I don't know how you found the strength to cope with that. But please, you must see there's no way we can be together now.'

Jim's look of love was replaced with despair as he opened his mouth to speak.

'Please, you've had your go, it's my turn now,' she said, not altogether unkindly. 'I feel for you, Jim, I really do. But you weren't honest with me about something so important and well, I don't reckon I'll ever get over that.'

'But Peggy—' he began.

'No, Jim,' she said, cutting him off firmly. 'I can see why you didn't tell me, but if we were to carry on courting, well it would always be at the back of my mind what else you hadn't told me. I don't want to live like that.'

Nodding miserably, Jim gazed down at the table as Peggy carried on.

'Like you, I was brought up to believe divorce was a sin. I was also taught that family is everything. Jim, if your parents are pushing for you to accept Hilda as your wife, then they would surely be against you and me starting a life together.'

'But I don't care about them,' Jim said hurriedly. 'I just care about you. I'll never see them again if they refuse to accept us. Please, my darling.'

Peggy shook her head. 'No. It's enough you're not speaking to your brother, which I understand. But don't lose your parents as well.'

Refusing to meet her gaze, Jim looked defeated.

'And let's not forget there's a poor innocent child mixed up in all of this, Jim,' Peggy said more quietly. 'I can understand you not wanting anything to do with Hilda and Ed, but if nothing else you could be a loving uncle to that child, Jim. If Edward won't take on the responsibility then I reckon you should. None of this is Iris's fault.'

Jim shook his head bitterly. 'I will not raise another man's child. I'm not strong enough for that.'

'You're stronger than you think, Jim Hudson,' Peggy insisted. 'Make the most of this opportunity. A child is a blessing.'

'But Hilda and I are divorced. She would never let me near that child without agreeing to keep up this ridiculous pretence,' Jim said, his tone full of resentment.

'That's something you and Hilda should sort out between

you. But don't let little Iris suffer because of her mother's bad behaviour.'

Peggy paused, but when Jim said nothing, she ploughed on. 'You have to see that there's nothing for us now. If you had told me the truth right from the beginning my feelings for you were that strong there's a chance I might've been able to deal with your divorce. Don't get me wrong, the staring, the rumours and the scandal would've been difficult to cope with, along with the fact we wouldn't have been able to marry in church, but together we might've managed. But now, I can't trust you, and that means any hope for a future together's over.'

'You can't mean that?' Jim blanched. 'Please, Peggy, say you don't mean it.'

Peggy pinched the bridge of her nose and took a deep breath to try and stem the tears that were threatening to spill down her face. 'When Hilda came to see me, she humiliated me, Jim. She all but ruined my career in the Army, she made me feel like a cheap tart you didn't care tuppence ha'penny for.'

'You know that's not true,' Jim protested fiercely.

'That might be so,' she continued, the tears now splashing down her cheeks like waterfalls, 'but I don't like secrets, Jim, never have, and this, well this is about as bad a secret as you could ever keep. Truly, Jim, I loved you with all my heart, but not any more. I'm sorry, we can't be together. Goodbye.'

With that she got to her feet and fled the teahouse without giving Jim so much as a backward glance. Saying a second goodbye to the love of her life had been the hardest thing Peggy had ever had to do, and she knew if she took one more look at his heartbroken face her resolve would fail. The fact was, Jim Hudson had taken a little piece of Peggy's heart, and it would be lost to him forever.

# Chapter Nineteen

Peggy raced down the road as if her life depended on it. All she wanted to do was reach the hotel and get away from Jim Hudson as quickly as possible. Rounding the corner, she picked up the pace, putting one foot in front of the other quicker than if she were taking part in one of her daily physical training sessions. The warm sunshine caused her to undo the buttons of her heavy jacket, but she was determined not to lose speed. Her legs and lungs were burning, but Peggy was enjoying feeling something besides the endless misery she had endured.

With just a few yards to go before she reached the sanctuary of her billet, Peggy turned left, only to collide head first into Kitty, causing her to fall to the floor.

'I'm so sorry,' she wailed, helping to pick her poor friend up from the pavement. 'Are you all right?'

Kitty brushed herself down and glanced sharply up at Peggy. 'I don't think there's anything broken. Whatever were yer running like that for anyway? Have yer robbed a bank?'

Peggy forced a smile at Kitty's joke. 'I really am sorry, Kit. D'you need to sit down or something?'

'Honestly, I'm fine, love,' Kitty replied, straightening her cap and running her eye over Peggy. 'Fancy a cuppa?'

Peggy shook her head. 'I've drunk more than enough tea to sink a battleship. I wouldn't mind some fresh air though.'

'A walk along the front then?' Kitty suggested. 'Ease my nearly broken limbs.'

Peggy nodded and the two girls linked arms and walked towards the sea in silence. Ten minutes later they had reached the water, and Peggy breathed in great lungfuls of the salty air. Taking in the view around her she smiled appreciatively. Hitler may have had a good go at destroying the town, but he couldn't destroy the beautiful Welsh landscape.

'It's beautiful, isn't it?' Kitty said, echoing Peggy's thoughts. 'I've heard the beaches here are lovely.'

'They are.' Peggy nodded. 'Just up ahead, the golden sands stretch on for miles.'

'Jim ever take yer?' Kitty asked casually.

Peggy shook her head. 'We were going to go. In the summer, if we were both still at our postings.'

'I see.' Kitty paused. 'And d'you think you might be going to the beach together in the future?'

Kitty's question prompted a fresh round of tears from Peggy. 'No, it's over. He's divorced.'

'Bloody hell!' Kitty said without thinking. Hurriedly she clamped her hands to her mouth. 'Language! Sorry, Peg. But divorce? Are yer sure?'

Nodding, Peggy started to tell her friend the whole sorry tale. She left nothing out, and by the time she had finished, Kitty looked as exhausted as Peggy felt.

'So let me get this right. This Hilda's pretending she's not divorced when she is?' Kitty quizzed.

Peggy nodded.

'And his parents are all right with that?' she asked incredulously.

Peggy nodded again. 'They don't want a scandal like this spoiling their family name.'

'Sod that!' Kitty fired angrily. 'What about Jim's reputation? What about yours, come to that? That dozy harpy caused you all sorts of trouble with her lies.'

Despite the sadness of the situation it was impossible not to giggle at Kitty's fury.

'She did. And that's just another reason why it's better things finish between me and Jim. I think he really believed that once he'd told me the truth we could start courting again, but it's not that simple.' Peggy sighed.

'No, it's not. But his ex-wife clearly is if she's telling folk she's still married to Jim,' Kitty fumed. 'She wants her bumps felt.'

'You've got a point, Kit,' Peggy agreed.

Lost in their own thoughts, the girls each reflected on Peggy's news.

'But he's all right, though?' Kitty asked, breaking the silence.

'Physically he's fine.' Peggy shrugged. 'I reckon he's lost a bit of weight, but now he's home he'll be right as rain in no time.'

'I didn't mean that,' Kitty said gently. 'I mean, was he all right when yer left him?'

Peggy blanched at the question. How could she admit she had been too distressed herself to check how Jim was? Instead she said nothing.

'So it really is all over between you now, then?' Kitty pressed again.

'Of course!' Peggy squealed. 'I told you, Kitty, too much has happened now. We'd have no chance of a future.'

Kitty stopped suddenly, causing Peggy to shift uncomfortably as her friend held her gaze. More than anything she wanted to tell Kitty the truth. That her heart was breaking at the thought of a life without Jim. That she wanted nothing more than to be with him. That sitting across the table in a tea house, having to tell him it was over was unbearable. With a start, a picture of Peggy bringing Jim home to meet Edie came unbidden into her mind, and it was all she could do not to burst out laughing. Edie would no doubt throw him out of the house immediately once she discovered he was divorced. She would call it a sin against God and refuse to even look at him. Peggy shook her head, no matter how much her treacherous heart may still long for Jim, there was no going back.

'And is that really what you want?' Kitty asked softly.

'Course.' She nodded miserably.

Kitty arched an eyebrow. 'This is me you're talking to, Peggy Collins. We've been through hell and high water together. If you can't be honest with anyone else, you can at least be honest with me.'

'Oh Kit, no, it's not what I want,' she moaned, hanging her head in shame. 'I want nothing more than for us to be together, but it's impossible.'

'Peggy, you daft thing, it's not impossible at all, if you love him,' Kitty said in a soothing tone.

'But he's divorced. The shame of it all,' Peggy sobbed. 'Even Edward and Wallis Simpson couldn't get over that hurdle.'

Kitty made a clicking noise with her tongue. 'Yes, but in a way they did, love. They're together, they realised love was more important, no matter what anyone else would think.'

'But their relationship didn't start out on a bed of lies, did it?' Peggy groaned, stepping out of the way of a couple of passers-by.

'P'raps not, but no doubt they had a fair few other issues to get out of the way.' Kitty smiled knowingly. 'This isn't hopeless, Peggy. It seems to me you and Jim truly love each other, and it's not like he didn't have his reasons for keeping the truth from you, is it? I mean, I can't say for sure how I'd have behaved if I had an ex-husband who was as mad as a box of frogs.'

Peggy laughed. Somehow Kitty always knew just what to say to cheer her up. There was no doubt about it, Kitty was the tonic she needed, but she couldn't go back, it felt entirely wrong. Peggy linked her arm back through Kitty's and together the girls carried on along the seafront, the dramatic coastline stretching out endlessly before them. If only it was as easy as Kitty seemed to think, Peggy mused. But there were just too many obstacles for her and Jim to overcome. Sitting across from him in the teahouse, she had longed to take his hand

and say yes to a future together. But then a heady combination of fear and reality had set in, bringing her abruptly to her senses.

'Yer know it wasn't easy for me when I realised I'd got feelings for Arthur,' Kitty said, breaking the silence between them. 'I felt as if I were betraying Joe. That to love someone else meant I was replacing him.'

Peggy squeezed her friend's arm affectionately. 'But it wasn't like that. Your Joe passed away and Arthur, well, you just fell in love.'

Kitty nodded. 'I never meant for it to happen. Didn't stop the awful guilt I felt as a result, though. I hated myself; I mean I still loved Joe – I never dreamed we wouldn't be together. Then when he was killed, well, the bottom fell out of my world.'

'D'you still love Joe now?' Peggy asked, suddenly curious.

'Naturally.' Kitty smiled as an image of him flooded through her mind. 'I will never stop loving Joe. But I love Arthur as well and I've realised my heart is big enough to love them both. Arthur understands that. I was lucky to find someone so understanding who gave me the time I needed to sort out my feelings. It wasn't easy for any of us.'

'It's only what you deserve, Kitty,' Peggy said loyally.

'Give over.' Kitty smiled. 'But what I am saying is that it's rare to find someone that special. And in these uncertain times, well, we all have to cling to a bit of happiness where we can. I think you're being too hard on Jim. He's said he's sorry for what he's done, can't you at least consider a fresh start with him now it's all out in the open? None of this was his fault and let's not forget, life's short, Peggy, if anyone knows that it's me.'

'No,' Peggy replied stiffly. 'My mind's made up now, I won't go back. I've my work in the Army to tend to and then when this war's done with, I'll go back to helping Mother in the shop. That's how life was always meant to be, I was a fool to think it could be any other way.'

The day after Jim's shock confession was Monday and Peggy woke feeling brighter and calmer. With so much on her mind she had expected another fitful and uneasy night's sleep, but the moment her head had hit the pillow she had fallen into a deep slumber, only waking when Kitty said goodbye.

'I'll be off now, love, say goodbye to Annie for me, won't yer.'

'Where is she?' Peggy asked, rubbing her eyes in a bid to come to.

'Guard duty, I think. Let's hope she doesn't have such an eventful time as you.' Kitty chuckled.

Peggy raised a smile and got out of bed to pull her friend into her arms. Leaning into her shoulder, she inhaled Kitty's familiar flowery scent and felt a pang of longing. It had felt so good to have her old friend by her side, like old times. Now she was leaving right when she needed her most.

As the girls broke away, Kitty looked at her knowingly. 'Think on about what I've said, won't yer?'

Peggy nodded. 'I will. I can't promise anything though, Kit.'

'I daresay yer can't.' Kitty nodded. 'But promise me yer won't throw away the chance of happiness just like that.'

'I know,' Peggy whispered. 'I'm not. I reckon I have to do what's right.'

Kitty bent down to kiss her friend's cheek before she turned to walk out of the door. 'As long as you do what's right for you and nobody else. Promise?'

'I promise.' Peggy nodded, waving her friend goodbye. 'I'll write to you at the weekend.'

Once Kitty was gone, Peggy washed and dressed quickly and made her way to the barracks, rejecting Ida's offer of breakfast. After Saturday night's revelations she needed to know how the land lay at work and felt a slice of toast and a cuppa in the mess was the best way of discovering if she was still a hero or was back to being a social pariah.

Walking into the mess, Peggy braced herself for the stares and whispers, and was amazed to find there were none. Joining the queue to collect her breakfast, she saw Sal and Annie drinking tea over by the fireplace and joined her friends.

'Morning, Peg. You recovered after Saturday night?' Sal asked cheerily.

Peggy nodded. 'Just about.'

'Annie filled me in on what happened with Jim,' Sal said softly.

'Did you also tell everyone else?' Peggy asked, turning to Annie.

She shook her head. 'What d'you take me for?'

'I just thought more people might be staring at me and whispering, that's all,' Peggy replied.

Sal shifted uncomfortably in her seat. 'I may have spread the word I'd make mincemeat out of anyone who said anythin' to you. What you need now is normality, not to be made to feel as though you're a circus act. The girls seem to have got the message.'

Peggy smiled at her friend. 'Thank you, Sal, that's ever so good of you.'

'It's the least I can do,' Sal replied warmly. 'I'm so sorry about all of this, pet, what a flamin' mess.'

'Mess is the right word.' Peggy sighed. 'Still, onwards and upwards now.'

'Have you seen Jim since you left him at the cafe yesterday?' Annie asked.

Peggy shook her head. 'No, and I don't want to neither. My mind's made up, there'd be no point seeing him. We've both got to get on with our lives.'

'And you're sure that's what you want, is it, flower?' Sal pressed gently.

Peggy rolled her eyes heavenwards. 'You're as bad as Kitty.

Yes, I'm sure. Divorce would have been difficult enough in itself to get over, but he wasn't open with me, Sal, I can't get over that.'

'Fair enough.' Sal nodded. 'You know what's right for you better than anyone else, just as long as you've thought it through properly.'

'I have, Sal,' Peggy replied earnestly. 'Anyway, I'm sick and tired of talking about me. What about you two, any news?'

Annie shook her head. 'We share a bedroom, Peg, you know all my news. Guard duty was thankfully quiet. Hooper's taken to sending us all out in pairs after your little escapade.'

'And about time too!' Sal exclaimed. 'I always said it was daft allowin' girls out on their own.'

'Well, to be fair, we didn't have much choice the other night, so many girls called in sick,' Peggy pointed out.

'Even so, I'll make it my business at my new postin' to make sure no girl is alone during a patrol,' Sal insisted, as she drained her cup. 'Right then, I must get on.'

'Hold up!' Peggy gasped, staring at Sal in undisguised shock. 'What's all this about a new posting?'

Sal gave her a watery smile. 'Oh, you caught that. I realised as soon as I opened me big fat mouth I'd said too much.'

'Is it true though, Sal? Are you really leaving?' Annie asked, aghast.

Sal nodded. 'Yes, it's true. I found out last week.'

'You never said nothing,' Peggy said accusingly.

'I didn't like to, flower. There was so much goin' on here, I didn't want to worry you with my news.'

Peggy felt a rush of affection for her friend. She was always so selfless. 'You should have told us. We wouldn't have worked you so hard at the show.'

'Why do you think I didn't tell you?' Sal laughed. 'I've not had so much fun in years.'

'Where are you off to?' Peggy asked.

'Southampton. I'm being made up to a section leader,' she said proudly.

Peggy flushed with pleasure at her friend's news. 'Congratulations, Sal. We'll miss you, but I couldn't be happier for you.'

'Peg's right, Sal. You deserve it.' Annie beamed. 'The place won't be the same without yer. There'll be nobody to sort out Pat and May for a start.'

'You'll manage.' She chuckled. 'I've no doubt you'll have the likes of those two firmly under control.'

'I dunno about that,' Annie muttered darkly, as she caught sight of the girls in question gossiping by the window.

'We all move on, Annie,' Sal said more gently now. 'Change happens to us all, we can be miserable about it or make the best of it.'

As Peggy watched Sal set her cup on the table, she felt a wave of sadness. She knew her friend was right, nothing stayed the same forever, but Peggy also knew she would miss the wise older woman's friendship and wisdom enormously.

'So when are you going?' Peggy asked eventually.

'Week after next,' Sal replied. 'I've a forty-eight hour pass next weekend and I'm hoping to get home and spend some time with me dear old mam.'

A look of surprise flashed across Annie's face. 'I didn't know you had a mam, Sal.'

'Well, how else do you think I got here, Annie? Did you think I was found under a cabbage?' Sal said accusingly.

Annie flushed. 'Well, I just meant—'

Sal held up her hands to cut her off. 'I know what you meant, young lady. I don't know how old you two think I am.'

'Old enough to know better.' Peggy smiled as she got to her feet and bent down to hug Sal. 'I'm so pleased for you. Keep in touch, won't you.'

'Try stoppin' me,' Sal whispered, a tear splashing down on to Peggy's jacket. 'Oh you. I never cry, look at what you're doin' to me.'

Peggy looked from Sal to Annie and was shocked to see how sad they both looked. She knew Sal would make an excellent section leader and it was no more than she deserved.

'Come on, you two,' she said, clapping her hands together. 'It's not like somebody's died, this is happy news not sad and we should celebrate with a drink or two on our next night off. In the meantime, I reckon we've all got work to do at the garage so let's get on, shall we?'

Annie and Sal got to their feet and followed Peggy out of the mess, grumbling behind her as they made their way out into the early morning sunshine.

'Since when did you become such a bossyboots?' Sal teased.

'Yes! I hope you're not getting ideas above your station, Peggy Collins,' Annie giggled as they made their way along the footpath towards the garage.

'You never know, pet,' Sal chimed in. 'I mean, she has got an award for bravery, who knows where that might lead.'

'Queen of the ATS.' Annie laughed. 'Complete with coronation ceremony.'

'Wearin' her best khaki jacket and passion-killers,' Sal mocked.

Peggy whirled around and laughed at the pair. 'Will you two shut up? Otherwise, when I'm Queen of the ATS, I'll have you both up for insubordination and thrown in ATS prison forever!'

As the girls collapsed into fits of laughter, a voice rang out behind them. 'Peggy Collins?'

Peggy stood up and saw Carmichael's assistant, Sergeant Jenkins, wanted to speak to her.

'Yes, sir,' she said, getting her laughter under control and together with Sal and Annie, saluting their superior officer.

'At ease,' Jenkins ordered the girls. 'Carmichael wants to see you in his office straight away, Collins.'

'Maybe you are getting that promotion,' Annie hissed

'Yes, that's exactly what's going on. Lieutenant Colonel Carmichael's polishing my crown as we speak,' Peggy fired back before following Sergeant Jenkins quickly across the grounds.

It only took five minutes to reach the office and as Jenkins showed Peggy in, she saluted Carmichael before he gestured for her to take a seat.'

'Collins. Good to see you.' Carmichael beamed. 'I wanted to see how you were feeling after Saturday night?'

Peggy flushed at the memory. She hadn't seen her commanding officer since that fateful incident with Jim. He had gone above and beyond what any superior officer would do for a volunteer and she was grateful.

Now she wasn't sure if she should thank him for his intervention, or if that would embarrass him? Peggy bit her lip as she fretted over what to do. What if he viewed her as a liability? What if he had called her in to dismiss her as his driver? She adored her job and would hate to lose it.

Shuffling on the chair so her back was ramrod straight, Peggy answered firmly, 'I'm fine now, thank you, sir. I would just like to say how sorry I am about what happened. I would like to assure you I have taken steps so nothing like that will ever happen again.'

Carmichael waved her concerns away with his hand. 'Don't be silly, Collins. And I hope you haven't got any silly notions that I want rid of you over this. You're a damn fine driver and a credit to the ATS. I meant every word I said on Saturday night, so if you're worrying about the incident then don't and that's an order.'

Peggy allowed herself to relax a little in her seat. 'Yes, sir.'

Carmichael smiled. 'Well, now we've got that out of the way, I've asked you here because I've got what I think is good news for you.'

'Sir?'

'Yes, I've been doing some thinking and I rather think you deserve a break, Collins. How does seventy-two hours' leave over Easter sound?'

Peggy's face coloured with surprise. 'Well, sir, I don't know . . .'

'Well, I do know,' he said firmly. 'Not only have you worked incredibly hard lately, I rather think a break away from the barracks, time at home with your mother perhaps, will do you the power of good.'

'That's very kind of you, sir, but are you sure you can spare me over such an important weekend?'

'Of course, Collins. There will be no meetings for anyone that week, save for emergencies, and I do hope we've seen the last of those, for a while at least. If I need anything I'm sure the redoubtable Sub-Leader Perkins can help.'

Peggy smiled at the mention of Sal. 'While she's still here, sir.'

Carmichael nodded knowingly. 'So she's told you her news? I'm delighted for her. It really has been a long time coming. She's been with the Army a long time and it's high time her efforts were rewarded. Although I shall miss her, as I'm sure you will, Collins.'

'I will, sir,' Peggy admitted. 'She's been a true friend to me since I got here.'

'All the more reason for a leave of absence then, perhaps?' Carmichael raised an eyebrow. 'Time away often helps us get perspective, break out of a rut, see things in a new light.'

'I'm not in a rut, sir, I'm very happy here—' she began before Carmichael cut her off.

'I am aware of that, Collins.' He chuckled. 'This isn't a punishment, it's a reward. Call it time off for extremely good behaviour.'

'Thank you, sir,' she said meekly.

'My pleasure. Now write to your mother and tell her you'll be back this weekend. Post should reach her by Thursday if you scribble a few words today. I'll see you in an hour for our drive to Wrexham,' he said, dismissing her.

Peggy stood up to leave and walked across the richly padded carpet. She had one hand on the door handle, about to leave, when a sudden impulse got the better of her and she swung around to address her commanding officer.

'I just want to say, sir, that I know what you did for me on Saturday night with Pilot Officer Hudson, sir,' she gushed. 'I know you didn't have to do any of that, and I don't know why you did it, but I want you to know that I will never forget the kindness you showed me and all the help you've given me. Thank you.'

Peggy could tell from Carmichael's face that her outburst had surprised and delighted him.

'You're very welcome, Peggy,' he said softly. 'We all need a little help every now and again and I was happy to do what I could. Do I take it the matter between you and Pilot Officer Hudson is now resolved?'

'Yes, sir.' Peggy gave a curt nod of the head.

Carmichael beamed. 'Excellent. Then let's say no more about it.'

As Peggy left his office and walked across the quad, she felt a flush of happiness flood through her. Despite all that had happened with Jim, she felt truly lucky to be surrounded by so many people who cared about her. Turning her face towards the sun, Peggy resolved to write a letter to Edie later that day and tell her she was coming home.

# Chapter Twenty

The drive to Bristol on Good Friday morning was uneventful, and Peggy was glad of the chance to do nothing more than peer out of the Lister truck window and gather her thoughts. She had been offered a lift down to her home town by a fellow spark girl who had deliveries to make in nearby Bath, and as a the familiar landmarks of Bristol slid into view Peggy brimmed with excitement at the prospect of being back home for a couple of days. By the time she was dropped off at Bristol Temple Meads station to meet her mother, it was all she could do not to run across the road towards her mother's batered old Tilly. Catching sight of Edie waiting by the arches, dressed in her trademark overalls, hair scraped under an old floral scarf, Peggy's heart skipped a beat – she hadn't realised quite how much she had missed her. Peggy waved in delight and rushed towards her.

'Mother, you came.' She beamed at her, setting her case on the floor and pulling her mother into her arms.

'Well, of course I came,' Edie replied, stiffly returning her daughter's hug. 'Come on, that's enough of all that nonsense now. I've gotta get back up the shop. We might be closed on this holiest of days but I've still got things to do.'

'Course,' Peggy said. Seeing Edie's truck parked nearby, she wasted no time clambering into the passenger seat.

'So how long have I got you for then?' Edie asked, firing the starter engine.

'Until first thing Monday morning,' Peggy said happily. 'We've got the whole of Easter together.'

'That's good news.' Edie smiled. 'You can help me this afternoon. I've a delivery that needs making.'

'But it's Good Friday!' Peggy exclaimed.

'I'm well aware,' Edie replied evenly. 'But it's just the one I didn't have time to sort out yesterday, what with me being alone.'

'I thought you had a delivery boy?' Peggy looked puzzled.

There was a pause before Edie spoke. 'I did – Robert. Only with his mother and father passing when we were raided not so long ago, and him moving to Bedminster to live with his aunt and uncle, I haven't liked to ask him to come and do the odd job for me.'

Peggy could have kicked herself for her insensitivity. How could she have been stupid enough to mention the Michaels so soon? She should have known Edie would still be upset, and here she was sticking her great big size nines in it before they had even left the station. If she wanted her mother to agree to her remaining in the Army then she had better learn to curb her tongue.

'Yes, course,' Peggy said quickly. 'As soon as I've dumped my stuff I can help you with whatever needs doing.'

'Good,' Edie replied quietly. 'So, you all right then?'

Peggy nodded as her mother swung the car on to the road towards Knowle. 'Fine. Nothing to report really.'

Edie paused. 'Is that why you haven't written to me in weeks?'

Peggy coloured with embarrassment. She should have known her mother would bring up the lack of letters sooner rather than later. The truth was such a lot had happened and she still hadn't worked out what to say about her mother wanting her out of the Army.

'We've been busy,' she said finally. 'I'm sorry, Mother.'

Edie pursed her lips. 'We'll talk about it later. Don't think I've forgotten though, my girl.'

'No, Mother,' Peggy said quietly.

'Anyway,' Edie continued as she turned the truck left, 'I s'pect you've heard that we've spent weeks without heat as a result of all these blasted bombs. The water cuts have been dreadful too, of course. I keep the tin bath full of water just in case, so if you were hoping for a good scrub while you're here you'll have to think on.'

'That's all right,' Peggy said hurriedly. 'I'll nip down the bathhouse. But what about the fire? Surely you've been able to light that?'

Edie snorted. 'What with? Coal? There's hardly any to be had anywhere. We keep praying up the church for God to provide, but so far . . .'

'At least you'll be able to make sure the kids get their Easter eggs this year. I'll deliver them later.'

Peggy smiled inwardly to herself at the thought of dropping off the little chocolate surprises to all the regular Sunday school children. The kids were all so happy to receive a little extra present from Edie and Peggy that the smile on their faces was almost as good as an egg itself.

'Easter eggs?' Edie laughed so hard, she nearly caused the truck to veer into the side of the road. 'The kids aren't getting Easter eggs this year. Times are hard, love. They'll be munching on a couple of carrots if they're lucky.'

Peggy said nothing. There was no talking to her mother when she was in this mood. The best way out of it was to either change the subject or go along with whatever Edie wanted. Instead she looked out of the window at the glimpses of familiar landmarks amongst the shelled buildings that gave the city an air of a ghost town.

But what was nice to see was that her hometown hadn't lost its sense of humour. Bristolians may have had their morale shattered in recent months, but they hadn't lost their spirit. Shops that were in ruins but still trading had a range of cheeky placards in their windows. One tailor had a sign that said,

'More open than shut', while a cafe with no ceiling had a slogan reading, 'Hitler's paid us a visit. Why don't you?'

After such a tough few weeks, it was precisely the lift Peggy needed and she hugged her kitbag close to her chest, feeling grateful once more to be home for a couple of days. Just under twenty minutes later, they were back in Knowle, and Peggy rushed up to the flat above the shop and changed into her shop overalls.

Pushing open the door to her old bedroom, Peggy was shocked to see a letter in a familiar hand lying on her bed. Gingerly she picked it up as if it were as dangerous as an unexploded grenade. Shakily, she shouted for her mother.

'What is it?' Edie asked, breathless from running up the stairs.

'When did this come?' she asked, holding the letter aloft.

Edie thought for a moment. 'Yesterday morning, I reckon, when I received your note telling me you were coming home. Why?'

'No reason,' Peggy said.

'You look like you've seen a ghost,' Edie said impatiently, her hands on her hips.

'No, I'm fine,' she replied, tracing a finger over the handwriting.

Edie shook her head in despair. 'Well if that's all, can you stop daydreaming and get a move on, Peg.'

Nodding, Peggy shoved the letter into her overall pocket. Whatever was inside this note could wait until later.

*

Sitting behind the wheel of the truck, Peggy smiled as she rattled down the familiar streets. Although it was cloudy and drizzling with rain outside, she wanted to feel the fresh air in her lungs. Peggy had forgotten how much she enjoyed dropping off goods to customers in her mother's truck. Not only did she enjoy a natter with all of the regulars she had grown up getting to know, she adored the feeling of freedom driving still gave her. Feeling the thin steering wheel slip through her small hands, she was grateful Edie had insisted she learned to drive as soon as she was old enough. There was no feeling like that of the open road, and Peggy was pleased the Army had recognised something in her that she had not and made her a spark girl. She shuddered to think of how she might have ended up spending the war working in the stores or kitchens.

Turning right into Redcatch Road to make her delivery, Peggy pulled up outside the house of a regular and felt a surge of happiness. Edie might despise Esme Hotchkiss but Peggy thought of the elderly customer as one of her favourites. Mrs Hotchkiss had always had a kind word or treat for Peggy, ever since she was small, particularly remembering to drop something special off for her at Christmas or on her birthday. She was a widow twice over, and had always shopped with her mother since she opened the shop just after Peggy was born. Pulling out her rationed box of meat and veg, Peggy walked up the little path towards the villa and knocked sharply on the door. Mrs Hotchkiss opened it almost immediately and rewarded Peggy with a bright smile.

'This is a treat.' She beamed at her, taking the box and walking through the house to the kitchen. 'Where's your mother? Too busy to do the deliveries herself now, is she?'

'No, never too busy for you, Mrs H. She's just trying to get ready for Easter, that's all. There's a lot planned for the service this Sunday, you know how it is.'

Mrs Hotchkiss sniffed as she invited Peggy to sit down at the little wooden table that stood in the corner. 'I know how it is with Edie Collins all right. Making her own daughter work on Good Friday, scandalous. Would you like a cuppa, love?'

Peggy shook her head. 'No thanks, I've really got to get back to help Mother.'

'Heaven knows that's a woman that needs all the help she can get,' Mrs Hotchkiss grumbled under her breath.

Rolling her eyes as Mrs Hotchkiss unloaded the groceries, Peggy wondered why on earth the older woman chose to shop with her mother. There had never been any love lost between the two women and yet Esme Hotchkiss had been one of Edie's most loyal customers over the years.

'Have you got many plans for Easter, Mrs H?' Peggy asked, keen to change the subject.

'Well, my daughter Betty's invited me over to her house for something to eat with her and the family after church,' Mrs Hotchkiss replied as she placed two tins of fruit in her pantry. 'Nothing more than that, it's a bit of a miserable Eastertide with everything what's happened, and of course no eggs for the little ones this year.'

'No, Mother said,' Peggy said sadly. 'I reckon she and the vicar are hoping to keep the children's spirits up with some games after the service at the very least.'

Mrs Hotchkiss's face darkened at the mention of Edie. 'Well, if there's one thing your mother knows all about, it's games.'

Wearily Peggy got to her feet. Mrs Hotchkiss could go on about her mother for a lifetime given the opportunity and Peggy had heard it all before. She had asked her mother once why the widow was always so rude, but Edie had merely mumbled something about it being impossible to get on with everyone.

Usually Peggy shrugged off Mrs Hotchkiss's barbed comments, but today she didn't want to waste what she had left of her precious seventy-two-hour pass listening to someone run her mother down. Peggy wasn't stupid, she knew her mother had her faults, but for the life of her couldn't understand what Esme Hotchkiss had against Edie.

Bidding Mrs Hotchkiss farewell, Peggy walked towards the front door. She was halfway there when suddenly she felt an urge to turn back.

'What did you mean just then when you said my mother

knows all about playing games?' Peggy asked, seeing the older woman standing at the sink.

Mrs Hotchkiss jumped at the sound of Peggy's voice. 'I thought you'd gone, lover.'

'I had,' Peggy replied, not moving from the kitchen doorway. 'But it just occurred to me that every time I see you, you're always lovely to me, but always have something nasty to say about my mother, I just want to know, I s'pose, what it is you've got against her when so many people around here think she's a pillar of the community.'

'Not everyone knows your mother like I do,' Mrs Hotchkiss muttered, still facing the sink.

'And what does that mean?' Peggy pressed.

Turning to look at her, Mrs Hotchkiss wiped her hands on a tea towel and paused as if deliberating over what to say. 'The thing is, Peg, you're a good girl,' she began. 'You're well-liked and always have been.'

'What's any of that got to do with my mother?' Peggy said defiantly, hands on her hips.

'Let's just say it's a good job you take after your father,' Mrs Hotchkiss said in a steely tone.

Peggy felt a flash of fury. Mrs Hotchkiss might be elderly but that didn't give her the right to keep on at her mother. Edie had her faults, nobody knew that better than Peggy, but she had always been a model of good behaviour, which was half the reason she expected Peggy to follow suit. She looked at Mrs Hotchkiss again, about to press her for more, but then decided to let the matter drop. What was the point of getting upset with an old lady who was clearly confused?

'Have a happy Easter, Mrs Hotchkiss,' she said crisply, turning on her heel.

Outside, she clambered into the truck, took a deep breath to calm down and started the engine. As she drove along the road she felt her fury melt away and, seeing the sun was trying to peep through the clouds, stopped the car.

The park was just up ahead and a good walk would no doubt help clear her mind. The moment she stepped on to the grass, she felt her mood improve. As her brogues sank slightly into the mud with every step, she simply smiled and enjoyed the feel of the sun on her face. Easter was her favourite time of the year, and she wasn't about to let one old woman ruin it for her with her thoughtless comments.

Besides, she had more important things to think about, such as the letter she had received from Jim.

Gaining speed, she walked past the entrance to the public shelter, and could wait no longer. Sitting on the nearest bench, she pulled the letter from her pocket. Running her fingers over the handwriting, Peggy hesitated for just a moment before tearing it open.

*7 April 1941*

*Dear Peggy,*

*I write this to you now from my new posting. After everything that has happened I have been asked to teach for a while so I'll be on terra firma for a bit, which will be a challenge and a blessing.*

*I have been thinking about you ever such a lot since you ran from me that day in Swansea. I don't blame you, I can imagine everything I told you was a dreadful shock. It has all been somewhat shocking for me as well, if I am honest. This last year has been frankly dreadful. When I found out about Hilda and Edward, Peggy, I thought my heart would break. I had never felt so betrayed and never expected to find happiness ever again. Consequently, I devoted myself to the RAF and being the best pilot I could be. My own life meant so very little to me any more, but then I met you and everything changed.*

*I will never forget your face as you stood in the middle of that country lane after I had ruined your vehicle. I have never seen a girl look more furious or more determined and* in that moment I knew I was ruined. My life before you didn't exist, there was no life. How I longed to sweep you up in my arms then and there, and tell you that I wanted you, that it was finally no longer just my country I would lay my life down for, but you.

When you agreed to let me take you to the pictures, I felt a happiness like no other. I knew then there was hope for me and that was something I never expected to find again. And Peggy, how I found that with you. My darling, I won't lie to you, I adored Hilda, but you, my God, Peggy, you I fell hard for. My love for Hilda was nothing compared to the love I felt and continue to feel for you. You gave me a reason to live again and that is something I shall never forget.

I should have told you everything, but I was terrified of losing you and so I took the coward's way, which I will never forgive myself for. All that time away in France, when you thought I was dead, I never stopped thinking about you. Trapped in that lonely basement with no windows, light and scarcely any food, I found I had plenty in my heart to give me sustenance. The very image of you was all I needed. I would close my eyes and the two of us would be together building a perfect and happy future. Alas, it appears that is not meant to be, but know this, Peggy. My love for you will never die, which is why when Carmichael told me he was going to grant you Easter weekend off, I took the liberty of writing to you at your mother's home.

I also wanted to let you know that I have done some serious thinking since you and I spoke. I have come to realise that you are right about Iris. Edward will never do the right thing by her and the girl needs a father. You, Peggy, have shown me that there are many forms of love and Iris shouldn't suffer needlessly because of poor decision-making on the part of her parents. I have made it abundantly clear to Hilda and my parents that I will never go along with *their ridiculous charade of pretending to still be married to Hilda, reputation or no reputation. However, I intend to do right by the child and become a father figure to Iris. I shall visit her on Good Friday during a stay with my parents and it is my intention to shower this child with love in the way that you showered me with love and affection.*

*I shall always cherish our time together, Peggy, my heart will always belong to you. I hope one day you shall find it in your own heart to forgive enough so our hearts can beat as one.*

*Yours forever,*

*Jim*

By the time Peggy had finished reading, her eyes were shining with tears. Even though she was absolute that they could never be together again, the fact Jim was going to be a guardian to Iris was proof that anything was possible. She was delighted he was looking to the future. Now it was just down to Peggy to try and do the same.

*

After a supper of Potato Jane, Peggy washed up the last of the dishes and set the kettle on the range.

'Not for me, love,' Edie bristled, removing her housecoat and reaching for her jacket. 'I'm off out. Listen, I forgot to pick up the books, would you mind popping down to the shop before you settle in for the night and I'll go over the day's paperwork later on.'

Confusion passed across Peggy's features. Edie's routine was like clockwork. After supper she had a cup of tea, and would then balance the day's takings while listening to the wireless.

'Where are you going?'

'Over to Bedminster. I want to look in on Robert,' she

explained, lacing her shoes.

'Why now?' Peggy asked. 'It's Easter, I thought you'd wanna be with me. It's not like I'm back for very long.'

Peggy was aware she sounded childish but her earlier conversation with Esme Hotchkiss had left her feeling unsettled and more than anything she wanted to spend time with her mother.

Edie gave her a pointed glare. 'Don't be daft, child. I'm going to see Robert precisely because it's Easter. In case you've forgotten, he's lost both his parents, I want to wish him well.'

Feeling suitably chastised, Peggy shuffled uncomfortably by the range. 'Sorry.'

'I should think so,' Edie said curtly. 'I won't be late. We'll have a cup of tea and say a prayer when I get back.'

As Edie turned her back to walk out of the door, Peggy rushed across the kitchen and reached for her mother. If she didn't do it now, then she might not have the courage again and she had to know where she stood. Jim's letter had shown her the future waited for nobody.

'What is it?' Edie sighed in irritation.

'I just . . . well, I wanted to talk to you about something,' Peggy said quickly.

'Spit it out then.'

Peggy inhaled sharply. 'I wanted to talk to you about the Army.'

Edie pursed her lips. 'Is this about the letter your Lieutenant Colonel Carmichael sent?'

Peggy nodded, feeling a surge of hope.

'And your Lieutenant Colonel Carmichael's very persuasive.' Edie frowned. 'Told me you'd been awarded a commendation for bravery, though wouldn't say any more than that. He told me you were one of the best ATS recruits he'd ever seen and it was his privilege to have you as his driver.'

'Did he?' Peggy's hands flew to her mouth in delighted surprise.

'Wipe that smug look off your face, young lady,' Edie said staunchly. 'There are no prizes here for showboating.'

Peggy bristled. 'I'm not being smug, I'm proud I'm serving my country and my superior officer reckons I'm doing a good job.'

'Well, Carmichael's always been over the top with praise. Nothing changes.' Edie sniffed, fastening up her coat. 'We'll talk about it properly when I get back, but in the meantime, I thought we could drive up Clutton tomorrow and I can show you the shop I'm on about.'

Peggy caught her mother's sleeve as she turned to leave. 'Hang on a minute. What did you mean when you said Carmichael's always been over the top?'

'Figure of speech,' she said quickly. 'Now, I've got to go, it might only be a couple of miles but it'll no doubt take me forever and a day to drive across in the blackout.'

But Peggy wasn't finished and rounded on her mother. 'Wait a minute. I don't reckon that is what you meant. You know him, don't you?'

Edie sighed and rolled her eyes heavenwards. 'All right. Yes, Peggy, I know him. He worked with your father years back.'

'Why did you never say nothing before?' Peggy blurted in surprise. 'Why didn't he?'

Edie's expression darkened. 'Well, I can't answer for someone else, but I personally didn't know you worked for him until now.'

'Yes, you did,' Peggy whispered in disbelief. 'I wrote to you and told you all about him in my letters. Why are you keeping something from me?'

'I'm not. You're reading far too much into this,' Edie said firmly. 'Peggy, we can talk about this later if you want, but right now I have to go out, I will see you later.'

'But what if there's a raid?' Peggy protested, eager to try and stall her mother, so they could talk.

'Then I'll find shelter. See you soon,' Edie replied.

With that she walked out of the door, slamming it behind her. As Peggy heard her almost race down the street, she cast her mind back to Mrs Hotchkiss earlier that day. Although Peggy had dismissed her ramblings as those of a confused old woman, she now wondered if she'd had been right. She had seemed so convinced that Edie had wronged her, what if there was something in it?

Sinking on to the hard grey settee that lined the back of the parlour, Peggy put her head in her hands and wondered just how well she knew her mother after all. She had always believed Edie told her everything. After all, she had drummed it into her since she was a young age that honesty was the best policy.

Peggy smiled as she thought back to the times she and her dad would roll their eyes discreetly at each other when Edie started off on one of her tirades. They knew that without fail she would always finish with that particular saying, and yet it seemed to Peggy that her mother didn't necessarily always practise what she preached.

Once the kettle boiled, Peggy made a cup of tea for herself, and sat at the table to drink it. She had only taken a mouthful when the screech of a bomb whistled through the air. She stood on tip toes to peer around the edge of the blackout curtain, and saw with horror that orange and red flares were descending on the city.

Fear tugged at Peggy's heart. She had hoped they would be safe from the Germans tonight. Yet one glimpse up at the sky told her the Jerries were likely to unleash a reign of terror if the full moon was anything to go by. She shuddered at the eerie moonlight, realising it was the perfect night for a raid. Sure enough, just moments later the scream of the bombs multiplied and rained down on the city as if the Germans were throwing confetti at a wedding. As they shrieked and hissed through the air, Peggy's thoughts turned to her mother. Realising Edie was more than capable of unleashing her own version of hatred that would rival anything Jerry had to offer, Peggy reluctantly made her way outside to find the books.

Inside the shop, it was a struggle to see anything in the gloom as she peered through the tin cans and groceries and walked towards the cash register. Reaching behind the till for the little file of paperwork her mother relied upon, the all too familiar wail of an air-raid siren sounded. Groaning, she took the file and hurried to the shelter at the back of the shop.

The shelter wasn't the most comfortable and she remembered how she and her mother had been holed up in the cupboard for hours in January. Now as she huddled inside, Peggy hoped she wouldn't be there for so long.

As her eyes got used to the darkness, she saw a candle on top of a shelf. Fumbling for the matches she knew would be next to it, she lit the wick and the room instantly appeared less miserable. In fact, Peggy saw her mother had done her best to make it as comfortable as possible. Although the make-do shelter was only big enough for one person and possibly a child to stand up in, Edie had ensured there were a couple of cushions and blankets to keep out the chill. There was also a jug of fresh water on the shelf next to the candle and what looked like a tin of biscuits.

Opening the lid and finding it filled with garibaldis, Peggy smiled, grateful for Edie's foresight, and sank her head back on to the cushion, listening to the shrieks and whines of the bombs that continued to ring out across the city.

Peggy wasn't sure how long she stayed in the cupboard but soon her eyes started to wander. This little storage room was where she used to play hide and seek as a child with some of the regulars in the shop. She thought back to those days, where if she wasn't playing games she would hide in the cupboard out of sight, playing dominoes on her own. Sometimes, if her father was around, he would try and squeeze inside with her and they would have a tiny tea party for giants while her mother filled the shelves with stock or served customers, always too busy for games. Peggy smiled at the memory. How she missed her father and would give anything for just another hour with him.

She would love to know what he would make of this business with Jim. Would he have been disappointed or would he have offered her support? Peggy didn't even need to ask the question. William Collins had always thought Peggy was the apple of his eye, he would have helped her through the mess, just as he always helped her through life.

Her eyes strayed to the shelf next to the door. It held necessities for the shop like files, spare keys and tea, but today Peggy saw something she hadn't seen for years – her mother's memory box.

Standing up, she plucked the black and yellow Huntley and Palmers tin from the shelf, and rubbed the dust from the top. Through the years, her mother had placed little mementoes in here and as a child she had loved rifling through the contents. There was the cinema ticket stub from her parents' first night out together, a precious photo of Edie and her mother when she was just a baby, and a lock of Peggy's flaming red hair, cut the day she was born.

She was just about to open it and relive the memories, when the all-clear sounded and she breathed a sigh of relief at the welcomingly loud noise. Putting the tin back, and grabbing her mother's precious books, she stepped out on to the street. The bitter smell of burning hit her nostrils instantly. Cautiously she looked around, but it seemed as though the bombs hadn't hit Knowle and this side of the city had survived another raid.

Pushing open the door to the flat, Peggy walked straight into the kitchen and was surprised to see Edie sat at the table.

'How long have you been here? There's been a raid on,' she exclaimed.

Edie shook her head as she sipped her cup of tea. 'I'm well aware of that, thank you. Not long. The all-clear sounded a bit earlier over Bedminster so I made my way back while I could.

There's plenty of tea in the pot if you want one, I've only just made it.'

Peggy said nothing. She set the books on the table then reached for a cup above the range. Pouring herself a drink, the steam from the brown liquid was already warming her stiff, cold bones.

'What were you doing in the shop?' Edie blurted as Peggy stirred in the milk.

'Getting the books you wanted,' Peggy replied, taking a seat next to her mother at the table. 'I was just there when the siren sounded so I had to lock myself away under the stairs. And guess what I found.'

'What?' Edie asked warily.

'The tin,' Peggy replied, her voice full of glee. 'I haven't seen it for years. I thought I'd pass the time by having a look through.'

Edie's face drained of colour. 'You never went in there?'

Peggy shook her head. 'No, I didn't get a chance. But I loved all those old things you kept hold of, Mother, thought they might while away the time.'

'They're my memories not yours,' Edie scolded. 'You've no right to go through things that are none of your concern.'

Peggy blanched at her mother's forthright tone. 'All right. I'm sorry. I didn't mean no harm. You always used to let me look through the tin before.'

'Well, that was then, when you were a child,' she said. 'Things change, Peggy, you should know that.'

About to open her mouth to apologise again, the wail of the air-raid siren punctured the air, swiftly followed by the evil drone of the Luftwaffe. The whine of the planes was so loud, Peggy covered her ears as she looked at her mother who seemed frozen with fear.

'Quick, Mother, under the table,' Peggy said quickly.

Like a frightened child, Edie allowed Peggy to pull her to the floor and together they scrambled under the table. As they huddled against one another for comfort, Peggy felt her mother tremble, and put an arm around her shoulders. Much to Peggy's surprise, Edie didn't push her away. Instead she nestled closely into her body as the incendiaries rained down quicker than a flurry of unexpected snow. Peggy said nothing. This was the first time she had ever seen weakness in her mother. The loss of the Michaels family must have hit Edie harder than Peggy realised.

As the planes began to fly over their home every couple of minutes, the angry and rapid fire of their guns proving they meant business, Peggy remained calm. Then more bombs studded the air, sounding for all the world like hail at the start of a thunderstorm. All too soon they exploded, and were so loud it felt as though they were falling directly on top of the house, every vibration causing Edie to tremble in fright.

Pulling her mother in closer, a cold chill coursed through Peggy's body. Every judder felt as though the Germans were making it personal, as if they wanted to snuff out their lives in an instant.

As another blast sounded, the noise ricocheted through the room and Peggy heard the faint sound of Edie reciting the Lord's Prayer. Peggy knew her mother only ever did that when she was overcome with worry.

'Come on, Mother, we'll have a sing-song, take our mind off it,' Peggy suggested.

'All right,' Edie agreed, her voice shaky and face white.

As Peggy started to sing, 'I've got sixpence, jolly, jolly sixpence', everything suddenly grew quiet outside.

Puzzled, she and Edie turned to one another in surprise.

'Is it over?' Edie begged.

'I don't know,' Peggy replied cautiously. 'I doubt it.'

'They were busy in the city tonight,' Edie said hopefully, the colour returning to her cheeks. 'Maybe they've had enough.'

Peggy smiled sadly at Edie's optimism. She had never known the Germans have enough of anything; her encounter with Hans had taught her that much. She was just about to say as much, when the sound of a soft crackle overhead made her look up. To her horror, Peggy saw the ceiling above them was bowing dangerously.

Quickly, she grabbed Edie's hand and half-dragged her towards the door.

'Where are you going?' Edie screamed, her legs rooted to the floor.

'To the shop. The ceiling's about to collapse – we can't stay here,' Peggy shouted.

Edie was trembling uncontrollably. 'We can't leave. The all-clear hasn't sounded. The Luftwaffe's everywhere, they'll get us out there if they don't get us in here.'

As the creaking sound above their heads grew louder, so did Peggy's sense of unease. Something told her they were in more danger inside their home than they were outside. 'Move!' she shrilled, pulling her mother roughly by the hand.

But it was too late as a ferocious crash sounded overhead and what looked like an avalanche slid into the front room, ripping through the wall that divided the two rooms. Most of the roof had collapsed, the blast so strong it lifted her clean off the ground, causing her to let go of Edie and fall to the floor.

With the rubble tumbling down around her, Peggy lifted her head, and saw with fresh horror that a beam from the ceiling had loosened and was now flying through the air. Everything was happening in slow motion as if she were watching a film. She opened her mouth and screamed again at Edie to get out of the way, but she just looked at Peggy blankly. It wasn't until the beam struck her mother cleanly on the back of her head, that Peggy saw the expression on her mother's face change from fear to shock as she was propelled from one side of the room to the other, flying through the air as though she were nothing more than a goose feather.

When Edie finally landed, a heap of bricks and rubble descended around her and Peggy screamed in panic as she realised she could no longer see her mother's body.

'Mother,' Peggy screamed, the air from her lungs sending more dust and debris everywhere. 'Mother, where are you?'

But there was no reply. Just the sound of the only home she had ever known collapsing around her ears, and with it a lifetime of precious memories and dreams.

# Chapter Twenty-One

A strange red glow descended on the room, transforming Peggy's home into a terrifying palace of despair. Glancing up at the ceiling once more, Peggy gasped as she saw there was now a gaping hole where the roof had been, and the smell of her burning hometown rapidly flooded her senses. Peering into the space where up until moments ago the front room had stood, Peggy realised with a thudding heart that she could now see straight into the shop below.

A scream caught in her throat at the devastation, but Peggy knew this was no time to fall apart.

'Mother, where are you?' Peggy tried again. But there was no answer.

The agonising silence left Peggy's blood cold, but she carried on, picking her way through the debris, her feet crunching across the broken glass, determined to help Edie. Outside, she could hear the screams of neighbours also hit by the blasts, while the echo of footsteps as they raced away from danger penetrated her soul.

Despite knowing the terraced street was teeming with people, Peggy had never felt more alone. She longed to find her mother, but the dust and smoke was too thick for her to see anything let alone breathe.

Reaching into the pocket of her skirt, Peggy pulled out a handkerchief and pressed it to her mouth. As her breathing slowed, the waves of panic started to grow as the sound of groaning told her precisely where her mother was. Hurrying towards the noise, she could see Edie was in a bad way, lying face down under the window, the beam that had catapulted her across the room still lying defiantly across her back. Crouching down, Peggy could see half of Edie's face was covered with rubble, while the other half was coated with a thick black grime. Blood was streaming from her forehead, the grazes on her cheek disrupting the steady flow. She tried to stem the bleeding with her handkerchief, and a surge of alarm coursed through her as she realised she couldn't make it stop.

Desperate to do something to help, she stood up to wrestle with the beam, and tried to move the wooden lintel. But no matter how hard Peggy tried, it was impossible to lift. She tried again, but the old oak support was wedged in between rocks and broken furniture, rendering the task impossible.

'Leave it, Peg,' Edie rasped.

'No!' Peggy cried, bending over double and flinging plaster and stones away from Edie's airways.

She glanced down and saw her mother's arthritic fingers creep towards her. As Edie's hand made contact with her daughter's she grabbed at Peggy's fingers.

'The tin,' she croaked. 'You must take the tin.'

'Stop talking, Mother,' Peggy commanded, as she continued to clear debris from around her mother's nose and mouth. 'You need to save your strength.'

'No, love.' Edie's voice grew desperate. 'Whatever happens to me, you must take the tin. There's something in there I ought to have given you a long time ago.'

Peggy paused for a moment and looked into the eyes that were as familiar to her as her own. 'Stop it, Mother, stop talking like that.'

'There are things that need to be said,' Edie wheezed.

'Not now, Mother. Tell me when we get out of here,' she insisted, as she cleared more of the rubble away from the beam.

'We both know I'm not getting out of here, Peg.' Edie's voice rang out clear and true in the darkness. 'At least not alive.'

Edie's prediction made Peggy feel sick. She did not escape from being held at gunpoint by a German pilot only to lose her one remaining parent. Now Jim was gone, her mother was her past, her present and her future. She was nothing without her; Edie had to survive.

'I promise I'm getting you out of here,' Peggy growled determinedly.

An agonising rasp sounded from Edie's lips. 'I can't breathe, love. It hurts too much.'

Peggy was almost in tears as she looked into her mother's pale blue eyes. She was frightened, she could see that. Edie had always faced every challenge head on. Even when her husband had died, Edie hadn't crumbled; in fact, Peggy hadn't even seen her shed a tear. You took what life threw at you and you got on with it had always been Edie Collins's motto. But then war had broken out and Edie's resolve had crumbled. It was down to her, she realised, to show her mother she could and would survive.

'That's no reason to give up, Mother,' Peggy soothed.

'I'm not giving up, Peggy,' Edie croaked. 'I'm facing facts, just as I need you to. I'm dying.'

Peggy caressed the worn skin of her mother's palm and felt a lump form in her throat. This was the woman that had given her life, had fed her, clothed her and in her own way loved her. As the bombs continued to fall all around them, Peggy suddenly felt very afraid. She wasn't ready to lose her mother; she never would be.

Glancing down, Peggy saw Edie's breathing was coming in ragged wheezes now. She had to do something. Frantically, she tried tugging at the beam once more.

'Not long now, Mother,' she panted, trying to move the beam just a fraction. 'You'll be up and out of here any minute now.'

'Peggy,' Edie whispered, slowly lifting her head to find her daughter. 'Please, there's something I needs to say.'

Anxiety fluttered through Peggy's heart as she saw just how much strength it took for her mother to move just an inch. Bending her head close to Edie's, she stroked the dusty hair from her eyes.

'What is it?'

Edie fixed her gaze on Peggy and opened her mouth slowly. 'When I'm gone, take the tin and then speak to your Carmichael.'

'What?' Peggy croaked in surprise. 'You're not making sense.'

'Please, Peggy, just do it. Promise me,' Edie replied, clearly agitated.

Peggy stemmed the tears that were threatening to fall. 'I promise.'

Once her daughter said the words aloud, Edie seemed to relax as she closed her eyes and smiled. 'You're the love of my life, Peg, my girl. My entire world, always know that. All I've ever wanted is for you to be happy, that's the only thing that matters in life, my love. The only thing, you hear? No matter what life throws at you, if you follow your heart you won't go far wrong.'

Peggy stared at her mother in shock. The words she had longed to hear all her life had finally been spoken.

'Mother,' she whispered in her ear, the familiar scent of Lifebouy soap filling her nostrils and wrapping her in love. 'Hang on, Mother.'

Just then a beam of light flooded the darkness and Peggy had to shield her eyes from the glare.

'Anyone here?' an ARP warden called, standing at the foot of what used to be the stairs.

'Up here,' she shouted. 'We need help, my mother's trapped.'

The ARP warden, who Peggy recognised as Bob Watkins, a long-time friend of her mother's, burst into view followed by two firemen wielding a ladder.

'Don't worry, Peggy,' the warden said kindly. 'If you'll come with me we'll get you to a shelter until Jerry's decided he's had enough of playing silly buggers.'

'But Mother, she needs help,' Peggy protested. 'I can't leave her.'

She felt a fireman grip her shoulder and raise her to her feet. 'We'll take care of her now, you go with the warden and get out of harm's way.'

As she followed Bob, she glanced back at Edie and saw her breathing had become even more shallow, every breath clearly more difficult than the last. Instinctively, she rushed to the woman who had raised her and planted a tender kiss on her forehead.

'I'll always be your girl, Mother, always,' she wept.

Then Peggy was reluctantly hauled to her feet by the warden and led away. Turning back to look at her mother one final time, she felt a rush of love for the woman who had finally found a way to open up. Peggy knew there would never be a sweeter gift, and she would cherish this moment come what may.

*

Outside, the street was lit up like a Christmas tree and amongst the chaos, Peggy confronted the damage for herself. It was clear to see that the street she had grown up in had been blown to kingdom come. A crater the size of two buses stood in the middle, while fires burned from almost all the houses along the row. As firemen and volunteers worked tirelessly to extinguish the flames, the smoke whirled around like a torpedo, ready to claim yet more victims.

It was a scene all too familiar now, Peggy thought bitterly as the ARP warden led her to the public shelter, past the shop, or what remained of it. It looked very much to Peggy that little was left of the treasured corner store. Wild-eyed, she glanced around the street, astonished to find cans of fruit and jam littered amongst the debris and dying embers of the fires that had been put out. Bending down to pick one up, she ran her hands over the lettering of what remained of the label. Only that morning she had delivered a tin exactly like this to Esme Hotchkiss.

At the thought of the woman who hated her mother with such passion, Peggy felt a tug of anger, and scowled all the way to the shelter at the top of Red Lion Hill. It wasn't until a volunteer pressed a hot cup of tea into her hands and guided her to a nearby bench that Peggy felt herself relax.

Resting her head against the dank tin wall of the shelter, she closed her eyes and listened to the friends and neighbours she had known since childhood gossip all around her.

Peggy was far too tired and overwrought to join in. Instead she thought about her mother, and her insistence she look for the tin then talk to Carmichael. What had she been talking about?

She knew with a certainty now that Edie was dead. The damage had been too great for her mother to survive, Peggy could see that. And when the all-clear finally sounded at dawn, she was greeted by Bob Watkins, the ARP warden who had taken her to safety, his face grave.

'Peggy love, I've some bad news,' he said haltingly.

In the dim early morning light, Peggy offered him a half-smile. 'It's all right, Bob, I know Mother's gone.'

Bob removed his hat and clasped Peggy's hand. 'She was a fine woman, Edie Collins, we'll never forget her.'

'No, we won't,' she said shakily, before walking out of the shelter and back towards her home.

It didn't take long to reach Priestley Avenue, or what was left of it. The street was unrecognisable, with almost every house bombed out. Fires continued to blaze all around her with soldiers and volunteers using stirrup pumps and buckets of water alongside the fire service to try and put out the infernos. Standing in front of what was left of the shop and her home, she saw it wasn't quite as bad as she had expected, with only the window blown out and the rest of the store seemingly intact. But the flat she had grown up in above was destroyed, the only thing obviously left, the kettle, that lay at her feet.

'You can still make a cuppa then?' a woman's voice said gently beside her.

Whirling around, Peggy saw it was her neighbour Brenda Smith. 'Yes, I s'pose so. How are things with you?'

Brenda shrugged. 'We're bombed out. Homeless now, me and the kiddies.'

'That's terrible. What will you do?' Peggy sympathised.

'We've got family over Nailsea way so we can stop with them,' she said quietly, her expression softening. 'I just heard about your mother, Peg, I'm ever so sorry.'

At the mention of Edie, tears filled Peggy's eyes. 'Thanks, it's all so sudden.'

'I know,' Brenda soothed comfortingly, giving the younger girl's arm an affectionate squeeze. 'That's the thing about this flamin' war. We're all here one minute, then gone the next. Edie'll be missed though, bab, she was the lifeblood of this street.'

'I don't know what I'll do without her. I wasn't ready to let her go,' Peggy cried out, the anguish of her loss hitting her squarely in the solar plexus.

'You never are,' Brenda told her knowingly. 'When I lost my mum in the raids last month I thought I'd never find the strength to go on. But I have, I had to for the kids' sake as much as my own.'

An uneasy silence descended across the two women as they each lost themselves in their own grief. They stayed like that for several minutes, until the sound of two boys rummaging through the rubble, pointing to where their bedrooms used to be, brought them back to the present.

'I reckon Jerry had a right good go at all of us last night, though,' Brenda said grimly. 'I'm told Broadmead was badly hit, as well as Bedminster.'

'Where's it's gonna end, Bren?' Peggy said sadly, getting her sobs under control.

Brenda shrugged as she leaned in closer to the spark girl. 'Course, I've heard a rumour Winston Churchill hisself is gonna be in town today.'

'Why?' Peggy asked in astonishment.

'He's some bigwig up the university, isn't he? I heard he was coming down to Bristol to give his chums some honorary degrees or something. All I can say is I hope he don't mind a bit of smoke damage to his jacket. It's a nightmare up round there, by all accounts, and of course the tramways have been destroyed.'

Peggy frowned at Brenda's news. 'The trams and the university was hit too? I didn't know that.'

'The bridge up by Philip St Norton, the university, Stokes Croft, Cotham, Cheltenham Road, fires still raging by all accounts.' Brenda nodded authoritatively.

At the mention of Stokes Croft, Peggy's blood ran cold. Jim had told her he was going to visit Iris and Hilda that day.

'How bad were they hit in the centre?' she asked shakily.

Brenda thought for a moment. 'Pretty badly, I reckon. Almost wiped out, I heard. You just hope the poor souls made it to shelter in time.'

In fear, Peggy thought about all that Jim had endured over these past few months. The thought of him ending his days at the mercy of the Jerries was just too cruel. With a start, she remembered Jim's expression as she had run from him in the cafe. His eyes had been filled with love, shock, but most of all hurt after revealing the betrayal he had suffered. A surge of guilt hit her as surely as if she had been struck. She was the one that had sent Jim to Iris, she was the one that had encouraged him to be a father figure. She had been so caught up in trying to do the right thing, to make up for past wrongs, that the only thing she had successfully done was send Jim to his grave. She felt sick at the idea of him surviving a plane crash, trekking across France, finding salvage with the Resistance only to die right here in his hometown. Trembling, Peggy looked down at her hands, convinced she could see Jim's blood all over her fingers. With horrible cruelty, she realised Kitty, Sal, Annie and, most poignantly of all, her mother had been right, life really was too short; happiness should be taken when you find it, but how awful to be realising that just now, when it was surely too late. With knees like jelly, she sank to the floor, glass from the rubble cutting clean through her stockings. But Peggy didn't care, instead she wept unashamedly for all the horrors she had endured and all the horrors this war was still waiting to throw at her.

Brenda crouched down on to her haunches and rubbed her back. 'Come on, lover. How about we go and find a nice cuppa somewhere, see what we can't sort out.'

Wordlessly, Peggy stood up and allowed Brenda to take her hand. For the second time in as many days, Peggy realised she was being led away as if she were no more than a helpless child.

*

A couple of hours later and Peggy was feeling considerably calmer. She was still gripped with heartache over the death of Edie, but she also understood that now was not the time for grieving, not when there was so much to do. Draining her teacup, she thanked Brenda for all her help and resolved to sort out as much as she could of what was left of the flat and shop before making her way back to Swansea. Although she wasn't expected back until Monday, Peggy felt she needed to get back and be with her friends who would understand.

Forlornly she left the volunteer van and picked her way back through the rubble. Outside, there was a definite chill in the air that reminded Peggy they were still a long way from spring. It was hard to ignore the sense of despair that filled the streets. Neighbours picked their way through what was left of their homes, keen to hang on to what they could before a gust of wind or, worse, looters took what was left. Up ahead, Peggy passed a man she recognised as the butcher her mother had always bought her meat from. He was curled up into a ball, crying silently next to the body of his wife who was lying in the corner of the street. The sight of it chilled Peggy to the core and as she quietly slipped him a clean handkerchief, she found herself thinking, there but for the grace of God.

By the time she reached the corner of Priestley Avenue, Peggy was relieved and surprised to see the damage didn't seem as bad as it had in the early morning light. It was true their small house was all but destroyed, but the shop would almost be serviceable by the time it had a new window and the front wall rebricked.

Mentally, Peggy made a note to ask Brenda if she would help her organise it all while she returned to the ATS. She knew there would be more to sort out in the coming days, including her mother's funeral, but for now she would do what she could.

Gingerly, she made a start. Thankfully, a lot of the debris had been swept away by volunteers, so it was a lot easier to sift through what remained of their possessions. Peggy got to work immediately, and realised she was surrounded by scores of other women doing just the same. Like her, she knew these women had not only lost their homes but loved ones too, in fact Mrs Ellis, four doors along, had even lost her two children in the blast. Peggy wasn't sure how she had found the strength to stand up, never mind sort out the mess of her home, but this terrible war taught her that there were times you had to find the strength to go on, even when you just didn't want too.

Catching the eye of Mrs Somers from two doors down, the older woman smiled at her then opened her mouth. At first Peggy thought she was going to offer her some words of comfort, but when the woman launched into song, Peggy realised her lively voice was just what the doctor ordered and soon joined in, finding strength in the simple act of using her voice.

In no time, the rest of the women from along the street were singing 'There'll Always be an England' and Peggy felt less alone. Along with everyone else she worked until her back ached and her fingers were cut to ribbons, shifting, carrying and cleaning. Thankfully, Peggy had been able to salvage most of the shop, though of course most of the food had been destroyed. What was left of the tins had disappeared, and Peggy wasn't entirely surprised. After all, food, along with coal, water and heat was scarce, so no wonder people were taking what they could, where they could.

Glancing at her watch, she saw there was an hour or so of light left. Incredibly, her mother's Tilly truck hadn't been damaged as it had been parked at the back of the store in their delivery yard. Consequently, Peggy was going to parcel up the things she wanted and drive over to Nailsea with Brenda who had kindly offered to let her store what she needed in her relative's outhouse until she could make alternative arrangements.

Peggy had been touched; with no family, she was hoping to call in on the vicar later and ask if it would be all right to use the church's facilities. But with so many other poor souls in need, she didn't want to be another burden to the parish. As she flung cups, plates and the kettle into boxes to give to the homeless, she realised that she was in many ways fortunate. Some people had nobody and nothing left. But Peggy not only had the love of her friends and neighbours, she had another family with the Army. It was the Army that would take care of her, work her hard and give her something else to focus on, eventually helping her face and deal with the grief that in time would ease just a little.

Pulling her greatcoat around her to keep out the chill of the early evening air, Peggy looked around her at the wreckage. She could have cried. All those happy memories destroyed in a single moment. The front room fireplace that now lay in tiny pieces had been where she had taken her first steps, and was where her father had hugged her tight when she left school at fourteen to work with Edie in the shop full-time. The upended settee that had once stood in the front room had been where she and her father had read stories side by side every night before supper. It was also the place they all sat and played charades on Christmas Day, with her mother never being able to get the clue.

Smiling at the memory, Peggy turned around and saw the fragments of glass that up until a few hours ago had one been their flat's kitchen window. With a start, Peggy realised that was where she had last seen Edie. Heart in her mouth, she saw the beam that had crushed her lying beside the glass. Running her fingers along the wood, Peggy found herself shaking. She hoped that her mother hadn't suffered too much and that the end hadn't been painful. Eyes bright with tears, Peggy suddenly remembered the promise she had made to look in Edie's memory tin.

Wiping the droplets away with the back of her hand, she quickly scrambled through the debris. Inside the shop she saw that looters had been busy once more while she had been working away at the front, but Peggy didn't care. As long as they had left the old biscuit tin, people could take what they liked.

Hands trembling, Peggy pushed open the door of the cupboard and looked around. It was exactly as she left it, right down to the cushion she had sat on during the earlier raid. Glancing around for her mother's tin, she felt a pang of relief as she saw it on the shelf, and reached for it, holding the metal as tightly to her chest as if it were a newborn baby.

Settling down on the cushion to honour the promise she had made her mother, Peggy took a deep breath and was about to pull the lid off when a loud voice calling her name stopped her. Exasperated, she put the tin to one side and looked up to see Mrs Somers standing in the doorway, a harried expression on her face.

'Everything all right, Mrs S?' Peggy asked.

'Well, love, there's someone here to see you.'

'Who?' Peggy asked.

Mrs Somers shrugged. 'A young man. Quite insistent he is.'

'But I don't know any young men,' Peggy replied, perplexed.

'Well, that's what me and the girls said,' Mrs Somers carried on, gingerly resting her head against the doorjamb. 'He was all set to come in here, all guns blazing if you please, but me and the girls wouldn't let him without speaking to you first.'

'Who is it?' Peggy asked again.

'It's me,' a gravelly voice boomed.

Stepping out from the shadows, his tell-tale fringe falling in front of his eyes, was Jim.

Peggy's mouth gaped open in astonishment. Getting to her feet, she did her best to recover herself, but found she was unable to take her eyes off the pilot before her. So many questions raced through her mind, but the thing she wanted to know most of all was why he was standing in what remained of her mother's shop.

Taking a step towards him, Peggy felt her heart race as she looked the pilot officer up and down. He had blossomed since she had last seen him. The gaunt, haunted look in his eyes had been replaced by his usual twinkle, and the hollow in his cheeks was gone. Instead, he looked like the Jim she had always known, and loved, a voice added silently in her head.

Coughing, Mrs Somers broke the silence as she caught the look of longing between the pair standing inches away from her.

'Well then, I'll leave you two to it,' she said, tactfully. 'Peg, you know where I'm to if you need me.'

'Thanks, Mrs S,' Peggy whispered, her eyes never leaving Jim's.

Once her neighbour had left, Peggy flung herself into Jim's arms. All thoughts of the mistakes that had been made and the hurt she thought would never heal were forgotten. All that mattered at this moment was that he was here, he was alive and she never wanted to let him out of her sight. Feeling him squeeze her tightly, Peggy leaned her head against his chest and closed her eyes, savouring his unmistakable musky scent.

'You're alive,' she wept. 'I was sure you hadn't survived.'

'Me too, Peggy,' Jim whispered, burying his nose in her hair and inhaling the scent. 'I thought I'd lost you when I heard about the raids over here.'

'I'm fine. I got out in time, but Mother . . . Mother's gone . . .' Peggy's voice broke off, unable to finish the sentence.

'Oh, Peggy sweetheart,' Jim soothed, kissing the top of her head with such affection.

It was the salve Peggy needed and as she let him pull her down on to the cushion, she nestled against him as though it were the most natural thing in the world. Closing her eyes, she tried to take it all in: her mother gone and Jim returned to her all in the same day was too much to cope with.

'I came as soon as I could; I had to know you were still alive,' Jim said softly.

Peggy opened her mouth to reply, but found she couldn't speak. All she wanted to do in that moment was commit every precious part of him to memory, in case she never saw him again. He was just as she remembered, handsome and strong, but that wasn't all. Jim Hudson had an air of confidence mixed with vulnerability that Peggy found intoxicating. She knew she would never meet anyone she loved and adored as much as this man.

'I'm sorry,' she said quietly. 'I should never have said all those things to you up the cafe that day.'

Jim shook his head furiously. 'No, Peggy. You were right. Every single thing you have ever said to me has been right. I will never forgive myself for not telling you about Hilda straight away, it was thoughtless and selfish.'

Peggy shot him a watery smile. 'We've all been thoughtless at some point. We shouldn't spend our entire lives apologising for it, though.'

He clasped Peggy's face between his hands. 'When I saw the state of your street, I was so scared I had lost you, Peggy. All the way up here I made a bargain with God. I told myself that

333

if you were living and breathing, that would be good enough, that I would walk away and I would be happy. But the thing is, now I have seen you, now I have held you in my arms, felt your skin against mine, I just don't think I can do that any more. I love you with all of my heart, Peggy Collins, I would die for you. Please tell me you feel the same way too.'

'You must know I do,' she breathed.

Tenderly, Jim bent down and brushed her lips with his. At the feel of his touch, Peggy felt as if fireworks were exploding inside her. How was it possible, she marvelled, to find such extreme pleasure in a time of such sorrow? As they broke away, Peggy's eyes roamed Jim's face and she saw with delight he was as spellbound as she was. Staring wordlessly at one another, she felt as though they were the only people in the entire world, and all the horrors of the night before were light years away.

With a pang of longing Peggy had never felt before, she rubbed her thumb over the back of Jim's hand, and to her dismay saw his eyes were filled with pain.

'What is it?' she gasped.

'I'm just sorry we've wasted so much time. It would have killed me if you and I had lost our chance to be together because I had been foolish,' Jim whispered.

'Don't say that, my love,' Peggy begged. 'We can have that chance now. If anyone's been foolish, it's me. All night I was terrified for you.'

'Why?' Jim asked gently.

'I got your letter, I knew you'd be up Stokes Croft visiting Hilda and Iris yesterday,' Peggy babbled, her words tripping over one another. 'I heard how bad the raids were, I heard there were scarcely any survivors. I couldn't stand the thought of you going to your grave with me having said all those terrible things. I realised everything people had been saying about life being too short to throw away happiness was true. More than anything I wanted the chance to tell you that. If I hadn't, I'd never have forgiven myself.'

With that, Peggy gave into the tears that had been brewing all day and let herself cry for the mother she had lost, and for the future she thought she would never find. Jim said nothing, instead he simply wrapped his arms around her and held her tightly until Peggy had sobbed her heart out.

'Sweetheart, if we're going to have any sort of life together there is something else I need to tell you,' Jim said, his tone filled with urgency.

'Go on,' she coaxed.

'The thing is, you were right about how bad the raids were in Stokes Croft last night. And I know that because I was there visiting Hilda and Iris just as I said.'

Peggy's hands flew to her throat in shock. 'But you're not hurt?'

Jim shook his head gravely. 'No, not me. But Hilda was killed. She was at home while I had taken Iris out for a walk. We managed to find refuge at the public shelter in College Green, but Hilda, well, she didn't have a chance, a bomb struck her home, killing her instantly.'

'That's terrible,' Peggy breathed. 'That poor child.'

Jim nodded. 'All day, all I have been thinking about was what you said to me in the cafe. That little girl needs a father figure now more than ever. Edward won't be remotely interested, even now Hilda has gone, and Mother, well, she and Father are too old to care for Iris.'

'And Hilda's parents?' Peggy asked softly.

'Dead,' Jim said matter-of-factly. 'Killed outright in the last war against Germany.'

'That poor child,' Peggy said again. 'What d'you want to do?'

Jim looked into Peggy's eyes searchingly before he spoke. 'I want to marry you now, Peggy, and I want you and I to adopt Iris and raise her as our own.'

'What?' Peggy spluttered. 'I don't know the first thing about bringing up children.'

'That doesn't matter,' Jim begged. 'You'll learn.'

Shutting her eyes, she listened to the sound of the wind whirling through the shop. Iris's face came slowly into her mind. She was gorgeous, a bonny baby, of that there was no mistake. But was she strong enough to be the girl's mother? Her own mother had been much more capable than Peggy. After all, Edie had always insisted Peggy wasn't tough enough to manage on her own, that she couldn't manage without her. And yet, wasn't it true that things had changed? Peggy thought back over the last few weeks. She had coped tremendously with heartache, loss, despair and even danger. She had felt her confidence grow and grow. Could she do this? With a shudder, Peggy thought of the alternative if she said no. She knew from Kitty just how hard an upbringing was in a care home. She wouldn't, she couldn't wish that on Iris.

'D'you reckon I'm strong enough, Jim?' she asked.

'Oh, my darling, you're more than strong enough. You're the most capable, incredible and amazing woman I have ever met, Peggy. You can do anything you want, and I know that you could be an outstanding mother for Iris. Besides, we love each other, doesn't this feel right to you?'

'But how would it work?' she asked wildly. 'I have a job in the ATS. I'm serving my country. If we got married, I would have to give all that up, and you, well you would be off serving, away from me and the baby, we would be alone.'

Jim held her hands and looked at her pleadingly. 'Peggy, I would do anything for you. But I also know that what I am asking is so much bigger than that. I'm going back to my posting tonight, and I want you to think over what I've said. You don't need to answer me now. I do know what I'm suggesting is not the future either one of us imagined. But I am asking you to please, at the very least, think about it. You don't have to give me an answer now.'

'I can do that.' She smiled weakly. 'I'm not saying no, Jim, more than anything I want to say yes. But this, well, it's a big decision and ever such a lot has happened today. I want to be sure I make the right choice for you, for me and most of all for baby Iris.'

As Jim cocooned her in his arms once more, suddenly Peggy felt very tired. She leaned her head against his chest and wondered just how much more this war would send her before she shattered into a million tiny pieces.

## Chapter Twenty-Two

All thoughts of the tin Edie had urged Peggy to open went clean out of her mind until the following morning. After Jim had left, Peggy had been overcome with tiredness and so when Brenda came to find her for a lift over to Nailsea, she had forgotten about the tin, and left it in the shop.

Consequently, when she realised later that night, she had barely slept a wink on the camp bed Brenda's cousin had kindly put up for her in the parlour. Instead, she had lain awake tossing and turning, willing Easter morning to come. The moment dawn broke Peggy had leapt out of bed and raced out of the door without even so much as a cup of tea, eager to discover the tin's contents.

Thankfully the weather was fine, but the early morning sunshine peeping through the pink-tinged sky of Easter morning did nothing to help calm Peggy's nerves as she drove the twelve miles back to the city. All the way there, waves of panic soared through her as she imagined the worst. Visions of looters raiding the shop, destroying the contents or worse, taking the tin altogether, ran through her mind. By the time she pulled up at the back of the shop's delivery yard, she was trembling so badly she could barely walk in a straight line towards the back door.

Stepping into the shop she walked straight into the tiny cupboard. Relief washed over her as she saw the black and yellow tin on the floor to the side of the cushion, just as she had left it. Gingerly, Peggy reached for it and carefully pulled off the lid and peered inside. It was like stepping back in time, with a treasure trove of memories waiting to be rediscovered. Inside lay keepsakes from days out to Weston-Super-Mare, a lock of hair, not to mention old photos. She found her favourite one of the three of them, taken just after Peggy was born, and felt a tug of longing as she looked at it with fresh eyes. She was an orphan now.

Every picture told a thousand stories, she thought, and this one suggested her parents had never been happier. Both of them were looking down at Peggy, their eyes bursting with pride and love. She traced her fingers over the image, almost as if she were willing herself back there to try and relive the moment of such joy.

So far she hadn't come across anything she hadn't seen before, so she rifled through the contents more urgently. Spotting a creamy envelope, Peggy froze – this hadn't been in the tin the last time she had looked inside. Picking it up, her heart pounding, Peggy saw at once that it was a letter addressed to her. Was this the reason her mother had wanted her to open the tin?

Turning the envelope over, she ran her finger under the flap and pulled the letter out. Her mother's handwriting swarmed before her eyes and Peggy's eyes filled with tears at the sight of it. Her mother suddenly felt so close, and yet so far away, it was overwhelming. She took a deep breath and began to read.

*My darling girl,*

*If you're reading this then you will know that I feel the time has come for you to know the truth about just who you are. Before you start to wonder, or panic, please know, my precious child, that you mean the world to me. You are, without doubt, the very best thing in my life.*

*Even though you are just a few days old, you have taken hold of my heart in a way no man ever has or will. My love*

339

for you is so strong, I would die for you, Peggy, and I will dedicate myself to ensuring your life is filled with nothing but love.

Your father and I both adore you, but Peggy, my love, there is something you should know about your father. For while I know that he will be a father to you in every way that matters, William is not in fact your birth father. Your real father is a man named Cecil Billington. I'm ashamed to even write these words down, Peggy my darling, but you should know who you are and where you come from. The truth is, your dad, William, and I had a very complicated relationship and the fact of the matter is I have often felt very lonely. When your dad came home on leave one week-end with a friend, Ian Carmichael, just after the war ended, we all went out together and met up with another friend of theirs from the Army, Cecil. The moment I saw Cecil, I fell in love with him. I told myself I was being stupid, Peggy, that I was a married woman who had taken vows. But it soon became clear that although he was married, he too felt the same about me, that we had something special and I saw a chance of some happiness and took it. The war against Germany taught me that happiness can be hard to find.

I'm not making excuses, Peggy, I know what I did was wrong. For a while we pretended we were just friends and wrote to one another. He stayed in the Army and wasn't based all that far away so we occasionally met up in Bath. Yet those meetings were torture, Peg, we were drawn to each other like moths to a flame, and of course one thing led to another.

When I discovered I was expecting you, I was over the moon. Me and your dad had always longed for a baby and had tried unsuccessfully for years, but suddenly, like a miracle, there you were. Then it struck me that you couldn't possibly be your dad's.

*Foolishly, I thought this was the chance for me and Cecil to be together and to start a new life. But Peggy, oh, he wasn't pleased and broke things off then and there. His family ran a chain of shops and he met me about a week later and threw a set of keys at me. Told me he wouldn't give me anything for the baby other than a roof over my head and the chance to put food on the table. The keys are for a shop in Knowle, love, and heaven only knows how we'll get on, I've never run a shop in my life, but I'll make it work for you, my love, I promise.*

*Course, I had to tell your father the truth eventually. I think he had always known he wasn't your birth father, and I didn't know what he would say. But he surprised me. He told me that he would never forgive me for what I had done, but that we were married, in sickness and in health, for better or worse, and that he would love you as his own.*

*Already I can see that's true. He's punishing me, Peggy, and I reckon he always will as long as he's alive. I can't say I blame him. I'm grateful to him for sticking by me, Lord knows I'm no good on my own. But the thing is, Peggy love, Cecil has just this minute been to see you. Oh, my love, he fell for you as soon as he saw you. There were tears shining in his eyes as he held you, his firstborn, and he didn't want to let you go.*

*I don't know what the future holds for any of us, but I want you to know the truth regardless. You were made out of love, and you are the most precious thing in the world to me. Whatever happens, I promise you I will dedicate myself to giving you the best life possible. Promise me you will do just the same. Live a life that makes you happy, that's the very best life you can live.*

*All my love now and forever,*

*Mother*

Peggy dropped the letter on to her lap as if it were alive. Her father was not her father. Her mother had lied to her since she was born. Her father, who she had treasured, was little more than a stranger, and her real father was a man named Cecil, who had wanted nothing to do with her. Waves of nausea rose within her as strongly as if she were on a boat crossing the Bristol Channel. Desperately, she breathed in great lungfuls of air but they did nothing to help her calm down. Her whole world was spinning on its axis, and she had no control.

Shakily she got to her feet and let the tin crash noisily to the ground. No wonder Edie had never wanted her to find the letter until she was dead, Peggy thought angrily. And what about her poor father? She had seen the way he looked at her mother as though he hated her sometimes. Peggy always assumed they must have had a row, now she knew differently. At the thought of her father, the man who had raised her with a love so strong, she felt a pang of sadness; even he had never truly belonged to her. All too soon, wracking great sobs rattled through her body and she sank to the floor and gave in to the grief of her past and the uncertainty of her future.

*

Several hours later, Peggy had dried her eyes and almost reached Swansea in her mother's Tilly truck. With a heavy heart, she had realised it was time for the truth to be faced and dealt with, and that no amount of crying on the shop floor was going to change the past. Yet there were so many things she didn't understand, and perhaps never would.

The biggest shock, Peggy thought as she turned into the road leading to Ida and Harry's hotel, was that she had thought she knew her mother so well when, in fact, it appeared she had barely known Edie at all. She had always assumed her mother was a God-fearing woman, with a husband she adored. The thought of that now almost made Peggy laugh out loud. What about her father? Whatever must he have thought of Edie's behaviour? And what had he really thought of her? she wondered, biting her lip. Peggy had always idolised William and she'd thought he felt the same way. Yet every time he looked at her, all he must have seen was betrayal. With a stab of realisation, she thought that was just how Jim must have felt when he discovered his brother had fathered a child with his own wife. Pulling up into a spot at the back of the hotel, she shook her head in despair and jumped out of the cab.

'It's all such a mess,' she wailed, slamming the door shut.

'What's a mess, love?' called a voice.

Peggy spun around to find Ida standing behind her, hands filled with rubbish.

At the sight of her landlady, Peggy felt a surge of hope flood through her body. She was a sight for sore eyes after such a terrible weekend.

'Oh, Ida, I don't even know where to begin,' she sighed.

Ida put the rubbish down and pulled Peggy into her arms. 'I heard about the raids down in Bristol. I'm so glad you're all right.'

'I'm fine, but Mother's not. Jerry dropped a bucket load of hate on us and she was killed, Ida, our home was destroyed,' Peggy said quietly.

At her news, Ida visibly paled, but closing her eyes rocked her as if she were no more than a baby. 'Oh, Peggy, my love, I'm so very, very sorry.'

'I don't know how I'll manage without her, I already miss her so much,' Peggy wept.

'Peggy, sweetheart, I know, I know. I never cared for my own mother, but when Harry's mum passed, I thought the world had ended.'

'So how did you do it? How did you cope?' Peggy begged, desperate to learn some magic trick that would take away this dreadful pain burning a hole through her very core.

Ida pulled away and looked at Peggy, her eyes brimming with

concern. 'There is no magic secret, my love. It's just time. You will learn to live with it, though there isn't a day that doesn't go by where you won't miss her, but it will get easier.'

Wiping her eyes with the back of her hand, Peggy attempted a weak smile. 'That doesn't sound like a very good magic trick, Ida.'

The landlady smiled. 'It isn't, precious. But it's all we've got. That and a cup of tea, is it?'

Peggy nodded and Ida led her inside into the hotel kitchen and got the kettle on. Peggy pulled out a wooden chair, scraping it noisily across the parquet flooring and rested her hands on the scrubbed pine table. The hotel kitchen had a lovely, homely feel and was one of Peggy's favourite places to while away an afternoon. The large bay window looked right out on to the hotel garden and the sea beyond. On a clear day, you could see all the way to Bristol, something Peggy usually found comforting, but today, knowing her city was still burning, it made her feel ghoulish to think she had the perfect spectator spot.

'Have I missed anything while I've been away?' she asked, changing the subject.

Ida rolled her eyes as she poured the tea. 'There's been a bit of trouble.'

'How d'you mean?' Peggy asked, grateful for something else to think about.

'Annie's had another one of those letters,' Ida said in a worried tone. 'The girl's been beside herself all day.'

'So she's told you about how she can't read then?' Peggy said quietly.

Ida nodded. 'I told her I'd worked it out when the letter was delivered here and her face dropped like a stone. Made me read it to her, she did, and it didn't half make her howl. Course I soothed her best I could, but nothing I said seemed to make a difference, so I got hold of Sal, and well, Annie admitted to us then about how you'd been helping her learn to read. I said nothing of course, but Sal was ever so good with her. Said she had nothing to be ashamed of, but she's still all over the place.'

'Poor Annie,' Peggy said softly. 'I had hoped that after the show these letters would stop.'

'You'd think people would have better things to do,' Ida grumbled as she poured the milk into the teacup and handed it to Peggy. 'You did say though, Peg, that you thought you knew who was doing it.'

Peggy nodded as she took the cup. 'I thought I did. Something in the letter gave me a clue, but I wanted to wait until the time was right and I could be sure of my facts. I also hoped they'd see sense, but it seems not.'

Peggy let the warmth of the cup soothe her inside and out before she spoke again. 'Have you got the letter?'

'Right here. Refused to let Annie take it away and torture herself with it,' Ida replied, reaching into the front pocket of her pinny and pulling out a folded sheet of lined paper.

Peggy unfolded the note and began to read.

*Hello Annie (or should that be girl what can't read),*
*How stupid are you that you still can't read and write? Since your sister died, I thought you'd have got the hang of it by now, what with that trollop with no morals teaching you what's what. Mind, if you'll take my advice, you'll be careful of what she's learning you, lover, seeing as her main talent seems to be nothin' more than being led in a bed with a married man for company. Don't worry though, we'll keep your little secret . . . for now!*

*A friend*

By the time Peggy reached the end, her cheeks had flamed as bright a red as her hair and her blood was boiling.

'This is flaming disgusting, Ida,' she fumed. 'Is Annie all right?'

Ida nodded. 'She's fine. Sal's taken her up the pictures.'

'This is the last thing Annie needs. She's been doing so well lately,' Peggy said, angrily handing the letter back.

Ida nodded, as she slipped the letter back into her pinny. 'I know, love. She could read some of it and she's said it won't put her off carrying on, which I'm pleased about. But she was ever so tearful a bit later on.'

Peggy shook her head in fury. The words made her feel sick. Girls in the ATS were meant to come together and support one another, not turn and destroy each other. Anger ebbed away at her as the culprit's face came to mind. She wanted revenge and suddenly she had an idea of just how she could achieve that very thing.

'Can you slip me that letter again, Ida?' Peggy asked.

As Peggy read it once more, her jaw clenched and her brow furrowed, causing Ida to worry about what on earth Peggy was thinking about.

'What are you going to do, love?' she begged.

'I'm going to make whoever's doing this pay. I need to talk to Annie, but come tomorrow morning, if I'm right, they're going to be very sorry indeed,' Peggy said menacingly.

*

Easter Monday dawned bright and clear, and Peggy woke early after sleeping like a log. After so much distress, she hadn't expected to sleep a wink, but miraculously had fallen asleep as soon as her head hit the pillow. Sitting bolt upright in bed, she threw the thick blankets back and saw Annie was not only wide awake, but almost dressed

'Morning, sleepyhead.' Annie smiled, catching sight of Peggy. 'I didn't like to wake yer when I got in last night, you looked so peaceful.'

'That was thoughtful, I needed the kip.' Peggy grinned as she got to her feet and washed her face.

'Ida told me about your mam, I'm ever so sorry,' Annie said, her voice faltering as she handed Peggy a towel.

'Thanks, babber. It's been a horrible time, it suddenly hit me last night that I'll have me mum's funeral to organise now. I've never sorted anything like that before, I don't know what I ought to do.'

'I'll help yer,' Annie said quickly. 'Me and Sal, we both will.'

'Thank you,' Peggy said again, smiling with affection at her friend. 'But today, I want to help you. I hope you don't mind but Ida showed me the new note.'

At the mention of the latest poison pen letter Annie's cheeks flushed crimson. 'I'm so angry, Peggy. All I want is to learn to read and write, why won't they stop tormenting me?'

'Because they're cowards,' Peggy said crisply. 'But they've made a few mistakes in these last couple of notes and I'm going to get back at them, if you'll let me. But it does mean you have to be brave.'

Annie's eyes widened with fear. 'How brave?'

'How about I tell you in the truck?' Peggy smiled. 'I'll give you a lift up the barracks if you like.'

By the time the girls arrived ready for drill practice, the sun was beaming down, flooding the garrison with a warm spring glow. As they marched towards the mess for a cup of tea before square-bashing began, Peggy closed her eyes and turned her face towards the sun. Her life might be crashing down around her ears, but the sun still rose and set each day and there would always be drill practice, she thought wryly.

Pushing open the heavy door to the mess, she felt the revulsion contained in Annie's letter burning a hole in her pocket. She seethed, she couldn't wait to wipe the smile from the vicious minds behind the letters, but she knew she and Annie would need nerves of steel. Turning to her friend, Peggy checked to see if Annie was showing any signs of wavering but her friend seemed as determined as her, with head held high and jaw set.

'All right then?' Peggy asked her nervously as they walked through the crowds of girls chatting away in the mess.

'Fine.' Annie nodded. 'I'll get the tea.'

'I'll go to the noticeboard,' Peggy said brusquely.

Pushing her way through the throngs of recruits, she looked around. Standing by the window, surrounded by small-minded gossips, Peggy spotted her prey.

Narrowing her eyes, she pulled the letter from her pocket and pinned it to the centre of the noticeboard then she pulled an empty chair across the floor and stood on it so she towered over the room.

'Excuse me,' she said, clearing her throat. 'I'd like to say something.'

At the sound of Peggy's voice, the idle chatter died down, and the girls turned to look with interest. Once she was sure she had everyone's attention, Peggy carried on.

'Some of you might've heard I've been running a few reading and writing lessons. I thought you might like to know my lessons are open to anyone who wants a bit of extra help with their English. I'm more than happy to lend a hand.'

Pausing to allow the girls standing before her to exchange confused glances, Peggy swung her attention back towards the window. 'Pat, May, d'you two want a lesson off me?'

Pat shot her a withering look. 'I don't reckon, Peggy. There's nothing you could teach me.'

'That right?' Peggy asked, a quiet steel to her voice. 'Only, judging by this letter what you wrote Annie over there, I reckon you could more than benefit from a lesson or two. I mean the content's horrible, but it's the spelling and grammar I had the biggest problem with. I've corrected it and stuck it on the noticeboard if you want to see, because I reckon that if you two want to write this kind of filth, then you ought to at least get your English right.'

Everyone's eyes swivelled towards May and Pat who had now gone a shocking shade of red. Peggy looked at them with triumph in her eyes.

'Don't be shy, girls,' she called. 'I s'pect everyone would like to know what you think of the letter I've had a look at. And the rest of you, please step forward and take a look.'

'You're mad, Peggy Collins,' Pat suddenly shouted from across the room.

'That's what happens when you're a tart,' May jeered.

'I'd rather be a tart than the writer of a poison pen letter,' she shot back defiantly.

Peggy watched in quiet amusement as Pat and May exchanged worried looks. Then with a confidence Peggy was sure they didn't feel, they strode over to her.

'You've got a cheek, Peggy Collins,' Pat bristled as she drew near.

'I'll second that. Accusing us of things we haven't done,' May added.

Turning to the noticeboard, Peggy stepped down from the chair and jabbed her index finger at the letter. 'So this isn't yours, then?'

'I've never seen it before in my life,' Pat exclaimed.

'Me neither,' May added. 'I'd never write anything so horrible.'

'Really?' Peggy's tone contained a hint of menace. 'Remind us, Pat, of the one thing you and I have in common that nobody else does.'

Pat smirked. 'I've got nothing in common with you, Peggy Collins.'

'Apart from the fact we both come from Bristol,' Peggy said quietly.

There was an agonising pause as Pat thought for a moment. 'All right, we've got that in common, that don't mean I wrote no poison pen letter.'

'Even though you've used words we would only ever use in Bristol and spelled things the way we talk.' Peggy chuckled. 'Really, girls, I can't think why I didn't spot it sooner, it was obvious, especially as you two are thicker than a bowl of Cook's porridge.'

The girls in the mess tittered and as the colour drained from Pat and May's faces, the crowd fell silent, every pair of eyes agog at the unfolding drama.

'You can't prove nothing,' Pat fired eventually.

'Maybe not, but we all know you two are the bitchiest pair of witches for miles,' Annie shouted from the tea counter.

Peggy looked over and saw Annie's face was filled with a heady mix of anger and determination as she continued her tirade.

'You pair of scrubbers are the only ones who would be horrible enough to write a letter like that; the poison that seeps out of you was all over those letters you thought you were so clever to send.'

'Now just you hang on a minute,' Pat snarled. 'Any more of that talk and I'll knock you out.'

'And I'll help,' May growled. 'Think you're smart, eh? You were doing your work all over the barracks. Anyone with half a brain could see you were learning to spell like a child. And you weren't smart enough to realise we were the ones sending the letters, you needed help from the tart you share a room with.'

A collective gasp sounded across the room as too late May realised her mistake.

'I'm not saying we sent those letters. It was just an expression,' she babbled.

'No, it wasn't,' a gravelly voice rang out.

There at the doorway stood Carmichael. Arms folded, his face was puce with rage. Peggy gulped in fear at the very sight of him, she had never seen him look so angry. Slowly and purposefully he walked towards the noticeboard and glared at the letter.

Deftly, he plucked it off and looked at Pat and May with disgust in his eyes. 'You two were warned about this behaviour a year ago and yet here you are carrying out this vile, cowardly act once more.' His eyes narrowed in fury as he turned to each of the girls. 'I will see each of you in my office now.'

With that he turned and walked out of the room, Pat and May following awkwardly behind him. Once the girls had gone, the rest of the recruits clapped and cheered both Annie and Peggy. While Peggy was pleased to be congratulated for her detective work, what made her feel even more delighted was the support the rest of the ATS girls offered Annie when they discovered her private battle. Standing back to let Annie take the praise she richly deserved, Peggy felt a burst of pride when Annie shyly told them all how she was learning to read and write, and that she was getting there. The girls were full of support, offering to help Annie with her lessons and lend her books to get her to read more. Looking at the glee and relief on Annie's face, Peggy knew without doubt that joining the Army had been one of the best decisions she had ever made.

*

Knocking sharply on the door of Carmichael's office, Peggy took a deep breath. She was due to drive him to Shrewsbury for a meeting and had spent the best part of an hour scrubbing the Humber so it was gleaming. Needless to say, she wasn't expecting to be called into his office so soon and as she sat down in her dirty overalls, she shifted uncomfortably in her chair.

'Wanted to say well done to you, Collins. You're quite the Miss Marple.' Carmichael beamed as he leaned across his mahogany desk, hands clamped together.

'Thank you, sir.' Peggy nodded.

'And very well done for educating young Annie. I understand you are the one who has got her reading and writing now,' Carmichael continued.

'Yes, sir. But it's Annie what's done the hard work,' Peggy explained, embarrassed at the praise. 'She's the one that deserves the credit.'

Carmichael nodded his approval. 'And she'll get it, believe me. The challenge she has undertaken is a great one. Not made easier by those two recruits. I don't normally go out of my way to explain the punishment of others, Collins, but I want to send a message. Those girls will be court-martialled, their future in the ATS is pending, shall we say.'

'It's no more than they deserve,' Peggy spat furiously, before colouring as she remembered who she was addressing. 'My apologies for the outburst, sir.'

'Not at all.' Carmichael chuckled, waving her concerns away. 'Anyway, that's not why I asked to see you.'

'No, sir?'

Carmichael's face became grave. 'Peggy, I heard about your mother. I am so dreadfully sorry. Is there anything I can do?'

She looked at his kindly features and was about to open her mouth to reply, when she suddenly remembered her own letter. Buried within the lines, Carmichael's name had been mentioned, along with her mother's last request to speak to him.

Peggy gave Carmichael a watery smile. 'Before she died, she told me to look in a tin, made me promise.'

Carmichael looked puzzled. 'Why?

'She wanted me to see this,' Peggy replied, reaching for the letter that she couldn't bear to part with. Handing him the thick creamy envelope, she gestured for him to look inside.

Taking the note, Carmichael's eyes ran across the words, drinking in every letter. Peggy couldn't tear her gaze from his face as his expression went from sorrow and amazement to despair.

'Oh, Peggy, I'm so very sorry you found out this way,' he said sadly, handing the letter back.

'Are you the Carmichael in the letter?' she asked bluntly,

The commanding officer looked down. 'I am. And ever since you walked into my barracks I've wanted to tell you the truth about your parentage, Peggy, but it wasn't my place. All I could do was tell myself that I would be here for you when the time came. You're a credit to your father, Peggy, you really are.'

'So you did know him then?' Peggy pressed.

Carmichael nodded. 'I knew both of them. Though I was better friends with your father than Cecil.'

'So why were he and my mother so unhappy? Why did she fall for Cecil?' Peggy's voice rose an octave.

Carmichael sighed. 'Edie and your father were together for a long time. They were childhood sweethearts, as I understand.'

'Yes, I know.' Peggy smiled, knowing the story well. 'They met in the playground.'

'That's true.' Carmichael nodded. 'But what's also true is that they were together for so long they didn't treat each other terribly well. Your father had a number of other women, Peggy, and I believe your mother became tired of competing for his affections, and of course it was a considerable source of distress when she couldn't have a child.'

Peggy looked at Carmichael in shock. She had no idea her father had been with other women. He had never seemed the type. Though, to be fair, with her limited experience of the opposite sex, she wasn't entirely sure what that type would be.

'Are you sure my father did that?' she gasped.

Carmichael nodded. 'I'm afraid so. And it was something he continued, secretly of course, after you were born. I rather think he liked to rub Edie's nose in it.'

Peggy let this new piece of information wash over her before she spoke.

Everything's been a lie,' she said quietly. 'My whole life. Even the shop Mother told me had been in the family for generations wasn't true. It came from Cecil.'

Carmichael said nothing, instead he let Peggy talk, thinking she needed to let everything out.

'I just don't know what to think,' she said at last. 'I had no ideal Mother was so unhappy, at least until she met Cecil?'

'Yes, Cecil changed her life.' Carmichael sighed, and drummed his fingers on the table as he cast his mind back. 'Cecil was married, but he made your mother feel alive again, as though she were a woman worth taking notice of. Edie was a formidable woman, Peggy, but your father somewhat overshadowed her. Seeing her with Cecil was like someone had breathed new life into her.'

'So what happened? It said in the letter that Mother hoped he would change his mind. What went wrong? Where is he now?' Peggy gulped, finally asking the question she had been both dreading and desperate to know the answer too.

Carmichael's face was grave. 'There is no easy way to say this, I'm afraid, Peggy. He died on his way back from seeing you in the hospital. Your mother never got over it, he had been so taken with you when he came to see you, she believed he would change his mind about a future with you. When she learned of his death, all the spirit and fun was knocked out of her in an instant.'

'What happened to Cecil's wife?' Peggy asked quietly.

Carmichael looked grave. 'Catherine killed herself after Cecil died. She discovered the truth from William about Cecil's affair with your mother and was heartbroken after he died. She couldn't live with the shame her husband had fathered a child out of wedlock or that he had fallen in love with someone else.'

Peggy let out a short gasp of horror. Poor Edie, Cecil and Catherine, and William. Could they ever have had a chance of a happy ending?

'So was my dad a consolation prize then? She seemed so unhappy and so strict, did I become a constant reminder of the mistake she had made and the love she had lost?' Peggy felt her cheeks flush with anger. Her life could have turned out so differently.

Carmichael leaned across the desk and clasped Peggy's hand. 'Your father, I believe, never knew of Cecil's visit. He had no idea of Edie's secret hope to run off with him after all. He was grateful for the shop, however, believed Cecil ought to pay something towards you. As for Edie, she adored you, Peggy, but she worried about you. She had seen how cruel the world could be and encouraged you to believe that the only way you would be safe in the world would be if you remained at her side, working in the shop, the two of you together forever. Your father treated her appallingly and she believed all men would ultimately bring pain, though I know how much she believed you should find your own happiness.'

'She was always so against me making friends, and when I was a child, if I ever talked about the day I would get married, she would always say no, Peg, you and me are all the other needs,' Peggy said quietly.

'Edie didn't want you to make the same mistakes she had. She had been hurt by your father and by Cecil in very different ways. She didn't believe relationships could be happy, and she so wanted you to have a very different, but very happy life,' Carmichael explained.

Peggy nodded, the picture of her mother becoming clearer. 'I understand that now. But at the time it felt like she was locking me in a cage. I wanted to live. I reckon that's why when my friend Bess encouraged me to join-up I didn't tell Mother. I wanted to be like my dad. He was the one who always got me to do things. It was thanks to him I was allowed to have Bess as a friend at all, never mind join-up.'

'And Edie knew that,' Carmichael put in. 'She wrote to me when you told her you were going into the ATS, asking my advice. I said she shouldn't fight you, and I said precisely the same thing again when she wrote to me recently suggesting you were removed. I always urged her to let you live your own life, I said it was important.'

'Did she listen to you?' Peggy smiled.

Carmichael returned her grin. 'You know your mother. She lived by her own set of rules. But I like to think that she heard me in her own way.'

A flicker of confusion crossed Peggy's face. 'Why did you stay in touch? You weren't friends.'

'No,' Carmichael agreed, 'but we became friends. Edie needed someone she could confide in once Cecil left her for good and things with her and your father became even more strained. I always liked your mother enormously and was happy to be a shoulder for her to cry on when she needed it, though until recently I hadn't spoken to her for several years.'

'And my father? William, I mean, not Cecil,' Peggy asked.

'Your father loved you. But he rather held your arrival over Edie, I'm afraid, used it against her on more than one occasion.' Carmichael looked pained, as if the very admission of his friend's guilt hurt him too.

Peggy shivered. How could her father have been so cruel and yet so loving at the same time? It didn't equate with the version of the dad she had known and cherished.

'And I loved him,' she said, her voice full of sorrow. 'How do I make sense of any of this?'

'You don't,' he said gently. 'All you need to know is that you were adored in very different ways by your parents. Humans make mistakes, Peggy, but don't hang, draw and quarter them over it. That's how wars start.'

A heavy silence descended on the pair as the wisdom of Carmichael's words began to dawn.

'Jim turned up Saturday morning,' she began shyly. 'He wrote to me at home, told me he'd thought about what I'd said about him taking more of an interest in Iris's life and that he was going to see them both on Good Friday. It turns out Hilda was killed in the raids, but he managed to get hisself and Iris to a shelter in time.'

'My goodness,' Carmichael said in surprise. 'That poor child growing up without her mother.'

'Jim has suggested we marry and raise Iris as our own,' she continued. 'He says his brother will never have anything to do with his kiddie and that otherwise she'll end up in care.'

'And how do you feel about that?' Carmichael asked quietly.

'I don't know,' Peggy cried in despair. 'I loves him, almost losing him twice over has taught me that. But I don't know if I'm ready to face the stigma of being married to a divorcee, it goes against the Bible. But most of all, I don't know if I'm ready to be his wife, or a mother to a child that's not even mine. I don't know if I'm good enough, I don't know what to do.'

Carmichael said nothing for a moment, allowing Peggy's words to sink in. 'The thing of it all is, Peggy, love is sometimes stronger than any Bible teaching. That is a private decision only you can make, but think carefully. As for whether you can love a child that isn't your own, your father said just the same thing to me when he discovered Edie and Cecil had made a baby. And look how loved and treasured you were throughout your childhood and beyond, Peggy. I'm not saying they got it spot on, but you and Jim are nothing like your parents: you two truly do adore one another. With the kind of love you two share, perhaps you are both more equipped to look after a baby that isn't biologically your own than you think.'

Just then, Carmichael got to his feet and gave her shoulder a gentle squeeze as he ushered her out. 'Don't give up on a chance of happiness because of fear, Peggy, promise me that much at least.'

As Peggy looked up at him, she thought she might dissolve with gratitude at the generosity of his spirit. So many people had shown her what love looked like today, and it wasn't always those who she was related to. Could she do the same?

## Chapter Twenty-Three

A fortnight after the Good Friday blast that rocked Peggy's hometown, she found herself back there on a bright spring day. As she stepped from the train at Bristol Temple Meads, she found herself looking for her mother by the entrance, before realising with a jolt that Edie wasn't there, and never would be.

Heart heavy, Peggy walked on to the street and basked in the warmth of the sun. It looked like a good day for Edie's funeral, and Peggy was glad; her mother deserved nothing less. Today had been a day Peggy had been dreading for some time, but as she pulled her cap straight before clambering aboard the bus that would take her up to Knowle, she found she didn't feel quite as bad as she had expected. It had helped that Edie had written her instructions on a separate piece of paper at the bottom of the biscuit tin, which Peggy had found a few days later. Edie said she only wanted a simple service, with few mourners and no flowers, 'a waste during wartime' she had written.

The only thing she had insisted upon was that she was buried next to her own mother in the graveyard at the church where she had worked tirelessly for so long. Peggy was pleased to oblige and had written to the vicar who had told her he would take care of everything.

And so, dressed in a newly pressed and starched uniform, Peggy found herself back in Knowle ready to say goodbye to her mother. She knew she had been lucky to receive the day's leave, and was only sorry that Annie couldn't come with her. Together with Sal she had been a tower of strength over the last fortnight.

Looking across at Sal now sitting next to her on the bus, Peggy's heart lurched. She missed her more than she'd expected now she had started at her new posting. Yet they had both helped with the funeral arrangements as much as possible. Annie had even presented her with a card, instructing her not to open it until she needed to.

Peggy smiled, remembering the seriousness of her friend's expression as she looked out of the window at the damage the city had endured. She could still scarcely believe what had happened, but the proof of what every Bristolian had gone through was there for all to see. The blitz so far had hit the city hard, with 180 killed and 382 injured. That on top of the raid in March which had seen almost 400 murdered at the hands of the Jerries, it was a wonder folk had the strength to keep going.

But as Peggy watched shopkeepers tidy their window displays, florists set up their stalls and window cleaners go about their business, she knew the Bristol spirit was still thriving.

'You all right, pet?' Sal asked, interrupting Peggy's train of thought.

Turning to face Sal, Peggy smiled. 'I'm fine. I'll be glad when today's over with.'

Sal's smile slipped. 'I know, pet. And it will be soon. At least you've no wake to get through, I always think that's the worst thing about a funeral, all that fake smilin'. Someone's died, its heartbreakin' to have to make idle chitter-chatter.'

'I must admit I was relieved when Mother said she didn't want any bother. She was very clear that she didn't want a do of any kind.' Peggy nodded.

'Was she always like that?' Sal asked as the bus turned left.

'She always hated a fuss,' Peggy admitted. 'I s'pose I'm the same way. I like to keep things simple.'

A smile passed Sal's lips. 'Nothing wrong with simple. When I got wed, it was just me, Norm and a handful of guests. We had a fruit cake that my Auntie Joyce had made and a few sandwiches in my mam's front room.'

'Sounds perfect,' Peggy said warmly, getting up as she saw their stop approaching.

Sal followed Peggy down the bus. 'It was perfect, even his old bat of a mother had a smile on her face for once. I wouldn't have changed a thing.'

Stepping from the bus, Peggy burst out laughing. It was typical of Sal to find a way of cheering her up on this very bleakest of days.

*

The funeral was just how Edie would have wanted it, Peggy thought as she watched the mourners file into the church. She, along with Sal and several of her mother's regular customers, sat at the front, along with Robert, the young man who had stayed with her mother until his family had been killed.

As she took a seat next to him, they exchanged knowing glances and smiled shyly. Each of them aware just how hard it was to lose a parent. Behind her, the steady stream of footsteps filled the cavernous church. Whipping her head around, Peggy was amazed that in spite of her mother's instructions for only a few mourners to attend, the church was filled to the rafters with people from across the city and beyond.

Scanning the people dressed from head to toe in black, she saw there were several faces she hadn't seen since she was a child, not to mention those she had never seen before. There were old neighbours, suppliers, fellow shopkeepers and even Esme Hotchkiss had turned up, much to Peggy's surprise. The older woman said nothing, just shuffled into the back pew and sat down. Bitterly, Peggy wondered if Cecil would turn up before remembering with a stab of anguish that he had died.

Yet another parent she had lost, she thought sadly.

Finally, when everyone was ready, the vicar began his eulogy. As he talked about Edie's work in the community and the support she gave to the church, Peggy was surprised to see several mourners around her dabbing their eyes with handkerchiefs. How wonderful it was to see this great outpouring of emotion for the woman who had loved her in her own unique way.

When the vicar was finished, the organist began to play the opening bars of 'Jerusalem', and Peggy, along with the rest of the congregation, got to her feet and picked up the little maroon hymn book that rested on the shelf in front of them. Peggy didn't need a reminder of the words, it was one of her and Edie's favourites, and she stood ramrod straight, her eyes resting on the cross behind the vicar, singing at the top of her lungs. If Edie was looking down, Peggy wanted her to know how treasured and respected she had been and always would be.

Once the hymn ended and Peggy sat down to listen to the rest of the service, it occurred to her that although Edie Collins had not always been the easiest woman to get to know, they had more in common than she realised. All her life, she thought she and her mother were worlds apart, but recently Peggy had come to see that was far from the case. Both she and Edie had coped with tremendous heartache and had been forced to face up to very different futures. Yet, despite her private pain, Edie had made her own way in the world, leaving a mark that would never be forgotten in this community and beyond.

Filing out into the sunshine for the burial, Peggy resolved to do much the same. Yet watching the pallbearers delicately balance her mother's coffin on their shoulders, she felt her resolve weaken as she realised this was the second funeral she had been too in almost as many months and she tried to stem the tears that threatened to spill down her face.

'Let it out, love,' Sal whispered as she walked alongside her towards the burial site.

'Mother wouldn't want me to,' Peggy whispered. 'She couldn't abide crying, especially not in public.'

Sal gave her a kind smile. 'Sometimes we have to do what's right for us, not what's right for our mams.'

With that, Peggy reached into the pocket of her khaki jacket, fished out a handkerchief and gave in. As Edie's coffin was lowered into the ground she wept silently. Then she walked towards the grave and lowered a single chrysanthemum on to the box.

'Goodbye, Mother,' she whispered. 'Rest in peace now.'

Afterwards, she turned to Sal and linked her arm through her friend's. Together they walked back up the hill towards the church, where the vicar was inside talking to the mourners.

'Do you want to come inside?' Sal asked.

Peggy shook her head. She needed some fresh air, and besides, she wanted to make sure she said goodbye to everyone and thank them for coming. It was what Edie would want.

'You go on,' Peggy insisted. 'I just need a few minutes to prepare myself for this next bit.'

Sal smiled in understanding. 'Course, pet.'

Peggy watched Sal's retreating back and shivered. Raising her eyes heavenward, she took a deep breath. She was strong, all she had to do was listen to her mother's friends and well-wishers tell her how special Edie was then she could get on the next train back to Swansea and say goodbye to this horrible day.

Looking down at her hands, she saw they were blue with cold despite the sunshine and she shoved them inside the pockets of her jacket. It was then she felt her fingers brush against the envelope Annie had given her that morning. She smiled at the memory of her friend insisting she open it when she needed. Well, if ever was a good time to open a letter from a friend, now was surely it.

Examining the thin white envelope, she was pleased to see Annie had taken great care to form her letters properly. She

362

had even attempted to join up the two gs in her name, Peggy noticed, feeling a flush of pride.

Pulling out a piece of thin card folded in two, Peggy turned it over and gasped with pleasure. On the front, her friend had drawn a picture of three ATS girls that were a very good likeness to herself, Sal and Annie. Underneath she had written in near-perfect penmanship, 'Friends are like family'. Inside, Annie had written:

*Dear Peggy,*
   *Just a note to wish you well today. I know how hard it is to say goodbye, but please know I will always be here when you need me, ready to say hello.*
   *Lots of love,*


   *Annie*

Peggy clutched the card to her chest and brushed away the tears that threatened to flow once more. How her girl had changed in the few short months she had known her. Annie had gone from a surly, inconsiderate volunteer, afraid to learn anything new or admit her mistakes, to a thoughtful, intelligent and committed member of the ATS. Looking at the note again, Peggy beamed with joy that she had helped her friend to grow into the wonderful woman she had become.

In a heartbeat she realised that must be what it was like to be a parent. The greatest pleasure would surely be to watch your child grow from incapable, dependent beings, into adults who were happy, successful and able to stand on their own two feet. Immediately her thoughts turned to Jim, and in that moment she knew she was more than ready to commit to what he was offering.

As the stream of mourners descended from the church led by the vicar, Peggy found the strength to smile with genuine warmth. As each one shook her hand and expressed their

363

sorrow, Peggy basked in the pleasure of hearing her mother spoken about in such glowing terms. However, by the time she came to face Mrs Hotchkiss, Peggy braced herself for an onslaught.

'I'm sorry, dearie,' Mrs Hotchkiss said gently. 'Your mother was a fine woman.'

'But you never had a good word to say about her,' Peggy exclaimed.

Mrs Hotchkiss cocked her head to one side and considered her point. 'That's true, but I always admired your mother. She was as strong as they come, and although I may not have approved of the way she conducted herself on occasion, she was resilient, I'll give her that.'

'Mrs Hotchkiss, did you . . .?' Peggy's voice broke off, as she tried to summon up the courage to ask the question that had just entered her mind. 'Is there a particular reason you disapproved of my mother so much? It wasn't anything to do with a man named Cecil, was it? Did you know him?'

The elderly woman patted her hand and smiled gently. 'Know him? He was my son, lover, from my first husband, before he was killed in the last war against Germany.'

Peggy's mouth fell open as she stared at the woman aghast. 'You're my grandmother,' she said eventually.

'Yes, lover, I am.' Mrs Hotchkiss smiled again, as she bent forwards and gently kissed Peggy's cheek, her papery thin lips bursting with love. 'I wondered when you'd find out. I wanted to tell you for years but Edie forbade it so I watched you grow up from afar. That was why I always insisted on shopping with your mother. You remind me so much of my Cecil. You come and see me next time you're home and I'll tell you a few things.'

With that, the elderly woman shook the vicar's hand and walked down the path, away from her. As Peggy shook the last few remaining hands, she did her best to focus, but her mind was full of Mrs Hotchkiss, her heart breaking at the thought of all those lost years. She thought back over her childhood, remembering how much she had always wanted a grandmother, just like the other girls at school. Watching the elderly woman push open the church gate, round the corner and disappear, Peggy made yet another promise, this time to herself. So much had been missed, she vowed she wouldn't miss any more.

'Thank you so much for coming, Mother would have been delighted to see you,' she murmured, barely glancing at the person standing before her.

'You're welcome. We wanted to be here for you,' a gravelly voice replied.

Peggy did a double take. She would recognise that voice anywhere.

'Jim,' she breathed.

At the sound of his name the pilot's face lit up as he jiggled a contented baby in his arms. 'You remember Iris?'

'How could I forget,' she gasped, brushing the infant's cheek with her forefinger and feeling a rush of love.

'We heard about Edie's funeral and thought you might like a little bit of moral support,' he said quietly.

'Thank you,' Peggy said gently.

Turning back to Jim, she felt suddenly shy around him. He had opened up a whole new world of possibilities for her, opportunities she would never have dreamed of if she hadn't met him. But could they really find a way back to one another surrounded by these ghosts of the past?

'I hope you don't mind us coming here today. It's just, it was selfish of me. I had to see you,' Jim began, his voice faltering. 'I couldn't wait any longer to find out if there was any hope at all for us. You must know by now, Peggy, that all my heart is yours. You are everything to me, you consume me and if there's the slightest chance you feel the same way, then I don't want to waste any more time waiting. I want us to start our lives together, right now.'

His voice trailed off and Peggy thought her heart would burst with love for this man standing in front of her, looking as vulnerable as the motherless baby he was holding. She knew then that though there had been times she had railed against her emotions, she had always loved him. Just as the waves always crashed against the shore, the sun always rose and a nurtured flower always blossomed, she knew that her love for Jim Hudson would always burn brightly in her heart.

Slowly, Peggy tilted her face towards him and closed her eyes. As his full lips tenderly brushed hers she could hear her heart roar in her ears and she kissed him back with a passion she had never felt before. She didn't want him to just hear her say how much she loved him, she wanted him to feel it.

Gently he pulled away, his face alight with joy. 'Do I take it this means you will do me the very great honour of becoming my wife?'

'Yes, a thousand times yes,' she cried, her eyes shining with tears of happiness.

Jim bent down to kiss her once more and Peggy allowed herself to give in to the sheer bliss she was feeling. Nothing had ever felt so right, so pure or so true and she never wanted the moment to end. Just then the gentle sound of a baby gurgling in her ear distracted her. Pulling away, she looked from Jim to Iris and saw the baby had her arms outstretched towards her.

'I think she would like to offer you her very own hearty congratulations,' Jim chuckled, as he handed her the baby.

Taking Iris in her arms, Peggy felt a warm glow sweep through her entire body. Looking from Jim and then back down to the baby, she knew, in that moment, she had found her family. This was her future, and it would be a happy one, that was something she could promise her mother.

# Epilogue

## January 1942

The warm fragrance of rich, sweet fruit wafted through the kitchen as Peggy pulled the cake from the oven. Placing it gently on the trivet by the open window to cool, she beamed at the sight of it. Despite the rationing, it looked every bit as good as the one her mother used to make, and the smell alone brought a thousand childhood memories rushing back.

'Gah,' Iris shouted, banging her tiny fist on the wooden table. 'Gah.'

'I know,' Peggy chuckled. 'This cake is definitely gah.'

Planting a kiss on her daughter's head, she made her way to the sink to wash her hands. As the water ran down her fingers she gasped in delight when she felt a pair of strong hands snake around her waist, and the gentlest of kisses flutter along her neck.

'Get off me!' she giggled in delight. 'I haven't got time for this, Jim Hudson. It's our daughter's first birthday party and the guests will be arriving any minute!'

'Typical. Everything changes the moment you marry a girl,' Jim groaned in between kisses.

As if on cue, the sound of a light rap at the door broke the spell and Peggy walked through the hallway to open it. Standing on the step was her old commanding officer and now very dear friend, Lieutenant Colonel Carmichael.

'Sir,' she beamed, stepping forward to kiss him gently on the cheek.

'Please, how many times, do call me Ian. You're a civilian now and as I gave you away at your wedding blessing, I rather think we're beyond sir,' he said, returning her kiss.

'Sorry,' she said, stepping back to allow him to pass.

Standing right behind him, in a smartly pressed khaki uniform complete with lance corporal pip on her arm, stood her old friend Annie.

'Hello, Peg, brought you a little something.' She beamed, pressing a piece of paper into her hands.

'You shouldn't have done,' Peggy chided as she gratefully took the gift. Unwrapping it, her hands flew to her mouth in delight as she saw Annie had done a little sketch of Iris.

'It's nothing.' Annie shrugged. 'Just a little something I knocked up in me spare time.'

Peggy chuckled as she shut the front door, and ushered her guests through to the kitchen. 'Spare time, working as chief driver for the lieutenant colonel? I think we both know there's not much of that.'

Carmichael roared with laughter. 'Well, I do keep young Annie busy, but she's up to it. Helping teach a new batch of spark girls some mechanical skills now.'

'Are you?' Peggy marvelled. 'That's brilliant, Ann, well done.'

Annie shuffled uncomfortably from foot to foot, embarrassed at the attention. 'It's nothing.'

'I have to disagree,' Jim said good-naturedly, filling glasses with home-made ginger cordial. 'Teaching is one of the hardest jobs there is, it takes a special someone to carry out a role like that.'

Peggy watched Annie relax at the kindness of her husband's words. When Peggy had left the ATS the previous summer to marry Jim and raise Iris, she had worried Annie might not cope on her own. Yet she had flourished, all under the guidance of Ian. He had recognised the quiet determination Peggy had seen when she taught Annie to read and write, and with his encouragement, Annie had progressed up the ranks and taken over from Peggy as his driver. It had turned out to have been the making of her.

'So how many of us are there this afternoon?' Ian asked, sitting at the table next to Iris and ruffling her hair.

'Gah, gah, gah,' she giggled delightedly at the attention.

'I think Peggy's invited everyone we know! By the way, is that a new word?' Jim asked, peering quizzically at his daughter.

'Yes, I reckon Esme has been trying to get her to say Granny,' Peggy chuckled.

'What, before she says Mummy or Daddy?' Jim scoffed. 'I don't think so.'

Annie pulled out a chair at the table next to Iris and sipped her drink. 'I take it things are still going well with your new gran, then?'

Joining her friends at the table, Peggy nodded. 'Esme loves the bones of her. She's been a godsend to us, what with helping out in the shop and taking care of this little one when I've been busy serving.'

'It's a wonder you got this place so shipshape and Bristol fashion, if you'll pardon the pun.' Ian beamed, sipping the cordial.

'It wasn't easy,' Jim admitted as he too joined them at the table. 'But several of my RAF pals helped us out and of course Mother and Father assisted. We had the shop up and running just a fortnight after our wedding last July, didn't we?'

'Yes, and it's been non-stop ever since,' Peggy groaned.

'Don't listen to her, you adore it, don't you?' Jim teased gently.

'I'm not admitting anything in front of witnesses.' She laughed.

But Jim was, of course, right. The moment he had suggested they begin their married life in the flat above the shop that Edie had passed on to her, and get the store up and running again, it had felt like the most natural thing in the world. Work had got under way quickly, thanks to a lot of help from Jim's friends.

But they had done it, and Peggy had been delighted to welcome customers old and new to the shop, complete with baby on her hip, just as her mother had.

'So, come on, Jim, how are you adjusting to life back down in the West Country?' Ian asked, interrupting her thoughts.

'Well, it's been a challenge, I won't deny it,' Jim admitted. 'As you know better than anyone, I always thought I would fight Jerry head-on in the skies, but after making my escape across France, well, I was more than happy to take up a teaching role instead. When a post came up here in Bristol, I jumped at the chance to be close to my wife and daughter.'

Peggy beamed happily at him. Not many men would admit to wanting to see their child grow up. But Jim had insisted that if it was possible, he wanted to serve his country and be there for the child they had adopted. Peggy couldn't help but admire him for it.

When they were going through the adoption documents, there was a small part of Peggy that panicked Edward would try to reclaim his daughter or fight it. Jim, along with his parents, who Peggy was relieved to find were as kind and gentle as Jim, assured her Ed would never want anything to do with his child. Yet Peggy had remained unconvinced, until the paperwork arrived last autumn assuring her they were Iris Hudson's legal parents.

Just over an hour later and the little room was filled with guests, all there to wish baby Iris a very happy first birthday. Next to her stood Sal, smiling gleefully as she waved at Iris. Peggy was delighted she had been able to come up for the day to celebrate. Now she was a staff sergeant, Peggy knew she was busier than ever and it meant a lot to her that she had been able to get away. Likewise, Kitty had suddenly managed a surprise appearance, showing up to press a gift and stay for a quick drink as she drove up to Manchester to make a NAAFI delivery.

Looking at her ATS friends gossiping wildly with one another, she felt a pang of envy. Her time as a volunteer, fighting for this country's freedom, had been one of the happiest of her life, along, of course, with driving. But thankfully Jim had made one concession, and peering out of the window she beamed at her second-best pride and joy. Receiving the Aston Martin Ulster from him as a wedding gift had been a wonderful surprise. But as Iris gurgled contentedly in her arms, Peggy knew she would trade it all in a heartbeat for the daughter she adored.

Covering Iris's face in kisses, Jim took a seat at the tiny piano in the corner of the room and struck up the opening chords to 'Happy Birthday'. Everyone joined in and soon the whole room was filled with song and Peggy thought she might just burst with happiness.

But despite her joy, her thoughts turned to the loved ones that couldn't be here: her father William who she would always adore, despite hearing the truth of her birth. There wasn't a day that passed where she didn't miss him, and looking at the vase filled with fresh red chrysanthemums that Jim had thoughtfully presented her with earlier that day, she knew her father would always live on in her heart, and little Iris's too. Then there was Cecil, and of course her mother. Through Esme, Peggy felt she was getting to know a little of what her real father was like, and discovering she had a grandmother, and even an aunt in Esme's daughter Betty, had been an unexpected delight Peggy was constantly thankful for. As for her mother, she knew that Edie would be thrilled to see her with a daughter and embracing this new life filled with joy. Consequently, Peggy often found herself yearning for the mother she had finally got to know in death. However, Peggy also realised there was no point wishing for things that would never be. She was grateful to have discovered the truth, and to be keeping the promise her mother had insisted on during her dying moments. Planting a tender kiss on top of her daughter's head, Peggy knew she had found a happiness she never expected, and she intended to make sure that Iris was encouraged to always choose happiness. With so many loved ones killed in the war already it was vital to treasure the time you had while you had it; after all, nobody knew how long this war was going to last. 'Do you think Hilda would approve?' Sal ventured as the song died down.

'I hope so. She adored her daughter and I reckon if nothing else, she would think a birthday party filled with her friends and family would be ideal,' Peggy said quietly.

'It's that all right, pet.' Sal beamed at her. 'And are you still takin' this little one to visit her grave?'

'Yes, we went up this morning. Said hello to Hilda, to Nanny Edie, Granddad William and Granddad Cecil as well.'

Sal raised an eyebrow. 'You were busy.'

'I s'pose we were.' Peggy grinned back at her. 'But, Sal, it's like I said to you when we adopted Iris: I'm her mother and will always love her, but I made a promise, when those official documents came through saying me and Jim were her parents, that neither one of us were to keep secrets from her. I know how damaging that is.'

'You're doin' all right, flower,' Sal told her.

'I am. I'm doing more than all right.' Peggy's eyes sparkled. 'Actually, I've got a secret of my own.'

'Go on,' Sal coaxed in hushed tones.

Peggy looked around to see who was listening, before leaning across to whisper in her friend's ear. 'This one's going to have a little brother or sister in a few months. I'm expecting, Sal.'

Sal gasped in surprise and pulled her friend into her arms. 'Oh, Peggy, pet, that's wonderful news. I couldn't be happier for you both.'

Peggy smiled as she pulled away from Sal's embrace. 'Actually, Jim doesn't know yet. I was planning to surprise him with it later, so keep it to yourself for just a little bit.'

'Course I will,' she said, her eyes filling with tears. 'Oh, look at me, I'm a daft old trout. I'm just so happy everything's worked out for you, pet. You and your Jim deserve it.'

'What do we deserve?' Jim asked, suddenly appearing behind Peggy and surprising her with a kiss.

'I'll tell you later,' Peggy vowed, placing his daughter in his arms to distract him.

'Promise?' he asked, holding his daughter close to his chest.

'I promise,' she said. 'Now, can you please take Iris over to her grandma. Esme's desperate for a cuddle.'

'Yes, ma'am.' He offered a mock salute with his free hand, and brushed her lips with his.

As he pulled away, Peggy's eyes locked with his and her heart swelled with love. This man, this child, this new life growing inside her, were her world. She would lay her life on the line for any of them. That was a promise she would never break.